FIVE PAST MIDNIGHT

Also by James Thayer

The Hess Cross
The Stettin Secret
The Earhart Betrayal
Pursuit
Ringer
S-Day: A Memoir of the Invasion of England
White Star
Man of the Century

JAMES THAYER

FIVE PAST MIDNIGHT

MACMILLAN

First published in Great Britain 1997 by Macmillan

an imprint of Macmillan Publishers Ltd
25 Eccleston Place, London, SW1W 9NF
and Basingstoke

Associated companies throughout the world

ISBN 0 333 66458 2

1 3 5 7 9 8 6 4 2

A CIP catalogue record for this book is available from the British Library.

Phototypeset by Intype London Limited
Printed and bound in Great Britain by
Mackays of Chatham plc, Chatham, Kent

For my mother
Buryl Stewart Thayer
and her parents
Constance May MacMillan Stewart
(1902–1996)
and
Thomas William Stewart
(1898–1988)

My heartfelt thanks to

David G. Knibb, Sally A. Martin, Daniel J. Niehans, John D. Reagh III, Jeano Riley, John L. Thayer, MD, Joseph T. Thayer, Dexter A. Washburn, Mark A. Washburn, and my wonderful wife, Patricia Wallace Thayer.

Victory is a thing of the will
– Ferdinand Foch

PROLOGUE

April 4, 1945
The White House

Donovan never recorded the meeting in his journal, but he would remember it in fine detail to the end of his days. It began when the usher tapped lightly on the massive oak door, then pressed a small button hidden in the wainscoting to notify the Secret Service watch officer that the spymaster was about to enter the office. Above the button a portrait of Andrew Jackson glared down at them.

'He's expecting you, General,' the usher said in a low voice appropriate for the august place. When he pushed open the door, the spymaster stepped through.

Franklin D. Roosevelt was sitting behind his desk, his face green in the light of a banker's lamp. The chandelier had been doused and the blackout curtains were drawn across the windows, so the walls of the Oval Office were a periphery of darkness. A mail pouch, copies of the *New York Times* and the *Washington Post*, a pitcher and glass, and several marble paperweights were on the desk.

The president waved the general into the room. Behind the desk, two tasseled United States flags hung from poles. The pennant Roosevelt had designed for himself when he was assistant secretary of the navy was displayed on a smaller staff near the fireplace. On a stand at the end of the desk was an intricate reproduction of the USS *Constitution*, one of the many ship models in the president's collection.

General William Donovan, director of the Office of Strategic Services, placed a manila envelope on the desk, pushing it across to the blotter so the president would not have to use the tongs he kept in a drawer. White House carpenters had raised the desk six inches to accommodate the president's wheelchair, and when Donovan sat in the low leather chair opposite the president, the desktop came almost to Donovan's shoulders.

Roosevelt chided the general by lifting the envelope and making a production of weighing it. 'You are a lawyer by profession, Bill. You write briefs. But you never write anything brief.'

Donovan should have chuckled dutifully. Not this night. The contents of the envelope precluded levity. Like most Americans, the general loved Roosevelt's voice, the fireside companion that had carried America through the bleak years. Every time the general heard that silky, compelling, faintly exotic voice, he felt rejuvenated and stronger. But again, not this night, not with the envelope.

Roosevelt pulled a Camel from its pack and stabbed it at a Bakelite holder that had white teeth marks on the stem. His hands trembled, and only after three attempts did he succeed in planting the cigarette. When he leaned forward for his Ronson, the president's face came into the lamplight. Donovan's breath caught.

Twenty-three of Roosevelt's sixty-two years had been spent in a wheelchair. Yet he had been the most vibrant man Donovan had ever met, exuding health and virility and energy. The president had possessed a sheer physical magnetism. But in the three weeks since their last meeting, Roosevelt's skin had taken on a ghastly pallor and a translucence that revealed the skull beneath. The bags under his eyes had darkened, and his lips had acquired a blue tinge. Stray strands of his hair flitted like insects in the lamplight above his head. The president was wearing a tweed jacket so old that it was shiny.

Roosevelt inhaled the smoke deeply then let it trail out his nostrils. He abruptly lifted his head in the manner that led many to suppose he was arrogant but which simply allowed him to see through his spectacles. 'Can you spare me all the reading, Bill? It's late.'

Bill Donovan was in plainclothes, as always. He was a small man, and scrappy, with a jutting jaw and a boxer's nose. Harry Hopkins called him the Irish terrier because the OSS chief always seemed on his hind legs at the end of a leash waiting for his master to let him go. Tonight he would try again.

'Mr President, I will summarize the contents of my envelope in three sentences.'

Roosevelt grinned appreciatively.

'First, each and every day the war in Europe continues, twenty-eight thousand men, women, and children die.'

The president's smile vanished.

'Second, a group of German staff officers is ready to assume leadership of the Third Reich if an opportunity arises, and will instantly surrender.'

Roosevelt's eyes lost their avuncular angle and became unreadable. He lowered the cigarette holder to an ashtray.

'Finally, Mr President, we have confirmation of General Eisenhower's report that the German SS is preparing a national redoubt in the Bavarian Alps, where Hitler may be able to carry on the war for another two years.'

President Roosevelt started to speak but his throat rattled, and he bent low over the blotter, caught in a coughing fit that left him breathless and even more pale. He lifted the glass of water with a shaking hand. Water splashed to the desktop. He sipped carefully.

He was finally able to rasp, 'The bastard is going to outlive me, isn't he?'

Donovan avoided the question. 'Hitler has recently pledged, and I use his words, that he will fight "until five minutes past midnight." '

The president blinked several times, and his mouth moved silently. He seemed awash in melancholy. He gripped the wheelchair rims and backed away from the desk. Carpet in the Oval Office had been removed to allow the wheelchair to move more easily. He rolled to a window overlooking the lawn. Most Americans had long before taken down their blackout curtains, but Roosevelt liked 'to remain on war footing,' as he once told Donovan. The president pushed aside the curtain, a small act that seemed to consume the last of his strength. It was ten o'clock in the evening. Streetlights and garden lamps and the Washington Monument were dark for the duration, so there was nothing to be seen through the window.

Yet he peered into the blackness for a full minute. Then, without turning away from the window, he said softly, as if in the presence of the dead, 'You take care of it, Bill.'

That was just enough. General Donovan rose from the chair, retrieved the manila envelope, and fairly sprinted out of the office.

PART ONE

The Castle

ONE

April 7, 1945
Berlin

Otto Dietrich was curled on the metal cot under a tattered blanket that smelled of urine and old blood. The blanket was alive with biting and burrowing vermin, yet he lay motionless, too uncaring to scratch. His eyes were closed tightly and his mouth was pulled taut in fear.

They always came at noon. A few more minutes. They had left him his watch so he would know when his moment had arrived. But his belt, shoelaces, gold badge, and wallet had been taken. And his bridgework, lest he try to slash his wrists with his false teeth, he supposed.

Dietrich's cell contained the cot and blanket, a chamber pot, and nothing else. The cell was belowground. Water seeped down the mold-encrusted stone walls to the floor, where it gathered in brown pools speckled with rotted waste. A single bulb was behind an iron grate in the ceiling, and it was never extinguished. The door to the corridor was an iron sheet with a viewing port at eye level. Another hatch was near the floor, through which a soup bowl and a cup of water was pushed once a day, and through which would come his *Henkersmahlzeit*, the condemned's last meal. There were no windows to the outside, and the cell walls were so thick that sounds could not breach them – not the guards' footsteps, not the wind, not the other prisoners' cries. The only noise in the cell was Dietrich's stertorous breathing and the steady dripping of water.

With an effort that made him moan, the prisoner struggled to a sitting position. He would meet his fate with dignity and would stand when they came for him. He had not bathed or shaved in three months, nor had he had a change of clothing. His skin was covered with dirt and insect bites and open sores that refused to heal. Grease and grime matted his hair and beard.

Dietrich doubled over with a grinding cough. Pneumonia, he suspected. His lungs rattled with each breath. He had lost two teeth while in the cell. His hands shook uncontrollably, and the skin around his fingers had shrunk for want of nourishment. They resembled claws.

Dietrich levered himself from the cot. He placed a hand on the oozing wall to steady himself. He spit into a hand, and pawed his face with it, trying to wipe away the filth. They had reduced him to an animal's existence, but every day he cleaned himself as best he could. He straightened his foul clothing and turned to the door. They were always prompt.

Dietrich's cell was in Wing B of the Lehrterstrasse Prison, across the Spree River from Berlin's Tiergarten. The prison was star-shaped, with three floors of cells. It had been built in the 1840s, patterned after London's Pentonville. The structure had no adornment. Brick walls and iron bars across small windows spoke of its sole purpose, to punish. Berliners found it impossible to pass Lehrterstrasse Prison without shivering. Many entered the prison. Far fewer left alive. Executions occurred in the cellar.

It had been a busy place since July 20, 1944. At Hitler's headquarters at Rastenburg in East Prussia, Colonel Count von Stauffenberg's briefcase bomb had only slightly wounded Hitler because the attaché case had been shunted aside by another officer, and Hitler had been shielded by the conference table's heavy leg. Colonel Stauffenberg, Generals Beck and Halder, Field Marshal Witzleben, former Leipzig Mayor Goerdeler and other plotters had already met their ends. Five thousand others – army officers, professors, writers, doctors, clergymen, district and town officials, most with utterly no knowledge of the plot – had also been executed.

Before his arrest Otto Dietrich had been chief criminal inspector with the Berlin police. He had joined the Kriminalpolizei, known to Berliners as the Kripo, after the Great War. Arguing that the investigation of criminal acts was irreconcilable with political police work, he had assiduously avoided involvement in the political police – then called the Schupo – and the growing National Socialist German Workers' Party and its strong-arm branches, the SA and the SS. He graduated from the Institute of Police Science in Charlottenburg. He won promotion to inspector that year.

Dietrich's investigative gift was clear from the start. In 1928 he solved the murder of the heiress Elisabeth Hoffer, whose headless corpse had been found in the Spree, put there, Dietrich learned, by her younger sister, whom he tracked to Buenos Aires. Two years later he was assigned to the highly publicized murder of Director Dräger of the Mercedes Palast cinema, who was killed during a kidnap attempt gone awry. Dietrich found the two killers in the German community of Seffert in central Ukraine. And in 1938 when Karl Schwandheist reported that two brigands had stabbed and carried off the body of his wife Marie, Inspector Dietrich found her alive and well in Geneva, spending with her husband the 400,000-mark insurance proceeds he had claimed. Otto Dietrich was a household name in Berlin.

From the door came the scrape of a key, followed by the shriek of metal on rusted hinges. Dietrich's fear welled up again. The executioner stepped into the cell.

In a land besotted with uniforms, even executioners had their own colors. Sergeant Oscar Winge's uniform was police green with yellow insignia and carmine-red piping. He had a drinker's face, blotched and purple, with red capillaries showing on his nose. His razor had missed spots below his mouth and under an ear.

A Gestapo case officer followed him into the cell. The agent had a pinched face, with deep lines like a cracked window. He wore street clothes and the ubiquitous Gestapo accessory, a black leather coat belted at the waist. The agent's name was Rudolf Koder, of the Gestapo's Amt IV 3a (counterintelligence). He was a senior-grade civil servant, a deceptively bland title.

The agent said, 'Let's see what today brings, shall we, Inspector?'

Winge brought Dietrich's arms behind his back to secure them with handcuffs. He prodded the prisoner through the door into the hallway. A line of dim overhead bulbs marked the way to the death chamber. When Dietrich's legs sagged, the executioner gently pulled on one of his arms to right him. Their footsteps echoed along the hall. They passed a dozen cell doors, behind which huddled the condemned.

Dietrich had always avoided cases that involved political controversies. He shunned the Drossler case in 1932 when it was clear the National Socialists had framed Drossler. And in 1939 he told his superior, Director Friedrichs, that he would not investigate crimes referred to him by the Gestapo. Only Dietrich's brilliant successes and his city-wide reputation allowed Friedrichs to resist the Gestapo's pressure to dismiss the inspector. When Director Friedrichs retired in 1940, Dietrich was passed over for the directorship because of his failure to join the Nazi Party.

There was more to it than that. Dietrich and the chief of the Gestapo, Heinrich Müller, had engaged in a ten-year feud, a running battle in which only Dietrich's skill and notoriety had allowed him to escape Müller's wrath. This time, skill and notoriety had not been enough.

And now Dietrich was an inmate in the very prison to which he had sent so many convicted criminals. His crime was as insignificant as it was damning. His brother Joachim had stolen from the Gettels Munitions Works in Hamburg the 'L' relay and detonator used in Colonel Stauffenberg's briefcase bomb. The Gestapo had taken only three weeks to discover Joachim's complicity in the plot, and he had been executed within twelve hours of his arrest. Otto Dietrich had known nothing of Joachim's involvement with Stauffenberg and was entirely unaware of the plot. But Dietrich's blood relationship to Joachim was an adequate indictment. His well-known anti-Party behavior over the years sealed his conviction.

The executioner and the Gestapo agent led Dietrich down three steps to the lowest room in the prison. Above the door was a crude keystone that jutted an inch into the hall. The ancient wood door hung on broad black iron hinges. Rudolf Koder opened the chamber door.

It is little known that the guillotine is the German execution device. Dissimilarities in the German and French guillotines may reflect their differences as people. Whereas the uprights on the French guillotine in the courtyard of the Fort d'Ivry in Paris rise to the heavens, the German machine is short and thickset, its purpose more readily evident. In France, the severed head drops into a woven basket, and while perhaps not a tender invention, the basket compares favorably to the rough plank onto which the German head falls. The French trestle, where the condemned lies while his head is slipped through the lunette below the blade, is decorated with a carved fleur-de-lis to remind the condemned of the state's authority by which he has found himself in this predicament. The Germans do not bother with such trifles, not wishing to waste the lesson on one who will be momentarily beyond caring.

Winge shoved Dietrich against the trestle and wrapped leather straps around his chest and knees. Lying on the board belly down, Dietrich was then lowered to horizontal. The trestle was on rails. The executioner slid Dietrich forward until his head was through the lunette. The neck beam was lowered and secured with a metal clasp. The Gestapo agent removed the safety bolt from the upright.

On his stomach Dietrich could see the plank and surrounding stone floor, blackened by a century of blood. He fought for breath, trying not to sob.

The Gestapo agent moved around the guillotine's ground beam so that Dietrich could see him out of the corner of an eye. 'Have you truly told us all you know about Joachim, Inspector?'

'I have,' he whimpered. 'I have nothing left to tell.'

It was the truth. The Gestapo had broken him. Dietrich had told them all he knew about his brother, his family, his career, and his religion. He had known nothing about his brother's treason, but Dietrich had held back nothing. He was bitterly ashamed of his weakness, but he was helpless against them.

'Well, it hasn't made any difference anyway, has it? Get on with it, Sergeant.'

Dietrich closed his eyes, blocking out the light for the last time. Winge stood motionless for a respectful ten seconds before pressing the button on the upright with his thumb.

With a searing squeal, the blade dropped in the post grooves. It fell for an eternity, for the blink of an eye.

And with a ringing crack, the blade stopped one inch above Dietrich's neck. The Gestapo agent had replaced the safety bolt.

'Not today, then, Inspector. Not today.'

The executioner released the neck brace and pulled Dietrich from under the lunette. The detective was quickly brought upright. When the straps were released, Dietrich swayed against the sergeant, who seized his arm to lead him from the execution chamber and along the hallway.

Dietrich was propelled into his cell. He collapsed onto his cot.

From the cell door Rudolf Koder said equably, 'We'll return again tomorrow. Right at noon. You may survive our next visit. You may not.'

The door creaked shut. Dietrich pulled the vile blanket over him and brought his legs up against his chest. For twelve consecutive days he had been taken to the guillotine, then returned to his cell.

Dietrich groaned, tightening the blanket around himself and laying his cheek against the cold metal of the cot. His entire frame shook with relief and with dread. His thoughts came only in simple pulses. All he wanted was to get out of this cell. Or out of this life. He didn't care which.

The POWs heard the crippled bomber long before they could see it. Allied planes based in occupied Italy now flew so often over the castle ninety miles south of Berlin that the prisoners could identify them by the pitch of their engines. This was an American B-25 Mitchell, and one of its engines was sputtering. Several POWs lifted to their toes for a better view.

'Stay in formation,' shouted Lieutenant Gerd Heydekampf. 'Close up there.'

Heydekampf was five feet three, and was known by the POWs and his fellow guards as Dreikäsehoch, Three Cheeses High. The lieutenant was wearing a greatcoat, short boots, and trousers with ankle-length gaiters, which the Wehrmacht had begun issuing that winter to conserve leather that would otherwise be used in the army's tall marching boots. He had a square chin and a gold front tooth. He was almost sixty years old, a reservist recalled to duty when the younger guards had been transferred to the front. Most Colditz guards were in their fifties and sixties.

'You there, Davis,' Heydekampf ordered, pointing to a POW in the first British line. 'Get back into line.'

Lieutenant Heydekampf was the camp's *Lageroffizier* (camp officer), senior to all guards but the commandant. He had lost his left arm in the Great War. The left sleeve of his coat was tucked into his belt. He spoke English well, learned on the job. He was a kindly man who tolerated no cruelty by the guards toward the prisoners.

Standing at sluggish attention, the British POWs were in five-by-five rows. The senior Allied officer, RAF Group Captain Ian Hornsby, stood at the front center. The Americans were in the northernmost group, nearest the chapel. Twenty-two guards were in the yard, and more on the catwalks and towers.

Captain David Davis of the Royal Ulster Rifles smiled evilly, then drew a finger across his throat in an exaggerated motion. Not once since D-Day had Davis been addressed by a German guard without responding with the slashing pantomime. Earlier in the war Davis would have been sent to the cooler for five days for such insubordination. Now Lieutenant Heydekampf bit down and turned away. An endless topic of conversation in the guards' mess was their fate when the Americans or Russians – pray God it would be the Americans – overran the camp. Surely the POWs would not slit their throats once the guards threw down their rifles. But, just in case, none of the guards was going to be anywhere near Captain Davis on that day.

Or anywhere near the nameless American who always lined up during the roll call in the back row, staring straight ahead, chewing rapidly on nothing. The American was captured six months ago, dressed in a US Army Air Force uniform. He had refused to divulge his name or rank to his interrogators at Dulag Luft, the airmen's reception camp at Oberursel. At Dulag Luft, he had defeated sophisticated interrogation techniques by simply saying nothing, not one word to the interrogator. Instead, after three hours of questioning, the American had reached across the desk to grab the interrogator by the lapels, used him as a battering ram to break open the interrogation room's door, then sprinted across the camp ground toward a command car, dragging the hapless interrogator along as a shield. The escape attempt had been foiled by a sentry who had shot the American in the leg, a poor marksman, as he was aiming for his back. After the American had recovered in the camp hospital, he was shipped in manacles to the castle.

None of the guards believed the American to be a flyer. He lacked the airmen's camaraderie and high spirits, unmistakable among flyers even in the meager conditions at the castle. There was a ruggedness about him, and a recklessness that bordered on indifference to his own safety. The American had attempted six escapes from Colditz, one a month since his arrival, receiving twenty-one days in a solitary-confinement cell each time. He was either escaping or serving time for it.

Still out of sight behind the walls of the prison, the Mitchell bomber drew closer. Its damaged engine drummed unevenly, fluttered, then quit altogether. One engine continued to thunder. Some POWs cocked their ears to better pick up the sound. They could tell the plane was on a northwesterly course. Perhaps its target had been the Leuna synthetic oil plant near Leipzig.

Several intoned silent prayers. Others whispered, 'Come on, old fellow,' and, 'You'll make it, friend.'

'Silence there,' Heydekampf ordered. 'Back to attention.' But he, too, turned to glance over the roof of the castle, searching for the plane.

Because they were in a forty-yard-square courtyard surrounded by five-story walls, the guards and POWs would not see the plane unless it passed directly overhead. The bomber sounded like it might oblige. Near the passage to the German yard the camp commandant, Colonel Erich Janssen, also stared into the sky. He monitored the roll calls but let Heydekampf do the work, and seldom said anything, merely nodding when Heydekampf gave him the completed roster at the end of the roll call. The sound of the failing bomber grew louder.

Built on a high promontory jutting out over the Mulde River, which flowed north to the Elbe, Colditz was perhaps the least attractive, least romantic castle in Germany. The citadel consisted of a series of wings erected over the centuries that had resulted in a figure eight, with two baileys in the middle of the wings. The south bailey was the prisoners' yard. The north was the guards' recreation area. The castle resembled a dormitory, with four and five-story edifices surrounding the courtyards. The windows were evenly spaced and barred, some looking into the yards, others looking over the apple and pear trees of Upper Saxony. Two Moorish cupola towers were the structure's only ornament. The lower walls were seven feet thick. The wooden roofs were sharply canted. Dormers extended from the roofs in a haphazard fashion, and brick chimneys dotted them. The entrance to the POW yard was over a moat and through mammoth oak doors. The ground fell away from the castle in terraces, on the west toward the town and in other directions toward orchards. The castle loomed over the medieval town of Colditz, where it was visible from every intersection.

With its guests' propensities for escape in mind, the castle had been modified. A machine-gun tower had been built in the northwest corner of the terrace outside the walls, giving a sight line down the north and west walls. Catwalks had been erected to eliminate guards' blind spots in the courtyard and on approaches to the gate. The castle's eighty-foot-high exterior walls were floodlit, as was the POWs' bailey. Microphones and primitive seismographs had been planted in the walls to detect digging. The lights went off only during air raids. Guards were on duty all night in the courtyard.

But since D-Day, escape had lost much of its allure, and attempts had largely stopped at Colditz and other POW camps. General Eisenhower had recently ordered POWs to stay behind the wire. 'We'll get to you soon,' Colditz's senior POW officer had heard Ike say over the camp's hidden radio. The prisoners knew Ike would keep his word, and so did the guards. The POWs could now hear Allied guns night and day to the south.

Only the American had tried to escape Colditz since Eisenhower's order. More interested in the American than in the approaching Mitchell, Lieutenant Heydekampf glanced at him again. Until last autumn, food had been adequate for the prisoners. Now the POWs were slowly wasting away. The lost weight had sharpened the angles of the American's face. With the wide cheekbones, cleft chin, and the three-day stubble he always wore, his face resembled a gnawed bone. His eyes were the gray-blue of smoke. He had thin, bloodless lips. His blond hair was sparse, and he kept it shorter than the POW fashion, little more than bristles along the sides of his head. He was taller than the other prisoners, and until recently his shoulders had sloped with muscles and his arms had filled his shirts. But he was thinning quickly, with the rest of them, and now the cords on his neck stood out and his clothes fit sloppily. The American had an aura of restrained violence about him, a brawler's presence. The guards knew he was incessantly calculating, searching for weaknesses and an avenue to exploit. The commandant had ordered that one of the guards on the catwalk above the potato-cellar stairs was always to watch the American when he was in the yard. Heydekampf and the other guards often speculated about the American. They had concluded that he was both dangerous and mad, an alarming combination.

The POWs' breaths showed in the raw air of morning, the steam almost filling the small bailey. Their eyes were on the gray sky. The bomber's remaining engine blustered, echoing between the walls of the courtyard and rattling the windows. The plane sounded as if it was aimed right at the castle. Then the second Wright engine quit, and the abrupt silence in the POW bailey was startling. Heydekampf followed the gaze of the prisoners to the small patch of leaden clouds visible above the castle walls.

The B-25 suddenly filled the sky over the bailey, eight hundred feet above the castle roofs. The bomber was canted on its starboard wing so that the POWs could see the white star on the fuselage. Fire had engulfed the engine cowling on that side. Smoke and flames soared behind the wing as far as the tail gunner's bubble. The plane's nose had been hit by flak and was a blackened and gaping hole.

The canopy behind the cockpit was a twisted mass of metal churned by white flames. The roof gunner's bubble was filled with flame, resembling a beacon. The hydraulics had gone awry; the left landing gear was down and the bomb-bay doors were open.

The Michell was a medium bomber, with a payload of over two tons. This plane was carrying incendiaries, fire bombs the size of milk canisters. The flak had detonated incendiaries that were still in their bomb-bay cradles. The plane had become a roaring torch.

Heydekampf swallowed hard, at once pitying the Mitchell crew and relieved that the bomber would fly well over the castle. The plane would land in the orchards north of the castle or in the Mulde River.

The lieutenant's relief was short-lived. Canisters were spilling from the open bomb bay. The plane was quickly out of sight again but the bombs remained, sprinkled across the sky in a ragged formation. And they were growing larger.

Heydekampf blew his whistle. 'Dismissed,' he yelled in English. 'Get into the building.'

The POWs were motionless, transfixed by the specks in the sky.

'Now,' he bellowed. 'Get going.'

A stampede began. Guards and prisoners dashed for the doors to the scullery, prisoners' kitchen, chapel, parcel room, solitary block, and the stairs down to the potato cellar, anywhere away from the courtyard. They quickly filled the barbershop, the guardhouse, and the shower room.

Heydekampf raced for the delousing shed at the southwest corner of the yard, where firefighting equipment was stored. The shed was a temporary structure made of clapboard with a shingle roof. The lieutenant yanked on the latch cord and rushed inside.

On one wall of the shed were shelves containing insecticide powders and solutions, an assortment of barber's shears, and a dozen flit-guns. A shower had been rigged but most of the delousing was done with the sprayers. A footbath was in the center of the hut. Tin tubs used to chemically wash clothes were in another corner. Nits, ringworm, fleas, chiggers; the shed had seen them all. Along another wall were stirrup pumps and buckets of sand.

The lieutenant grabbed a pump and was turning toward the door when an incendiary bomb shot through the shed's roof, showering the room with shingles. The canister slammed into the cement floor and burst open, spewing phosphorus to all corners of the shed and immediately igniting. A second canister blew through the roof, splintering the storage shelves before it split open on the floor and splashed more chemically fed fire across the room.

Furious flames blocked the door, crawled up the wood walls, and surged into the shower and tubs. Acrid black smoke blinded Heydekampf. Fire climbed his legs. The German was surrounded by shimmering sheets of orange flame. He tried for the entry, but the inferno beat him back. He doubled over, his lungs unable to draw in the baked air. He dropped the pump. His cap fell to the pool of flames on the floor. Fire splattered onto his uniform. His hair ignited. He sank to his knees, keenly aware that he was about to die.

And he journeyed straight to hell, surely, for out of the wall of fire stepped the devil, his skin leaping with flame, his eyes sinister red embers. Fire roiled around Satan's head in a profane imitation of an angel's halo. The devil's arms – limbs of flames – reached for the German.

Satan had the same features as the crazy American. It figured, was Heydekampf's last thought. He toppled toward the footbath.

The American scooped up the lieutenant and charged back out the delousing-shed door trailing flames. POWs immediately smothered the two men with their coats. They wrestled them to the cobblestones and rolled them over and over, choking the flames.

Two other incendiaries had landed in the yard. Guards and prisoners used shovels and sand from the fire station in the British orderlies' quarters to douse them. Other POWs returned to the yard and ran over to the lieutenant and the American.

The blankets were lifted. Lieutenant Heydekampf's clothes had become charred shreds. The hair on the left side of his head was scorched. His neck and wrist and calves were raw. The soles of his boots had been burned off.

The crowd around them grew larger. The American rolled to his knees. Smoke wafted from his blackened jacket and pants. His right ear was singed and his right arm would require salve. His eyebrows had been burned almost to the skin.

Lieutenant Heydekampf opened his eyes. Through heat-blistered lips he gasped, 'You!' He coughed roughly and panted for breath. 'I thought you were the devil.'

The American grinned and spoke to a German guard for the first time since his capture. 'I've been called that before.'

TWO

The American scraped a rusty nail with a fingernail file. The filings dropped to a tiny red pile on a copy of the *Overseas Kid*, the German propaganda newspaper for POWs, used mainly for toilet paper. The American worked rhythmically until the nail shone like new.

Next he began filing a piece of charcoal. A cone of shavings grew on the paper. Also on the table was a tin marked NUR FÜR KRIEGSGEFANGENE (FOR POWS ONLY), a grainy jam distilled from sugar beets. Leaning against the wall was a baseball bat he had carved from a pole stolen from the castle shop.

He was on the first floor of the British ward. At his elbow was dinner: one-seventh of a loaf of black bread and three small potatoes. At the stove near the door Lieutenant Reginald Burke of the Royal Tank Regiment was stirring tomcat stew, a catchall for anything available that day.

'Are yours in, Yank?' Burke called from the stove.

The American threw him the three potatoes. Burke sliced them, letting the wedges drop into the kettle. The stew also contained a handful of barley and kohlrabi, a plant resembling a turnip. He tossed in a pinch of salt. Pepper was not issued because a POW who was attempting escape had once thrown it into a guard's eyes. Tomcat stew was inedible to anyone but the starving.

The POWs knew the American as John, and they knew it was a pseudonym adopted to protect his life, for reasons they could only guess. Cray had told only the senior Allied officer his true name.

Burke was a Londoner, with hooded eyes and ears that stuck out at ninety degrees from his head. The turret of his Churchill tank had been on fire when he fled through the hatch, and the burn scar on his neck resembled purple crêpe. He lifted a pot from the stove, then moved to the table to fill the American's cup. The ersatz coffee smelled like a wet dog.

Two other kriegies were lying on their bunk beds, weak from pneumonia and dysentery. The Colditz infirmary was full. The American opened a D-bar from a Red Cross parcel. He cut the chocolate into fourths. Then with his spoon he gathered the crumbs that had fallen from the bar while he quartered it. He placed these atop the chocolate pieces, careful to apportion the crumbs evenly.

Burke ladled stew into a bowl. 'This is as ready as it'll ever be.'

The American rose from the table to take a bowl and cup from Burke. He carried them to a bunk where Captain Lewis Grimball of the Wiltshire Regiment was shivering under his blanket. The spring thaw had not reached the castle's interior. The American helped him to a sitting position. Grimball coughed raggedly. The American wiped spit from the corner of Grimball's mouth then held the cup to his lips.

Grimball sipped, then wheezed, 'This tastes like bloody dirt, John.'

'Here's your chocolate.' The American placed the candy in his hand, then stirred the nail rust and charcoal powder into the ersatz coffee, and handed it to the Brit. Rust prevented anemia and the charcoal helped control dysentery.

Grimball coughed again. He nibbled on a piece of bread.

The American also served a meal to Lieutenant Richard Cornwall of the Essex Scottish (Canada) Regiment, who was lying on his bunk near the stove. The walls of the ward were gray stone, and the slate floor was set in a rococo pattern, perhaps designed by a Saxon duke. The bunks, table, a few chairs, and a stove filled the small room. Nails had been hammered into the ends of the bunks to hang clothes. One shirt was hanging on a nail near a wash bucket filled with water and with prunes, raisins, and sugar from Red Cross parcels. Fermented a month, the concoction would have a horse's kick. When guards approached the ward, a POW would yell, 'Goons up,' and the hanging shirt would be tossed into the wash bucket. The guards assumed a POW was doing his laundry. When the Jerries left, every drop of the brew would be twisted from the shirt. Two barred windows overlooked the prisoners' yard.

When the American returned to the table, Burke placed a soup bowl in front of him. As they reached for their spoons, the door opened and the senior Allied officer entered the ward, followed by the ranking American officer.

The American and Burke dropped their utensils and quickly rose to attention.

'At ease,' the SAO said. 'May we have a few words with you, John?'

Group Captain Ian Hornsby had lost his Handley Page Halifax and three fingers of his left hand over occupied France, and had been caught attempting to walk out of Stalag Luft at Barth dressed as a chimney sweep. Hornsby had seemingly taken all of Colditz's privations onto himself. He had lost sixty pounds, and his body had become spindly. He had a mulish mouth and a wisp of a mustache. Hornsby shook his head at Reginald Burke's offer of coffee.

'We thought perhaps you could tell us what's going on,' said Harry Bell, the senior American POW. Bell liked to complain that his position as senior American officer didn't amount to anything because there were only five Americans at Colditz. Major Bell's bomber and fifty-one other B-17s – one-fifth of the attacking force – had been shot down during the Regensburg raid, August 17–18, 1943. Bell's face had been pinched by his months in captivity, and deep lines were around his mouth. His eyes were surrounded by a network of wrinkles.

The SAO said, 'We've gone along with your determination to remain anonymous, believing that you faced a firing squad or service in a slave-labor gang if the Jerries found out who you were. You told only me, and we've told no one. Except London, when you first arrived here.'

The American might have nodded. His face lost its usual trace of merriment. He was wearing a wool sweater under a duffel coat and black watch cap. His angled face, harsh in good times, had become bony. The skin had sunk around his cheekbones and jaw.

He had not lost teeth like many of the POWs, and they were even and white. He asked, 'A message on your radio?'

The POWs knew a radio was in the camp somewhere because BBC war news was known almost immediately after a broadcast, spread by Hornsby's runners, who would memorize ten sentences of news, then repeat it verbatim to gatherings of POWs. For security reasons, only Hornsby and two others knew that the radio was hidden in a table leg, or that half a year ago Hornsby had devised a wireless code, a multiple substitution with frequent changes. When a Geneva Red Cross official visited Colditz, Hornsby had asked him to take a message for his wife, and cable it to her from Geneva. It had contained the code, which England accepted. Hornsby had been receiving coded instructions since then.

Working his mouth silently and frowning, Bell had been staring at Jack Cray. Finally he spoke, clipping his words for emphasis. 'Captain Cray, we've been ordered to get you out of here.'

The corners of the American's mouth lifted. 'My friends call me Jack.'

'You've told us nothing about yourself,' Bell said angrily. 'All we know about you is that you are a crazy escaper.'

The last had been a particularly crazy attempt. When an electrician's truck was entering the yard through the main gate, the American took off, madly running past the guardhouse and over the moat bridge. Three Rottweilers tackled him seconds later. Then the guards reached him. A melee ensued, resulting in four guards being thrown into the moat, one with a broken jaw and another with a shattered kneecap. It took three blows to the American's skull with a rifle butt to bring him down. The American required 140 stitches in his legs and buttocks from the dogs' slashing fangs.

Bell demanded, 'Why have we been told to spring you from this place?'

'Did the message say?' The burns on Cray's arm were covered with gauze.

SAO Hornsby said, 'We thought you might have a clue.'

Cray shook his head.

Glowering, Major Bell shifted on his seat. 'I suspect you *do* know, goddamn it, and – '

Hornsby interrupted. 'There have been almost no gone-aways from POW camps in the past half-year. It's just not worth it anymore, with the Allied armies getting closer every day. And now when there is an escape, the Gestapo takes over the facility.'

'Things are hard enough here without letting the Gestapo have an excuse to run the castle,' Bell said, still glaring at Cray. 'Christ, our men are going to start dying if those bastards mete out a camp penalty, cutting the ration any further.'

Reginald Burke poured more coffee. 'Can I go with you, Yank?'

Hornsby ignored him. 'Captain Cray, the Germans are no longer toying with escapees, giving out the twenty-one-day confinements. The Gestapo has issued an order that all escaping POWs are to be handed over to them. That means if you're captured you'll either be shot outright or sent to the Grandenz Military Prison, which might be worse.'

'There must've been more to the message,' Cray said.

Hornsby looked at him closely as if trying to divine his thoughts. 'A Berlin address and a code word. Horseman. Does that mean anything to you?'

'Not a thing.'

Bell asked: 'Captain, why would they send you to Berlin, of all places? If you're so valuable, why aren't they getting you out of Germany, instead of further into it? And why do anything at all, with the war weeks from ending?'

Cray shrugged.

'And the message directs you to divert and distract on your way to Berlin,' Hornsby said. 'That's the term it uses. Divert and distract. Why, do you think?'

Cray rubbed his chin. 'So the Germans will use up a lot of men and material searching for me, I suppose. Maybe my mission is just to be a feint.'

Hornsby stared pensively at the American. Finally he said, 'Well, we've got to get you out of this castle. I've got an idea, a good one. You willing to try it?'

Cray grinned widely. 'Can I go today?'

Katrin von Tornitz walked carefully along Lasslerstrasse, stepping around a crater filled with murky water, then around an uprooted tree, torn from its planter by a high explosive blast. It was ten in the evening, and the city was black, with no streetlights or neon. The few cars in the street had tape over their headlights. She carried a heavy suitcase, a prewar Rugieri from Milan. On Katrin's lapel was an ornate lily pin designed by the Berlin goldsmith Emil Lettine and given to her on her twentieth birthday. The case and the pin were among the last bits of the life she had once known.

She ducked into a doorway to let a column of Home Guards march by, some with Panzerfausten – antitank rocket launchers – over their shoulders, most carrying only shovels. They were old men, bedraggled and ridiculous. At the intersection to the north an apple-red Post Office van also waited for the guardsmen to pass. Amid the chaos of Berlin was a berserk normalcy: mail was delivered daily, newspapers were printed morning and evening although most had been reduced to single sheets, and telephone calls could still be made from Berlin to any part of Germany.

Like many Berlin automobiles and trucks, the van had no hood over its engine. Hoods and trunk lids had been sucked away by the vacuum that follows a bomb detonation. On a reader board on the side of the Post Office van was the message THE FÜHRER'S WHOLE LIFE IS STRUGGLE, TOIL, AND CARE. WE MUST TAKE PART OF THE LOAD OFF HIS SHOULDERS TO THE BEST OF OUR ABILITIES. An elderly woman walked by, wearing a scarf around her hair and a briefcase with shoulder straps, a recent Berlin invention for shoppers who spent most of their days in lines.

Across the street was a building that had been a bakery. Most of the top-floor roof had been blown away. On the bakery door was a placard reading ACHTUNG! MINEN! An unexploded bomb was inside.

The old men's footfalls faded. Katrin glanced nervously along the street. Most of the tenements on the road had been destroyed. At the end of the block, a bathtub was perched in the air, attached to a pipe above a mountain of shattered masonry.

Katrin saw no one, so she briskly crossed the street. She had developed the *Berliner Blick* (the Berliner look), the habit of glancing over her shoulder for the Gestapo. She wore a gabardine coat with the collars pulled up against the wind. On her feet were 'Goebbels shoes,' flats with pressed-cardboard soles. They were sodden with rainwater. Most of Katrin's high heels had been broken on Berlin's perilous sidewalks and streets. Hats had not been rationed, and so had come into their own. Hers was green felt, peaked in two ridges, approximating a hat she had seen on Vivien Leigh in an English movie before the war.

Again Katrin surveyed the dark street. Still no one. She pushed against the bakery's shattered door. Her coat brushed against the bomb warning, and she stepped inside. Glass shards snapped under her shoes. The darkness was thick, black shadows on shadows. She held her hand up to ward off hanging wires and timbers. Her fingers found an oven built into a wall, and she barked her shin on an overturned chair.

She vaguely saw another warning poster tacked to a wall at the back of the bakery. The bomb lay under the pile of wreckage. A ragged hole had been punched through the ceiling above the mound of debris. She stepped around support pillars that gleamed like oilskins, damp from the rain dripping from the floor above. She felt along a wall of the room until she came to a stairway. She was met with the smell of decaying flesh. The Rescue Squad had missed a body somewhere under the rubble.

She climbed the stairs, splintering clumps of plaster with her shoes. The second floor was mostly open to the sky. Rain had dampened beams and the floor. She stepped on a broken mirror, cracking it further. Moving slowly, she crossed the room to the window, which had only slivers of glass sticking up from the frame. No one was on the street below.

Katrin found a barrel chair and placed her suitcase on it. She flipped the clasps. Inside was her radio, a pack wireless once used by a Wehrmacht infantry squad for unit messages. A powerful amplifier and frequency multiplier had been installed. She pulled a small compass from her pocket. It had been a toy, issued to a member of the Deutsche Jungvolk, the branch of the Hitler Youth for ten- to fourteen-year-olds, but it worked well enough.

Before Allied bombing had begun in earnest, she would have known which direction was northwest, but most of Berlin's landmarks had been toppled, and it was dark. She squinted at the compass's tiny needle, then squared herself to the northwest, toward another smashed window.

Unrolling one of the wire antennas, she picked her way across the room to the window's fractured casing. She retrieved a thumbtack from her coat pocket. The end of the antenna had a tiny loop. Bending close to the casing, she pressed the tack through the wire circle and into the wood. She did the same with the second wire antenna.

The two wires made a broadside array antenna, boosting the transmitter's radiation along the plane of the wires toward London. In directions lateral to the plane the broadcast waves largely canceled themselves out. Each half-wave wire was a precise length, and they ran to the window exactly three feet apart, all to put the radiation waves in phase.

She brought up her wristwatch. Still five minutes to go. She righted a captain's chair, brushed dampness from the seat, and lowered herself into it. She turned her head to gather in the wrecked, black room. Through the gaping holes in the ceiling, she could see the red night sky, colored by the fires set by American bombs that day. She wanted to grin at fate's irony but she lacked the energy.

Katrin von Tornitz had not visited Berlin until her twenty-third birthday, seven years ago. In 1902 her grandmother, Countess Voss-Hillebrand, had been one of the Ladies of the Palace. When the Kaiser changed the title Lady of the Palace to Lady-in-Waiting, and appointed new Ladies of the Palace ranking above them, the countess stormed out of the court and left Berlin for the family estate in the Mecklenburg area. She raged anew when she learned from a family friend, Ludwig Count Oppersdorff, the court marshal, that the kaiser enjoyed making jokes at the countess's expense, vulgarly approximating her bosom. The countess swore her family would never return to the city, and her iron will had prevailed for decades. Not once in her fifty-five years had the countess's daughter – Katrin's mother – visited Berlin. Only when her grandmother died – of an accumulation of bile, the family suspected – could Katrin venture to the great city.

During her first evening there, at the Hotel Esplanade, Captain Adam von Tornitz had approached her as she was standing near a terrace fountain. Cosseted away in the Voss-Hillebrand estate most of her life, Katrin was defenseless against the gallant Wehrmacht officer. That evening he had whispered into her ear that she was *das Ewig-weibliche*, the eternal feminine, a phrase from Goethe. They were married ten days later.

Their love was a gift from God, she knew then. Their years together played themselves out joyfully, even though they were together only a few days here and there when the captain received a leave. What they lost in those days apart they made up for in intensity when they were together. She was convinced then – and still fervently believed – that their love was a unique creation, unattainable by other humans. With Adam she had found her fulfillment.

Adam von Tornitz was arrested on July 28, 1944, tried before Judge Freisler in the People's Court for complicity in Colonel Stauffenberg's plot, then taken to Plötznsee Prison, where he was hung by piano wire from a meat hook. Rumours circulated in Berlin that a motion-picture camera had been in the death chamber, and that Hitler watched the movies at night. She never learned what, if anything, her husband had done to assist Stauffenberg.

Her grief had made her a traitor to the Fatherland. At Adam's funeral, one of his friends, Colonel Wilhelm Becker, expressed his sympathy, then added cryptically, 'Katrin, if you would like to do something in memory of Adam more substantial than tossing flowers onto his casket, let me know.' Becker was with the Wehrmacht Administration Office in Berlin.

She had been doing her part for the Reich for three years,

working as a radio operator for OKW assigned to G Tower, the thirteen-story antiaircraft complex built on the grounds of the Berlin Zoo. She had known nothing of the messages she sent or received. They were always in code, and she knew radios, not codes. She had spent her days over a Morse sender.

She had been fired at OKW the day Adam was arrested. Had she not been so disconsolate after Adam's death, she might have feared for herself because the Gestapo often arrested the accused's family members. But she was numb to everything but grief. And then rage began to kindle.

So she had visited Colonel Becker at his home in Dahlem. Three days later she received the pack wireless and a one-time pad, a booklet with codes printed in red for enciphering and black for deciphering, and made of cellulose nitrate, which burns quickly and leaves no latent images. Each page of the book contained a new, random key character, to be used only once for each plain text character. A one-time code is unbreakable because it never repeats.

She was also given a route that took her from the Tiergarten to Kreuzberg south of the city center then back to the Friedrichstrasse Station, during which she checked three drops. She was to transmit whatever message she found, but there had never been any, until today. She had found in her southerly drop a message that the sender asked be transmitted immediately. Katrin did not know that a milkman had made the drop. She had transmitted his message that afternoon.

Colonel Becker had also told Katrin of the Gestapo's new radio direction finder, a circular antenna mounted on a black Opel. She was not to broadcast twice from the same location, and she was never to send for more than thirty seconds. Buildings with ACHTUNG! MINEN! on them were free from squatters and looters. She knew the risk of treading inside buildings where high-explosive duds had fallen, but she no longer feared anything.

Berlin was a city of widows, and they had grown to look alike, with vacant eyes, compressed lips, and the timid expressions of those eternally fearful of more dreadful news. Katrin had fought this sameness. She wore lipstick and a light stroke of eyeliner, though not much because heavy use of makeup was unpatriotic. Her face was slightly overfeatured, with vast Prussian-blue eyes. Adam had said they were the color of the Havel River. Her eyes had once been able to switch from glacial to gay in an instant. They had an inexhaustible supply of expressions. Now they were only mournful. The slightest of webs had begun around her eyes, giving her a delicate majesty. Her nose was sharp. Her smile had been luminous, as if lit from within. She could not remember the last time she smiled. Adam had reveled in her black hair, and had called her 'my little raven.' The ebony hair, blue eyes, frost-white skin, and her full rose lips were jarring in their kaleidoscopic colors. Adam had trouble finding his voice that day they had first met each other on the Esplanade terrace, he had later admitted.

She removed the one-time pad and a pencil from a pouch in the suitcase. She waited until the dial on her watch clicked onto the hour. Her radio was set at 13,500 kilocycles. She removed her hat to place the headset over her hair. The set painfully pinched her ears. She tapped her call sign, *PAT*, arbitrary letters she had chosen during her first broadcast. Then she sent a series of *V*s so London could precisely tune to her signal. She repeated the *dit dit dit dah* three times. Her next letters were *NA*, meaning she had no message to send that night.

From her headset came a series of *V*s. England was acknowledging her signal. The Morse ended. That was all she ever received. She was about to remove her headset when the receiver stuttered into life again. An actual message. She fumbled for the pad. Unable to see the paper clearly in the dark, she jabbed her dots and dashes across the pad. Twenty seconds later it ended. She clattered an acknowledgment of *V*s.

Deep clefts grew between her brows, and a moment passed before she could take off the headset and lift herself from the chair. The message was brief, so she decoded it as she sat there, squinting hard, as if that might help her see better in the dim light. Decoded, the message said only, 'Follow Horseman's instructions.'

She knew of no one named Horseman.

Her sudden responsibility slowed her as she wound the antennas and packed the suitcase. Carrying the case, she cautiously descended the stairs, again whiffing the body hidden in the ruins of the bakery. She paused at the door, checking the street. A dozen refugees were tramping along, looking for shelter for the night. She waited until they had passed, then darted from the building, and she was worried.

And she would have been more worried had she known of the black Opel two blocks away. The car had been traveling back and forth along the roads, but always closer and closer to her, its radio direction finder moving left and right. But when Katrin ended her broadcast, the car slowed, then stopped, having failed again to find her in time.

Dietrich was staring at his wooden bowl, attempting to occupy his mind by guessing whether the white bits floating in the clear fluid were rice or maggots. He tried to push aside hopes that his doctor might visit again. One week had passed since the first visit, and the doctor had said he would return again in a week, if possible. He had come at mealtime, seven days ago. The chance he might return had been a spark of hope for the prisoner, as faint and improbable as it was persistent. Seeing somebody other than the executioner and Gestapo agent Koder come through the door was a glittering prospect. Dietrich slowly lifted the spoon, having determined that once he sipped the soup, all possibility of the visit would end.

The latch sounded. Wearing a knotted frown, Rudolf Koder pushed open the metal door and stood aside to let the doctor into the cell.

Dietrich closed his eyes a moment at the answered prayer. Then he carefully put the bowl to one side and stood to greet the visitor.

'Otto, you look even worse than last week,' Kurt Scheller said, gripping his friend's arms.

'You humor me.' Dietrich's voice cracked, and he failed to make himself sound anything but pitiable.

The doctor helped lower Dietrich back to the bench. Scheller's face was narrow, with cheeks so drawn that the outline of his teeth showed on them. His neck was as thin as his wrists, and he was so slight he was lost in his clothes. His smile was warm.

'Did you find out anything about Maria?' Dietrich's words tumbled forth. 'Could Golz find out anything? Did you talk to Wunninburg? Did they get anywhere?'

Scheller shook his head. 'I'm afraid not, Otto.'

Dietrich closed his eyes. Erwin Golz was director of Berlin police, Dietrich's superior. And Alfred Wunninburg was general of police, Golz's superior. Maria Dietrich had been arrested because of the new practice called *Sippenhaft* – the arrest of kith and kin.

'I spoke with both Golz and Wunninburg, Otto. Several times. They tried hard, but they couldn't locate her.'

'Maria is alive, though?'

'They couldn't even tell me that. She was arrested soon after you were, and has disappeared somewhere in the political prison system. They told me police officers don't have any influence in those places. Director Golz said he has used all his chits just to get me inside Lehrterstrasse Prison to see you these few times.'

A roach crawled along the floor toward the bucket that served as the privy. Dietrich rubbed his forehead, hiding his eyes. He didn't want the doctor to see his tears. But Dr Scheller had served the Dietrich family for a generation, and knew his patient. He lowered himself to the bench and gripped Dietrich's hand.

'Don't give up hope, Otto,' the doctor said in a low voice. 'You are still alive. You have survived this long. Don't give up.'

Dietrich looked up. He whispered, 'Did you bring it?'

Scheller answered lamely, 'The guards took my black bag away from me before letting me into your cell and – '

'You aren't answering my question, Kurt. Did you bring it?'

Scheller inhaled hugely. 'I'm dead set against this, Otto. It's against all my beliefs and all my training.'

'And that's damned easy for you to say, because in two minutes you are going to waltz out of here back into the sunlight.' Dietrich gripped the doctor's arm. 'You brought it. Give it to me.'

Scheller glanced at the closed cell door, then he pulled off a shoe and held it upside down. A silver pill dropped into his hand. Dietrich reached for it, but the doctor closed his hand.

'Otto, you must pledge something to me.'

Dietrich scowled with frustration.

Scheller continued, 'You won't use this until all hope has ended, and you can no longer endure.'

Dietrich nodded noncommittally.

'Do you pledge that to me?' Scheller persisted. 'Do you swear? Maybe there will be good news about Maria. We can still hope. Wait until you hear.'

After a moment Dietrich answered quietly, 'I'll wait until I hear.'

Indecision written on his face, the doctor slowly opened his hand and let Dietrich claim the pill.

'What do I do?' the detective asked.

'Bite down on it, and close your eyes. It'll do the rest.'

'How long does it take?'

'Thirty seconds.'

The cell door opened. Agent Koder said, 'Your time is up, Doctor.'

Scheller rose from the bench. 'Remember your pledge, Otto.' He stepped toward the door. 'I'll try to get in next week again. Wait for me. You'll wait for me?'

The cyanide pill in his hand, Dietrich lay back on the cot and turned to the wall, not strong enough to watch his friend disappear through the door.

THREE

Lieutenant Heydekampf detested these marches, but the Geneva Convention allowed them so he bit down and paced along the wall near the chapel, waiting for it to end. Every time news of an Allied victory reached Colditz Castle, the POWs would march in brisk formation, to and fro in the tiny yard, flaunting the Allied achievement. The British and American POWs had become expert in tight about-faces.

Today the POWs were marching to celebrate the United States Ninth Army's capture of Essen, an event that had happened just the day before, April 9. Heydekampf knew the POWs had a radio hidden in the castle because the entire POW population learned the BBC news on the same day it was broadcast. Despite searches that had entirely destroyed the wards of the SAO and Captain David Davis – who Heydekampf suspected was chief of X-Organization, the POW escape committee – Heydekampf's flying squads had been unable to find the radio.

The left side of Heydekampf's scalp was open and raw from the fire, so he was without his cap. Bandages were patched around his neck and wrist, but he seemed to hurt all over. Even his missing left hand seemed to be pumping pain into him.

The POWs were using an American marching chant: 'She left. She left. She left, right, she left. You had a good home. You had a good job. You had a good life, but she left, right, she left.' The interminable refrain crawled up Heydekampf's back. With the war going as it was, the POWs marched every day.

The chant abruptly stopped, and Heydekampf's head jerked up

at a new sound. The wail of a cat whose tail was being pulled. Or the screech of fingernails dragged across a blackboard. A chilling noise he had never before heard. Coming from the formation of marchers.

He blew his whistle and the parade halted. The sound continued. The devil's dog braying, it sounded to Heydekampf.

'What is that noise?' he demanded in English. 'What have you got?'

Harold MacMillan, of the Argyle and Sutherland Highlanders, called out, 'Bagpipes, sir.' He was standing at attention at the back of the POW formation.

Heydekampf charged across the yard to the POW. MacMillan held the bag under his arm. His fingers were on the chanter. Three drones lay across his shoulder. MacMillan was the shortest man at the castle, barely five feet one. He said in a thick Scots brogue, 'The windbag has the Black Watch pattern. Lovely, isn't it?'

For a moment the German lieutenant was frozen by the sheer brazenness of the bagpipes. This musical instrument – if it could be called that – lifted the POWs' impudence to an outrageous new height.

He sputtered, 'Where did you get that, MacMillan?'

'Lieutenant, may I speak with you?'

Startled at the voice, Heydekampf turned to find the camp commandant, Colonel Janssen, standing at his shoulder.

'Of course, sir.'

The colonel led him to a spot near the blackened ruin of the delousing shed. The ward wall above the shed had been colored by the flames. That section of the castle, called the Saalhaus, was for senior POW officers, and in ancient times had been the armory. The stone had resisted the fire.

Janssen had won the Iron Cross at Flanders in the Great War, and he wore the decoration on his tunic. With the shortages, he had lost weight, and his gray uniform coat hung loosely on him. He had a miser's face, with tiny features and suspicious eyes.

He said, 'Lieutenant, about the bagpipes.'

'Yes, sir?'

'I am allowing the prisoners to accompany their marches with that infernal instrument. I see no harm in it.'

The parade resumed. The bagpipes' caterwauling made Heydekampf ball his fists. The prisoners marched in time, their wood clogs clacking against the cobblestones.

Lieutenant Heydekampf said through teeth clenched against the din, 'Where'd it come from, sir?'

Colonel Janssen's face was carefully deadpan. 'I purchased it at a curiosity shop in Leipzig yesterday.'

A puzzled moment passed, then understanding creased Heydekampf's face. 'And you received a safe-conduct pass in return, is that it, sir?'

The colonel drew himself up stiffly. 'You are being insubordinate.' Then he softened. 'I know you are dedicated to the service of this camp, Lieutenant Heydekampf. Thanks to you, no POWs have escaped in all your time here as camp officer, a remarkable achievement considering the escape artists interned here. But your dedication to the Reich should not cloud your understanding of what is to come for us.'

Heydekampf asked with acid sweetness, 'You are saying that we must look out for ourselves, is that it, Colonel?'

'POW Captain MacMillan signed a document saying that I had treated him humanely during his two years at Colditz. This piece of paper may get me through difficult times in the weeks to come. To insinuate that I've acted traitorously is unfair to me, Lieutenant.'

Heydekampf chewed back his anger. The colonel was right. Janssen was a patriot and a fine prison administrator. And he was always fair. He had divided evenly among the guards the American airmen's emergency rations found in the downed Mitchell bomber, which had crashed in a pear orchard a kilometer from the castle. Heydekampf's portion had come to half a can of Spam and a Hershey bar, his first chocolate in three months. None of the American crew had survived. Their bodies had been pulled from the wreckage and buried in the military cemetery near the river. Their dogtags would be given to the Red Cross.

The good-conduct passes had lately become a currency in the

camp. Heydekampf knew that Colditz's other *Lageroffizier*, Lieutenant Birzer, had traded a precious kilo of bacon for one from the POW tank officer, Lieutenant Burke. Some of the guards were gathering them like children collected stamps before the war, believing that if they could present twenty of the testimonials their blamelessness would be proven beyond doubt.

Heydekampf smiled crookedly. 'Couldn't you have made it a trumpet, Colonel? I don't know how much of this racket I can endure.'

'POW MacMillan was a difficult bargainer, and . . .'

Shouts came from the marching formation. Janssen and Heydekampf turned to the sound. A fight had erupted among the prisoners. The bagpipe was thrown into the air. Two prisoners fell to the ground, flailing at each other. The other POWs roared, quickly choosing sides.

Heydekampf rushed toward the fray, then hesitated, quickly swinging his gaze the length of the yard. Fistfights were classic POW ruses, designed to draw attention away from an escape. The lieutenant saw nothing unusual. He started again for the two brawlers. One of them was Harold MacMillan.

'Break it up,' he bellowed in English. He waded into the crowd.

Another shout, a desperate animal shriek of fear, instantly halted the fight. The cry came from the direction of the Saalhaus, the same corner of the yard where the remains of the delousing shed were.

Heydekampf pivoted to the sound. He saw a body slam into the ground.

'No,' he gasped, then sprinted toward the body, pushing aside POWs. He came to the broken form.

It had come to rest face down at the base of a five-story wing of the castle. A brown cardboard suitcase made from a Red Cross bulk food box had hit the ground nearby, as had two moss-covered shingles.

Heydekampf rolled the body over.

'Damn,' he said softly. 'Damn it to hell. It's the crazy American.'

Blood was coming from the American's ears, which Heydekampf knew from his Great War service was evidence of a fractured skull.

The blood was gathering at the American's neck, staining his coat and flowing onto the ground. One of the American's eyes was blackened and filling with blood. A ruptured eye socket. The POW's arm must have crashed into the ground first, because it projected behind his shoulder at a twisted, unnatural angle. The American lay on the cobblestones like a rag doll.

Commandant Janssen and Group Captain Hornsby came to the front of the crowd.

Heydekampf opened the suitcase. A spare sweater was inside, along with ration tins containing escape fudge, a treacly molasses, raisin, and chocolate mix made by the POWs for cross-country journeys.

Heydekampf reached for the POW's wrist. He waited a long moment with the American's wrist between his finger and thumb before he announced, 'No pulse. He's dead.'

'Of course he's dead, Lieutenant,' Group Captain Hornsby said bitterly. 'He fell five bloody stories and hit your goddamn stone courtyard.'

A sentry on the catwalk over the yard gate called out, 'Halt. Hands up.'

Heydekampf spun to the new sound. The guard had his rifle at his shoulder, aimed at the roof above the Saalhaus. Heydekampf moved quickly through the crowd and across the yard almost to the chapel door across from the Saalhaus, where he could see to the roof.

POW Burke was hanging from the ridge line of the roof with one hand. A suitcase was in his other hand. His feet were scrabbling for purchase. He managed to catch the peak with a heel, and he levered himself to a sitting position. A track of missing moss indicated where the American's body had slid down the roof before pitching into space.

Burke raised his free hand and yelled, *'Schiessen Sie nicht. Ich ergebe mich.'*

Don't shoot. I give myself up. It was a lifesaving phrase memorized in German by all would-be escapers.

Heydekampf waved at three guards. 'Go get POW Burke from the roof.' He returned to the Saalhaus wall.

Colonel Janssen was kneeling next to the American's body. He, too, was searching for a pulse, his hand wrapped around the POW's other wrist. He exhaled heavily. 'He's dead.'

'*Scheisse*,' Heydekampf muttered.

Dabbing at a tear, Ulster Rifleman David Davis turned away. The American had been a good sport, someone to enliven an evening with a story or two. Ike and Monty were coming as fast as they could but the war had not ended quickly enough for the American.

Janssen ordered a nearby guard, 'Get a bag from the infirmary.'

Heydekampf moved along the crowd of POWs to the senior allied officer. 'Your fight over the bagpipes was a ruse, was it not, Captain Hornsby? A little choreography to distract my guards?'

Hornsby said nothing.

Anger clipped Heydekampf's words. 'You see what has resulted from your game? A good soldier is dead, thanks to your escape pranks. You live with that for a while.' The German's voice carried emotion he could not control. 'And why in the world would you try to free this man when your troops are days or weeks away? You can hear your own guns every day as well as I can.'

Commandant Janssen also addressed the SAO. 'Tell me what you saw, Captain Hornsby.'

Hornsby stuck his chin out.

'I am asking you if you witnessed any German action in this matter. Any brutality? Any involvement by a guard?'

Hornsby's voice was brittle with contempt. 'Protecting your record, Colonel? Hoping none of us will testify at a war crimes trial in a few months?'

'You have been treated as civilly as possible by me and my staff. You know that and so do I. Now I demand that you clarify in front of these British and American and German witnesses what was seen here.'

The RAF officer looked along the line of the prisoners. 'I didn't see anything untoward,' he admitted. 'Anybody else see anything?'

The prisoners murmured they had not.

'Good.' The commandant walked rapidly between the POWs across the yard toward the underpass to the German yard.

Lieutenant Heydekampf said quietly, 'We'll bury him today, Group Captain Hornsby. I will issue some wood and white paint from the shop if you will have one of your men construct a cross.'

Heydekampf glanced again at the American, a pile of broken bones, a parody of a human. The lieutenant began toward the gate, stepping through the crowd of POWs. But he was brought up by David Davis, who would not get out of the German officer's way.

Davis glared at the German, then slowly drew a finger across his own throat.

Heydekampf shuddered. He brushed past the POW and hurried toward the shop.

SS Private Bruno Patzer knew the garden had once been a lovely atrium, with fountains, a tea pavilion, and a greenhouse full of hyacinths and jasmine, the blossoms the Führer preferred on his table. The garden would have offered little solace on this bitter night, though, even if bombs had not destroyed it. The private shuffled his feet, trying to keep warm. His post was the camouflaged guard tower that had a clear view of the entire Reich Chancellery garden. His sentry box was fifteen feet above the ground. It was unheated, but a roof was over his head. The day had been unusually cold for April, and now rain was falling heavily.

It was nearing ten o'clock in the evening. Landscaping lights had once illuminated the cherry and linden trees, boxwood hedges, and azaleas, but the lights were subject to blackout regulations. A wind was picking up, pushing the rain sideways onto Patzer. The Führer had personally designed a yellow-and-white standard, and earlier in the war it had flapped on its pole above the New Chancellery whenever he was in Berlin. Now that enemy armies were near, the standard never flew.

Patzer heard footsteps in the gravel. He straightened his back and brought his rifle to the ready. A conversation carried to him on the wind.

'The Führer should go at once. There is no sense remaining.'

Patzer recognized the voice as that of the Führer's secretary, a stocky bulldog of a man named Bormann. The private knew nothing about the secretary, not even whether he held a rank in the military or the Party. He wore no insignia on his ill-fitting brown uniform. Patzer had been told by his captain to stay out of Bormann's way but the captain had not clarified his warning. Bormann was walking with Dr Morell, the Führer's physician. They made their way toward the blockhouse.

Private Patzer shifted his hands, trying to keep his cold fingers away from the colder steel of his Mauser, gripping instead its wooden stock. He blew air into a hand. Christ, it was frigid in the watch-tower, standing still, hour after hour. The Reich Chancellery was across the garden from Patzer. The façade on Vosstrasse was intact, but Patzer's view was of the back of the vast building, and it had been heavily damaged by bombs. From his watchtower perch most of Private Patzer's view was ruin. The greenhouses had been destroyed by a bomb blast, and glass splinters littered the garden. Uprooted trees and broken statuary seemed to have been tossed casually about. The wooden cistern containing water for firefighting had been repeatedly repaired by the air-raid wardens, and was still on its stand. A wandering trench had recently been dug in the garden for the guards to jump into during the Allied bombings. A cement mixer had been abandoned near the shattered greenhouse, and had been there, forgotten, ever since Patzer was first assigned to the Chancellery. The largest structure in the garden was the blockhouse, a thirty-foot cube of concrete near the rear of the Old Chancellery. The blockhouse's steel door led to the Führer's bunker. The private had never been through that door.

Patzer smiled to himself. Two LSSAH men – members of the Liebstandarte-SS Adolf Hitler, an elite SS bodyguard unit – were stationed at the door, and even that pompous ass General Keitel was asked for his pass each time he entered the bunker.

From his tower Patzer could also see the damaged Foreign Ministry's office across Wilhelmstrasse. The ministry's windows overlooked the garden and had been boarded up. The SS patrolled the vacant building, insuring that no one would be able to find a window looking into the garden. Silhouetted against the purple sky was an antiaircraft battery on top of the New Chancellery. The fifteen-man crew of No 1 Flak Division were behind their weapons at the division's duty station.

SS Private Patzer was one of fifteen guards on duty in the garden. Two SS patrols were responsible for the east and west sections. An additional guard, called the *Hundführer*, roamed the western portion near the blockhouse with a German shepherd.

The private was proud of his service in the Liebstandarte-SS Adolf Hitler. LSSAH soldiers took a personal oath of obedience to the Führer, and on that day two years ago when Private Patzer had taken his oath, Hitler had walked down the line of soldiers, shaking each hand and looking into each pair of eyes. When the Führer reached him, it was the greatest moment of Patzer's life. Patzer and other soldiers had sworn they could see a halo around Hitler's head. Although the Führer had not spoken to him that day or any day since, Patzer was as close to the German savior as he was to his mother. He loved the man. And knowing where Hitler was – in the Chancellery or the bunker or the garden – when few in Berlin had any idea, fed the familiarity. The guards referred to Hitler as Grofaz, short for *Grösster Feldherr aller Zeiten* (the greatest general of all time), and even with the Soviet barbarians on the Oder and their American, Canadian, and British dupes marching into central Germany, there was not a trace of irony or mockery in the guards' voices when they used the nickname.

A guard at the blockhouse blew a bosun's whistle. Patzer's thoughts instantly returned to the garden. He quickly squared his helmet and his belt, and brought his Mauser in line in front of him. He cleared his throat, not that he would have occasion in the next few minutes to use his voice. But, perhaps, someday.

The blockhouse guards jerked themselves to a rigid attention, a snap that would have broken most backbones. From the black doorway, emerging slowly, his figure congealing out of the darkness, walked the Führer. Beside him was Blondi, his white Alsatian. The dog leaped to the end of his leash, eager for the trees and bushes of the garden. Hitler let the animal lead him along the gravel path.

The Führer was wearing a gray greatcoat, a scarf, black gloves, and a field-gray peaked cap.

He moved slowly, cautiously, as if testing each step. Patzer wanted to weep for the man. The private had seen Hitler walk up the long flight of steps to the podium at the 1938 Nuremberg SS rally. Now Hitler wobbled like a drunken sailor when walking, and lurched to the right with each step. He used his right hand to both grip the dog's leash and to hold his dead left arm close to his body. In better days Patzer had seen him guide Blondi over a two-meter wooden wall, then up a ladder where the dog would beg for a treat. Hitler kept the treats in his coat pocket. He shuffled along the gravel path. In the darkness Patzer could not see his face, only a small glint off the gold-rimmed spectacles he always wore except when in front of cameras.

Blondi danced in a circle, almost pulling the Führer off his feet. At the fork in the path the dog pulled Hitler south toward Patzer's tower. The private could see Hitler's breath in the cold air.

Patzer removed his gaze from the man to stare precisely ahead, as ordered when the Führer passed. The private stiffly held his rifle at present arms.

Hitler's awkward footsteps sounded in the gravel, yet closer. Then they stopped. At tense attention, Patzer braved a look down the side of tower.

The Führer's head was tilted back, and he was peering straight up the tower at Patzer. Even in the dim light Patzer could see the diamond-blue eyes. Astounded, the private swayed on his feet and let his mouth fish open.

'It's cold up there,' Hitler said. 'Much too cold for April.'

Patzer tried to bark out his response as he had been trained. Instead, his voice was tremulous. 'Yes, my Führer.'

'Your hands are wet, and are going to get blue.'

'Yes, my Führer.' A little better. Almost the proper tone of absolute attention, utter subservience, and panting eagerness.

'Here.' Hitler peeled off his gloves, juggling the leash between his hands. 'Can you catch these?'

'Yes, my Führer.' Patzer lowered his rifle.

Hitler tossed the calf gloves skyward. Patzer could catch only one of them. The other fluttered back down to the ground. Blood rushed to the guard's face.

Hitler stepped off the path into the mud to retrieve the glove. 'We Germans don't play cricket like our enemies. So you can't blame me for a lame toss.'

'No, sir.'

Hitler reared back again and launched the glove. Patzer snatched it easily.

'Put them on your hands,' Hitler lectured lightly. 'Don't stick them into your pocket to keep them for a museum somewhere.'

'Thank you, my Führer.' Patzer shoved his fingers into the gloves. The rabbit-fur lining still radiated Hitler's warmth. Patzer was giddy with the intimacy.

'And thank you, SS-Private.' Hitler tottered off, following his dog, the gravel snapping under them.

Patzer lifted his rifle again. He breathed deeply of the sweet moment. He had taken his SS oath in the presence of his leader. Now he took another one, in silence, to the Führer's back as Hitler hobbled away. The end of the struggle was coming. If the Führer stayed in Berlin at the Chancellery, Patzer swore he would stay with him to the end, to the very end.

FOUR

The farmhouse was fifty yards off the road, down a dirt drive. Cray walked toward the house, avoiding ruts and potholes. An apple orchard was to the north, the trees new in their spring leaves. Poles for supporting the apple-laden branches in autumn were stacked alongside the driveway. On the other side of the drive was a moss-covered stone wall that might have been two centuries old.

Cray surveyed the farm as he approached. To one side of the house stood a goat shed and an open machine shed in which there were a two-bladed plow and stacks of apple boxes. Leather rigging hung on pegs behind the plow. Grass along the stone wall was long, wooden planks had fallen from the goat shed, shingles were missing from the farmhouse roof, and ivy had grown up and over the porch. The farm was in decline.

Cray neared the house. No automobile in the driveway. No one at a window looking at him. No farm animals. The house was made of clapboard, with a stone chimney. The porch creaked when he stepped onto it, then he leaned to his right to peer into a sitting room. Empty. He walked to the rear of the house, where a garden contained a row of bean stakes and a torn bird net that was hung over small pear trees. A potato patch had been turned over, perhaps again and again, though the potato harvest would have been last year. A shovel was still in the ground, planted rather feebly. He searched the goat and machine sheds.

Cray moved to the back door. The knob turned easily. When he stepped into the kitchen, he was met by the smell of fresh baking, a fruit pastry of some sort. Tendrils of scent wrapped around Cray, making him feel lightheaded. Shrunken and ill used, his stomach loudly rolled over at the prospect of being filled. A strudel and several old newspapers were on a sideboard near a woodstove.

Cray gazed at the pastry. A flaky crust around apple halves. He wiped a corner of his mouth. A table and two chairs were in the kitchen. He looked into a pantry. Near it was an open cupboard containing pots and pans. A wooden box held a dozen small potatoes and two cabbages with brown leaves.

Cray stepped into the sitting room. An overstuffed chair, a wall clock. He opened a closet near the front door. Empty but for two coats and an umbrella. Then he walked across a hooked rug past a fireplace to the bedroom. A poster bed, a hat on a wooden rack, a dresser and a mirror. Leather boots were on the floor in a corner. A farmer's spartan home. Cray was satisfied no one was home. The house was cold. Cray could still see his breath.

He rifled through the dresser. In one drawer he found a man's clothing. Cray peeled off his shirt and pants. He found a shirt with wooden buttons, too tight but wearable. Next were a pair of pants and a work coat.

He returned to the kitchen and opened a drawer for a fork. He lifted the strudel reverentially. He sniffed the pastry, but only slightly, lest smelling it might somehow diminish it prematurely. He lowered the plate to the table, sat on a sturdy chair, and squared himself to this grand task. He carefully cut off a small piece of the pastry, monitoring where all the crumbs fell so he could return to them, and lifted it to his mouth.

The muzzle of a shotgun bit into the back of Cray's neck. His fork froze.

'This is my house,' a voice behind Cray said. An old woman's voice. 'And that's my strudel.'

Cray sat utterly still. His knife was under his belt.

The shotgun barrels lifted from his neck. The woman came into his view. She was wearing a long green coat, a crocheted shawl, and a frown. The shotgun was held comfortably in her hands. She sidestepped to the end of the table opposite Cray, the barrel never wavering. She sat on a chair, propping the bird gun on the table edge, its barrels pointed at Cray's throat.

'You are an escapee from that awful castle over in Colditz.' It was not a question.

He answered in German. 'Yes.'

'So you must be dangerous.' The woman wore her silver hair in a bun on top of her head. Her face had deep lines like dried and broken mud. Her eyebrows had grown together above her nose. She was thin, with her coat hanging loosely from narrow shoulders, and with wrists the width of broom handles. Her dark eyes were far back in her head. They were alert. Cray suspected they missed nothing.

'And you speak our language,' she said. 'I should shoot you now.'

'Will you wait until I eat this strudel before you shoot me?'

An eyebrow rose. Then a corner of her mouth lifted slightly. 'If I wait until you eat the strudel, then I'll have a dead body in my kitchen and no strudel. But if I shoot you now, I'll have a dead body but I'll also have the strudel. So it would be smarter to shoot you now.'

Cray suggested, 'How about if I eat half, then you shoot me?'

'All right,' she said. 'Cut the strudel in half, then I'll choose which half you eat.'

Cray visually measured the pastry, then cut it precisely in half with his fork. The old lady nodded at the piece to Cray's left. He instantly dug into it with the fork. The strudel seemed to burst inside his mouth, filling him with flavor down to his feet.

He took three more bites, then said, 'You are a good cook, ma'am. This would taste wonderful even if I weren't about to be killed.'

'I didn't have fresh fruit, so I used apples I canned last fall. And I had to stretch the flour by adding some sawdust.'

'I wondered about the piny taste.'

'How did you learn German?' the woman asked.

He hesitated. 'My parents came from Berlin.'

'I have an unerring ear for the truth,' she said. 'And I didn't hear it just then. Maybe I should shoot you now, just so I don't have to listen to lies.'

Cray chewed. 'How's this then? After I received a degree in mechanical engineering in the United States, I did postgraduate work at Berlin Polytechnic. This was in 1936. I learned the language in Berlin.' He lifted more strudel on his fork. 'And then in the army when I was training at a base in East Anglia, northeast of London, I often traveled to a POW camp near Stowmarket to practice German with Wehrmacht POWs.'

'Why would good German soldiers teach you their language, even if they were in a POW camp?'

'I'd bring them candies and cakes, and I never asked them anything regarding the military. We just chatted.' He looked down at his pastry. 'I find that as I get near the end of my strudel, I'm eating more slowly.'

'You aren't a regular soldier, are you?' she asked.

'Why is it so cold in here?'

'I don't have any firewood.'

Cray said, 'But I saw a big stack of wood just outside your kitchen door.'

'I have bad arthritis in my fingers and hands and shoulders. I can't swing an ax at all. So I sit in here all day, cold. I made that strudel using only woodchips for heat. Those I can carry in.'

Cray scratched his nose. 'Why don't I cut some firewood for you. In exchange for the other half of the strudel.'

'Then when do I shoot you?'

'After I chop the wood, and after I eat the last half of the strudel.'

'The ax is out by the woodpile.'

Cradling the shotgun in her arms, the old woman followed the American out the kitchen door. A maul, a wedge, and an ax were lined up against the house. She stayed by the door as he centered a log on a chopping block, then lifted the maul and the wedge. He tapped the wedge into the center of the log end, and then swung the maul in a large circle. It landed on the wedge with a flat crack. He swung again, then again, and the log split in half. He pushed the halves to one side and reached for another log.

Cray said, 'May I ask your name, ma'am?'

'Helga Engelman.'

'I searched the house, Frau Engelman. Where were you?'

'Outside. I saw you coming, and walked around the house in front of you, always keeping a corner between me and you.'

'You walk pretty quietly, sneaking up on me like that, Frau Engelman.'

She laughed sharply. 'I'll bet it hasn't happened often to you, has it?'

He glanced at her. 'No, it hasn't.'

'I was in the kitchen when I heard the front porch boards squeak. So I grabbed my dead husband's bird gun, which I keep in the kitchen to discourage refugees looking for food.'

'Well, I was just looking for food, too.'

'At least they knock', she chided. 'You were concentrating on the strudel and didn't hear me sneak up on you.'

'I'll profit from that lesson, then.'

'No point in profiting from a lesson you don't survive,' she said. 'What with me about to shoot you.'

'Are you running your farm alone, Frau Engelman?'

'Two summers ago during the harvest my husband lay down between two apple trees and never got up again. A heart attack. You look better in his clothes than he did.'

Cray worked the maul, pushing the halved wood to one side.

She added, 'My husband used to split wood, just like you. I miss the firewood more than I miss him, I'm afraid.'

Cray split another log, then another.

'You are a commando,' Mrs Engelman said. 'Am I right?'

'Well, not really . . .'

'Remember.' She wiggled the shotgun. 'I have an ear for the lie.'

'I'm a commando.' Cray put the maul and wedge to one side, then lifted the ax.

'What is your group called?'

'Rangers, ma'am.' Cray placed one of the split logs on the block. The ax whistled and the wood split in two.

'Have you done your commando work in Germany?'

'Some.' Cray swung the ax again. He was breathing quickly from his efforts.

'What's the worst thing you've ever done to my homeland?'

Cray turned to her, the ax hanging at his side. 'Why in the world would I reveal that to a German woman holding a shotgun on me?'

'Because I'm holding a shotgun on you.'

He lifted another piece of wood. Again he worked the ax. 'I sank a submarine once.'

'You sank a submarine? By yourself?'

Cray nodded. 'The submarine belonged to the Kriegsmarine's Tenth Flotilla, and was in a pen at Lorient, on France's west coast. The sub pens were under twenty feet of concrete and had proven impervious to bombing raids.'

'How did you do it?' Frau Engelman's face was expectant, as if she were about to hear tantalizing gossip.

'I was parachuted into Brittany, twenty-five miles inland, north of the base. Traveling at night and avoiding the roads, I made it to Lorient in three days.'

'Don't we Germans defend submarine bases?'

'I got inside the base by burying myself in a locomotive's coal car. Then with a satchel charge in a rubberized bag, I swam to *U-495*, which was in the yard for fuel and provisions.'

'The *U-495*?'

'Kapitänleutnant Rolf Strenka's boat that had sunk HMS *Valiant*.'

'So what did you do to our poor submarine?'

Cray bent a little to look at her hands. 'You know, Frau Engelman, the safest way to hold a shotgun is to have your finger resting on the trigger guard, not around the trigger.'

'I'm perfectly safe with my finger on the trigger.' She smiled, revealing yellowed teeth. 'So what did you do to my submarine?'

Cray began again with the ax. 'I used blow ports for handholds, and climbed the hull, and dropped the satchel into the forward hatch. Then I slid back into the water. The blast tore *U-495* in two. The sub sank in the pen.'

'I presume you survived.'

'I swam three miles to sea and opened a dye pack. I was plucked out of the water by a float plane captured from the Luftwaffe's sea-rescue service. The plane still had its Luftwaffe markings.'

The shotgun barrel lowered slightly. The old lady studied him as he worked. A line of sweat formed on Cray's forehead. The pile of split wood grew rapidly.

'I told you I have an ear for the lie.'

'Yes, ma'am.'

'That submarine isn't the worst thing you've done to my country, is it?'

Cray didn't stop his mechanical motion. 'No, ma'am.'

After another moment watching him, she asked, 'I don't suppose I want to know the worst, do I?'

'No, ma'am.'

She said, 'You may be an enemy commando, but you aren't a bad man, are you?'

Cray stopped the ax. 'Pardon, ma'am.'

She put the shotgun down, leaning it against the wall, then brushing her hands together as if to fully rid herself of it. 'You could have flicked me aside like a bug, shotgun or no. Isn't that so?'

Cray replied, 'The thought never crossed my mind, Frau Engelman.'

'But someone like you, it would have been an easy thing, less work than chopping wood. And you didn't, so you are a kind man, despite what your army orders you to do.' She smiled again. 'Will you help me put the firewood inside before you go?'

Cray filled his arms with wood, then carried the load into the house.

'To the kitchen stove,' she instructed. 'The wood will last longer if I only heat the kitchen.'

Cray stacked the wood in the cradle near the stove. Then he made five more trips.

When the hopper was full, she said firmly, 'It will be my duty as a German patriot to report that you were here.'

'Can you wait three hours?'

'One hour.'

'Ninety minutes?'

'All right. Ninety minutes.'

Cray opened the grate to place several logs into the stove. He gathered a handful of chips from the hopper and shoved them under the logs. When Frau Engelman handed him several newspaper pages, Cray crumpled them and pushed them into the stove. He lifted a match from a ceramic cup and scraped it against the stove top. It flared, and he placed it under the newspaper, which quickly caught fire.

Frau Engelman held her hands out to the stove. 'That's better.'

'I'm off, then,' Cray said.

She wrapped the rest of the strudel in a sheet of newspaper and passed it to the American. 'I've got more canned apples and sawdust, and can make another. You'd best hurry. Five of your ninety minutes are already gone.'

Cray tucked the pastry under his coat. 'Maybe I'll come back and visit you, Frau Engelman. After the war.'

'If you survive, which you probably won't, you being a commando.'

'I'll survive.'

Cray was at the door when the old lady added, 'It's going to be hard around here for a long time after the war, isn't it?'

'Yes.'

'Bring coffee when you return. I won't have any, most likely.'

Cray smiled again at Frau Engelman, then left her house.

He heard her call after him. 'And cream. I take mine with cream.'

The Reich Security Service (RSD) office had been moved three times in as many weeks, the victim of fires caused by the Allied terror flyers: from a building on Wilhemstrasse near the Reich Press Office, to one east of the Brandenburg Gate on Unter den Linden, to the current one on Potsdamer Platz near OKW's Cipher Branch. The structure had once been an apartment, but the RSD had evicted the tenants. The only heat was a fire on the grate. SS Lieutenant General Eugen Ebenhardt sat at his desk with his uniform coat over his shoulders.

Although Heinrich Himmler often acted otherwise, the RSD was a separate Reich agency, subordinate only to the Führer himself.

Gestapo leader Heinrich Müller, known as Gestapo Müller, had offered the RSD space in the Gestapo's office on Prinz Albrecht Strasse. Eberhardt might have accepted the kindness had he been able to tolerate being in the same building as Gestapo Müller, whom the RSD chief viewed with equal amounts of revulsion and fear. So Eberhardt made do with the makeshift office. His red mahogany desk had been moved just ahead of the Unter den Linden fire, and one leg was singed. An electric cord hung from the ceiling to a desk lamp. Six file cabinets lined a wall. Two telephones were in front of him, one with an outside line and the other with a direct connection to the RSD's small office in the New Reich Chancellery basement. On the wall behind him was a portrait of the Führer.

The closest General Eberhardt had ever been to suffering an apoplectic fit was in May 1942 during a midnight conference at Wolf's Lair, the Führer's military headquarters in East Prussia, when Hitler had said over the rim of his glass of mineral water, 'I owe my life not to the police but to pure chance.' Eberhardt had purpled and gripped the table in anger. He had opened his mouth but a hard glance from General Jodl had throttled him. Only one person in that room was allowed to rage, and it certainly was not Eberhardt. But the general still remembered the words in acid detail. Hitler's casual slight had wounded him. Eberhardt's RSD protected the Führer. Since the beginning of the war, the RSD had thwarted no less than eighteen credible attempts on Hitler's life.

The largest Allied bombing raid on Berlin of the war – over two thousand planes – had occurred the night before. The government quarter had not been hit, but ash was building up on Eberhardt's window ledges like snow. Sirens had been sounding all day.

Eberhardt's face was too narrow for his features, and his mouth and nose and eyes crowded it. In the past few years his mouth had become pinched and his suspicious eyes had moved even closer together, a face rearranged by his vast responsibilities. Eberhardt never removed his gray uniform jacket while on duty, not even during Berlin's sweltering summer days. High collars pressed his neck. On his jacket was the Golden Honor Badge, indicating he was among the first 100,000 Party members.

Eberhardt studied a photograph of the POW who had escaped from Oflag IV C at Colditz that afternoon. The photo had been taken on the prisoner's admission to Colditz. The POW stared back at him, not with the apprehension and exhaustion always displayed in camp admission photographs but with a studied disdain. The prisoner's mouth was slightly arched, and his eyebrows were lifted as if he were amused. From the black and white photo Eberhardt could not tell the prisoner's eye color, but the man had fair skin and short blond hair. His jaw was aggressive, and he had pug ears. A boxer's face. Each time Eberhardt returned to the photo, the prisoner's countenance seemed to have shifted slightly, from one issuing a challenge to one broadcasting enormous competence to one about to laugh. It was a chameleon's face, changing even in the stillness of the photograph.

Colditz's commandant, Colonel Janssen, had reported the escape an hour earlier to General Hermann Reinecke, who was in charge of the Armed Forces General Office (AWA) a division within OKW that had authority over prisoners of war. If more than five POWs escaped from a camp, or if only one escaped from Colditz, a national alert was issued, and Eberhardt's RSD and many other Reich organizations were notified. Copies of all prisoners' admission photographs were on file at the RSD.

General Eberhardt had just spoken with the Colditz commandant by telephone. Colonel Janssen had not determined how it had occurred, but he had apparently buried a man alive in the castle cemetery. Janssen was perhaps Germany's leading expert on POW escapes, and Colditz Castle had an escape museum toured by POW administrators from all over the Reich. Nevertheless, Janssen and his experienced *Lageroffizier* Lieutenant Heydekampf had been fooled. Janssen had sworn again and again to Eberhardt that the prisoner had been dead when taken in a cart to the castle's cemetery.

After the Colditz prisoners and guards at the graveside service had gone back to the castle, the minister who had said words over the grave had begun searching for edible portions of apples on the ground at the orchard next to the cemetery. The minister saw the POW emerge from his grave, like a demon from the center of the earth. According to Colonel Janssen, the minister was still trembling from the ordeal.

Eberhardt idly scratched his chin, still staring at the POW's photograph. The general was suspicious of everything untoward. There had been few escape attempts from POW camps in Germany for the past half-year. Eberhardt was aware of General Eisenhower's order to POWs to remain in their camps. The POWs were following the directive. Yet today a POW escaped from Colditz. The method of his ruse was not yet known, but clearly it was a plan unique in POW administration history. Was it possible that larger forces – those outside the Colditz wards – had ordered the escape?

And this POW was not the usual inmate. He seemed to have surrounded himself in mystery, telling neither the guards nor his fellow prisoners anything about himself. Even his name was unknown. All that Janssen knew of him was that he had been a frenzied escaper. And he had courageously rushed into a burning shed to rescue the castle's *Lageroffizier*.

The general's deputy, Major Gustav Busse, came to the office door. Busse was also wearing his uniform overcoat. He held a yellow TDX sheet. 'Sir, AWA has just sent another report. The Colditz POW was spotted at Böhlen, a village ten kilometers north of Colditz. An elderly woman found him in her house, eating pastry.'

General Eberhardt had never heard of the town of Böhlen. 'You say north of Colditz? North?'

'Yes, sir.'

American and British and Canadian POWs were incarcerated in the eastern parts of the Reich to make their potential escape routes longer. So these escapees, from camps in Saxony and Thuringia and Brandenburg, usually headed east toward the Soviet lines. It was known among POWs that the Red Army would gladly assist them in getting home and, in fact, treated them as honored guests, sating them with brandy and caviar. An Allied escape organization in Odessa sent the escapees to Leningrad, then Stockholm. Then why had this Colditz escapee journeyed north toward the heart of the Reich, not east?

'There's more, General,' Major Busse glanced at the TDX. 'It seems the old lady and the POW had something of a talk. She said the POW belongs to an American army unit called the Rangers.'

'Rangers?' Two deep clefts formed between Eberhardt's brows. 'That unit climbed the cliff at Pointe-du-Hoc, on the Normandy coast, last June.'

'And this one claims to have sunk the submarine in the pen at Lorient. Remember that? Our office was alerted about that sabotage.'

'Could the POW have been lying to impress the old lady?'

Busse added, 'He knew the submarine was the *U-495* and that it was captained by Rolf Strenka.'

'Why is this American Ranger chatting with an elderly German lady, telling her this?'

Busse shrugged. 'She was charmed by him, sounds like. So maybe he's just talkative and friendly and a bit of a braggart. You know how Americans are.'

'I've never met one,' Eberhardt said drily. 'And neither have you. And why is this American escaping when the war – pardon the treasonable defeatism – is weeks or months from ending?'

'I don't know, sir.'

The general's expression shifted as he glanced again at the POW's photograph. Eberhardt was the Führer's last shield against his enemies. Adolf Hitler's very life testified to the general's skill. Eberhardt had not lasted for twelve years as Hitler's personal security chief by being tentative. His method – the means by which he had kept the Führer alive all those years – was simple: apply overwhelming force immediately to the slightest of suspicious circumstances. And the general had learned to heed his hunches.

He held out the photograph to Major Busse. 'I want this enlarged, then I want five thousand copies made. Do it immediately.'

Busse's eyebrows climbed his head. 'Five thousand, sir?'

Eberhardt dipped his chin. 'Our enemies are up to something with this POW. So I'm going to flush him out.'

FIVE

Otto Dietrich woke to the rasp of the key. He was on the metal cot, rolled into a ball under the frayed blanket. He had become attuned to the rhythm of Lehrterstrasse Prison. The sound at his cell door was out of turn. He pushed himself to his feet and brought his wristwatch up. It was an hour past noon. He had been to the blade and back an hour before. Now they were coming for him again. The precious pill was in his hand. He put it under his tongue so they wouldn't find it. Dietrich had promised the doctor he would wait until he heard about Maria. But now the detective did not know if he had the strength to wait.

'This is against your rules,' he said meekly as the door opened. 'I've been to the guillotine once today.'

The executioner, Sergeant Winge, entered the cell carrying two buckets of water. A towel was draped over his shoulder. He worked his dappled red face into a smile. 'You have an appointment. You need to get ready.'

Agent Koder came next. He was holding a pair of pants, a shirt, and a leather bag. His face was hard with thought. 'This is unprecedented, Sergeant. There are no regulations governing such things.'

'Take your clothes off,' Winge ordered.

Dietrich surprised himself by finding a reserve of dignity. 'I'm not going naked to the guillotine.'

The sergeant's pudding face lightened even more. 'Our plumbing is out and the shower stalls don't work. So I'm going to give you a shower like we did in the trenches thirty years ago. The bucket brigade.' He lowered one bucket to the stones.

Rudolf Koder's voice was bitter. 'You are to go to the Prinz Albrecht Strasse headquarters as soon as possible. Would you know why?'

Dietrich removed his ragged shirt and pants. He pulled off his shoes and socks and his shredded underwear. He stood nude in the middle of the cell, his arms away from his sides. The pill was still under his tongue.

The executioner swung a bucket. Icy water doused Dietrich from face to toes. Then the sergeant gave him the towel. He lifted the other bucket to the cot.

'Here's a razor and soap and scissors,' Winge said. He took the bag from Koder and put it on the cot. 'You'll find shoes to fit you in this bag, along with your wallet, cop's ID, and your bridgework.'

'I don't understand why I was not consulted by General Müller,' the Gestapo agent complained, lowering the clothes he was carrying to the cot. 'He knows I'm your case agent.'

Dietrich tried to cut his beard with the scissors.

The sergeant said, 'Your hands are shaking so badly you're going to stab yourself.' He took the scissors and quickly cut back the beard to stubble, letting the hair fall to the stones. Then he dampened an edge of towel, rubbed soap on it, and worked it into a foam with his fingers. He dabbed the soap lather on Dietrich's face.

'My father was a barber – did I ever tell you?' the executioner asked. 'I was going to enter the trade, but I found the army first. So instead of cutting off hair, I cut off heads. Funny how life works.'

The sergeant rapidly shaved Dietrich, dipping the straight razor into the bucket several times. Then he wiped the detective's face with the towel. He stepped back to admire his work.

'Good as new,' Winge said proudly.

Dietrich inserted his bridge, and snapped his jaw several times to test it. He was too weak to stand on one leg so he leaned into the sergeant to pull the pants on. His fingers shook so, the sergeant buttoned his shirt. Winge tried tying Dietrich's tie from the front but finally stepped behind him to knot it correctly. Dietrich pulled on the coat. Nothing quite fit him. Then the sergeant pulled Dietrich's pistol – a Walther – from the bag and passed it to him. Dietrich shoved it into his belt. He had never determined how to make a shoulder holster comfortable.

Koder and the sergeant led him from the cell, along the dim hallway, through a gate manned by a guard, then up the stairs to the main floor. When they stepped through the doors, Dietrich had to bring his hands to his eyes. He had not been aboveground for three months. Daylight was blinding. The sergeant grabbed his elbow to lead him across the sidewalk to a waiting car.

Koder's face registered surprise at the automobile, a 7.7-liter supercharged olive-green Mercedes with silver swastika medallions above its fenders. He exclaimed, 'General Müller's car.'

Sergeant Winge opened the door. Dietrich tried to lower himself to the seat, but his legs buckled. Winge caught him and gently placed him on the seat.

Executioner Winge said, 'I like my work, Inspector, but not enough to hope to see you again.' He closed the Mercedes's door.

Dietrich had smelled nothing but mold and rot and his own fear for months, and the limousine's odor of leather and cigars was intoxicating. He still could not open his eyes. He was thrown against the seat back when the car pulled away from the prison.

He blinked rapidly, his eyes slowly adjusting. He saw the black cap of an SS driver. The detective turned to the window. The car was passing through a valley of rubble that rose steeply on both sides. Dietrich could see nothing but debris, hills high enough to cast the street in shadows. At an intersection the car slowed for a tram pulled by a horse.

When he was sure the driver was not examining him in the rearview mirror, Dietrich spit out the pill and put it into his pants pocket. Then he asked, 'What's that new trolley?'

'With all the wreckage many streets are too narrow for cars and trucks. So we've brought narrow-gauge locomotives and cars from the Ruhr mining valleys, and laid the tracks for them.' The SS driver spoke pleasantly, almost in a rehearsed manner, as if he frequently gave tours to visiting dignitaries. 'If all the rubble in Berlin were put in one pile, it would be taller than the tallest of the Harz Mountains, the Brocken, eleven hundred and forty meters.'

Dietrich craned his neck left and right, taking in Berlin's wilderness of devastation. Some of the mountains of waste were new, others had weeds growing from them. The debris consisted of concrete, mortar, brick, glass, plumbing, limestone, sandstone, and shattered furniture. Above many mounds were solitary chimneys, still standing.

They passed a line of decrepit nags pulling carts. Dietrich saw almost no automobiles or trucks. He still had to squint against the bright light. The sky was dust-laden, and the sun was an outsized fiery red orb like a biblical omen. The Mercedes came to a rubble peak blocking the street.

The driver put the car into reverse. He turned to look through the back window. He had a long face with a flared nose. His dimples were at odds with the SS tabs on his collar. 'Can't go anywhere directly these days. I know some detours, but they change every day.'

The Mercedes veered around a crater, then tried another street. The car bumped over abandoned fire hoses. They passed sandbagged storefronts and the Mitte Cinema, still in operation. The epic *Kolberg* was playing. The marquee also advertised that a Fritz the Cat cartoon opened the show. Dietrich rolled down a window. The air smelled of sewage, cordite, and escaping gas. When he coughed against the dust, he cranked the window up.

A line of fallen telephone poles blocked the road. The driver again backed up, then turned onto another street, but here high-tension cables lying across the pavement were marked with a warning sign. Again he put the car into reverse, this time going two entire blocks backward before finding a clear roadway, but one that had not been swept. It was a river of glittering glass, sparkling gaily from curb to curb and crackling under the Mercedes's tires. At the next intersection they passed a field kitchen with a long line of haggard women and blank-faced children waiting with tin bowls in their hands.

The Mercedes turned onto Berlinerstrasse, then came to the

Tiergarten. The two massive flak towers at the zoo had so often been strafed that their concrete walls were scabrous. Piles of concrete chips lined the bases of the towers.

Dietrich's mouth turned down at his first view of the Tiergarten's lawns. They were a moonscape of room-sized craters. Many of the chestnut and lilac trees had been blasted down. Others had been cut down for firewood. The park reminded Dietrich of the no-man's-land at the Somme, where he had spent much of the Great War. Once the Tiergarten's ponds had been blue gems but now were filled with rubble pushed there by bulldozers clearing nearby streets. Because the trees were gone, the park's statues were plainly visible. Without their usual camouflage of leaves and branches, they seemed naked and embarrassed. Goethe stared moodily at the victory garden that had been planted at his base. The statue of Frederick William II was newly headless. The Victory Column was undamaged but was surrounded by ramshackle squatters' huts. Columns of refugees flowed westward across the park.

The Brandendburg Gate came into view. Its twelve Doric columns and the Quadriga – the female charioteer with her four bronze stallions – was pocked and cracked. The gate's copper roofing had been removed early in the war.

The driver said, 'Remember the fog crows that always spent the winter and spring in Berlin? They're gone. Bombs chased them away. Nobody knows where they went.'

Dietrich was more interested in the two policemen they passed. 'When did Berlin police start wearing steel helmets and carrying carbines?'

'Two, three months ago. We'll make them fighters yet.'

They drove along the once elegant Kurfürstendamm, where the café society had reigned. The street was bombed out and boarded up, the restaurants' striped awnings lying along the gutters. The Kudamm was filled with filthy rainwater. At the top of the avenue they came to the Kaiser Wilhelm Church where the tower clock had been frozen at seven-thirty since the day in November 1943 when Allied bombers destroyed a thousand acres of the city.

'The city will never be rebuilt,' Dietrich said.

'That is defeatist talk,' the driver said lightly. 'I'm charged with arresting you and taking you to Gestapo headquarters.' He laughed. 'And I would arrest you, too, if you weren't already on your way there.'

A wave of Dietrich's fear returned. 'What for?'

The driver shrugged. 'I'm a chauffeur. General Müller doesn't often consult me regarding his appointments.'

'An SS trooper with a sense of humor,' Dietrich said. 'They must be lowering their standards.'

The driver laughed again. 'I'll say.'

The detective was inordinately grateful for the small talk, a flicker of normalcy even if it was from an SS storm trooper. Dietrich said, 'The city has changed so much since I last saw it, it's unrecognizable.'

Another shrug. 'I'm not going to worry until you can get to the eastern front by the underground.'

'Berlin will cease to exist, I think. Farmers will plant wheat and barley here.'

Dietrich continued to stare out the Mercedes's window at the disfigured city. Those features that gave Berlin its unique personality had been ravaged. While Munich embraced art, Hanover its spas, Nuremberg its fourteenth-century gables and frescoes, and Hamburg its lovely lagoons, Berlin once had the splendor of its architecture. But since Schinkel, no Berlin architect had seen his work survive his era. And so it would be again. Berlin had become a second Carthage.

The car traveled under a camouflage net strung from building to building, then stopped in front of Gestapo headquarters on Prinz Albrecht Strasse. The structure had once been an industrial arts school, but now the business in the building's dungeon was so ferocious that Berlin mothers warned their children not to walk by the building because of the sounds coming up through the sidewalk grates.

After an SS guard opened the Mercedes's door, a Gestapo agent showed the detective into the building. The agent was in street clothes but Dietrich had long been able to identify them from their walk. He had often wondered if the Gestapo had a class that taught the peculiar gait. The hallway led straight to the back of the building, and was lined with doors, all closed. At the end of the hall was a plainclothes guard carrying a machine pistol.

Dietrich was led to the third floor, to Müller's office. Dietrich was astonished when the door was opened to reveal all of the chiefs of the Reich's criminal and political police organizations sitting around Müller's conference table, silently waiting for him.

'Please sit down, Chief Inspector Dietrich,' Heinrich Himmler said.

Dietrich had never before met the man. He was smaller than his photographs portrayed. And more kindly in appearance. Dietrich had never seen a photo of Himmler without his cap, which was on the table next to a leather folder and a vial of pills. The SS chief had sparse sandy hair. His undersized chin, delicate mustache, and watery eyes behind rimless spectacles gave him the look of a clerk. His hips were wider than his shoulders, his double chin extended from his lower lip to his chest with only the slightest interruption for his neck, and he had gained a potbelly over the years sitting behind his desk. Himmler excelled at desk work.

Dietrich's immediate superior, Erwin Golz, said with feeling, 'Good to see you, Otto.'

Golz was the senior Berlin criminal police officer. His background was as a homicide investigator, and he still wore the clothes of a civil servant: striped pants and a jacket. Golz had not allowed the hardships in Berlin to cause him to miss meals. His small features were almost lost in the moon of his face. The bulk of his stomach kept him a good distance from the table. Strangers often mistook him for a jovial incompetent, a mistake. Golz had tried in vain during the first weeks of Dietrich's incarceration to free him. But the Berlin police's long arms did not reach into Gestapo prisons.

Displaced from his chair at the head of the conference table by Himmler, Gestapo Müller sat stonily to the Reichsführer's left. Müller was as barbarous as he was anonymous to most citizens of the Reich. He had been too long inside Gestapo headquarters, and his skin had faded to a leprous white and was marred by pockmarks near his ears. His nose was flat as if it were pressed against a window, and his mirthless brown eyes were set deep in his skull. His dark hair was combed straight back and kept in place with gleaming pomade. He wore plain clothes; a white shirt and emerald tie under a herringbone jacket. Müller stared at Dietrich with undisguised hatred.

Gestapo Müller was Dietrich's great nemesis, the ever-present threat and the constant danger. Ten years before, in 1935, Dietrich had arrested Müller for the murder of Müller's mistress, a teenager from the Bavarian mountains who arrived in Berlin on a train with twenty marks, a beguiling innocence, and an angelic face. Müller made her his, set her up in a flat just off the Kurfürstendamm, and purchased or stole for her everything the country girl desired. Dietrich had never determined what had driven Müller to his murderous fury, but the girl's body had been punctured with a knife eight times. Based on the report of a neighbor in the building who had seen Müller leave the premises with a bloodstained overcoat, Dietrich arrested Müller, who spent two months in the Lerhterstrasse Prison awaiting trial before the Nazi Party could effect his freedom. Despite Dietrich's pressing the issue, Müller was never rearrested or tried. And Müller had been after Dietrich for ten years, trying to waylay him, trying to catch him in a mistake, trying to find him in an exposed and vulnerable position. Finally the Stauffenberg plot had been enough. Müller himself had signed the warrant that had taken Dietrich to the same cell where Müller had spent those two months.

Although Dietrich did not have the slightest idea what was occurring, it was clear to him that his release from Lehrterstrasse Prison represented a victory of the criminal police over the political police, over Gestapo Müller.

RSD General Eugen Eberhardt was also at the table. Dietrich had worked with Eberhardt before and knew him to be highly competent.

Müller's office contained a Regency desk, a Louis Seize long-case clock, and the conference table. Because the windows had been boarded, several lamps with radiant orange and red leaded glass had been placed around the room, adding to the illumination provided by the electrified crystal chandelier hanging over the table.

'I have flooded the Reich with copies of this photograph,' General Eberhardt said.

Dietrich was finally able to remove his eyes from the lofty gathering. He followed Eberhardt's gaze to the white wall, where the image of a man's head was projected.

'His name is Jack Cray,' Eberhardt continued. 'He is an American.'

Himmler said, 'He may be the most dangerous man in Europe.'

'There is no question that this American was the guerrilla who entered the Vassy Château,' Eberhardt said slowly, letting his words take full effect.

All German police and military personnel knew of the Vassy Château disaster. On a moonless night last August, the 4th Company, 3rd Lancers of the Wehrmacht's 15th Light Division was bivouacked in a vineyard's château near St Lô. Sleeping soldiers were scattered about the main room, some on davenports, some on a Turkish rug. An enemy commando crawled into the château, put his hand over the first sleeping soldier's mouth and slit his throat. It was believed the commando was in the room less than ten minutes. He knifed eight Germans, every other one he came to. He dispensed death and granted life alternately. Soldiers woke up sandwiched between two dead comrades. The Wehrmacht and the Waffen-SS began fearing the night. They went to watch and watch, where fully half the soldiers served as sentries each night. OKW had not expected irregular warfare behind its line. The German army was forced to divert enormous resources to protect itself.

Eberhardt leaned slightly toward the projected photo and said, 'One of the sentries patrolling the château that night is now posted to the Lechfeld airport. He reports that the American snuck up behind him and spun him around.'

Dietrich now realized that he had been released from prison for his investigative skills. He was determined to prove himself to avoid a return to his cell. He asked quickly, 'Why would he bother to do that? Wouldn't the American have been smarter to blindside the sentry?'

Eberhardt replied, 'The American gave the sentry two seconds to look at his face before he smashed him with the pommel of his knife, knocking him out. The sentry believes the American deliberately let him see him.'

'And the American let the sentry live?' Dietrich asked. 'Why?'

'I don't know, Inspector.'

Director Golz speculated, 'Perhaps he wanted his description to become known, as a terror tactic.'

Himmler nodded. 'That is an American trait, you know. I have studied our enemies. Soldiers reflect their homeland's national peculiarities. British soldiers are courteous even when killing you. French servicemen refuse to fight on empty stomachs. Wanting to become famous for his exploit is certainly American.'

'Thank you, Herr Reichsführer.' It was far too dangerous for Eberhardt to allow the slightest inflection of sarcasm to touch his words. 'This same American singlehandedly sunk a Kriegsmarine submarine at the base at Lorient.' The general described the sabotage at Lorient. Then he added, 'This man belongs to an American army unit called the Rangers, and the – '

The room went dark as the electricity in the building was interrupted, for perhaps the tenth time that day. The slide projector blinked off and Jack Cray disappeared from the screen. When Eberhardt reached for the table to get his bearings, he brushed the slide projector.

'Our generator will come on momentarily,' Müller said, a disembodied voice in the murk.

Himmler snapped open the pill vial. 'I've got to take these for my breathing. It's the dust and ash.'

The lights flickered back on. The projector came to life, throwing Jack Cray's face onto the screen in stark blacks and whites. Because Eberhardt had nudged the projector further from the screen, the American was bigger, as if he had moved up on them in the dark, a perilous presence in the room. His countenance seemed even more fierce. Himmler was heard to gasp, a slight sound he covered by clearing his throat.

General Eberhardt centered the projector on the table to reduce Cray's image. 'We have another report about the American, this from a professor at Berlin Polytechnic. Jack Cray was his student for two terms in 1936. Cray was taking postgraduate work in mechanical engineering.' He glanced again at his notes. 'He took the fluid dynamics course from Professor Jörgen Hock, who remembers him well.'

'Tell Inspector Dietrich of the information on the American's enrollment forms,' Director Golz said.

Eberhardt lifted several sheets of paper from the table. 'Cray was born in the western United States, in a town called Wenatchee in the state of Washington. His father was an apple-grower and a school principal who apparently gave Cray his bent for education.'

'Who gave him his bent for commando operations?' Dietrich asked.

'Americans routinely circumcise their male children,' Reichsführer-SS Himmler commented. 'Irrespective of race or religion. Did you know that? Doubtless it makes them prone to brutality.'

Eberhardt chewed on his lip a moment before continuing. 'From his records at Berlin Polytechnic we know that in 1935 Cray graduated from Princeton, a university in the state of New Jersey. His marks were excellent, and he received a Wallingford scholarship to study advanced engineering courses at Berlin Polytechnic. He had a Kreuzberg address while in Berlin. Professor Hock does not recall him ever saying anything in class.'

'But you said Hock remembers him well,' Dietrich prompted.

'Not from anything in class. Professor Hock was walking across Berlin Polytechnic's commons one day, between the administration building and the engineering building. A half-dozen Wehrmacht cadets were taking turns dueling with sabers.'

Himmler interrupted, 'The party has not purposely encouraged dueling, of course. But our lads have caught the Prussian martial spirit, and who's to blame them?'

Eberhardt went on, 'Apparently the students had been practicing with each other, perhaps trying to gain scars on their cheeks like von Rundstedt's. Professor Hock says the students were boisterous, and were showing off, making sure passersby saw their skills with the blades.'

'And this Jack Cray joined them?' Dietrich asked.

'Not exactly. Cray was also on the commons, swinging at a ball with a bat, a baseball bat. He was hitting the ball against the side of the engineering building again and again. The cadets began to taunt him, questioning his manliness.'

'Are you sure it wasn't the other way around?' Dietrich asked.

'Professor Hock saw the entire sorry episode,' Eberhardt answered. 'The duelers called out things like "Do all Americans play with sticks instead of swords?" That kind of puerile thing. Cray ignored them for a while, batting his ball. But then the cadets walked over to the American, taunting him.'

Director Golz wagged his head. 'You can see it coming, Otto.'

'Finally one of them, a cadet named von Dehm, challenged the American to a duel. At this point the American finally ceased batting the ball and turned to the cadets. Professor Hock says that other students had begun gathering around, watching. The American said, "I don't know anything about dueling." Cadet von Dehm shoved a cutlass under Cray's nose and replied, "I'll teach you the rudiments – the Prussian thrust and the Mecklenburg parry – but it'll be a painful lesson." The other cadets hooted.'

'Professor Hock heard all of this?' Dietrich asked.

'He admits to having been among the assembling crowd. In any event, the American smiled winningly, Hock says, and then very suddenly and unexpectedly charged von Dehm with the baseball bat.'

Golz shook his head again.

Himmler sniffed, 'Not very sporting, I'd say.'

'It was over in two seconds,' Eberhardt concluded. 'Von Dehm was on the ground, his cutlass in the grass beside him, his right wrist and right collarbone broken. And Jack Cray said, "That's called my Babe Ruth thrust." '

Golz laughed but saw Himmler's scowl and promptly quieted himself.

Gestapo Müller asked, 'Who is Babe Ruth?'

'I'll find out.' Eberhardt bent over the table to write a reminder to himself. 'But, more important, Jack Cray is loose and appears headed to Berlin.'

'Are we certain he is not still in Böhlen, near Colditz?' Müller asked.

'AWA General Reinecke ordered a class-one search. The village was circled by over five thousand members of the Home Guard, Hitler Youth, BDM, police, and prison-service guards. Böhlen was searched house to house. The American is no longer there.'

Himmler said, 'This Jack Cray is coming to Berlin to attempt to assassinate the Führer.'

'How do you know that?' Dietrich asked.

Himmler was so unaccustomed to questions that his mouth snapped shut.

General Eberhardt said, 'At this point in the war the enemy can accomplish virtually all of its military objectives by using their bombers. There is simply no need for the Americans to go to extreme lengths to free this commando unless they had some very delicate but very important task in mind.'

'Like a murder,' Golz added.

'You are only making suppositions about this American's mission,' Dietrich said.

'We do not preclude the possibility that he may have some other mission, some other target,' Golz said. 'But we must assume the worst, and so we will undertake a massive effort to find and defeat this Jack Cray. Everyone around this table will be involved.'

'You have very little evidence,' Dietrich persisted.

Eberhardt replied, 'That's the difference between your job and mine, Inspector. As a policeman, you must find enough evidence for a jury to convict a criminal. But my duty is to protect the Führer, and I can and must act on supposition, on the slightest of suspicions, on the hint of a rumor.'

'If the Reich is to survive, the Führer must survive, it is as simple as that,' Himmler said. 'Director Golz tells me you are the best manhunter in the Reich. You are to stop this American.'

He removed a pen from his breast pocket and opened the folder. As he wrote on a piece of stationery, he continued, 'I have spoken with Jodl and Goering. They agree with me regarding the urgency of your task, and they have pledged that whatever you need for your search – manpower, communications, equipment – will be yours instantly.'

He passed the letter to Dietrich, who lifted it to his eyes. At the top of the page was the embossed emblem of the Reichsführer-SS above Himmler's printed name. The letter read in scratchy handwriting: 'This is Chief Detective Inspector Otto Dietrich. You are to obey his orders as if they were my orders. Himmler.'

The Reichsführer said, 'This note will assist you, I trust.'

Otto Dietrich would go to his grave wondering where he found the courage to next say, 'Where is my wife?'

Himmler's eyebrows rose. 'General Müller?'

'At a facility outside Munich,' Müller said. 'She is being detained pending investigation as your accomplice.' His eyes had not left Dietrich since the inspector had entered the room.

'I won't do anything until she is set free.'

'You are hardly in a position to bargain,' Gestapo Müller said in his gravel voice.

Dietrich brought a finger around like a turret gun to Müller. 'You release her from that place or I won't do a goddamn thing.'

Müller colored and half-rose from his chair. His mouth opened, but Himmler's cold glance cut him off.

The Reichsführer waved his hand airily. 'She will be released within one hour, and will be brought directly to Berlin. You have my assurance.'

General Eberhardt handed the detective the RSD file about the American. Eberhardt said, 'This American, this Jack Cray.'

'Yes, sir?'

'He is a genius at military violence. It will be far too dangerous for you to try to take him alive.'

'Don't let Cray even get a look at you,' Director Golz cautioned. 'It might be fatal.'

Eberhardt advised, 'Put a bullet in him. From a great distance, if possible.'

'I understand, sir.' Dietrich started toward the door.

He was brought up by Müller's piercing voice. 'You are to report your every move to me.'

Dietrich hesitated, then turned back.

Müller added, 'Your wife will be released. But the Gestapo is like the Lord. What it gives, it can take away. Remember that.'

Reichsführer Himmler clucked his tongue at Müller's boorish threat. But he added in a pleasant tone, chilling only if the source was considered, 'Now, Inspector Dietrich, kindly begin your work, and do not fail us.'

SIX

'Go ahead,' Otto Dietrich urged. 'They aren't poisoned.'

Lieutenant Heydekampf translated his words into English.

Dietrich had spread out the French crullers on butcher's paper on the table. The tops of the doughnuts were ridged with white icing. The ward was filled with the rich scent of the pastry.

David Davis and Harry Bell held their breaths and stared at the senior Allied officer. Ian Hornsby let indecision cross his face, but he was clearly agonizing over the decision.

Dietrich helped him. 'Offering pastries isn't some new German interrogation technique.'

Heydekampf again changed the words to English.

When Hornsby slowly reached for one of the doughnuts, Bell and Davis leaped for them.

Ulster Rifleman Davis crammed one into his mouth, then mumbled, 'You almost had a bloody mutiny on your hands, Captain.'

Bell chewed frantically. 'I would have joined Davis. A mutiny, I swear. Christ, this is good.'

The inspector said, 'You, too, Colonel Janssen and Lieutenant Heydekampf. I know you don't eat well anymore.'

Heydekampf could not keep the gratitude from his face. He passed a cruller to the camp commandant before taking one for himself. The skin on Heydekampf's neck was still blistered and oozing from the delousing-shed fire. Bracelets of burned skin were around his wrists. Everyone chewed in silence for a moment.

The first thing Otto Dietrich had done after leaving the Gestapo headquarters was to reenter Heinrich Müller's Mercedes. When the

SS chauffeur balked at driving the inspector without further instructions from Gestapo Müller, Dietrich produced Himmler's letter. With a laugh, the driver started the engine. On the inspector's orders, the driver took him to the Adler Bakery on Hermann Goering Strasse. The bakery provided cakes and bread for senior party members. The baker swore he had no pastries that day. Flashing Himmler's letter quickly resulted in four dozen crullers. The SS driver had then volunteered around a mouthful of pastry, 'We could have a lot of fun with that letter. I know some places on Friedrichstrasse.' The street was home for Berlin's elegant brothels, some of which still stood. Dietrich declined with thanks.

Then Dietrich had visited his precinct station to requisition the talents of Peter Hilfinger, his assistant for the past six years. On first sight of Dietrich, Hilfinger had grabbed him in an unprofessional bear hug, and then had been quick to drop whatever he had been working on to join him.

They had stopped briefly at an orthopedic surgeon's clinic on Krummestrasse, where Dietrich and Hilfinger conducted an interview while the driver waited at the curb. Then they drove to a haberdashery. The inspector had given the driver six more of the pastries when they arrived at the new airstrip at the Tiergarten.

Gestapo Müller's Fieseler Storch airplane had then taken Dietrich and Hilfinger from Berlin to Colditz. The inspector had eaten four crullers on the flight. The pilot had juked the plane from cloud to cloud during the flight, hiding from prowling Allied fighters. Dietrich did not know whether his nausea during the ride was motion sickness or was from the rich pastries. Between bites of crullers and bouts of nausea, he filled in Hilfinger on the assignment.

Dietrich walked around a bunk to a barred window, giving the POWs more time to sate their sweet tooths. On Dietrich's suggestion, Peter Hilfinger waited in the hallway so they would not give the impression they were trying to overwhelm the prisoners. Dietrich looked out into the prisoners' yard. At least a dozen guards were posted in the small area. The Gestapo had assumed administration of the prison camp, and six agents were also in the yard, all wearing the telltale trench coats. Colonel Janssen had been relieved of command but had not yet been arrested or ordered to Berlin, which offered him hope.

'If you will continue to translate for me, Lieutenant Heydekampf,' Dietrich said over his shoulder. To help support himself, he put his hand against the window frame, hoping the POWs wouldn't notice. His legs were still weak from his time at Lehrterstrasse. The charred remains of the delousing shed were below him to his left. 'Group Captain Hornsby, you are the senior Allied officer at Colditz. Major Bell is the senior American officer. Colonel Janssen believes that you, Captain Davis, are the Colditz escape committee chief. He doesn't know for sure, but I trust his instincts.'

Dietrich paused, allowing Heydekampf to render his words into English. Then he said, 'I asked you to meet with me because you three undoubtedly planned and assisted Jack Cray's escape.'

More translation. The three POWs were still eating with zest. But now their eyes were locked on the back of the German inspector as he spoke.

Dietrich turned from the window. 'After your capture, each one of you was questioned at Auswertestell West at Oberursel. Techniques there are sophisticated and successful. I'm sure that you have discussed your experiences there, and now understand fully our interrogation techniques. You know the water-glass trick, and the escape ruse, and the Red Cross questionnaire subterfuge, all designed to get new prisoners to divulge information.'

Hornsby furrowed his brow at Heydekampf's translation, then glanced at Bell, who shrugged and reached for another cruller. Captain Davis licked icing from his fingers. They had no idea where the detective inspector was leading.

Dietrich continued, 'So it would be impossible for me to trick you into divulging information about the American's escape.'

'Too right,' Davis said after Heydekampf's translation.

'But I don't need to.' The inspector patted a bunk, then picked up a paperback copy of John Steinbeck's *The Moon Is Down* from a tray at the bunk's headboard. 'I am going to tell you how you and the American did it.'

Colonel Janssen blurted in German, 'You know? How do you know?'

When Lieutenant Heydekampf translated, the three POWs stopped chewing in unison.

Ignoring the commandant, Dietrich lifted Jack Cray's baseball bat that had been leaning against a wall. He rolled it in his hands, examining it. 'How do you hold this?'

Harry Bell wiped his hands on his pants before reaching for the bat. 'You right-handed?'

When Heydekampf changed the words to German, Dietrich nodded.

'Right hand over left, feet a little wider than shoulder-width, a bit of a crouch.' Bell swung the bat slowly a few times then passed it back. 'I'd toss you a few easy ones, but we don't have a ball.'

Dietrich swung awkwardly several times. He shook his head. 'Balls should be struck with the feet, not a piece of wood.'

Bell smiled at the interpretation, then lifted another cruller from the table.

SAO Hornsby said drily, 'You have succeeded in disarming us, Inspector Dietrich. Why don't you continue?'

Instead, Dietrich resumed his examination of the ward, not a wild flying-squad toss, but a visual inventory, respecting the POWs' few possessions. He did not open the fruit crates that served as trunks near the bunks. He did not rifle through packets of letters. He stepped around a support post in the center of the ward. He still carried the American's bat. He came to the laundry bucket in which was floating a shirt. All eyes in the room followed him.

Dietrich dipped a finger into the wash bucket then brought the finger to his mouth. He inhaled sharply, then grimaced. 'Needs a little more soap.'

Heydekampf translated. Captain Davis laughed around a cruller.

Dietrich said, 'Your challenge was to make Jack Cray look dead. A fractured skull – one smashed against cobblestones from a great height – has a certain damaged appearance.'

Colonel Janssen protested, 'It looks just like Cray's did.'

'He had a ruptured eye socket, or so it seemed.' Dietrich breathed on a hand. His cell in the Lehrterstrasse had been warmer than the Colditz ward. 'But what Cray did, or one of you did, was to pull down his lower eyelid and put a small slice on the inside of the eyelid with a knife. The tiny blood vessels there bleed profusely, and will fill the eye with blood. And, although Colonel Janssen and Lieutenant Heydekampf didn't report any blackening around the American's shattered eye, you POWs may have dabbed a little chimney soot on his cheekbones to make it look bruised. Altogether, it would have been a convincing replica of a ruptured eye socket.'

Heydekampf had fallen into meter with the detective. He interpreted as Dietrich spoke, not waiting for pauses.

'Bleeding ears are a classic sign of a fractured skull,' the inspector said. 'And Jack Cray's ears had blood in them. But it wasn't Cray's blood, was it? One of you gentlemen cut yourself with a blade, on your arm or thigh or somewhere else, collected the blood in a cup, and at the right time, poured it into Cray's ears. If I were to search you, I would find such a gash.'

Ian Hornsby wiped cruller crumbs from the corners of his mouth. His face was a carefully composed mask.

The detective was wearing black trousers and a fur-lined waistcoat that he had procured from the haberdashery with Himmler's letter. Dietrich's shoes were also new, and squeaked when he walked. He said, 'Cray also appeared to have shattered his shoulders and arms when he hit the courtyard.'

Heydekampf nodded fervently as he translated. Then he added, 'His arms were bent crazily, as loose as rope. His elbows were touching behind his back.'

'It must have been a difficult task, Group Captain Hornsby.' Dietrich walked to the support post, a roughly milled timber felled in a Saxon forest in the eighteenth century. 'Cray stood with his back against this post, or another post somewhere nearby. One or two of you pinned him in place so he wouldn't slip around the column. Then two more of you dislocated his shoulders.'

Colonel Janssen's mouth opened. He shifted his gaze to Senior Allied Officer Hornsby.

Dietrich explained, 'The shoulder socket is shallow. A few people can dislocate their own shoulders, called a voluntary dislocator. But it's a rare talent, and more probably you had to force Cray's shoulder from the socket. You used this post as a fulcrum.'

Heydekampf held up his hand. 'Inspector, I don't know the English word for fulcrum.'

Dietrich flicked a finger, indicating it did not matter. 'You used this post as a brace, gripped his arm, and levered the ball of his shoulder bone out of the socket. The result was a grotesque, inhuman shape, a hollow in Cray's shoulder where the joint once was, and the arm sticking out behind. The pain must have been excruciating, but I doubt Cray called out. Am I right?'

Harry Bell helped himself to a chair. He gave Hornsby the slightest of glances.

Dietrich had not expected an answer. He continued, 'The Reich's Office of Medical Information gathers statistics regarding accidental deaths and suicides.' The inspector brought up the bat again, peering at the label carved midway along the wood. 'Who is Lou Gehrig?'

'A baseball player,' Bell answered after Heydekampf's interpretation.

'Like Babe Ruth?'

Bell raised an eyebrow. 'Yes, like the Babe.'

'Why would Cray carve this Gehrig's name on a bat?'

'Most baseball bats have famous players' names on them. Cray carved Gehrig's name on his homemade bat to make it look authentic.'

Dietrich pursed his lips, examining Gehrig's name. 'The Office of Medical Records reports that a person who falls three stories has a fifty percent chance of surviving. A person who falls four stories has a fifteen percent chance. And someone who falls five stories, like Jack Cray ostensibly did, has virtually no chance.'

Janssen nodded vigorously.

'Lieutenant Burke, who is now in the punishment ward, was escaping with Cray,' Dietrich said. 'Both were on the roof above us. Cray must have lost his grip, slid down the steep shingles, then fallen five stories to a certain death. But none of that happened.'

'I saw him fall, Inspector,' Heydekampf almost shouted.

'Lieutenant, you saw him land.' Dietrich moved to the barred window for the second time. The bars were iron, with a width slightly less than a man's wrist. 'Cray landed in the yard below this very window.'

Dietrich walked along the wall to the next barred casement. 'These bars would resist almost any force.'

He gripped the baseball bat as Major Bell had instructed him. He brought it back, then swung mightily at the iron bars. With a ring the bat bounced off the iron. The bar left a sizable dent in the wood. Dietrich smashed the iron a second time, and again the bat ricocheted off the iron. The bat suffered a second scar. The iron was unscathed.

'But now I go to the window below which the American landed.' Dietrich moved along the wall. 'This time I'm just going to yank the bars with my hand.'

Dietrich lowered the bat to the floor. He gripped the bar and pulled. It easily came off in his hand. When he gripped the second rod and tugged, it also came away from the window.

The inspector held up both metal shafts. 'Burke was up on the roof, five floors above the courtyard, and had two escape suitcases. Sitting on the peak of the roofline, he shoved one case down the shingles, where it fell five floors to the courtyard. It left a swath of broken moss, and the roof looked like a man had slipped down the shingles.'

Janssen added in a bemused tone, 'And Burke must have thrown those two loose shingles along with the suitcases to make it seem like the American had desperately grabbed at something as he slipped, and had pulled the shingles loose.'

'The fistfight over the bagpipes was a planned distraction,' Dietrich went on. 'The instant the brawl began, Burke pushed the suitcase down the roof and, at the same instant, you POWs pulled aside the bars and Cray leaped from this first-floor window. Cray fell ten feet, not five floors.'

'But I saw him fall,' Heydekampf objected.

'You heard Cray scream, and turned in time to see him fall a few feet and bounce off the courtyard stones. Lieutenant, your imagination filled in much of his fall. He dropped only from this first-floor window. To further convince you, Burke kicked his legs and slid around a bit up on the roof, and made it look like he had almost fallen.'

Heydekampf did not bother translating these last revelations.

Apparently resigned to the course of the conversation, Commandant Janssen offered, 'If you look at the tips of those bars, you'll see the mortar used to stick them back in place.'

Dietrich brought up an iron shaft. Dry powdery paste was at the tip.

'It's made from the old mortar in the stone walls,' Janssen said wearily. 'They probably scraped it off the wall with a nail or spoon, then mixed the powder with water. The mortar reconstituted and became sticky, just as it was when these walls were constructed many years ago, and they dabbed it onto the ends of the bars and replaced them right after Cray went through the window.'

Dietrich held up his hand to Heydekampf to stop him from interpreting, then asked Janssen, 'Where do you suspect the POWs got the metal saw or file to cut the bars?'

The commandant lifted his palms. 'From a maintenance crew probably. The POWs will steal absolutely anything left untended for more than two seconds. Or perhaps they have picked the shop lock. They can get into the shop and infirmary and kitchen at will, it seems. The prisoners undoubtedly have a hardware store's inventory hidden around the castle.'

Dietrich nodded to Heydekampf, who again began translating when the inspector said, 'Jack Cray's willpower can be measured by his posture after he landed on the stone court below this window. His arms were dislocated, and surely he was in a great deal of pain. He hit the stones, and he remained motionless in a rag doll's limp posture. A man who is badly wounded will reflexively curl up into a ball, but a dead man has a sprawled, boneless look to him. That's how you found Jack Cray. His flaccid posture alone would have led you to think he was dead.'

'He wasn't breathing,' Heydekampf blurted in German.

'He was breathing, very shallowly and slowly under his loose coat, and in checking everything else, you missed it.'

Dietrich placed the bars on the floor and returned to the table. Hornsby and Bell had finished their crullers, but David Davis still had one in each hand, taking bites out of each alternately and as rapidly as he could, as if afraid the German inspector might abruptly take them back.

'But he had no pulse,' Heydekampf argued. 'I swear it.'

'You are correct, Lieutenant. Jack Cray had no pulse. You and Colonel Janssen are not surgeons, so you cannot be faulted for failing to detect the American's ruse.' Dietrich brought out two lengths of rubber tubing from his jacket pocket.

Bell again glanced at Hornsby.

The inspector said, 'This is surgical tubing. When a surgeon amputates an arm or does some other invasive procedure on an arm, he wraps this tubing around the patient's upper arm, right under the shoulder. He pulls it tight. It prevents bleeding during the operation. And it blocks off all detectable pulse.'

Colonel Janssen's face whitened. His eyes darted to SAO Hornsby, whose features remained unreadable.

'The tourniquet can remain in place for up to two hours without damage to the arm,' Dietrich went on. 'Cray had tourniquets around both arms under his shirt and coat. Maybe not surgical tubing, maybe lengths of twine. But the tourniquets were there.'

As he interpreted, Heydekampf's voice lowered to a chagrined whisper. The POWs leaned toward him to hear the translation.

The inspector asked, 'You remember the blood on Cray's neck? It seemed to have flowed there from his bleeding ears and eye. In fact, it had been smeared there just before he went through the windows. Probably the same POW's blood that was in his ears.'

'Whatever for?' the commandant asked. His shoulders were hunched forward, as if the inspector's revelations were blows with Cray's bat.

'So you wouldn't check his carotid pulse in his neck.'

Heydekampf closed his eyes. 'Of course.'

'When it's easy to check his wrists, no sense bloodying your hands by checking the pulse in his neck.'

Janssen said quietly, 'So that's how he did it. It's clear now. And I've never heard of anything like it, not from Colditz or any other POW camp.'

'That's not quite all of it,' Dietrich said, a note of apology in his voice. 'Your report indicated that Major Bell and Captain Davis placed the American in the burial bag. To make him fit into the gunnysack, they had to relocate the arms. Another excruciating ordeal for Cray, who again remained silent, not calling out in pain. They also surreptitiously threw a knife into the bag, if Cray didn't already have one in his clothes, so Cray could cut himself out of the bag. And they may have removed the tourniquets, or Cray might have done it himself. The POWs who dug the grave made sure it was shallow.'

Janssen only nodded.

'And then there was the shortness of the ceremony at the grave,' Dietrich continued. 'None of the POWs offered to speak a few words over the body, saying they didn't know Cray well enough. Group Captain Hornsby, you and the others knew that Cray could last only a few minutes belowground.'

David Davis struggled, trying to keep a grin from his face.

'How did Cray know when the burial party had left?' Heydekampf asked.

'Maybe as he lay underground he could hear you. More likely he simply waited as long as he could, until his air was gone. The minister who read the service and who saw Cray rise from the earth estimates Cray was in the grave less than ten minutes. There was some air in the gunnysack. When it ran out, he came up, hoping no one was watching. Cray didn't know the pastor was nearby, in the orchard. The American probably never saw the pastor.'

Hornsby's head came up. He had not known about the minister seeing Cray emerge from the ground. So that was how the Germans were alerted so quickly.

Otto Dietrich replaced the American's bat where he had found it, leaning it against the wall. He stepped toward the ward's door.

'Colonel Janssen assures me that you have a radio hidden in the castle, and that in all likelihood you received coded orders over the radio to help Jack Cray escape this castle.'

The POWs remained impassive.

'You probably were not informed of the reasons Cray was to escape. He may not know the reason himself as yet. But he is going to try to commit a murder. Knowing this might reduce your pleasure from Cray's escape.'

After the translation, SAO Hornsby said in a crabbed voice, 'We need a lot of things in this castle, but moralizing from a German isn't one of them.'

Dietrich locked his gaze onto Hornsby's. After a moment the investigator replied, 'No, perhaps not.' He buttoned his coat. 'Goodbye, gentlemen. You told me nothing, but I learned a lot.' He stepped to the door. Janssen and Heydekampf followed.

The line of refugees at Sergeant Hans Richter's checkpoint was growing. His post was on the road between Colditz and Leipzig, at the small town of Rötha. His company had erected a barricade across the road and was checking all vehicle and foot traffic. He took documents from the next traveler in line.

Richter was a member of the Police Group General Goering, a guard unit originating in Prussia, where, in the early years of the Reich, Goering had become commander in chief of the Prussian police. The unit was now under the auspices of the Luftwaffe, with Goering at its head. On the left sleeve of Richter's green greatcoat was a dark green cuff title with silver Gothic letters spelling LPG GENERAL GOERING. The sergeant wore a service knife and a canteen on a belt at his waist.

Richter's unit had been at the road barricade for the past twenty-four hours. At their barracks in Berlin the sergeant's men had been given thirty minutes to pack their kits and climb into troop trucks headed south. Fire police, barrack police troopers, railway protection police, waterways police, police tank crews, motorized traffic police, female police auxiliaries, Party member volunteers, members of the

Security and Help Service, the Air Raid Warning Service, National Labor Service guards, Richter had seen them all heading south to isolate a portion of Saxony. The size of the operation awed him. Three of his mates had been killed in a British strafing run during the journey south.

The checkpoint was on the outskirts of Rötha. Pastures were on both sides of the road. Fields were overgrown because cattle that would have grazed the grass down had been added to the Reich's ration. Police patrolled the fields, insuring that the refugees kept to the road, funneling them to the checkpoint. The company's first duty when arriving on the Rötha road had been to dig a slit trench to dive into if Allied planes were spotted.

Richter was only twenty years old, and his face was moist and undefended, a twelve-year-old's countenance, he knew. He compensated by scowling while on duty, molding his face into one of authority. The Schmeisser submachine gun he carried across his chest helped.

He passed the identity card back to the refugee and waved him through. The refugee grabbed his suitcase with one hand and his daughter with the other, and continued on. Richter rose to his toes to glance back along the line. Must be three hundred people waiting to pass through, he guessed. They were hollow-eyed with fatigue. They wore a mixture of cast-off military uniforms, peasants' field clothes, and city attire. Some had blankets over their shoulders. Many had stuffed newspapers into their coats and down their pants because nights were cold. They pulled carts and pushed wheelbarrows. Horses led wagons piled with furniture and trunks. Richter even saw a cart drawn by a white goat.

Low clouds had moved in over the hills to the south. The clouds were about the only defense Germany had left against Allied planes. Richter was glad for the respite from skyward vigilance. It let him do his job, searching the line of refugees.

He looked again at the clipboard attached to the back of his Borgward troop transport at the side of the road. On the board was a large print photo of an American. At the briefing that morning

Richter's captain had warned that the fugitive was to be shot on sight.

A horn bleated, and a Horch limousine parted the refugees as it approached the checkpoint. The auto had a lieutenant general's ensign above its sweeping black fenders. The driver stopped the automobile at the crossbar and rolled down his window.

Sergeant Richter bent to the window. 'May I see your papers, please?'

From the back seat came a bark, 'I am Wehrmacht Lieutenant General Karl Dräger. Let me through immediately.'

'I must see your identification, General. And your driver's. Those are my orders, sir.'

The general leaned across the seat back to bellow, 'And I'm giving you new orders. Raise the barricade right now.'

Sergeant Richter put his hand around the Schmeisser's pistol grip. 'Sir, I'm a guard, and spend most of my time at factories and government buildings. I have gone the whole war without shooting anybody, and I'd hate to begin with a Wehrmacht general.'

Accompanied by a spewing curse, the documents were passed through the window. Richter took his time with them, flipping through the pages with a studied insolence. He held up the general's identity card to the daylight as if to detect a forger's mistake, and earned more profanity from the back of the Horch.

From somewhere in the growing line of refugees came a shout, 'The bigshot gets to ride while we walk.'

Another angrily yelled, 'That's all this war got us, a bunch of bloodsuckers.'

Richter waved them to silence. Carrying a carbine in his arms, one of his men moved back along the line, shaking his head, warning the travelers. A cargo truck slowly approached along the road, pausing frequently while walkers stepped aside.

The sergeant bent low to stare at the general's face, which was crimson from indignation. The Wehrmacht general's hooked nose could not be mistaken for the fugitive American's. The general was wearing a tailored gray-green greatcoat with scarlet facings, buttoned at the neck.

Next Richter examined the chauffeur's papers. The driver was a fifty-year-old corporal undoubtedly called from the reserves. No American there, either. Richter glanced at the Horch's floor to make sure no one was hiding there. He handed the documents back through the window.

'Stay where you are while I search the boot,' Richter ordered. He lifted the trunk lid, then pushed aside several camouflaged travel bags. Nothing but changes of uniform. He closed the trunk and then walked slowly to the Horch's hood. He opened it to reveal the eight-cylinder engine.

Richter glanced at one of his corporals across the road. The corporal was grinning. Seldom could one thumb his nose at a general, and a rude one at that.

'You idiot,' the general shouted from inside the cab. 'Nobody could hide under the hood.'

Moving even more sluggishly, Richter latched the hood. He used a mirror mounted on a pole to look under the car, then walked to the cross arm, a red and white bar with a counterbalance. Even his words were slow. 'Please proceed, General.'

The Horch shot forward, trailing curses like exhaust. Richter joined the corporal in a laugh. The truck neared the checkpoint. Richter was able to pass several more refugees through, and then the truck arrived at the crossbar. It was an Opel Blitz two-axle vehicle with an enclosed bed.

Richter stood on the running-board to ask the driver for his documents. The corporal was on the other side of the truck, and another guard positioned himself at the rear. The checkpoint guards had been ordered to bracket all trucks so no one would be able to escape.

As he passed his papers and his cargo manifest through the window, the driver asked, 'You looking for anybody in particular?' He had a Swabian accent, which to Berliners sounds lisping.

Richter returned the papers. 'Not you. Your ears stick out too much and you're about a foot too short.'

The driver smiled thinly. 'I guess a lad carrying a submachine gun is allowed to have a smart mouth.'

'Your cargo doors locked?'

The driver shook his head.

While one of his men searched the truck's underside with the mirror, Richter went to the back of the truck, where the guard there lifted his rifle to cover the sergeant. Richter lifted the hasp and pulled open the doors. The cargo was beef carcasses, hung from rods in two rows. The carcasses were still swaying from the truck's stop. They dripped blood from their butchering. They hung there, teasingly rocking on their hooks, five tons of meat not seen by most Germans in two years.

Gasps came from the refugees. Several stepped toward the truck. The guard moved his rifle to the ragged crowd.

'My God, look at all the beef' came from someone in the crowd.

'Enough to feed a village.'

'Another load for Wilhelmstrasse?' came from another refugee. Wilhelmstrasse was Berlin's diplomatic and government quarter.

'Goddamn Berliners,' another roared. 'The countryside is sucked dry to fill Berliners' bellies while we starve.'

An old man atop a horsecart cried, 'We've given them our sons and our grandsons, and they still aren't satisfied.'

A woman dropped her cloth bag to shake a fist. She raged, 'My boy starved to death in the east. And look at that truck. Look at all the meat.'

The crowd had transformed into a mob. Fists were raised and oaths yelled. The swarm moved tentatively, then, fed by its own momentum, it surged toward the truck.

Sergeant Richter raised his Schmeisser until the stubby barrel was pointed at the sky. He squeezed the trigger. The submachine gun bucked and brayed. Spent shells flew to the roadway.

The mob instantly halted.

'I'm not going to have to use this goddamn gun in earnest, am I?'

The refugees stared at him with fear and hatred and hunger, but slowly the crowd ebbed from the meat truck. The corporal held his carbine at the ready while the refugees listlessly re-formed their line at the barricade. Sergeant Richter stepped onto the Opel Blitz's bumper, then into the cargo bay.

The cattle carcasses had been skinned and dressed out. They hung by their rear legs. Short poles passed between the two bones of each hind leg, and the poles were hung from hooks on short chains. Some of the animals were bulls, with torsos much larger than the others, reaching from the hook almost to the truck bed. As hunger mounted, the Reich had begun slaughtering its breeding bulls. Richter pushed the carcasses aside. He searched the length of the bed, looking behind each swinging bovine cadaver, making sure no one was hiding behind the suspended carcasses. Blood from the carcasses stained his uniform. He also checked the corners of the van.

He peeked back out the truck, then stepped behind a side of beef, drew his service knife, and cut a dozen jagged sirloins from the hanging beef. He was no butcher, and he struggled with the beef cuts, taking several minutes. He tucked them into his coat under an arm. For a month his men had been eating nothing but *Eintopfgericht*, a wartime stew consisting of butcher-shop sweepings, the men suspected. Tonight would be different. Richter made his way between the rows of hanging beef carcasses back to the door. Holding the sides of his coat so he wouldn't drop his prizes, he jumped down to the road and closed the truck's cargo doors.

Sergeant Richter returned to the cross arm to lift it, then waved the driver through the checkpoint. He placed the beefsteaks on the front seat of his troop transport. The sergeant again began checking the refugees, one at a time, occasionally glancing at the photo of the American to refresh his memory. When the woman who had shouted that her son had starved in the east passed for inspection, he returned to the transport to slip her one of the sirloins. Her startled and grateful expression almost made the war worthwhile for the sergeant.

When the meat truck was two kilometers west of the checkpoint, Jack Cray's knife emerged from between the breastbones of a bull carcass. The blade slashed through the twine he had used to tie the ribs together after he had entered the organ cavity. He wrestled with the bones, grunting with the effort. He slithered out of the bull, dropping like a newborn calf to the truck bed. He was covered with blood and offal. His hair was matted with pieces of sinew and blood. His clothes were sodden. A veil of red slime covered his face.

He squeezed between the swaying and jolting carcasses to the cargo door, then slipped his knife between the door edges to lift the hasp. He pushed open a door, waited until the truck slowed for a corner, then leaped into the overgrowth at the side of the road. He rolled twice before finding his feet. He put his knife into his waistband, then pulled a compass from his pocket.

The compass had been made by the Colditz escape committee out of a molded phonograph record, a sewing needle and a magnetized strip of razor blade. Cray sprinted across the road, climbed over a pole fence, and entered a glade of trees.

The compass needle pointed north, and Cray headed in that direction. North, toward Berlin.

PART TWO

The Armory

SEVEN

Otto Dietrich stared between the blast tape crisscrossing the bay window out onto Kammler Street. Fractured and charred pieces of his neighbors' homes had been pushed into piles at even intervals along the sidewalk. Across the street, old Frau Fodor tended an iron pot hung over a fire, stirring it with a wooden spoon. Passersby stopped to stare into the pot and nod, enjoying the steam that wafted across their faces. Turnips and a potato were in the pot. Frau Fodor's home resembled a pile of kindling, and she was living in a tool shed in the back, but did her cooking on the sidewalk so she could share the scents and steam with her neighbors.

Dr Scheller asked, 'They said they'd bring her here?'

'Two o'clock. They are three minutes late.' The detective rocked back and forth on his heels, his eyes still at the window. His knuckles gripping the window frame were white. 'Those people are never late.'

The detective had pushed aside a lamp table so he could stand at the window. The doctor sat on an overstuffed sofa. Fabric on the sofa's corner was ragged where Maria's cat had sharpened its claws over the years. The cat had disappeared, Dietrich suspected into Frau Fodor's pot. The telephone rang, but Dietrich stayed at the window. His hands abruptly began to tremble, so violently that he grabbed his pant legs. Since his release from prison, his hands would begin shaking, for no reason and at any time.

'Are you prepared to see her?' Scheller asked.

'Prepared?' Dietrich wiped away his breath from the window so he could continue to peer through it.

'Maria won't look the same, Otto. I've treated a few of my patients lucky enough to have been released from that place outside Dachau. I hardly recognized them. You should prepare yourself.'

Dietrich nodded absently. He was wearing the same clothes in which he had met Himmler and Müller and Golz and the others, the ill-fitting suit. His Walther was in his belt and his ID card in his pocket. Mounted on the wall were gas lamps that Maria had insisted remain because the flues were made of pink glass resembling flames. A winged draft chair, designed to keep drafts from the sitter, was next to a drawing table on which was a chess set and Dr Scheller's black bag.

'Mister, do you have anything to eat?' The voice came from the doorway to the kitchen, a child's voice.

Dietrich turned to the boy, who was about five years old.

'A loaf of bread and strawberry preserves. Would you like some?'

The boy nodded shyly.

Dietrich opened a net bag he had placed on the floor near the door. He pulled out a knobby loaf of black bread, then tore a chunk from it. He twisted open a jar of preserves. The boy drew near. Dietrich poured jam onto the bread, spread it with his finger, then passed the bread to the boy, who gripped it with both hands and jammed it against his face to chew frantically.

'What's your name?' Dietrich asked.

The boy mumbled something around the wad in his mouth. He might have said 'Rolf.'

The boy's mother appeared at the kitchen door. She wore a green knitted scarf around her neck and a blue coat ragged at the seams. Dark patches were under her eyes. With wide blue eyes, she might have once been lovely, but deprivations and grief and weariness had worn it away. She was scarlet with embarrassment. She spun her son by his shoulders and gently pushed him toward the kitchen door.

When Dietrich said 'Ma'am,' and held out the bread and jam, she hesitated, then accepted them with a nervous smile. She led Rolf from the room.

The doctor asked, 'Who are they, Otto?'

'I found them here when I arrived a while ago. She and her son have been living here a month. After their Dahlem home was destroyed in a bombing raid, she found my place, all the windows dark. So she broke open a glass pane in the back door and let herself and her son in.'

'Squatters? They have no right to take over your home. Why don't you call the police?'

Dietrich smiled. 'I am the police.'

'Where is her husband?' the doctor asked.

'He was a submarine officer, so he's most likely dead.' Dietrich turned back to the window. A million Berliners were without homes. 'She kept this house cleaner than it ever had been, and hadn't touched a thing she didn't require. So I told her she could stay.'

'What's her name?'

'I haven't asked.' The detective wiped mist from the window. His voice rose suddenly. 'There's my wife.'

Dietrich yanked open the front door and hurried down the four steps to the black Horch. The driver and front-seat passenger made no move to get out of the vehicle.

Dietrich pulled open the rear door. 'Maria, I'm here, and – ' Emotions chopped off his words.

She sagged out the door and he had to catch her. He was startled at how little she weighed. And instead of smooth muscles on her arms and shoulders, Dietrich found only bone. She was skeletal and spindly.

'Maria,' he blurted. 'It's me. It's Otto.'

She was unconscious, her eyes closed, her body limp. She was wearing a coarse brown dress and no coat.

'Let's get her inside.' Doctor Scheller had followed Dietrich.

Dietrich was unable to move. The doctor put his arms around Maria's still form and pulled her from the car. In the front seat two Gestapo agents chatted about dinner plans.

Dietrich was finally able to help. He and Scheller formed a fireman's grip to carry her up the stairs. Dietrich kicked open the door. The Horch pulled away from the curb. When Dietrich and Scheller lay her on the davenport, her head flopped to one side.

'I'll . . . I'll get her some water.' Dietrich fled to the kitchen. He could not bear looking at her, her shrunken face, her convict's haircut, her dulled skin. He dipped a ladle into a bucket and poured water into a glass. After a moment he could return to the sitting room.

Scheller was using a tongue depressor to look at her throat, holding her head up with his other hand. A deflated blood-pressure cuff was around her thin arm. His black bag was open at his feet.

Dietrich held the glass. 'I hardly recognize her, Kurt.'

The doctor held her wrist and silently counted. He didn't look up.

After a moment Dietrich said in a low voice, 'She has always been the lively one, you know, the funny one in our marriage. If I was too dour – and I was dour a lot, looking at murdered people for a living – she would stick me in the ribs.'

Scheller lifted one of her eyelids, then the other.

'And she has always been stronger than me. When I was pressured to join the Party, and when I refused an order to investigate a political crime, I would come home afraid, and she would pour courage into me.'

Scheller unbuttoned the first three buttons at the back of Maria's dress so he could examine her skin.

Dietrich's voice was dark with sorrow. 'And when our only child, Bernd, was killed at Stalingrad, she helped me through the agony.' A moment passed. 'I can't lose her, Kurt. I can't.'

Scheller placed his hand against Maria's forehead, then he said, 'She's got typhoid fever, Otto.'

Dietrich blinked. 'Typhoid fever? How can you tell?'

'This rose-colored rash on her skin. I've seen this before.'

'Is she going to be all right?'

Scheller hesitated. 'Otto, I don't think she's going to make it. She's too far gone. She's bleeding internally.'

Dietrich's heart was a hammer in his chest. 'Too far gone? She . . . she . . . There must be something you can do.'

Scheller slowly shook his head.

'Some medicine?' the detective demanded. 'What medicine is used to treat typhoid fever?'

'Ampicillin. But there isn't any in the entire city.'

Dietrich stabbed his hand into his jacket pocket and brought out Himmler's letter. He held it up for the doctor. His words were frantic. 'We can get some ampicillin with this letter. This letter'll get us anything, anything we want.'

Doctor Scheller reached for his friend's shoulder. 'Otto, there's none in Berlin. There's none in Germany. And it's too late for the medicine anyway.'

Dietrich felt as if a cable were tightening around his chest.

'Let's take her upstairs, Otto. She'll be comfortable in bed.'

The detective's voice was a rough whisper. 'How long does she have?'

'A day. Maybe several days. No longer than that.'

They carried Maria up the narrow stairs, past the hunting prints on the stair walls, then by a tiny carved wooden truck that must have belonged to Rolf, then by a plant stand, and into the bedroom, Dietrich seeing none of it because of the tears in his eyes.

Twilight lingered in Leipzig. The sky was washed in reds and purples. Dust and ash from the day's bombing runs had not yet settled. They never settled, persistent Allied airmen saw to that. The particles softened the city by obscuring the distance, letting citizens occasionally forget that the skyline of their ancient city – the spires and towers – was now a series of rounded mounds. Leipzig's great publishing houses were in ruins, their university – opened a half a millennium ago – cratered.

All a flying execution squad needs is a standing wall, and Leipzig still offered a selection. When the Kübelwagen pulled to the side of the brick road, and when the troopers inside began spilling out of the enclosed cargo bay, only one man seemed to notice. He was apparently a refugee, who glanced over his shoulder at the troopers. He then shuffled on, walking into the wind, arms across his chest, the tails of his thin coat flapping behind, his feet crunching the rubble. A scarf was around his head, covering his hair and ears. He turned into an alley between two destroyed warehouses. The alley was filled with debris, but he found sufficient space to pause out of sight.

A railroad track lay down the center of the street. The building opposite the alley had been a depot, with six loading bays looking out onto the street. Because a high-explosive blast had torn the roof off the building, sky was visible through the bays. Three smokestacks were behind the depot, the northernmost stack missing its top third. Just north of the depot was a power substation that bombs had reduced to a blackened knot of wire and steel. The refugee peered back at the Kübelwagen.

SS troopers dragged two men from the truck. They wore Wehrmacht uniforms stripped of badges and stripes and even buttons. They had no boots or hats. Their faces were twisted in terror.

An SS sergeant pushed one of the prisoners toward the wall, and said in a bored voice, 'Let's go, let's go, let's go.'

When one prisoner tripped over a fallen beam, two troopers righted him and shoved him toward the wall. That prisoner turned to the troopers and held up his hands, as if he had anything more to surrender. The second man was pushed against the wall. He too turned, but his legs gave out, and he slid to the ground. His mouth opened and closed like a fish.

'Let's go, let's go.' Now the sergeant was addressing his troops.

There apparently was no time for the protocol of a firing squad. Without any further commands, four troopers formed a haphazard line, raised their rifles, and fired several shots each. The standing prisoner was blown back into the wall, then bounced back to hit the cobblestone street face down, a red stain spreading below him. The sitting prisoner slumped sideways, blood gushing from his chest, his face frozen in his last unimaginable passion. The shots echoed among the ruins, racing up and down the street several times.

The sergeant pulled a placard from the truck's cab. He leaned it against the wall behind the dead men. It read in black paint written by a hasty hand, DESERTERS FROM THE FÜHRER'S ARMY. The paint had not fully dried, and beads ran down the placard onto the cobblestones.

'Let's go, let's go, let's go.' The sergeant waved his arms at his men, hurrying them back into the truck. A day's work was never done.

One trooper made it only as far as the running-board before the truck accelerated away, and he clung to the door, laughing about something, his rifle across his back. His helmet reflected red sparks of the long sunset.

The witness to the executions stepped out of the alley. Jack Cray continued down the road, the third time he had walked this circuit. His gait was a perfect imitation of a refugee's, a dispirited, halting walk that broadcast hunger and despair. Cray had found the neighborhood by walking in the direction from which came loaded military cargo trucks. He had found an armory on the bank on the Parthe River.

Cray had only been able to get within a block of the building. Einheit and Borgward trucks in camouflage paint with black crosses on their doors passed a checkpoint where Wehrmacht soldiers looked at the identification cards of all drivers. Part of the armory had been destroyed in a bombing raid, but the portion that remained was still being used as a storehouse. The armory was surrounded by concertina wire, and soldiers patrolled the exterior of the building. Many important buildings in the Reich were now being patrolled by Werksschutzpolizei, the Factory Protection Police, who at this point in the struggle were the old and infirm or were pubescent boys. But this Leipzig armory still commanded regular troops, and a good number of them, and they were well armed. Cray had found no way to penetrate the wire and the patrols. He hobbled along the street.

When a troop truck passed, its wheels throwing mud, he felt the eyes of the driver on him. Cray reached down to the cobblestones for a discarded tin can, running his fingers inside the container, searching for anything edible. He licked his fingers. The truck's driver did not look a second time at Cray.

Cray passed an antiaircraft battery, four soldiers manning a Flakvierling 38. Next to the flak crew was a twisted skeleton of the last

AA battery that had tried to defend the armory against Allied dive-bombers. The Reich thought the armory still worth protecting. Down a side street ten refugees stood with their hands out toward a bonfire. When one of them threw a broken wood siding onto the fire, a pillar of sparks rose skyward.

Three blocks from the armory Cray turned toward the Parthe River. He passed a coal yard, ash capping each mound of coal, resembling a miniature Alps. The yard was guarded from looters by two protection police who gave Cray no notice. He passed a row of five gutted trucks, reduced to blackened hulks in a bomb raid. Then came a machine shop, a bindery, and a glassworks, all intact and operating, slits of light coming from under their doors. Workers' shadows were visible on blackout paper on the windows. The sweet scent of brewery malt turned Cray's nose. Their city was devastated, yet Leipzigers could still run a brewery. He grinned quickly at the thought of a beer, his teeth flashing like a half-hidden knife.

On the riverbank were the remnants of a warehouse, hit long ago. Brick pickers and iron scavengers had been through it, leaving only a concrete foundation, burned and fractured timbers, and scattered brick and glass shards. Glass crunched under Cray's feet as he moved across the warehouse floor toward the water. He stepped around a pile of broken barrel staves. Ash partly covered a stack of rotting gunnysacks. The American walked carefully in the grainy purple light, leaving the warehouse by wooden steps that went down to the river. He crossed gravel, then passed through damp grass as he neared the water. He stabbed his shoes into the mud for traction as the riverbank steepened.

The veil of darkness was beginning to obscure buildings across the river. Most of the structures had been damaged, and brick walls had spilled into the river, forming rough piers of rubble. Smoke rose from a few stacks across the river, and wind whipped the haze away. Power lines crossing the river were still up. Blackout curtains hid the window light from occupied buildings, and as night fell, the black city's gloom became palpable.

Defenders usually overestimate the value of water. Cray was guessing that he would be able to approach the armory from the river side. He removed the scarf and his jacket, then gripped the branch of a small elm tree that grew next to the river, and lowered a leg into the water.

The Parthe was shockingly cold. Yet Cray let himself sink into the river, and shoved himself away from the bank. He idly kicked his feet, doing most of the work with his arms, a silent breaststroke with the current. An observer would have thought the swimmer – pulling himself along the river with a powerful motion – was indifferent to the frigid water, but there were no observers. In the failing light the surface of the water shone like oil. Cray bumped into something floating in the water. A dog's body, its belly and eyes eaten out by rats. He ignored it and pulled himself along, keeping on the armory side of the river, avoiding fallen telephone poles and a truck that had been blown into the river by a bomb.

On the opposite shore was a railroad yard. Two locomotives and a coal car were turned on their sides. Boxcars had been burned down to the wheels. Cray dug into the water again and again, slipping toward the armory.

A barbed-wire fence ran along the edge of the armory property and into the water. Cray kicked around the fence posts and drifted toward the shore. When his feet found the soft bottom, he started up the bank, mud sucking at his boots. Then he heard a laugh to his left. Two cigarettes glowed near an armory door. Two more guards joined the group, and a match flared as they lit cigarettes. One of the guards shouted, and was answered by laughs from yet two more soldiers further along the brick wall. The water side of the armory was well guarded.

Cray slipped back into the river. An icy hand seemed to be squeezing his chest. The water had begun its work of killing him. He closed his eyes. His face hardened, resolution rekindling, and when he opened his eyes again, he was ready for more of the river. He was no longer shivering.

He drifted along the bank. The south end of the armory had been destroyed by a bomb, and only the north portion was in operation. But all of it was guarded. Cray glided through the water. A new scent caught him. Sewage. In the dim light he saw an effluent pipe that jutted from the bank, most of it underwater. He paddled up to the pipe, which was about five feet in diameter. Cray gripped the edges and held himself against the outflow. The human waste was warm, surging around him. He began to feel his chest and shoulders and arms again. He soaked in the warm fluid, his head above the pipe as he surveyed the armory's yard. The foul odor smelled like life to him.

The troops strolled back and forth, rifles on their backs. One lit a piece of paper and dropped it into a barrel, then fanned it with his hands. Licks of flame appeared. Several guards held out their hands to the heat. When an officer barked at them, the guards resumed their rounds.

The sewage pipe seemed to head underground in the direction of the armory, and alongside the toppled south end of the building. Bombs had mangled that end, and a wall had fallen into the lot to the south. The underground pipe appeared to lie below this cratered rubble.

Cray studied the effluent. The stream carried the brown and unspeakable. Cray was comfortable hanging in front of the sewage pipe, and was tempted to stay awhile, leisurely coming up with another plan. But a splinter of wood drifted into him from the pipe, then more small pieces of wood, and then bits of floating plaster not yet fully soaked.

Detritus was falling into the sewage not far up the line. The pipe was open to the air nearby. As if doing a pull-up, Cray lifted himself on the pipe to peer into the armory's yard. Two men in overalls had just entered the yard from a vehicle lot to the south. The lot had camouflage nets strung over it on poles. The men were negotiating a path through the bomb rubble, their heads visible to Cray one moment, then not the next as they climbed and descended hills of debris. They reached the armory's river-side yard. One of them carried a toolbox. They might have been mechanics, and perhaps their regular route between the vehicle lot and the armory had been obstructed when the south part of the armory was destroyed, so now they had to pick their way through the piles of bricks and beams and around craters. The mechanics had kicked debris into the open sewage line.

Cray smiled thinly. He had found the breach. He lowered himself again to peer into the pipe. He might have seen a slight suggestion of indigo down the pipe – a reflection of the dying day's light – but he could not be sure. He breathed deeply, lifted his legs until his feet found the concrete lip, and crawled inside.

Sewage filled the pipe except for the top seven inches. Cray twisted his neck so that his mouth and nose remained above the surface. The air was putrid, but Cray knew it wasn't the scent but rather the methane and the absence of oxygen that would kill him if he was too long in the pipe. He scrambled along, his feet slipping on slime that coated the pipe walls under the surface. He held his breath as long as possible, then let it slowly out. When he at last had to inhale, the fumes seemed to lock in his lungs, and on his second breath neon spots began appearing before his eyes. He dug his feet into the walls and pushed off again and again. He used his hands as paddles, struggling up the sewage stream. His head scraped along the top of the pipe, loosening crusted filth that dripped into his eyes and ears.

That distant purple spot seemed to draw no nearer. Blackness pressed in on Cray. He could see nothing except more neon colors, now dancing in front of him. He lost his bearings and drifted sideways, his shoulder bumping the pipe wall. He could not tell which direction was up. And then he could not detect the surface of the sewage. His mind was going. He kicked and kicked against the slime-covered walls, vaguely hoping he was still going toward that patch of purple. Soft fingers of unconsciousness reached for him.

Abruptly his head no longer had contact with the pipe. He rose in the waste. He had found the cleft in the pipe caused by the bomb blast. Cray gulped air.

The mad colors in front of his eyes dimmed. His thoughts began arranging themselves. The opening in the pipe was twice the breadth of his shoulders. Cray was in a conical bomb crater, with a short horizon of dirt all around, as if he were standing at the bottom of a funnel. He stood slowly so that the muck dripping off him would be soundless. He wiped his eyes and lips. He placed a foot on the dirt to test his weight. When several pebbles fell into the sewage, Cray froze to listen for the guards. He heard only good-natured chatter. With small and careful steps, he rose to the crest of the crater.

He could see nothing but bomb wreckage in all directions. He crawled over two beams that had fallen across each other, then up a hillock of bricks. He lay on the rubble pile like a lizard, sodden and stinking and once again getting cold.

Laughter came from a patrol near the river. Piles of debris hid Cray from the German guards. He crawled toward the armory, moving one limb at a time, testing each handhold and each foot placement. He moved down a hill of bricks, then along a valley between more mounds. He slipped through a tangle of bent pipe and split wood. He moved without thought, his limbs silently finding their way through the twisted ruins, his mind on the guards.

When he heard new voices, he paused to cup both ears with his hands, then rotated one cup downward, a hunter's trick that allowed him to better gauge the direction of the conversation. Sentries were both to his left and his right, to the street and the river sides of the building. Footfalls came from the rubble near the street, but they were even and unconcerned. Again Cray crawled forward.

In lieu of the fallen wall, tarpaulins had been hung from beams. They warded off the weather and acted as blackout curtains. They billowed in the wind. Cray moved the last few yards to a tarp. He slowly lifted a corner.

Sounds of machinery and men came from the far end of the building. Down a long aisle of wooden boxes, workers were pushing containers into two Wehrmacht trucks that had backed into loading bays. Cray's end of the building was dark. He slipped under the tarp and moved to a stack of boxes.

Many of the containers had apparently been salvaged from the destroyed end of the building, because they lay about in disarray uncharacteristic of the Wehrmacht. But toward the center of the building the rows became more orderly. Some stacks were almost to the ceiling. Weapons were against the east wall. Crates were stamped with STIELHANDGRANATE, FLAMMENWERFER, and MP/2 and contained stick grenades, flamethrowers, submachine guns. Many more crates were filled with other weapons.

Cray's clothing clung to him. He would turn to the weapons after he obtained a change of clothes. He left damp footprints as he moved to the closest container. The crate was painted in camouflage brown and gray, and was not latched. He opened it and pulled out green fabric. Cray held it up to his eyes. It was a field service tunic with the national emblem sewn on the breast. He found trousers and blouses, and windproof anoraks and boots and greatcoats, and caps with short cloth peaks. A dozen complete uniforms. From the cleated boots and anoraks, Cray guessed these were mountain troop uniforms. He set aside a full outfit.

Then he lifted out a canvas bag. He dug inside to find shoulder patches showing rank. He brought out a patch with the two pips, for a captain. He stared at it a moment, then caught the sewage smell of himself.

Cray whispered, 'I deserve a promotion.'

He bought out two braided major's patches.

'That's better.' He added the patches to his cache.

EIGHT

Sergeant Ulrich Kahr was passing the cement mixer when the air-raid siren began its low growl. He continued with his leisurely pace because the siren usually gave ten minutes' warning, and in a few dozen meters he would enter the most bombproof structure in the Reich, maybe in the world.

He had walked by the cement mixer countless times, and wondered why it had never been removed from the Chancellery garden. No new construction had occurred on the bunker in months, yet the mixer had remained. Painted in green three times on the round mixer was the name of its owner, Hochtief, the Berlin construction firm. The concrete guard tower was to his right.

Ahead was the Old Chancellery, a dark building made darker by low clouds. The side of the Chancellery facing the street was intact, but the rear, which was Kahr's view, was severely damaged. Most of the windows on the ground floor were boarded, and the sky could be seen through windows on the upper floor. Zigzags of strafing pocks decorated the stone walls, courtesy of enemy planes that roamed the Berlin skies virtually at will.

The siren's wail played back and forth among the buildings, washing over Kahr again and again. Ahead was the cement blockhouse with its steel door and two SS guards. Kahr was wearing his gray-green army uniform, the new model that was made of cheap cloth. To save fabric the tunic had only two pockets instead of four. So he didn't need to walk Berlin's streets to know the war was lost.

The SS guards eyed him as he approached, just as they did every day, looking at him as if he were some species of vermin. Kahr detested the haughty SS bastards, the lot of them. And he'd heard some stories about the SS.

The sergeant slowed, not wanting to enter the bunker one moment earlier than he had to. He glanced at his wristwatch. A few more minutes.

Kahr instinctively ducked when the AA gun atop the Chancellery opened fire, filling the garden with hollow pounding. He glanced skyward to see a stream of tracer shells arcing across the sky. The gun battery was hidden by the roofline. Didn't the sirens always give ten minutes? Kahr began to run toward the bunker entrance. The wand of tracers slashed across the sky, the gunner frantically cranking, trying to catch up to his target.

Then the daylight flickered. An airplane soared across the garden, east to west along the length of it, there and gone almost before Kahr saw it. But he did see it, an enemy plane, American, a small plane, flying so low Kahr could see the white stars on its tail, however fleeting. Undoubtedly a reconnaissance plane, sent over the Reich's capital, right over the Chancellery, with stunning impudence. Kahr had seen these recon planes before, many times. Enemy bomber command surely had a detailed map of Berlin, updated frequently, so the bombers wouldn't waste their payloads on buildings that were already destroyed, as if the British and Americans had to worry about a shortage of explosives, goddamn them.

The last of the tracers sped away across the sky, then blinked out in the distance, their own small admission of their folly. Wisps of smoke rose from the Chancellery's roof, from the AA barrels. Kahr heard the battery officer on the roof berate his men for slowness and poor aim. An SS guard was in a concrete tower to Kahr's right. The young guard looked unperturbed by the American flyover, and was examining with minute care a black glove he held in his hand, and smiling.

Kahr's right boot had a hole in the sole, and dampness had worked its way to his sock. He knew his foot wouldn't dry all day, and he didn't dare remove his boot to air out the sock because the last time he did so no less a personage than Dr Goebbels upbraided him for being out of uniform. Kahr had wondered later how the minister of propaganda had time to be concerned about a sergeant's bootless foot.

At the blockhouse door Kahr lifted his stiff gray linen identification card from a pocket. On the card was Kahr's photograph, a gold seal, a yellow diagonal bar, and the signature of the Führer's chief adjutant. Kahr had lost such a card three months ago, and had reported the loss immediately, and all Reich Security Service offices, the Wehrmacht Berlin regiment, the Gestapo, the Berlin police, and the Liebstandarte-SS Adolf Hitler were notified of the loss. But Kahr was not reprimanded because the authorities did not want to deter reports of lost passes. His lieutenant had ordered him to be more careful.

The sergeant had no idea how he had lost his pass. He didn't care about it anymore, anyway. Much had happened to Kahr since then, none of it good. He did not have the energy to care about such things as a piece of stiff linen, or these rude guards, or the destroyed garden behind him, none of it. The war's toll on Kahr had been so great that he could not find refuge even in bitterness. Ulrich Kahr was spent. Little was left of him.

The SS guard studied Kahr's face, comparing it with the photograph on the pass. Sergeant Kahr's mouth was crooked, lower on one side, giving him a carping look, even though he seldom carped. His eyes were dark and faded, with only a suggestion of life left in them.

The two guards were all polish and creases, brittle in their importance, guarding this hole in the ground. Every day this same guard glared at the ID photograph and then Kahr with renewed suspicion, and each time the guard handed back the pass slowly, as if he might change his mind at any moment. Finally the guard nodded, a grudging, almost imperceptible movement. When the other guard opened the heavy steel door, Sergeant Kahr entered the blockhouse. The door clanked shut behind him with the deep finality of the last sound on earth.

Kahr descended the stairs to one landing, then another, circling counterclockwise. The fetid smell reached for him, dank and sour. The bunker was surrounded by groundwater, and with every heavy rain the sewers backed up, filling the toilets with waste that would spill out into the halls. Added to the sewage smell were the odors of coal-tar disinfectant and damp wool uniforms. Kahr was sure these foul aromas chased away the good air, depriving his brain of oxygen, and so every shift he became dumber and dumber.

Then he heard the whine, his whine. Sergeant Kahr may have been the only person assigned to the bunker whom the ventilator system's incessant caterwaul did not bother. Most compared the sound to a dentist's drill. Constant, always on, reaching every room in the bunker, inescapable. But Sergeant Kahr was one of the bunker's ventilation technicians. His duty was to maintain the equipment that sucked in new air and blew out old air. He took pride in his task and appreciated the whine because it constantly reminded bunker denizens of his importance. Kahr might be the lowest-ranking person in the entire complex, but the whine was suffered by everyone irrespective of rank, which gave him some satisfaction.

At the bottom of the stairs was a foyer, lit so brightly by overhead bulbs that Kahr had to squint up into the faces of the two SS guards posted there. Schutzstaffel guards were all tall. One examined his pass, then checked the duty roster on his clipboard, marking off Kahr's name. The other guard searched Kahr, running his hands up the sergeant's uniform to his armpits, then along his lower back, then down and up his trousers, rudely probing his crotch. This guard carried a Schmeisser submachine gun across his stomach on a sling.

The guard captain worked at a small desk to one side of the door. He glanced up at Kahr, but quickly returned to his rosters and bulletins. Four telephones and several loose-leaf binders covered his desk. The guard captain wore a livid purple burn scar on his right cheek and the right side of his neck.

'All right, Sergeant,' the guard with the clipboard said. 'You can go in.'

'Bleib übrig,' Kahr said pointedly. Survive. Lately, Berliners had been using the phrase instead of goodbye. Kahr knew it irritated the SS guards, who viewed the new saying as defeatist. So he said it again. *'Bleib übrig.'*

'I'll survive, old man.' The clipboard guard laughed meanly. 'From the looks of you, you may not.'

Kahr could only nod agreement. The war had beaten up Ulrich Kahr, had ravaged his face and his body, and he knew it. Perhaps he shouldn't feel sorry for himself. He hadn't seen frontline duty, after all, not in this war, anyway, because he was fifty-five years old, born the same year as the Führer. But the war had etched deep lines into Kahr's face, running from his nose to the corners of his mouth, fanning out from his eyes in expanding webs. The skin below his eyes was a ghastly mottled green, looking as if it had been bruised. He walked now with a stoop like an old man. And he was hesitant, the boldness gone from him. Everything, from climbing a flight of stairs to rising from a chair to spreading ersatz butter on black bread, seemed an insurmountable physical challenge. Last week the Führer's physician, Dr Morrel, a kindly man, had offered to examine Kahr. The sergeant had politely said no. Kahr's decline was not due to a physical ailment but to news from the fronts, and in the last half-year he had taken Germany's sufferings upon his shoulders.

Karl had been a widower for fifteen years, and had raised his sons on his own. Last summer his oldest boy, Eswald, a Wehrmacht infantryman, had been killed by the American naval bombardment on the Normandy coast. Then just this past Christmas, Kahr had learned that his second son, Theodor, an armored scout-car driver, had been killed during the Ardennes campaign when his vehicle rolled over a mine.

Now all that was left of Ulrich Kahr's family was his youngest son, Max, who was on the eastern front. Every time Kahr saw the regimental chaplain, Kahr held his breath, hoping the chaplain wasn't bringing bad news, as he had already done twice. Kahr took little solace in knowing that he was not alone in having lost two sons. German families had been gutted by this war, their boys torn from them. A pall of grief lay over the land.

And there was no one to turn to. Every man in his regiment had lost someone. To talk of one's own loss was to rekindle someone else's heartache. So he suffered alone and in silence. Ulrich Kahr knew he could never again be whole, but he had one tender hope.

The chance he might see his son Max again, home and alive, was a fragile prospect, too perilous to nudge by dwelling on it, but it was all that was left for Kahr.

He stepped into a long central corridor used as a lounge. A Persian carpet brought from the Chancellery was on the floor, its edges folded under to fit the space. The furniture was an odd mix: a utilitarian bench resembling a pew, three ribbonback Louis Quinze chairs, several camp stools, and a long oak table against a wall under two enormous Schinkel landscapes. Dome lights cast the concrete walls in pale yellow. There were ventilation grates along the walls near the ceiling at three-meter intervals. Emergency telephones were mounted on each of the hallway's walls. The first door to his right was to a cloakroom.

Just then General Keitel emerged from the second door, from the conference room. In those two paces into the hall Keitel transformed his face. In the conference room he had been a worried supplicant, earnest but unassuming, offering nothing to offend. But as he stepped into the hall, Keitel's chin firmed, his head lifted haughtily, and his gaze became imperious. Even his dueling scar remolded itself, from an insignificant welt to a magnificent testament to Prussian honor. He must have been meeting with the Führer, the only person on earth who could drain the Wehrmacht chief of staff's face of its arrogance.

Then Kahr heard the golden voice, the remarkable tones that had once lifted Germany. 'And, Keitel, you tell him it must be done. He must wheel around. There can be no other course of action.'

The general half-turned, and answered, 'Of course, my Führer.'

Kahr gave the conference room the swiftest of glances. The leader was bent over a map table. He was wearing the pearl-gray tunic with the olive shirt and black trousers that he always wore in the bunker. On his left breast were his golden Party badge and the Iron Cross won in the Great War. Then General Jodl stepped around the table, and Sergeant Kahr's view of the leader was blocked, and Kahr knew it best to quickly move on anyway.

He walked straight ahead. Lockers were to one side, where Foreign Minister Ribbentrop was conferring with an SS general Kahr did not recognize. Ribbentrop fidgeted with a tunic pocket that contained a package of cigarettes, and he politely herded the general toward the door, apparently anxious to get outside for a cigarette. Smoking was forbidden in the bunker. Even matches were prohibited, some said for security purposes but most believed their banning was an extension of the Führer's loathing of cigarette smoke. Huddling at the rear of the corridor were the Luftwaffe's Chief of Staff General Koller, Major General Walter Buhle, and Hitler's adjutant, General Burgdorf. Aides to these officers – young men, eager and efficient, fairly panting – lined the wall opposite the lockers, waiting. The corridor was crowded.

Kahr glanced at his watch, wondering if he had time to visit the galley, which was through the door at the far end of the hall, then up the stairs to a second group of rooms, which included the servants' rooms, the communal mess, the pantry and galley. One of the cooks was sweet on Kahr, and would slip him pastry or a plate of veal. She liked to pretend the extra rations were her surreptitious gift to Sergeant Kahr, and she would make a production of looking over her shoulders to insure no one was looking as she passed the food to him, but in truth no one belowground cared that Kahr often carried extra food from the kitchen to his post in the ventilation room. The SS guard at the door to the stairway would glance at the food and say nothing. Kahr's wristwatch indicated he had better forego visiting the cook this day.

The sergeant had noticed a stratification in the bunker's society. Those who spent most of their time belowground – the Führer's cooks and secretaries and waiter, his personal aide and bodyguard SS-Colonel Günsche, his valet Heinz Linge, Martin Bormann, the blond woman with the chirpy Bavarian accent Kahr had heard called Eva, the SS guards at the bunker's entrances, and a few others, including Kahr and the other technicians who ran the ventilation system and generators and telephone banks – were treated as family by the Führer. He listened to their problems and gave them advice, sometimes scolding, often encouraging. When one of his secretaries, Trudi Reymann, weepingly reported that her fiancé had jilted her, Hitler sat beside her for half an hour, patting her hand and cooing softly. When his waiter, Walter Gademann, broke his wrist in a fall, Hitler stood by the operating table in the bunker's surgery, chatting to Gademann to distract him from the pain as Dr Morrel set the bone and applied a cast. And a month ago Kahr had been promoted from staff sergeant to master sergeant, and was astonished to find the Führer's signature, rather than the signature of Kahr's captain, on the order of promotion.

The second level of bunker society were those who visited the complex often, both the military men whose duty brought them underground and the sycophants who had somehow gained both the Führer's favor and valid passes. The former included Keitel and Jodl, Generals Krebs and Guderian, Admiral Doenitz, and Ministers Goebbels and Speer. The latter included General Hermann Fegelein, the SS liaison who was married to Eva Braun's sister, and who did little more than gossip with anyone he could slow long enough to catch an ear. These visitors were not considered family by the Führer, and were handled with less patience and less solicitude.

Battlefield commanders – Manteuffel and Busse and many others – arrived at irregular intervals, mud on their boots, uniforms often torn, faces haggard, anxious to report and get away from this place. Often as not, they would be summarily promoted or transferred or dismissed, and they rarely knew their fate when they arrived. In their demeanor and haste, these generals brought shocking reality into the bunker, where eight-foot-thick concrete walls muffled both bombs and the outside world. The contempt felt for those safely ensconced belowground was visible on every battlefield commander's face, and those in Führerbunker society were just as relieved to see them go as the commanders were to leave. These frontliners were certainly not members of the underground family.

This bunker had been built just the year before, but had not been completed. Construction was halted after the place had been made habitable but before it had been made comfortable. No one knew why construction had stopped, at least no one Sergeant Kahr had spoken with. He skirted the crowd, passing the first door on his left, which was to the telephone switchboard and guards' room. Here the overhead lights were for some reason orange, giving everyone's face a malarial hue. In other rooms the light was white, almost incandescent, a light that flattened perspective and revealed blue veins beneath skin. Older rooms were dusty with new concrete, while newer rooms were damp, the concrete not fully set. Some walls seeped water and were discolored by mold. A few walls were carefully painted to match furniture, but others had been left as unpainted concrete. Some rooms were as warm and humid as a hothouse, others were dry and cool. Everywhere was the soprano hum of the ventilator fans, and in some rooms this sound was supplemented by the gurgle of the toilet plumbing or the rumble of the sump pumps or the clang of exterior doors. Each underground room had its own combination of scents and colors and sounds, and there seemed to be no reason to any of it. And Ulrich Kahr liked none of it, except the ventilator's hum.

The sergeant thought of the Führerbunker as a concrete submarine, the walls always pressing in on him. As the end of each shift neared, the place became more and more oppressing, and Kahr always emerged from the bunker gasping, eternally grateful for the sky, whether it was clouds or sun or firestorm smoke or the darkness of night. He dreaded those days that called on him to sleep at his post, on a Pullman cot in his generator-ventilator room.

He rang the buzzer of the second door on the left with that day's signal: two rings, then one, then one more. The door was a solid steel plate with a deadbolt that could be opened only from the inside. Because of the room's critical equipment, the door was kept locked at all times. A Wehrmacht sergeant pulled open the door, and Kahr entered his domain, a cubicle filled with machinery. At the far end were two diesel generators, quiet for the moment because electricity had been patched through to the bunker. Many times a day the bunker would plunge into the absolute darkness of a coal shaft. The beating heart of the Reich would be utterly still until Ulrich Kahr came to its rescue. Helped by a flashlight, Kahr would pull the cord on a gasoline starter motor, then engage the diesel generators, and within a few moments the bunker would again have light and ventilation. The generators each produced sixty kilowatts, and supplied emergency electricity for the lights, heating system, water pump, and switchboard.

The ventilator whine was loudest in this room. Kahr asked the Wehrmacht sergeant who had admitted him, and was now standing in front of the control panel making the final entries of his shift into the log, 'Anything new?'

Sergeant Hans Fischer lowered the notebook. 'Power was out four times for a total of ninety-three minutes. The generators were up and running within two minutes each time.'

It was a boast. The diesel generators were complicated to start, and it was a nervous business because the most important people in the Reich were a few feet away in thick blackness waiting for the return of light.

'There is still a small oil leak at the base of starter one. No better, no worse. I telephoned Erwin and he said he was on his way, but he must have been detained.'

Erwin Göckel was a Wehrmacht mechanic, and he was scheduled to look for the reason for the oil leak. In any event, the room had a second starter engine, the spare. The room also contained yellow canaries in a wicker birdcage.

Fischer signed out on the roster, nodded goodbye to the canaries, and left the room, still stretching the aches out of his limbs. The job involved mostly sitting on a hard chair staring at dials.

The generators and starter engines and the fan boxes occupied much of the room, and an instrument panel took up most of the remainder. The panel – gauges and toggles and warning lights – monitored the generators and the ventilating system, some of which Kahr had designed. He had caught the Führer's attention once, when Kahr had insisted to his captain that an air-intake grate behind a juniper bush in the Chancellery garden should be raised as protection against an attack with heavier-than-air gas. Due to his experience in the Great War, Hitler feared gas. The gracious captain had mentioned Kahr in the report that had resulted in the grate being raised. Later a note of appreciation from Hitler himself had been taped to the ventilator control panel. On stationery decorated with the national eagle and a swastika, the note had read, 'Sgt Kahr: I appreciate your work with the grate. Hitler.' Kahr had often wondered if the Führer had taped it to the panel himself, perhaps having had to first search for pen and paper, then the tape, finally entering the generator room to put up the note, wondering where just the right place was so Sergeant Kahr would be sure to see it. This little scene pleased Kahr greatly, and he had replayed it endlessly in his mind.

Kahr looked at the oil- and water-pressure gauges, making notes in the machinery logbooks attached to the panel by cords. He lifted a rag from the wall hook behind his chair and checked six dipsticks, two for each of the diesel engines and one each for the starter motors. The room was dimly lit by a single overhead bulb, and Kahr had to bend close to his work, making sure the lines of oil were up to the marks on the sticks. Then he wiped away the few drops of oil that had leaked from the starter motor. Two jerrycans of gasoline were next to a box of gas masks. A diesel fuel tank was also squeezed into the room, and Kahr twisted off its cap and checked its level with a dipstick. The tank contained only two hundred liters of diesel, a small amount due to the possibility of fire. The two or three liters that were consumed by the engines each day during the blackouts were replaced daily through a fuel pipe with its outlet in the garden above.

Also squeezed into the room were two metal cots with mattresses. When more than one mechanic was on duty, there was no rule against one taking a nap. And in an emergency, the generator-ventilator mechanics would quarter in this room.

Sergeant Kahr returned the rag to the hook, then lifted a pinch of birdseed from a cloth bag and dropped it into the wood cup at the side of the cage. The canaries sidled along the perch to look at the offering, then ignored it, returning to their preening. The birds were an alarm, as they would die from gas poisoning before humans, and thereby would allow people in the bunker time to find their gas masks. Frequently, Kahr and Fischer were both on duty during the same shift, and after a week of hearing Fischer say in a falsetto voice, 'Heil Hitler, Heil Hitler, Heil Hitler' to the canaries, Kahr told him that it was parakeets that could talk, not canaries. Not appreciating having been revealed as a moron, Fischer had been cool toward him ever since.

Kahr lowered himself to the chair. Exhaust from the engines was piped directly outside, but the room still reeked of fuel. The Daimler company had known where these two diesel power plants were destined, and so had covered them with ornamental twists of chrome and brass, and they more closely resembled tea samovars than engines. Air flowed into the room from a grate above the rag hook, but the place was always too warm. On the wall above the panel was a diagram of the ventilation system, showing routes of the piping and the locations of the fans, filters, belowground grates and aboveground outlets and inlets, even the locations of the four cages of canaries. Switches on the panel activated dampers and gates, allowing Kahr to direct the flow of air. In the event of a gas attack he had been trained to shut off the fresh-air intakes and allow only captured air to circulate. Many of the ventilation pipes passed through this cramped room, along the ceiling and the long wall opposite the control panels. These were ribbed pipes, eighteen of them that entered the room from the walls and connected to the fan boxes. Half the pipes were painted red and half were green because they made up two separate, independent systems. If for some reason smoke or noxious gas were to breach the red set of pipes, that set could be closed off, and the fresh air and exhaust run through the green pipes. The fans were powered by outside electricity or the generators in the room next to them. Each air pipe in Kahr's room had a hatch that could be opened so the pipe could be pumped out in the event of flooding, which had never as yet occurred, or to insert poison to kill rats, which occurred frequently. The ventilation pipes were purposely too narrow to allow even the smallest of men to crawl through them. Near the fan boxes were two air purification systems, each in metal crates the size of a desk, and each with pipes running up the wall to join the other ventilation pipes. The air purification machinery was serviced daily by an outside technician, and Kahr knew little about them, other than how to switch them on should air in the bunker be fouled with smoke or gas.

A large red button on the panel activated the *Notbremse*, the emergency brake, which was to be punched only in case of fire, explosion, or assassination attempt. This button sealed all the doors and activated the sprinkler system. An identical button was located at the guard captain's station. Also in Kahr's room were emergency controls for the firefighting system, large valves to shut off water pipes.

With the dipsticks checked and the canaries fed, Kahr had completed his work for the shift, until the lights went out and he had to bring the generators to life. And with nothing to do, his thoughts invariably returned to his lost sons and his one hope, the return of his boy Max. Kahr had avoided religion all his life, until the death of his second son, and now had turned to it with fervor. Perhaps if he loaded God with prayers, much like loading artillery shells onto the bed of a transport truck, God would allow a small mercy. Kahr did not know theology, but suspected the sheer number of his prayers would not be overlooked. God would not overlook Ulrich Kahr's thousandth plea, or his ten-thousandth. Kahr closed his eyes and whispered a new prayer, softly, hardly audible under the sough coming from the air grate and the ventilator fans' whine. Even soft prayers were all right, Kahr figured, because God was not deaf.

The signal came from the buzzer above his desk. Two rings, then one, then another. Kahr was puzzled. Few people visited the generator room, because of the noise. He threw the bolt and opened the heavy door.

'Sergeant Kahr,' the visitor said.

The voice, the golden voice. Kahr stepped away from the door so quickly that his chair spilled backward against the gas-mask crate, and the startled canaries chirruped and frantically fitted around their cage.

Kahr straightened his backbone, slapped his arms against his sides, thrust his chin up and sucked his belly in.

'Sergeant Kahr, we are a family here belowground,' Adolf Hitler said, entering the room slowly, more a shuffle than a walk.

'Yes, my leader.' Kahr fought for breath. Most Germans, even high-ranking officers, suffered an inability to breathe while being addressed by their leader, so powerful was his effect.

'I have tried to take some of the burdens off my family, especially now that we must live down in this terrible place.'

'Yes, my leader.'

Even though Kahr worked within two dozen meters of the Führer almost every day, he seldom more than glimpsed the man, usually through a door or between several generals, sometimes partly hidden behind his dog as Hitler kneeled to pet it. So Kahr's image of Hitler had remained fixed, the glowing giant on the posters. Now Kahr was startled at Hitler's rapid decline. The Führer's pale blue eyes – his one distinctive feature – were bloodshot, the pupils filmy. Hitler's face was bloated and the skin was chalky and yellow. The bags under his eyes, which Hitler blamed on mustard gas in the trenches, were purple and puffy. Deep lines ran from his newly pulpy nose to the corners of his mouth. His hair had turned gray within just the past two months, not a dignified silver but a drab mouse gray. Hitler's left arm was palsied and useless, and he gripped it with his right hand to prevent it from shaking. The contrast between Hitler and his SS guards, chosen for their health and beauty, had become appalling.

But, still and ever, the voice. 'I cannot let my intimates suffer alone.'

On his nose were the gold-rimmed spectacles that most Germans knew nothing about. He brought up a sheet of paper to his eyes, and then Ulrich Kahr knew the reason for the visit.

The sergeant uttered a low groan and swayed. Only by replanting a foot could he stay upright.

Hitler said in a tender voice, 'Your son, Max, has been lost near Stettin, on the Oder.'

'Lost?' Kahr said in a fogged voice. His face was suddenly flushed, and he was dizzy.

'His commanding officer writes that Max did not come back from patrol. He is presumed dead. The Bolsheviks are not taking prisoners. I thought it better that I inform you, rather than have you hear this news from someone else.'

Kahr blindly reached for his desk. His legs were suddenly unable to support him. Hitler stepped into the small room to help the sergeant into the chair, not much help, with only one hand.

Then Hitler put his good hand on Kahr's shoulder. 'I am very sorry,' he said, bending forward so as to gaze into the sergeant's watering eyes. 'But at least you know that his loss was for the Fatherland.'

Kahr gulped air.

Hitler squeezed the sergeant's shoulder. 'I will be thinking of Max, too. So you will not be alone in your loss.' He stood upright and left the room.

Kahr turned back to his control panel. The dials and gauges were scrambled by his tears. His boy Max. This dreadful news. His last son. Kahr's thoughts were broken and dulled. He could not see beyond that minute, that hour, that day. His business with this world was done. Ulrich Kahr's last hope was gone forever.

The Bavarian Motor Works plant near Munich had been reduced to wreckage, but their motorcycles still worked well enough. Jack Cray straddled the machine, his hands out in front of him on the handlebars. The 900-cc engine rumbled under him. Wind blew in his face. The dirt road was pocked with puddles from the rain. He drove slowly, never more than thirty miles an hour. He did not know where in Saxony he was, somewhere north of Leipzig about fifty miles south of Berlin, he figured. He was in a shallow valley with hills rising on both sides of him. He guessed that any road headed north would take him to the city.

The motorcycle belonged to the Wehrmacht, and was painted in camouflage brown and black. After washing himself in a stream – he still smelled faintly of sewage – Cray had liberated the motorcycle from a military checkpoint north of Leipzig. In saddlebags hung over the rear fender were six stick grenades and four satchel charges, all stolen from the armory by Cray. He wore a pistol in a holster on his hip, also from the armory.

German countryside passed by. Small homes and barns, fenced

pastures, wood glades. He crossed a stone bridge over a stream, then paralleled a rail line for several miles. Clouds hid the sun. He sped through a village, nothing more than a train station and a dozen other buildings built around a crossroads.

Just north of the town was a rail siding occupied by a steaming locomotive and six cars. The top of each car was painted in bold white with a red cross. Four wooden buildings had once stood by the siding, but three had been destroyed. Hundreds of German soldiers lingered near the remaining structure, and the neighboring field was filled with soldiers, some leaning on crutches, some lying on cots and blankets. Bandages were everywhere, and even passing by quickly, Cray could see blood on many of them. This was a staging area for wounded, probably from both eastern and western fronts. Smoke poured from the locomotive's stack. Injured soldiers were being loaded onto the rail cars. Fifteen ambulances – trucks with red crosses painted on top – were parked by the siding, and three more approached the field on the road behind Cray. He accelerated to outdistance them.

Next, Cray passed a train that had been attacked by dive-bombers some time ago: twenty cars and a locomotive, so heavily damaged the field resembled a junkyard. The railcars had been carrying armored scout cars. Apparently unimpeded by enemy fighters or AA fire, the bombers had made leisurely extra runs, and the scout cars had been torn apart and flung all around and burned to black, and were now hardly recognizable. The tons of twisted metal and charred rubber had been pushed aside to let other trains pass, and the line had been repaired.

Cray was wearing a gray greatcoat opened to the midriff button to allow him to ride the BMW. Under the coat was the field uniform of a Wehrmacht major. His eyes were covered with bottle-bottom goggles, and he wore a leather cap with flaps over his ears. He chewed on a raw potato. Three more potatoes were on the seat of the BMW's sidecar, as was a Schmeisser submachine gun. A pistol in a holster was on his belt, and a Wehrmacht service knife in his boot. He passed another farmhouse at the side of the road, then drove alongside another field. He twisted the throttle just to hear the satisfying rumble of the engine. He might get a motorcycle after the war. Jack Cray hadn't felt this good in months.

Geysers of dirt and stone shot up from the road, so much soil and pebbles and muddy water that the road seemed to turn on its side. The motorcycle bucked. Cray lurched forward over the handlebars, his legs suddenly in the air behind him. The BMW spun left. Then the careening front wheel caught on a stone. The sidecar rotated up and over and the cycle rolled. The gas tank smacked into Cray, launching him into a ditch at the side of the road.

The motorcycle continued a few more yards onto the field. Then its gas tank exploded in an orange plume. Bullets had passed through various parts of the BMW. The motorcycle and sidecar and Cray's new weapons burned furiously. A stick grenade detonated, casting motorcycle parts across the pasture.

Cray pushed himself to his knees in time to see the Thunderbolt bank out of the valley. The fighter skimmed the eastern hill, rising to make another run at the motorcyclist. Cray knew the plane had six .50-caliber Colt-Browning machine guns, and that in a moment they would all be aimed at him again. He could see the silhouette of the American flyer under the cockpit's glass. The pilot was probably smiling.

Cray mentally checked himself. Nothing broken. But his rib ached where he had bounced against the BMW's tank. The sound of the eighteen-cylinder Pratt & Whitney engine filled the valley. The Thunderbolt leveled off, coming at the road at a ninety-degree angle. Now sunlight glinted off the cockpit glass, hiding the American flyer, making the plane seem pilotless and even more sinister. The Allies must be running out of targets, to take after a lone cyclist with that fearsome machine, then to bother to come back to make sure the job was done.

Cray leaped from the ditch and sprinted across the road toward a barn. He could see muzzle flashes from the Thunderbolt's wings. Spouts of dirt rose from the road and rushed toward him. Cray dove behind a corner of the barn – his ribs jolting him with pain – then scrambled on his hands and knees along the side of the barn away from the road.

Behind him, the barn's corner disintegrated in a cloud of splinters as bullets poured through it. The roof sagged and creaked. The plane soared by a hundred feet above the ground, the bellow of its engine dropping to a low growl as it passed. The fighter sped away down the valley. Cray smelled its exhaust.

He lifted himself from the ground and brushed the mud and straw from his uniform. He started back the way he had come, south down the dirt road. The Thunderbolt disappeared to the west. Cray splashed along the road and in ten minutes came to the field of German casualties. The locomotive was pouring smoke into the sky. A white banner with a red cross was draped across the front of the locomotive, hung between a marker lamp and the bell, and two more red crosses covered the side of the boiler below the steam dome. The red crosses had spared the train the Thunderbolt's deadly attention.

Looking for sentries but seeing none, Cray stepped onto the muddy field and began walking among the injured German soldiers. They were scattered across the field, many lying on greatcoats and blankets. A few wore the black uniforms of tank crewmen. Most were in the Wehrmacht's grey-green. Several SS troopers wore their black. Blood was everywhere, on the uniforms, on skin, smeared across the mud. Most of the casualties wore bandages or splints or some combination of both. Cray smelled the stink of gangrene and the sourness of sulfa powder. Many of the soldiers had died here waiting for help, and were lying on the ground with their eyes and mouths open, often wearing startled expressions. Litter bearers carried the wounded toward the train. Those who could walk waited in lines near the cars.

Cray searched for fifteen minutes. He was asked no questions by the wounded or the nurses or the train crew. He had a large selection, soldier after soldier who had gone to war and had paid the price. Cray finally found what he wanted. He knelt by a dead Wehrmacht major – a fair-haired man about Cray's height – who had suffered a deep shoulder wound. The hole was packed with cotton wadding. Judging from the red ground under him, the officer had bled to death.

The American glanced up to confirm no one was watching, then pulled off the dead man's dressing. He tied the bloody rag to his neck. A medic had pinned the dead major's papers to the man's stained coat. Cray attached the documents to his own coat.

He walked slowly toward the train, stepping around groups of wounded soldiers. Some smoked, some talked in low voices with each other, but most were in too much pain to do anything but wait. Cray joined a line of walking wounded, most with blood on them in colors from bright and fresh to brown and old. The soldiers had haggard faces and thin necks. They had been hungry longer than they had been injured. The line made its way slowly toward the railcar.

When Cray reached the car's step, a medic glanced at his documents, but the man was so tired he was not seeing anything. A brigade medical officer with a white band on his right arm and a greatcoat covered in blood helped Cray aboard. He asked Cray a question, but Cray pointed to the bandage on his neck and shook his head. The medic nodded his understanding that Cray could not speak, and led him to a seat on the car.

Most other seats were filled. Soft moans came from some passengers, the blowing rasp of tortured breathing from others. After a few minutes the locomotive's whistle blew. The sound of couplings under sudden stress rolled from front to rear. The train lurched forward, leaving most of the injured to wait for yet another train.

Cray trusted his German only enough to hide it in a rough whisper. He asked the soldier next to him, who had a bandage around his head covering his eyes, '*Wo gehen wir?*'

The soldier answered, 'Berlin.'

The American nodded to himself and said just above a whisper, 'Berlin.'

NINE

Otto Dietrich slumped on the three-legged stool next to the bed. His wife's hand was in his. She lay there, her breathing shallow and occasional. Her face was rose-red and splotchy, the same rash that covered most of her body. She had moaned much of the morning, but now she was quiet, and Dietrich knew the end was near. Her lovely face was sunken and her hair was sandy gray against the pillow.

She was bone-thin, and Dietrich had been told by the doctors at the Charité that it was her time in detention and not the disease that had wasted her away. Her eyes were dark hollows. The skin of her face was so thin he could see capillaries. She had always had an inexhaustible supply of expressions, and now the stillness of her face was alien to Dietrich. She seemed a stranger.

Dietrich's physician, Kurt Scheller, had given her a few days, and he had been generous. Now her time was up. Dietrich sat in their old house, the back two rooms boarded up from a bomb blast fourteen months ago, squeezing her hand, wondering how he would continue after today. Long ago he had determined that only two things were certain in his life: the love between Maria and him, and his investigating skills. Two things he could always count on, the two constants that would get him through a hard day, a hard week. Now one of those constants was leaving him.

Christ, he loved his wife. He blinked and blinked. A photograph framed in silver was on their bedside table, and he turned to it rather than look at her. She was her old self in the photo. A flash of teeth, merrily angled eyes, mischief right there for all to see. Dietrich glanced behind him, to the dresser, to a photo of them on their wedding day, as handsome a pair as had ever been joined together at the Charlottenburg Lutheran Church. Next to the photo was his service pistol and a manila envelope containing the photograph of the escaped POW.

Feeling he was being unkind – looking at her in the old photographs rather than as she was now before him, drawn and skeletal – he turned back to the bed. Her chest rose and fell, just a suggestion of movement. He wiped a bit of spittle from the corner of her mouth, then caressed her forehead. Her fever had ended only because her body no longer had the strength to generate heat. Her eyes were closed as they had been since the Gestapo had delivered her.

The telephone rang for the tenth or eleventh time since he had brought her home from the hospital. He ignored it again.

Time and time again when he was in the Lehrterstrasse Prison, Dietrich would reconstruct their wedding day. Each time he remembered more detail, until after several months in his cell he could play it out before his closed eyes like a cinema, even though it had been twenty-five years ago. All the bouquets, the champagne, his father-in-law's lederhosen, the cream and strawberries, every faux pearl on Maria's dress. Their wedding, all the way through, over and over.

As he stared at his wife, Dietrich was about to begin again with his memory, with his arrival at the church with his brother who was best man. But Maria shuddered and gasped. Her body straightened as if pulled from both ends. She inhaled loudly and let it out, her nose flaring.

Then her head moved on the pillow and her eyes opened. She looked at her husband a few seconds, and she whispered his name, 'Otto.'

The she was still. The life went out of her, her eyes still open. He knew she was dead: he had seen enough dead people to know. But he checked the pulse in that thin arm, and there was nothing there.

Otto Dietrich stared at his wife for five more minutes, or it might have been thirty. Grief bore down on him. He held her hand, then he held his head in his hands, vaguely wondering how he would ever leave this room. Then he closed her eyes with his fingers, and bent to kiss her forehead.

He stepped across the room to the dresser. She was gone, and now if there was anything left of him, it was his ability as a policeman. He did not know if it would be enough to carry him through the days to come.

He pulled Jack Cray's photograph from the envelope, staring at it with the same intensity with which he had gazed upon his wife. He put the envelope in his pocket, then lifted his pistol. He went downstairs and out of the house to his automobile.

The train moved in fits and starts, often on hastily reconstructed tracks that sank under the train's weight. At the Plane River all the wounded soldiers disembarked to lighten the load because the bridge had been heavily damaged in a bombing raid. Soldiers limped across or were carried across on litters, and reboarded on the other side. Often only a mile would be gained in an hour, and the train was frequently shunted onto sidings for no apparent reason. Twice American dive-bombers soared low along the train, looking for evidence that the train carried anything but wounded soldiers. The locomotive was using peat for fuel, which caused sparks to gush out the stack like fireworks.

Cray's car was hot and fetid. The odors were of unwashed uniforms and old dressings. The soldiers rocked and swayed. When a Wehrmacht corporal slumped sideways and fell to the floor, he was returned to his seat even though he was dead because there was no other place for him. Medics occasionally passed through the car, but they had few supplies and so relied most often on kind words. An infantry NCO in the seat in front of Cray had suffered a head wound, and blood seeped from under the gauze pads onto the seat back. Cray surreptitiously dipped his hand into the blood and dabbed it at his neck to freshen the appearance of his dressing.

Across the aisle, a tank corporal in a black uniform wore a wrap around his right wrist where his arm newly ended, and softly dictated a letter to his seatmate, a grenadier lieutenant. The lieutenant's left pant leg had been cut off and replaced by a white wrap that was dappled with blood. The soldier behind Cray moaned softly.

Through the fogged window Cray saw a sign announcing the town of Linthe. The train passed a thicket of trees, then a station house where four armed guards patrolled the platform. Next came a water tower and an equipment shed. Then the couplings sounded and the train began to slow. Out Cray's window was another guard, this one in a coal-bucket helmet and the padded gray anorak of the Waffen-SS, and carrying a submachine gun. Then into Cray's view came four, then eight more Waffen-SS troopers, a line of them. Behind them were officers in gray greatcoats. And further back were a dozen or more members of the rural police in their brown knee boots and old-fashioned double-brimmed caps. All eyes were on the train. The Waffen-SS troopers were taking their submachine guns off their shoulders. Brakes shrieked all along the cars.

Cray quickly rose from the seat and moved to the rear of the car. The other passengers were too exhausted to glance up at him, except for a Wehrmacht captain with burn blisters across his right cheek and down his neck. He nodded at Cray, who pushed open the rear door and stepped into the coupling housing. The slatted floor shifted beneath his feet. Out the small housing window Cray saw more Waffen-SS troopers. The housing was made of ribbed canvas. The train slowed. Cray inserted his hand between the rubber flanges that connected the two cars' housings. The rubber was pliable, but only when he struggled against it. The car came to a stop. He again glanced out the window. A guard walked past the coupling, saying something to another guard who was out of Cray's sight, then the guard disappeared behind the corner of the car.

Cray knew it was a gamble. Policemen and soldiers would be watching the car doors, not the couplings, but even so, a guard might step into sight of the coupling. The guards were undoubtedly going to start a car-to-car search, and Cray had to get off the train. He squeezed an arm and shoulder through the rubber so that the flanges gripped his trunk. He struggled against the frame, and forced the ribbed canvas back like an accordion. He pushed himself further through.

Cray was extruded through the gap. With his trailing leg still squeezed between the rubber flanges, he dropped to the gravel and ties below. He frantically kicked his leg free, then crawled under the train.

He was below the coupling. Arm over arm, he moved back a few feet until he was hidden by wheels. Black boots walked on the gravel nearby. Two guards laughed at something. Cray grabbed the brake hose with one hand and the top of the iron wheel with the other, then lifted himself up to the undercarriage of the car. He inserted a foot between the hose and the bottom of the car, then an arm, and so could hang onto the undercarriage. He pulled himself up tightly against the slats.

Troopers and policemen and a German shepherd on a leash walked by, only boots and paws visible to Cray through the triangular gap between the two wheels and the car bottom. Cray heard guards walk overhead as they searched through documents and looked at faces. And he overheard guards standing along the siding talk about the American they were searching for.

Ten minutes after the train had stopped, it began again, quickly picking up speed. The last of the black boots passed from Cray's view. Then he saw tree trunks and undergrowth as the tracks took the train into a forest. The motion of the train jarred Cray again and again, the slats slapping into his arms and chest and legs, and he knew he could not hang on long. Railroad ties passed beneath him in a blur.

Sergeant Georg Keppler stepped on the starter, but the truck's battery was dead and the engine wouldn't turn over. He had been traveling south on a road paralleling the rail line. When he had stopped the truck at an intersection, it had stalled. And now it wouldn't start.

'Get out and check the generator belt,' he ordered. 'Maybe it's gone.'

Private Werner Enge opened the Krupp's door and slid off the seat to the ground. He struggled with the latch before he could push up the hood.

'Gone,' he called. 'We've been running off the battery.'

Sergeant Keppler slapped the steering wheel. 'The lieutenant is going to hang us from a power pole, Werner.' He climbed down from the truck.

The private nodded. 'I suppose he will.'

Private Werner Enge was sixteen years old. His green eyes were still lively with innocence, and his mouth seemed permanently set in a smile of wonder. His Wehrmacht uniform hung loosely on him.

'The lieutenant does not listen to excuses,' Sergeant Keppler said darkly. Keppler was a veteran of the eastern front, and wore fresh maps of scars on his legs from a Russian mortar shell that had found him in the Ukraine. Keppler had been transferred to a transport battalion while he recovered. His face was doughy, with loose jowls and a bulbous nose. He wore his field cap back on his head, showing a tossed crop of seal-brown hair. 'He might just hang us.'

Pasture too stony for crops was on both sides of the rail line. A dilapidated barn was to his left. The crossing road was muddy. Bunches of spring grass grew alongside the road. The sun was a flat gray disc seen through a cloud layer.

Keppler turned to the sound of an approaching train. 'They must be done with their search. Goddamn it, we should be back at that field by now, picking up our unit.'

Keppler and Enge had dropped off their squadron, then traveled to Linthe to look for fuel, and had been returning for their soldiers when the Krupp broke down.

'It could be worse,' Enge laughed, eager to please the sergeant. 'Our truck could have stalled right on the tracks.'

'Here they come, poor bastards.' Keppler leaned against the truck's fender. 'Blown up, shot, burned, and broken, the lot of them.'

Private Enge watched the train approach. The red cross on the boiler front rippled in the wind. Smoke from the stack blew across the field. Enge's view was along the length of the train as it came toward them. The cars rocked sideways on the unstable track. The locomotive's main rod rose and fell. A coal tender followed the locomotive. The engineer leaned out the cab window to stare at the track ahead. He lazily saluted Enge and Keppler. The locomotive was a monster of rivets and cylinders and hoses and rods and plates. It seemed to roar by them, even though it was only traveling at fifteen kilometers an hour.

Six cars passed, each with a red cross on a white banner below the windows. Keppler scanned the sky for enemy planes. He had lost two trucks to them in the past week. Whipped up by the train, wind cuffed his face.

Enge squinted at the train. Window glare hid most of the train's passengers, but Enge could see a few bandaged heads as they sped by. The last two cars were converted cattle cars used for the wounded on litters. The cars' slats had been covered with tarpaulins and the red cross. The train had no caboose. The last car rolled by.

'Let's start walking.' Sergeant Keppler pulled Enge's rifle from the Krupp's floor and passed it to him, then reached for his own Mauser.

As the last cattle car pulled away from them, a mound on the track caught Enge's eye. The train had left something behind. A lump between the two tracks. As Enge watched, the lump rose from the ties and gravel and transformed itself into a man. Someone had been run over by the train, maybe. The man rose, turning toward them.

Enge was relieved. The man couldn't be hurt too badly, even though he had a bandage at his neck. The man's Wehrmacht uniform was soiled. He was an officer, a major. Enge and Keppler hurried toward the man.

The major staggered and fell. Then as the soldiers neared him the man rose again with something in his hand.

Private Enge gasped when he saw the major's face. Enge awkwardly grabbed for his Mauser. Sergeant Keppler also brought his rifle around.

The man moved with startling speed, two steps toward them, bringing his hand around in a vicious arc. Enge saw only a crease in the day, a horizontal blemish against the background, and then heard a solid thump. Keppler collapsed to the ground, a stone the size of a fist hitting the ground next to him. The man had thrown a rock at the sergeant.

Enge's rifle strap snagged for an instant on a shoulder button. He yanked it free and brought the barrel up, wildly searching with his finger for the trigger, too late. The man in the Wehrmacht major's uniform moved so quickly he seemed to be a haze rather than a man, and he grew in front of Enge, a wall rushing at him.

The day blinked out. Nothing but blackness.

The private woke a moment later, his nose in the mud, the side of his head a mass of pain. He coughed raggedly, blowing dirt from his mouth. He pushed himself up with one hand. Sergeant Keppler was still on the ground, his forehead bleeding onto the mud. Many Sergeant Kepplers, swimming in front of Enge, whose eyes refused to focus.

'Is this all you have to eat?' the voice above him asked in German with a flat accent.

Enge rolled over, and shaded his eyes with a hand. The man was backlit by the dull sun, and his features were obscured, a dark mountain hovering over Enge. The man rustled around in Enge's pack. The private pushed himself to sitting, and carefully probed the side of his head. No blood. Not too bad, he vaguely decided. Sergeant Keppler moaned.

Enge tried to rise, but dizziness kept him on the ground. The man's hand reached under his arm to help him up. Enge shuddered and stepped back. The man's face seemed cut from wood with an ax, with cheekbones so prominent they threw shadows on his face below. His chin was angled. His blond hair was short and spiky, and his nose was blunt. He was thin, and his skin was stretched tautly across his face. His hands looked like a logger's, with thick fingers and solid knuckles.

'You're the American, the one who was at the Vassy Château.' Enge's voice wavered as if from the wind. He clasped his hands together so they wouldn't shake, but instead they trembled in unison.

'You know about me?' The American handed Enge the pack.

Private Enge's head pounded. He still had no idea how the American had blacked him out. A hit to the head, for sure, but Enge had seen nothing, just a blur. He pulled a flyer from his coat pocket. Jack Cray's face was printed on it.

Cray studied it. 'That's me, all right. Where'd you get this?'

'Everybody in my unit has one. And they are posted all over Berlin, all over Germany.'

Groaning, Sergeant Keppler rolled onto his belly.

Cray chewed on nothing, staring at the flyer. Below the photograph of his face were the words NATIONAL ALERT, and then in slightly smaller type, VASSY CHÂTEAU KILLER ESCAPES POW CAMP. And below that was a description of Jack Cray's actions at the château. On the bottom of the flyer was Cray's name, and under that SPEAKS GERMAN FLUENTLY.

Cray returned the flyer to the private. 'Let's go.' He lifted Enge's rifle.

Enge was startled. 'Go? Go where?'

'North.'

'If you wanted to go further north, why didn't you stay on the train?'

'I held on as long as I could,' Cray replied. 'Let's go.'

The private shook his head solemnly. 'I'm not going anywhere without my sergeant.' He pointed at Keppler, who was now sitting with his legs splayed out in front of him, a hand touching his head, his jaw open and his eyes closed.

'You don't have a lot to say about it,' Cray said. 'Get in your truck and let's go.'

Enge said with satisfaction, 'The truck doesn't work.'

Cray stared at Private Enge's face, an open face incapable of a lie. 'Then let's walk.'

The private shook his head. 'Not without Sergeant Keppler.'

'You read that flyer.' Cray smiled. 'You are talking to a dangerous fellow here. You should do what I say, and quickly.'

Another adamant shake of the private's head. His lip was out.

Cray shrugged. 'All right. Let's get him to his feet.'

One on each side of the sergeant, they pulled Keppler upright. He swayed, but could move his legs as Cray and Enge began walking north along the road. The sergeant's rifle was left behind. Cray carried the other Mauser in his free hand.

'That's quite a bloody wrap you have on your neck,' Enge said. 'Are you really injured?'

Cray shook his head. 'I do it for sympathy.'

After a while Sergeant Keppler shook off their help and walked unassisted. He said nothing. Red welts were forming on his forehead where the stone had hit him. Blood seeped into an eye and he wiped it away with a finger. Cray dropped a pace behind so he could watch both of them.

High in the east, a bomber formation moved south, the rumble of the Fortress engines rolling softly over the fields. The country lane paralleled the railroad tracks, and the three of them passed several farmhouses.

'Where did you get that Wehrmacht major's uniform?' Enge asked. 'Did you kill some poor guy to get it?'

'From a box in a warehouse.'

'I'll bet you killed somebody for it,' Enge insisted. 'Took it off a dead body.'

Sergeant Keppler scowled at Enge.

'I promise I didn't.' Cray moved his hand across his uniform. 'Cross my heart.'

That satisfied the private.

Keppler said his first words to the American, 'Where are you taking us?'

'As far north as I can get.'

'Why don't you kill us now and save us the walk?' Keppler asked.

Enge's eyes widened. 'You think he's going to kill us, Sergeant?'

'Christ, Enge, you read about him. That's what his country pays him to do. I'll bet he's got a knife half a meter long hidden under his coat, and he's going to stick it into us.'

Enge stared at the American. 'He's not going to do that.'

'Why would it be any different for you and me than it was for those poor bastards at the château?' the sergeant said.

'But he seems friendly and all,' Enge argued.

Cray smiled to prove it. 'Americans are friendly people.'

'Enge, you are stupid even for the Wehrmacht,' Keppler said. 'You and I are already dead. This man here just needs to decide exactly when.'

'What town is that?' Cray nodded north.

'The outskirts of Potsdam,' Enge answered. 'I can see the white steeple. I've been in that church.'

'And then what town is next?'

'Berlin is only a few kilometers beyond.' Enge paused and squinted down the road. 'Something is coming.' He pointed. 'A motorcycle and sidecar.'

The motorcycle had rounded a bend in the road. The two riders bounced high as the motorcycle found pocks in the road.

Cray reached into his boot and brought out a two-edged knife that gleamed like evil in the gray sunlight. He removed the clip from the Mauser and put it in his pocket, ejected the shell from the chamber, then handed the rifle to a startled Enge. He abruptly caught Sergeant Keppler around the neck, the knife at Keppler's throat, but the blade hidden in Cray's hand.

'Tell them I'm your major, and that I've been injured.'

He put his other arm across Private Enge's shoulders. Cray let his head slump to his chest. He pressed the blade into the skin of Keppler's neck.

'What if they don't believe me?' Keppler's voice was a frightened, ragged whisper.

'Make something up,' Cray said. 'The minute I sense they are doubting you, I'm going to cut your throat from ear to ear. So you'd better put your heart into your acting.' He dragged his left foot as if it had been injured, and sagged so that Keppler and Enge had to lean into him to support his weight. They each held one of his arms.

Keppler gasped, 'The knife, it's cutting into my skin.'

'Not yet it's not,' Cray replied under his breath as the motorcycle closed on them. 'You won't have any doubt when it does, though.'

He held the knife high on the blade, the blade and handle hidden by his hand. His left arm was around Keppler's shoulder, and his hand at his neck. Cray's head seemed to hang loosely.

The BMW and sidecar stopped in front of the three walkers. The passenger was holding a Schmeisser, its barrel pointed at the ground just in front of Cray. Both driver and passenger wore rubberized motorcycle coats and shiny metal ornaments that read FELDGENDARMERIE around their necks. They were military field policemen. The BMW's engine popped and roared.

'Get out of my way,' Keppler yelled at them. 'I've got to get to the aid station.'

A bit defensively, the sidecar passenger said, 'We've been ordered to look for the American commando. He's been – '

Keppler growled, 'I know all about him. Everyone does. Do the three of us look like an American commando? Now get out of my way or you'll be responsible for my major's death.'

'I need to see your – '

With his free hand, Keppler brought out his identification card and waved it at the policemen. 'Give me your motorcycle. We'll take the major back in the sidecar.'

The driver shook his head. 'This belongs to my unit.'

Keppler half-stepped toward the motorcycle. 'This is life or death.'

The driver shook his head. 'I hear that every day. It's all life or death.'

'I'm giving you an order,' Keppler barked. 'Get off the motorcycle. I'm commandeering it.'

'Goddamn know-it-all lifer sergeants.' The driver turned to his sidekick. 'Hang on.' The driver accelerated the engine and kicked the motorcycle into gear. The rear tire spun gravel as it passed Cray and the Germans.

The driver called over his shoulder, 'LMA Sergeant.' The abbreviation was universally understood in the German services, and was short for *Leck' mich am Arsch* – lick my ass.

The motorcycle sped away to the south. Cray brought his hand away from the sergeant's neck. The American said, 'Shakespeare it wasn't, but not bad.' He pulled the Mauser away from Enge and inserted the clip.

'You weren't really going to kill Sergeant Keppler, were you?' Enge's eyes were wide. 'With that knife of yours?'

'Nah. I was pretending.' Cray's knife had disappeared.

Keppler said, 'Enge, you are dumber than a stone.'

'I'm going on alone,' the American said. 'You two walk back in the other direction.'

'Really?' Enge blurted. 'We can go free?'

'Walk back the way you came.'

The sergeant said sourly, 'He's going to wait until we are five meters away, then shoot us with your Mauser.'

Cray spread his hands in a gesture of reasonableness. 'Would I do that?' He started north, his boots splashing puddles of rainwater. He rested the rifle on his shoulder.

Enge followed him. 'Our lieutenant is going to murder us for being absent without leave. He's a real bastard.'

'That really isn't my concern, Private.' Cray picked up his pace.

Enge matched the American step for step. 'Well, it's your fault.'

'My fault? The whole war is your fault.'

'And the SS is shooting soldiers for running away. Maybe some Blackshirts will find Sergeant Keppler and me and shoot us. You'd have that on your conscience.'

Cray sighed, something he didn't like to be heard doing. He turned to the private. 'What do you want me to do?'

Enge pulled out his flyer of the American commando. 'You can write a note to my lieutenant.'

'Write him a note?'

Enge nodded earnestly. He pulled a pencil from a front pocket and pushed it and the flyer into Cray's hand.

'Enge, you are a moron,' Sergeant Keppler called.

The private turned around to offer his back as a surface for the paper. 'Write this: "I am the American terrorist whose photo is on this poster. I kidnapped Sergeant Keppler and Private Enge so they were late to return to their duty." '

Cray transcribed the dictation. 'Anything else?'

Enge thought for a moment. 'They acted honorably and bravely, especially Private Enge.'

Cray added the sentence. 'Anything else?'

Enge pursed his lips. 'How is the lieutenant going to know it was really you who signed this?'

Cray offered, 'I'll add something about the Vassy Château that very few people know, that you couldn't know.'

'Like what?'

Cray scratched his chin. 'The third soldier I killed had a white patch over one eye. How's that?'

'Perfect.'

Cray finished the note, signed his name, then passed the flyer back to Private Enge.

Enge grinned his thanks before trotting back toward Sergeant Keppler.

'The Russians will overrun this place someday soon,' Cray called. 'Don't let them kill you, Private.'

Enge cackled victoriously as he rejoined his sergeant. 'If you couldn't kill me, neither can the Russians.'

Cray resumed his walk north. 'No, probably not.'

The weight of the message slowed her, seemed to be a yoke around her shoulders, and she had to will her legs to carry on. She could feel her heart in her chest. Katrin von Tornitz suspected she was a coward.

She had yet to decode the message, but its length terrified her. She had transcribed the dots and dashes, and toward the end of the message her hands had been shaking so badly she could hardly keep the dots from being dashes. She had come to calling the faceless sender of the messages the Hand, and the Hand was asking her to break its own rule about her making long broadcasts because the information it had wanted had then taken five minutes to send. She had signed off with her *V*s and fled the ruins of the abandoned house a kilometer from her own home, and now walked in the darkness of Berlin's Nikolassee neighborhood, carrying the radio in her suitcase.

Night covered the neighborhood. Streetlights were out, blackout curtains hid windows, and the few automobiles on the road had tape over their headlights that allowed only thin beams of light. Katrin made her way along the street, stepping over stray branches of oaks and elms that had been cut down for firewood. A slight scent of smoke hung in the air, but she could not tell if it was from her neighbors' fireplaces or from that day's bombing runs in the eastern part of the city.

When she passed the home of Gauleiter Eckardt, the smell of pastry made her slow, made her glance up the brick walkway to the door. The gauleiter had an inexhaustible supply of food because he controlled the city's warehouses. The day after Adam's arrest, Eckardt had appeared on her doorstep offering her the benefits of his pantry and the protection of his household if she would help him overcome the loss of his wife and children, who had left for the safety of Switzerland. Katrin had politely declined, but such was the power of her hunger that she always slowed as she passed the gauleiter's walkway. She would detect the scents of beef or venison, or chicken soup, which Berliners like to sip through straws, and once she had smelled a blackberry strudel, she was sure of it. She wondered if now – all these months of hunger later – she would be able to resist his offer should it come again, whether her mouth would be able to form the words to turn him down. She shook off her revolting speculation.

Thoughts of food were a familiar companion, and they calmed her. She walked steadily, the vapor of her breath trailing over her shoulders. On these cold spring nights Berlin was as silent as a country pasture. The citizens had fled or were dead or were inside their homes huddling before small fires, if they had somehow found wood. At least until the British bombers came at midnight, Berlin's residential neighborhoods sounded as the areas must have a thousand years ago, with the soft sough of wind and the occasional lupine cry of a dog. On these long walks she could will away the war.

And she could will back Adam. She was still two blocks from her home, so she still had time to recreate one of their dates. Shc smiled to herself as she picked his birthday dinner – his last birthday dinner ever – at Horcher's. They had sat near the window at the tiny restaurant at Lutherstrasse 2, and had begun the meal with sherry and caviar surrounded by shaved ice, followed by consommé Marcelle, then crabs in a dill sauce served over red rice, then venison in sour cream. Then a 1928 Lieserer Niederberg and peaches flambé, which was brought to the table by two waiters. The peaches and sugar were placed in a silver bowl and cooked over an alcohol lamp for five minutes. Then the skins were removed and the fruit cut in half and placed over shaved ice in another bowl to chill. Finally the peaches were layered on ice cream and topped with crushed nuts and apricot brandy.

Katrin ruefully wiped the corner of her mouth. She had begun to salivate like a dog. And she was painfully aware that, as she had brought back that lovely and departed day, she was focusing on the food rather than on Adam. Her home was now just half a block more along the street. It rose in front of her, a dark shadow on a black night, unleavened by a light or the hope of a warm greeting at the door. Instead of a sanctuary, her home had become a roof and a bed to her, offering no joy that was not a memory. She wondered what she would eat that night, could not think of a single item left in her pantry. Maybe there was a potato in the bin on the back porch. She would cut away the rotted black spots. She passed the laurel hedge that marked the edge of her lot.

The sound of auto tires came from behind her. Katrin looked over her shoulder. A black sedan was moving slowly, was following her, and was running without headlight slits. The cab was dark and she could not make out faces. Then she saw a circular antenna on the car's roof. This was the Opel that Colonel Becker had warned her about. The agents inside the car must have been able to fix on her broadcast, and had been following her since she left the abandoned house. A window rolled down on the car's passenger side, and a hand holding a pistol emerged.

Desperation and fear abruptly wrapped around her like a coat. She walked faster, approaching her brick walkway. She held the wireless in front of her, as if she could possibly hide it now. Anything she could do, any thoughts she might have, seemed useless and small. Then she broke into a run, slipping on the brick, but catching herself. She hurried up her walkway toward the front door, aware her attempt to escape was so hopeless it was comic.

Maybe she had known she could never accomplish what the

Hand wanted. Maybe she had known they would find her. Without Adam waiting for her in the living room with a fire roaring on the grate, it didn't seem to matter if she reached her door.

The Opel accelerated to her walkway, then slowed. Two men in dark coats leaped out before it was fully stopped. The driver stayed in the car. Katrin braved a glance at them. Both wore belted coats and both carried pistols. One yelled at her to stop.

She thought vaguely that perhaps she could make it into her house. She climbed the eight steps to the porch, passing ivy planters on both sides. The home had been in Adam's family for eighty years, but she and Adam had planned after the war on finding a house with more light and fewer rooms. The enormous black oak door had a wrought-iron grate over a center portal. She uselessly fumbled for her keys. Maybe if she could get inside, look at their wedding portrait once more.

The Gestapo agents scrambled up the front steps and onto the porch behind her. Perhaps only because it was habit, the taller agent clubbed her with the butt of his handgun. Katrin sagged against the door, then slid to the mat.

The second agent caught her suitcase as it fell. He was a plug of a man, with his weight in his chest. He slipped his pistol into his belt and opened the suitcase. The plug grinned. 'A pack radio.'

The first agent said, 'We've been looking for you a long while. You've kept a lot of us busy.' He bent to dig roughly into her pockets. He pulled out her one-time pad. 'Looks like we've found ourselves a professional.' He continued his search of her, patting her down, but found no weapons.

'They all talk down in the cellar, professional or not.' The plug laughed. 'They talk and talk and talk.'

The agents lifted Katrin by her elbows. She found she could focus her eyes. Pain from behind her ear poured down her neck and into the rest of her body. Her legs were rubbery, but the agents held her up. They carried her down the stairs and along the walkway toward the car. They chatted about something, but she could not think beyond the agony of her head. They approached the Opel, with its sweeping fenders and long hood shaped like a coffin. Darkness hid the driver.

The taller agent opened the back passenger door. Gestapo cars have the cab lights disconnected to hide comings and goings. The tall agent bent to enter the cab first.

The plug waited behind Katrin. He said tonelessly, 'You can tell us about your radio broadcasts on the way to Prinz Albrecht Strasse. It'll save us time once we get there.'

She thought she heard the tall agent cough from inside the cab.

The plug put a hand on her head and pushed her down toward the door. He shoved her onto the back seat.

Everything inside the car was entirely wrong. Instead of the tall Gestapo agent, a blond, chop-jawed man sat in the middle of the leather seat, a knife in his hand. Blood dripped from the knife onto his trousers. The body of the tall Gestapo agent was pushed against the far door, crumpled and slack, blood gushing from a wound in his throat. In the front seat, the Gestapo driver was bent over his steering wheel, his hands loose at his side. Katrin could hear blood from the driver's neck splashing onto the floor. The radio direction finder was on the seat next to the driver, its gauges glowing amber.

The blond man held a finger to his lips. He was smiling narrowly behind his hand. He wore a Wehrmacht major's uniform. For all his concern, he might have been sitting in a pew in church.

The plug had heard nothing. When he bent to enter the cab, the blond reached across Katrin, gripped the agent by a coat lapel and jerked him into the cab.

The agent did not even have time to register surprise. The blond brought the agent's head down over the knife, and the blade worked swiftly. The momentum of the plug's body carried him across Katrin. The agent shook violently and then relaxed in death, his last sound in a liquid sigh. His body came to rest on the first agent. In one smooth motion, the agents had entered one door alive and ended up against the other door dead. The agents seemed a pile of leather. Less than ten seconds had elapsed since the first agent had entered the car.

The blond man wore stubble across his chin. His face was full of harsh angles. The knife disappeared somewhere.

With a broad accent, the blond man asked, 'Do you have anything to eat?'

TEN

Katrin sat on the only piece of furniture left in her bedroom, a Gothic armchair of carved and gilded wood with velvet upholstery. The one-time pad was on one knee and her pages of dots and dashes on the other. The room was meagerly lit by an oil lamp resting on a windowsill at her shoulder. On a bitterly cold night three months ago, with no electricity and coal, Katrin had ripped apart her bed and used the frame for firewood. Then onto the fire grate went the dresser and her antique desk on which she once wrote letters to Adam, and even the chair with the scroll legs and ball feet made by the Huguenot Daniel Marot two centuries before. She had huddled near the fireplace and watched the flames blacken and eat away the old wood, so happy to be warm she hadn't given the heirloom furniture another thought.

She decoded the last line and stared at the page. The message made little sense to her, and it was not meant to. It was addressed to the Horseman. She fumbled with the sulfur match, her hands so cold she had difficulty grasping it. She scratched the match head, then put the flame to the pages she had torn off the one-time pad. After they had curled and turned dark, she blew out the flame and used the bottom of an ink bottle to crush the embers.

Katrin's head snapped up at the scent of meat. She had not had any kind of meat in six weeks, maybe longer, she could not remember. The heady smell was almost foreign to her. Tendrils of the aroma seemed to lift her from the chair and pull her from the room. She carried the message with her as she descended the stairs.

Her head throbbed with each step, and her ears were still buzzing from the Gestapo agent's blow.

The American was in the kitchen. She held out the message. 'It's for you.'

He looked up from the frying pan. He must have been more interested in the meal, because he put the message on the counter without looking at it. He salted the meat. She shuddered at the sight of the American, and found herself taking a step back. But the scent of the meat – it looked like flank steak, sizzling and browning, the juice gathering at the bottom of the pan – held her in the kitchen.

'I don't bite,' he said, shuffling the meat in the pan.

She glanced at the flyer on the counter. It had been delivered to every door in the neighborhood by a Pimpf – a member of the Jungvolk – that afternoon. This man's face was on the flyer.

'I had no idea . . .' Her voice faded.

'You had no idea the Horseman would be the man on the posters all over the city, the Vassy Château soldier?'

She shook her head.

He smiled. 'I had no idea I was the Horseman either, until a few days ago. Somebody gave me the name. I'd like that job. Sitting in a room, dreaming up code names.'

He took another pinch of salt from a bowl and sprinkled it over the pan. He concentrated on the steak and seemed to exclude all else in the room. Also on the stove were potatoes and carrots in boiling water. On the counter and table was a vast treasure of food. The kitchen seemed to be bursting with jars of jam, cheeses, potatoes, three dressed-out chickens, dozens of sausages, tins of butter, loaves of bread, and bottles of wine. And pastries. French éclairs, an apple tart, Bismarcks, and a blackberry strudel.

She moved toward the pastry. She knew she should show some restraint. Her finger dipped into the icing on an éclair. She brought it to her mouth. She tested it with her tongue, then like a child licked it off her finger. The sweetness of that small taste made her giddy, overwhelmed the pain in her head. Her finger went back for more.

'Don't spoil your dinner,' the American said lightly. His German was gnarled by an accent, but fast and understandable.

Katrin picked up a cloth bag from the counter and held it to her nose. She closed her eyes. 'Coffee. Real coffee.' She glanced at him. 'Is the gauleiter still alive?'

He looked up, wearing a startled expression, perhaps for her benefit. 'Of course he's still alive.'

'Then how did you get all this food?'

In the Opel, after the American had told her he was the Horseman, and with blood still pouring all around, he had asked where the nearest food was. In a daze, she had pointed at the gauleiter's home. He had told her to go into her house, and that he would be along in a few minutes, all the while speaking with a bank clerk's dispassion. He had returned while she was upstairs decoding the message.

The American said, 'The gauleiter was upstairs, drunkenly bawling out some beer-hall song. And a lady was up there too, giggling and singing. I went in the unlocked back door into the kitchen. They didn't hear a thing, and so much food was in his larder he won't miss the little I took. I made three trips, my arms full of food each time.'

'Where did you put the car, the car with the bodies?'

'I left it in a park a kilometer from here. From there I walked to the gauleiter's.'

She nodded at the stove. 'And the wood?'

He grinned again. 'It's coal, not wood.'

'I've been out of coal for months.'

'Do you know anything about your furnace?' he asked.

'Only that it doesn't have any coal, like I said.'

'This is a large house, and you have a huge furnace. A coal bin with a feed into the furnace usually has a few pieces of stray coal that the feed screw couldn't collect. And I found a few more chunks that had fallen into the ash bin below the furnace.'

The scent of the meat was powerful, was making her act strangely and inappropriately. She was talking with a cut-throat, a merciless killer, chatting away and making small gestures, all as an excuse to monitor the progress of the steaks in their pan.

She had heard a few things about America and Americans, mostly on the radio. They were naive and full of energy, children really. They were easily swayed and easily distracted. Churchill had duped the entire country. American women shaved their armpits and New York City lay in ruins after Luftwaffe bombings. That was all she knew about them. She had never before met one.

Now an American was making a meal in her kitchen. If Americans all looked like him, the war was certainly lost. His smile was there and gone, there and gone. A killer, yet he had a veneer of urbanity and good cheer. In fact, she thought, he looked rather German. At least, he looked like the exaggerated caricatures of German soldiers on the propaganda posters Goebbels had placed all over the country. Stout and blond and agate-eyed. Except this one looked like he'd been run over by a truck once or twice.

'Are you German?' she asked abruptly.

'I'm an American. I thought you knew that.'

'What I mean is, is your heritage German? You look German. Were your grandparents from Germany, maybe?'

He pulled at an earlobe. 'I had an uncle who was German. He came to America to work in a baby carriage factory.'

'Yes?'

Cray said, 'He was fired after two weeks.'

'Why?'

'Because every time he tried to build a baby carriage, it turned out to be a machine gun.'

It took her a moment. Then she said, 'You are a child.'

'Looks like the steaks are done.' He slid them onto two plates, then fished out the potatoes and carrots. He broke the potatoes open and spread butter on them. He tore off large chunks of bread. He buttered hers, but with his he scraped the meat pan, letting the grease soak into the bread. When Katrin pointed at the pan, he did the same with her bread, cleaning the pan with it. He handed her a plate. So much time had passed since her last full meal, she was startled with the plate's weight. He gave her a knife and fork.

She followed him into the adjacent room, where a fire was on the grate. The coal was of a poor quality, and it gave off more smoke than heat. Even so, it warmed the entire room. He had placed a bucket containing a few more pieces of coal to one side. He lifted two pillows from a sofa and tossed them in front of the fireplace. He lowered himself to the pillow, his feet out to the flames. She followed him down to a pillow.

The fire was the only light in the room, which Germans call the good room. This good room still looked as it had since the turn of the century, everything in its place in a rigid geometry. In the middle of the room was a carpet, and centered on that carpet was a table; in the middle of the table was a crocheted mat, and in the center of the mat was a flower vase. Around the table were six chairs with plaited cane seats and red plush backs. Dark curtain hung over the windows. In one corner was a wicker flower stand for a miniature rubber tree. A small portrait of the German patron saint, St Boniface, occupied one wall and a copy of Brehm's *Animal Life* was on a pedestal table under a lamp with a silk shade. Katrin could not imagine anyone ever laughing in the room. Except her and Adam. They had laughed here a lot, rolling and groping crazily in front of the fireplace on these very pillows. Then Adam had been taken away.

'Aren't you going to read the message?' she asked.

'Until I eat this steak, I don't care what's in that message.' He cut off a large portion of meat and shoved it into his mouth.

She bit into the grease-soaked bread, then said around the wad in her mouth, 'I've never tasted anything better than this.'

They ate in silence, the only sound the rush and pop of the fire. She could not take her eyes off him. He ate with a singular dedication, his hand moving mechanically between plate and mouth. She thought she was repelled by him, but no emotions and few thoughts could compete with the flavors of the meal. She ate quickly, as if the American might decide to take away her food. She had also heard they were volatile.

He cleaned his plate with the bread, and only when the last of it was gone did he go to the kitchen for the message. When he returned, he was also carrying an open bottle of wine and two glasses. He sat next to the fire and used its light to read. Then he read it again. He brought his head up slowly and stared at the Brehm print, not appearing to see it. Then he returned his gaze to the message.

He asked, 'Do you know what this asks me to do?'

She shook her head. 'It's in English. I transposed the letters without understanding it.'

The American poured wine into the glasses and passed one to her. 'What's your name?'

'Katrin von Tornitz.'

'Why was I sent here to you? Because you have the radio?'

'That's the only reason I can think of.'

'Your hand is shaking.' His mouth turned up. 'You're splashing wine out of the glass.'

She dabbed at the drops of wine on the floor. 'I'm afraid of you.'

He seemed genuinely puzzled. 'Why?'

'I just saw you kill three men with a knife. Three hard men, all of them armed.'

He grinned. 'Oh, that.'

'Then you use your same knife to cut the steaks. Then you eat a huge meal, and now you're having a glass of wine and sitting cozily in front of this fire as if nothing happened at all, your charm on display.'

He shrugged. 'I'm a soldier.'

'And you are frightening to look at.'

He scratched his nose.

'Look in a mirror someday,' she insisted. 'Your face is as tough as you are. You'd frighten any child and most adults.'

'We'll get along better if you don't try to flatter me.' He grinned again.

'And your smile won't work with me. It's a tool for you, like your knife.'

'I'm not the tough one.' He leaned back on his elbows. 'You are.'

She looked away, into the fire.

After a moment the American said, 'I need to visit the Reich Chancellery.'

She turned to the fire and brought her knees up under her chin. 'The Hand has ordered you to kill the Führer, hasn't it? That's the only reason someone like you would be sent to Berlin.'

He drank from the glass. 'Are you going to help me?'

She was silent.

He said, 'The Hand must think it will help win the war.'

Her gaze swept back to him. 'Winning the war? I'm not going to help you Americans win the war.'

'Your radio transmissions are – '

She cut him off. 'I'm going to help stop the war, not help you win the war. I would never do anything to harm Germany and my people.'

'Well . . .'

She pointed angrily at him. 'And before you tell me how good I am at rationalizations, let me tell you – '

'I wasn't – '

' – that you fat and happy Americans – up in your big comfortable bombers and . . . and strolling through your Yosemite Park – don't know anything about anything.' Again she looked away, in time to hide her tears from him. After a moment she said, 'I just want it all stopped.'

He watched her for a while. 'Is your husband dead?'

'All our husbands are dead.'

'How did it happen?'

Her voice lost its anger, but her tones were full and bitter, 'He was a German and he believed Germany should have a future. That's how it happened.'

'Was he my size?'

For a moment the American's question did not register on her. Then her head came around like a hydraulic tank turret. 'You are asking if you can have his clothes?'

'Sure.'

She stared at him, trying to dampen her anger. Then he grinned again at her. So preposterous was his request, and so preposterous was he, that she finally laughed. 'No, you can't have his clothes. You can't have anything. I don't like relentless people. That's what you are, and that's all you are. I'll be glad when you leave my house.'

'I like this wine. How about you?'

Baffled, she stared at him. Then she said emptily, 'Utterly relentless. No wonder the Hand is using you.'

The fire filled the room with beautiful heat. She was warm all the way through, not just on one side, not just a part of her. She watched the fire. The amber and red and gold colors, flickering across the furniture and walls, almost made this room bearable, and almost brought Adam back. Her husband was almost sitting here with her, instead of this American stranger.

'I've lost my loved one, too,' he said, his voice just above a whisper.

'Please don't share anything with me,' she said. 'I already have enough of whatever you are going to tell me.'

He might not have heard her. 'Wenatchee is a little town in the state of Washington in the United States. And although I've not been to all the small towns in America, Wenatchee is probably the loveliest, right there on the Columbia River. We grow apples there, and in May the valley is covered with apple blossoms. I was raised there, and so was my wife. My memory doesn't run back to a time when I didn't know her.'

She didn't want to know any of this, but the American was now staring into the fire and speaking in a low voice, and she found she could not stop him. She took a sip of wine. She thought it safe to look at him. The wine, even these few swallows, had begun to play with her mind. The American seemed softer, his eyebrows less prominent, his mouth not so wintry, and his eyes less cruel.

'My wife – her name was Merri Ann – once told me that she knew from first grade that we would be married someday. I suppose I knew it, too.'

Even his German was getting better, she thought. And he seemed forgetful of himself.

'I've heard old people say that they wish they had known how happy they were when they were younger, because they would have made a point of enjoying it more.' He chuckled, a hollow sound. 'Well, I knew how happy I was.'

'What happened to your wife?'

'Apple cider is made from apples, and you can get as drunk from apple cider as from anything.' His mouth silently worked a moment. Finally he said, 'Merri Ann was killed by a drunk driver.' He might have been talking to the fire. 'So I know something of what you are going through. Some mornings I wake up and wonder whether it's worth getting out of bed.'

'What happened to the drunk?' Katrin asked.

'I don't know.' His face re-formed into hardness. 'Not yet I don't.'

After a moment, she asked, 'Do you know why the Hand has chosen you?'

'The Vassy Château and a few other reasons, I imagine. And that I speak German.'

'More than that.'

He finally looked away from the fire and at her.

'The Hand knows about your wife,' she explained. 'It knows of your sorrow. You don't have much to live for, or so the Hand believes. And so you will go places and do things that a person who wants to survive will not.'

He shrugged.

'The Hand is sending you on a suicide mission,' she insisted.

'I don't go through a door unless I know I can get back out.' The American lifted the message and reread it.

Katrin thought he was deliberately making light of the message. She said quietly, 'And I'm telling you, you are being sent to your death.'

A dead dog in a wheelbarrow was Cray's ruse, and it was working. Stooped and limping, he walked southwest from the park and onto Hermann Goering Strasse. The Reich Chancellery garages and guard quarters were on his left. SS guards stood at the doors to the barracks. Others manned machine guns behind sandbags. Rolls of razor wire had been spread along the curb to keep passersby from nearing the barracks. Two antiaircraft guns – Flakvierling 38s with quadruple barrels – were at the corners of the barracks. Their regular-army crews stayed near their weapons, away from the SS guards.

Cray walked among a slow stream of refugees, pushing his wheelbarrow. They were a sullen, dispirited lot, shuffling ahead, slowed by despair and grief and hunger. Many glanced covetously at the dead dog, knowing its owner would eat well that night. One man wore rags wrapped around his legs like puttees. A woman with an empty sleeve pinned to her coat led a ten-year-old girl with a bandage over her eyes. Some refugees wore pieces of cast-off uniforms, some little more than rags, more than likely picked off bodies, including a Soviet flyer's thigh-length fur-lined boots and a Danish army officer's black greatcoat. Many carried their possessions in blankets over their shoulders, some wore rucksacks, and others carried dilapidated suitcases. Two dead chickens hung from a pole over one man's shoulders, and another used a birch switch to herd a goat. Crutches and canes were common on this street. Cray's was not the only wheelbarrow. Others pulled small hay carts loaded with possessions, and one family nudged along a railroad porter's cart.

Walking among the refugees, but with brisk steps in an effort to appear to be on business, were many servicemen in Wehrmacht gray and Luftwaffe blue and even a few Kriegsmarine sailors in navy-blue pea jackets. Were any of the soldiers or sailors to mill about, they would be pounced upon by roving SS squads demanding identification and orders. Cray guessed that many of these servicemen were from destroyed units and were seeking – with various degrees of diligence – to hook up with new companies.

Berliners had become expert at judging shell trajectory from the sound, and when a Red Army shell sailed overhead, sounding like a dog's growl, few looked up. They knew the shell was destined elsewhere, and an instant later it detonated three blocks away, a muffled and dull sound indicating it had found rubble rather than a standing structure.

Up ahead, a horn bleated, and the refugees were shunted toward the curb as six Wehrmacht Phänomen and Auto-Union trucks carrying troops rolled down the street, the last one pulling a fifteen-centimeter infantry-support gun. They were followed by three enormous Famo half-tracks whose steel treads ground stray bricks and plaster to powder. When the convoy had passed, the refugees refilled the street.

Cray was wearing two wool jackets, one over the other, a grease-stained felt hat, and pants so short they showed his ankles. His eyebrows and hair were blackened with fireplace soot, and a bandage was over his left cheek and ear. He shuffled along, bent and slow, indistinguishable from hundreds of others on the street.

He turned his wrist to look at his watch. Only he among the crowd knew that an American air strike was due in twelve minutes.

The dead dog stared up at the American with unseeing eyes. Its back was bent unnaturally, probably the result of falling bomb debris. Cray pushed the wheelbarrow nearer a row of five-story apartment buildings, once the elegant homes of Reich officials, now vacant, many with façades pushed in, others sagging out onto the street. Rubble rose in front of the ruined buildings like foothills. Pipes and support posts jutted uselessly into the sky. Mounds of rubble seemed like rolling fields. A toilet hung in the air on a pipe, the new Berlin weathervane.

American and English bombers had not settled for changing Berlin's landscape. They had also changed the language. Berliners now called a sunny day a bombers' day. A cloudless night was now known as a smoking night because of the smokescreens from oil-burning canisters placed all over the city. The Elbe River was now Bombers' Alley because the Allies flew along the river toward the city.

Air-raid sirens began their plaintive wail. The sirens were on posts and atop buildings, and the sound eerily came from all directions. Cray was nearing Potsdamer Platz, still within sight of the Chancellery, now behind him. The sirens usually gave Berliners ten minutes. Many refugees looked around wildly, searching for bomb shelters. Cray pushed the wheelbarrow to the curb, passing a poster on a telephone pole that read OUR WALLS MAY BREAK, BUT NEVER OUR HEARTS, then climbed the steps of an abandoned building. The door frame was empty, the door sucked off the building by a bomb sometime before.

Cray walked into the apartment, toward the stairs to the cellar. Perhaps because he had abruptly begun walking like he might know where he was going, Cray was followed by a dozen refugees and a serviceman looking for shelter from the coming attack. He led them down the stairs, ducking under a wall that had collapsed over the steps. He pushed away dangling boards.

The floor had collapsed into the back of the basement. Cray passed a boiler, empty crates, and an overturned cement washtub. Light leaked into the cellar from fractures above. A woman behind him held an infant in her arms, and she followed Cray as if she knew him. The baby sucked on a checkered rag that looked as if it had been torn from a shirt. Cray found the civilians looking at him. He sat on the floor against the concrete wall, and the woman with the baby followed him, and then the others also lowered themselves to the floor. A Wehrmacht private sat at the other end of the room. He had a nose with a knot in it, and eyebrows and hair the color of straw. He tore a piece of paper from a notebook, chewed it for a moment, then stuck wads of the damp paper into his ears. He was missing his cap and was not carrying a weapon.

A low sound came from the north, a persistent and growing rumble. Dust fell from the ceiling. The baby grinned at Cray.

The American rose to his feet and crossed the floor to the washbasin. He tried to drag it across the floor, but it slid only a few inches. The Wehrmacht private obligingly rose to help Cray. They pushed the sink to the wall, then rolled it over and leaned it against the wall, forming a solid shelter. The bombers grew closer, and antiaircraft guns began their stuttering clap. Cray motioned to the woman, and she smiled hesitatingly at him, then scooted under the upside-down basin, her baby waving his rag at Cray. The soldier returned to his corner.

Cray couldn't see the sky, but he knew what it contained. It would be laden with bombers, perfect formations. Smaller planes – American fighter escorts and spotter planes – flitted about, daring the Luftwaffe to send planes skyward. The bombers had taken off from England, but the fighters had joined the formation from captured German airfields, and unlike earlier in the war, fighters could now escort the bombers during their entire mission. The sound of the massed planes seemed to be pressing the basement dwellers into the ground.

High above, the planes' bellies opened. Sticks of explosives fell away from the B-17s, so high the bombs would seem tiny and insignificant to anyone watching from the ground. At first they fell horizontally, resembling ladder rungs. Then the bombs squared away to their purpose and dropped nose down.

Cray could hear the woman's teeth grind together. She shivered, waiting for her country's due from the sky. Cray reached under the basin for her hand. She gripped his hand fiercely.

Another civilian scrambled down the stairs, tripping over a crate as he stared up at the sky, as if he could see through the tumbledown building. Then an SS officer followed him down the stairs. The collar tabs on his gray-green greatcoat collar identified him as an SS-Standartenführer, the equivalent of a colonel. The SS version of the national emblem was on the coat's upper left arm, and a silver cord adorned each shoulder. Under the coat were a brown shirt and a black tie. A silver death's head was on the gray peaked cap. He carried a briefcase. His mouth was a stiff, pedagogic line. He had spent the war indoors, and his face was as white as a skull. The man was an SS bureaucrat, an author of orders and a keeper of files and an attendant at meetings. He glanced at the Wehrmacht private, who ducked his head. Then the colonel sat next to Cray.

The first bombs tore into the neighborhoods. Debris flew skyward and had started its descent before the sounds reached Cray. And it was less a noise than a pulse. Then fireballs rose, mushrooms of bubbling flame, out of sight of the troglodytes in the cellar. The basement's walls trembled, then bucked. Cray's ears popped with the sudden changes in air pressure. The sound was as if thunderclaps were going off between his eyes. A shroud of dust drifted down from the flooring planks. The bombs roared, one indistinguishable from another. The room shimmied. The baby wailed. A bicycle that had been leaning against a wall fell over. Empty canning jars fell from a shelf and shattered on the floor. The SS officer coughed, then brought a handkerchief to his mouth. Added to the bombs' deep retorts were the eerie sibilance of fire-driven wind and the shriek and moan of structures giving way.

Cray's thoughts – those that could form between the pounding of the explosives – settled on Katrin, and their conversation last night. She had thought his comments about Merri Ann to be manipulative, offered to show that Cray and Katrin were kin in suffering, offered to open her up and get her to help. But Cray's memory of his wife, and of her death, had come forth unbidden, as it did every hour of every day, and would until he left this earth, he grimly supposed. This time, though, someone other than a combat-hardened Ranger had been near him when a wave of sorrow washed over him, and Katrin's grief had caused his own to escape his mouth before he could control it.

Only part of it had escaped him, a fragment of the story. He was surprised by his unexpected moment of confiding in Katrin, but he had reined himself in and had not told her all of it. The horror of that day, and of the subsequent weeks and months when Cray had almost left this life, had remained locked within him, available only to torment him and to push him. Katrin had been right. The Hand knew of his wife's death, and of Cray's wild grief and guilt, and was using it. The Hand knew that Jack Cray gave most of his energy to accomplishing his assignments, and little to getting back to safety. Cray would seldom be diverted from his goals by the frivolous complications of escape plans. He had lied to Katrin when he said he didn't go through a door unless he knew he could get back out. If he got out, fine. If not, well, he deserved to find the door closed.

He had never allowed this knowledge of himself to fully form. It had been partly hidden by his vast pool of self-loathing. But Katrin had put it bluntly, had thrown it up in front of him. Cray sat in the trembling cellar, realizing fully for the first time – just as the Hand had perhaps long known – that Cray didn't care if he returned from his missions. If Cray didn't have the courage to resolve his overwhelming guilt, perhaps the Germans would do it for him. And the dreadful days would end, and the long, long nights. Despairing and angry, Cray squeezed the bridge of his nose, his mouth pulled back in a snarl. Jesus, if he could just have that night back. Just that one night. The woman under the basin yelped, and Cray lessened his grip on her hand.

Time in the cellar had an odd elasticity. With the crushing noise and the heated rushes of air and the basement's jarring, Cray could not determine whether the raid – and his dreadful memories – lasted five minutes or half an hour, but finally the last bomb detonated, and the weight of the sound was lifted from the cellar's occupants.

Cray kept his hat between him and the SS officer, and rose to push aside the concrete basin. The baby had cried himself to sleep. His mother squeezed Cray's arm in thanks. Others opened their mouths to crack their jaws, trying to clear their ears. They dusted their shoulders.

'You.' The SS officer stabbed his hand toward the Wehrmacht private. 'Your ID and orders, quickly.'

The private, no more than seventeen years old, whitened and stammered, and it was instantly apparent he was a deserter. The civilians in the cellar hurried up the stairs, anxious to get away from the SS colonel and his young prey. Except Cray.

The colonel reached inside his greatcoat for his service pistol. The young soldier backed into the wall, his hands out. His mouth formed a word, an entreaty, but no sound came. A civilian looked back, hesitated, but hurried toward the stairs.

'You are a deserter,' the colonel exclaimed, leveling his Walther on the soldier. The war had put him behind a desk, and perhaps he saw this as his moment of glory, a chance to use the weapon he had carried on his hip for a decade. 'A disgrace to the Fatherland and the Führer.' The colonel held the pistol at full arm's length, and hesitated, maybe wondering whether to arrest the young soldier or to shoot him straightaway.

Cray saved him the trouble of making the decision. He quickly stepped to the colonel, and put his arm around the man's waist. The colonel stiffened.

Cray said, 'Let's give the lad a break. What do you say?'

The SS officer's mouth moved silently. His head turned to Cray, but still he said nothing. His white face turned ashen, and his knees wavered. Cray held him tight, a friendly embrace, except for the knife deep inside the colonel's chest cavity. Blood bubbled at the SS officer's lips. The pistol lowered, then dropped to the floor. Cray held the colonel up, the blade hooked in his ribs. The officer's head nodded forward. Blood seeped from under his coat and down his leg.

'Beat it, Private,' Cray ordered.

The soldier rushed away, stumbling over paint cans and chicken wire that littered the basement floor.

Cray yelled after him, 'And find a helmet and a rifle, for God's sake. You look like just what you are.'

The private hesitated, nodded at Cray, then climbed the stairs two at a time. Cray could hear the soldier's footfalls on the planking above his head. The American let the SS officer sink to the floor. The greatcoat wicked up blood.

Cray searched for the man's identification and found it in the inside breast pocket of his service tunic. He studied the gray linen card for a moment. The documents identified the colonel as Kurt Schwenninger, an SS liaison officer to the Chancellery.

Jack Cray understood the benefit a commando operation might glean from confusion. Shake things up, see what happens, move when others are frozen, exploit any weaknesses. Bedlam cracked open barriers. It waylaid the best-planned defenses. It threw up targets that had been well concealed. And, as here, it presented tools for the commando's trade. Even if his mission were a feint – as Cray increasingly suspected – undertaken to consume German manpower and *matériel*, he still needed the tools.

Cray had called in the bombing run so that he might study the government quarter, so that he might see the fire and rescue services in action, learn the guards' emergency routines, and observe evacuation plans, searching for a flaw in the Chancellery's defenses. But when the SS colonel found himself too far from a bomb shelter and had to seek refuge in the cellar of a ruined building, Cray had been offered more than an opportunity to study.

He emerged from the cellar ten minutes later wearing the

colonel's uniform, with its black belt and shoulder strap. A rose of blood was around a gash in the greatcoat. The American still wore the bandage on his face. Cray stepped with purpose into the daylight, no longer shuffling like a refugee. He carried the colonel's briefcase.

Potsdamer Platz was obscured by smoke and dust, so thick that a fierce fire across the plaza could be seen only as a golden glow. The all clear mixed with the thin wail of fire-truck sirens. Cray walked along Hermann Goering Strasse, stepping over newly fallen telephone poles. Water flowed from a broken main. A bomb had landed among four Mercedes limousines, and their wreckage was thrown about, a headlight here and a fender there. Other automobiles were on fire, sending black smoke into the sky. Bricks blown out of buildings covered the street. The neighborhood had been bombed so many times that most of this day's explosives had merely churned rubble. Berliners crawled from their basements and bomb shelters.

A truck had been overturned by a bomb blast. Citizens surrounded it and climbed into its cargo bay, frantically grabbing cases of tinned plums and peaches. In the gutter were two bodies, naked, their clothes blown off them. A grocery store had been hit, and a stream of fluids – honey, condensed milk, and marmalade – oozed out the front door. Berliners rushed into the store to plunder it. A horse pulling a newspaper vendor's cart had been killed by flying debris. It had not fallen over, but had sunk to its haunches. Three women with carving knives whittled at the horse's shanks. More starving Berliners hurried to join them.

Cray quickly approached the city-block-long Reich Chancellery. Not until he was within fifty yards of the smoke-hidden structure could he see that it had been hit. The westernmost end of the building was a tangle of masonry and wood and tiles. Smoke drifted from the wreckage, but fire trucks were already parked near the building, and hoses were pouring water into the debris. That end of the building was being used as a hospital, and when Wehrmacht ambulances arrived on Vosstrasse in front of the Chancellery, their crews rushed toward the building carrying litters to bring out the patients. Cray walked closer.

Guards at the Chancellery door nearest the ruined part of the building were diligently checking the rescue crew's identification papers. Ninety percent of the structure still stood, and Chancellery personnel – senior service and Party officers, secretaries and cooks – who had been out of the building at the start of the raid now returned, holding their hands over their faces against the dust.

As Cray approached the door, he saw that despite the smoke and sirens and firemen and confusion, the SS guards were closely examining the faces and identification cards of those who entered the building.

Cray turned away from the guards, brought his knife up to his forehead, and slashed the skin above his eyebrows, left to right, leaving a trench, dragging the blade against bone. Blood instantly poured down his face. He pulled the bandage off his cheek, pretended to dab at the cascade of blood. The shirt collars and tie were quickly soaked. The knife disappeared, and he turned back to the Chancellery.

He waited behind a Wehrmacht general, and pulled out the colonel's identification card. Pulling his mouth back in pain, he held up the card and stepped forward when the general was allowed into the building.

The guard looked at the blood covering the American's face, then asked, 'A splinter?'

Cray nodded, wincing, fingers to his face as if to stem the blood, but which only smeared it. Blood dripped down his hand to his sleeve. More blood dripped from his eyelashes, and ran down on both sides of his nose. It collected around his mouth and streamed down his chin.

The guard looked at the identification card. A second guard patted Cray down, keeping his fingers away from the blood. He opened the briefcase and flipped through the documents. He snapped the case shut.

The first guard then said, 'Dr Niedhardt is inside, Colonel. He'll fix you up.'

Cray nodded and stepped through the door into the Reich

Chancellery. He entered a hallway with a green marble floor, then turned left, in the direction of the new ruin. Smoke filled the room.

A woman stepped out of the haze, stared with wide eyes at Cray, then took him gently by the elbow. She said, 'The doctors are this way, Colonel.'

Cray let himself be led into a conference room with a thirty-foot-high marble ceiling. The room was dominated by a table around which were two dozen Empire chairs. The seat back of each chair was decorated with an eagle and a swastika. A green cloth covered the table, with gold tassels hanging at the ends of the cloth. In front of each chair was a blue leather folder and a writing pad with a minister's name embossed in gold. Landscapes in gilded frames were on the walls, and a red and blue Kermanshah carpet covered the floor. This was the Chancellery's cabinet room. Hitler had never convened a meeting here. Cray's blood dripped onto the carpet.

The woman led him into an anteroom, where a surgery had been set up to treat Chancellery personnel. An examining table, three beds, a medicine cabinet, and an X-ray machine filled the room. Two of the beds were occupied by guards who had remained at their stations during the raid rather than seek shelter. One moaned and turned his head back and forth. A physician tended to a third guard, probing a wound on his arm.

The woman lowered Cray into a chair by a window and patted him on the arm. 'He'll be with you as soon as he can.' She continued to stand near him, waiting to catch the doctor's eye.

Prompted by the sudden good fortune of an SS uniform and documents allowing him entry into the Chancellery, Cray's makeshift plan had been to see as much of the building as he could, open a few doors and walk into a few rooms, and if he found the target, take advantage of the opportunity. At the very least, he would discover the layout of the seat of German government. At best, he would accomplish his mission.

The American wiped blood from his eyes, wondering when this good-hearted woman would leave him so he could continue his reconnaissance. He turned in his seat to peer out the window.

Behind the Chancellery was a garden. The smoke was lifting,

and Cray saw that it must have been an elegant park at one time, with pergolas and fountains and symmetrical planters and walkways. But the fountains were dry, and air-raid ditches had been dug in irregular patterns. A tower was occupied by an SS guard.

Cray again brushed blood from his eyes. At the west end of the garden was a massive concrete block with a steel door in it. The block stood by itself, not connected to the Old or New Chancelleries, and its door surely led belowground to a bunker. Two SS guards stood at the door. And to one side of the block General Keitel and General Jodl were bent in conversation, smoking cigarettes.

Cray recognized both generals from photographs. Wilhelm Keitel was known as Lakaitel (*lakai* means 'lackey') and carried out Hitler's orders without question. Alfried Jodl attended Hitler's twice-daily strategy sessions and turned the Führer's strategy into tactical operations. Cray knew that neither Keitel nor Jodl ever allowed himself to be far from Hitler. And when Keitel and Jodl threw aside their cigarette butts and reentered the blockhouse, Cray knew that Hitler was no longer ruling the Reich from the Chancellery, but instead was in a fortified bunker below the Chancellery's garden.

When the helpful woman walked to the physician to alert him that a badly wounded SS colonel needed his attention, Cray rose quickly and left the room, then crossed the conference room, still carrying the briefcase. The Chancellery was filling quickly as personnel returned from bomb shelters. Many stared at the mask of blood on Cray's face, but the wounded were as common as stray bricks in Berlin, and no one paused to ask after him. Cray walked out the same door by which he had entered the Chancellery.

He walked toward Hermann Goering Strasse, and grinned to himself, the drying blood around his mouth cracking. He had located the Führer. In a bunker below the Chancellery garden. Adolf Hitler had gone to ground.

ELEVEN

Otto Dietrich walked through a canyon of flesh. Corpses were on both sides of him, stacked like firewood as high as his head, presenting walls of white feet bottoms, bodies filling every space except the narrow walkway to the examining room. The path zigzagged left and right because some corpses were longer than others. In one corner were piles of severed arms and legs, and in another corner were heads, resembling a stack of cannon shot.

Some of the bodies were clothed, others had had their garments blown off, others burned off. Most in the room had died during bombing raids. Many injuries were visible, but other people seemed alive, lying there, eyes open, not a wound anywhere. Bomb blasts near them had created instant vacuums in their body organs, hemorrhaging brains and spinal cords, and they had collapsed, dead before they were prone, their insides turned to mush.

Dietrich had spent a career examining bodies, but he locked his gaze straight ahead as he made his way to the wide door, wide enough for a gurney. The stench of decay seemed to have removed useful oxygen in the room, and Dietrich panted as he walked. Behind him two workers brought in another corpse, and searched for a spot in the crowded room they might be able to wedge it in. The detective's shoes crackled through dried blood.

As he passed through the door, the scent shifted from rot to formaldehyde. A stainless-steel examining table filled most of the room, white and green institutional tile under it. The table was ringed by a blood gutter, and three buckets of fluid were at one end.

Bone cutters, scissors, hemostats, scalpels, forceps, and an oscillating bone saw were arrayed on an implement tray.

A naked corpse lay on the table. Dietrich was embarrassed for it. Blue-white flesh in folds, mouth hanging open, filmy eyes staring dumbly at the ceiling, stripped of its humanness. The only color to the dead man was at his throat, which was open ear to ear, a gaping black and red maw of a wound, with sinews hanging about.

'I knew you couldn't keep away, Otto.' Emil Wenck smiled at the detective. Wenck was Berlin's chief medical examiner. He wore rubber gloves and a dappled apron. The doctor's eyes were kindly and bagged, and a horseshoe of white hair was around a bald head. The base of his nose was almost as wide as his mouth. His forehead was half the length of his face. His ears stood out at right angles.

'You could have been a baby doctor, and you chose this instead,' Dietrich said. 'Shows what you know.'

Inspector Dietrich had worked with Wenck for years. In addition to being the city's chief coroner, Wenck held a chair in anatomy at the University of Berlin. He raised one finger to his chest and moved his eyes in an exaggerated way toward the rear door. A warning.

Dietrich dipped his chin. 'The bodies have piled up, Emil. You are behind in your work.'

'The morgue is full. The cemeteries are full. So when Berliners find a body – and there are many to be found – they often bring it here, thinking the coroner must know what to do with corpses.'

'And what do you do with them?'

'Usually they are brought in one door and taken out another, a parade of the dead. These bodies are being taken to a new open-pit grave at a farm near Zehlendorf, not too far from here. But our truck has run out of fuel, and there's none to be had, so the cadavers are backing up, just like the plumbing.'

Dietrich heard voices from the doorway behind Wenck. Because paper would quickly become bloodied, a chalkboard was against a wall for the physician to mark down observations. A reflector light hung over the table, and another was on a stand at one end, adjustable by two universal joints. On a wall to Wenck's right were three enlarged photographs of bodies, showing the portion of each body from the breastbone to the nose. The bodies looked remarkably similar. Each wore a Wehrmacht tunic, and each neck was creased with a wide and ghastly wound, and each set of eyes was open and staring, giving each corpse an appearance of modest surprise. Blood was pooled under each dead soldier, obscuring what might have been a Persian rug below the bodies.

Gestapo Müller entered the examining room from the rear door, followed by General Eberhardt. Müller's mouth was pressed into a thin line, and his lip curled contemptuously when he saw Otto Dietrich. Apparently having lost an argument, Eberhardt was flushed from neck to hairline, and his jaw was set at a mulish angle.

Müller's raincoat was buttoned to his throat. His eyes shone with anger. He chopped his head at Wenck and demanded, 'Tell him what you just told us.'

The coroner pursed his mouth a moment before he began, Dietrich guessed to annoy the Gestapo chief, who seemed to quiver with impatience, rocking on his heels and clenching and releasing his fists, his gaze cutting between the body on the table and the three photographs on the wall.

Wenck stepped toward the wall. 'These are photographs of three of the soldiers killed at the Vassy Château. You can see that all have severe wounds to their throats, which caused their deaths. These photographs were taken by a military police lieutenant right after the deaths, and are of an inferior quality to photographs I would normally insist upon from my investigators.'

'Can we cut this short,' Müller said. It was not a question.

Wenck said, 'Skin on the neck is in a state of tension because of elastic fibers that align on a particular axis – '

'Shorter,' Mueller ordered.

Wenck inhaled sharply. 'I have examined all three – '

'This is one of my agents lying here.' Müller stabbed the table with a finger. 'He and two others were knifed last night in the Nikolassee district.'

Doctor Wenck said, 'There is a certain artistry to the wound that killed this man and the other two last night.'

'An artistry?' Dietrich repeated.

'An economy is perhaps a better word.' Wenck bent over the table to lift a flap of the corpse's skin, exposing the neck wound. 'This sharp force wound was a straight penetration. The assailant used a knife approximately twenty centimeters long. And although it is difficult to tell if the knife had one or two edges, I believe the one used here was a double-edged blade.'

'A commando knife,' Müller added.

Dietrich stepped closer to the table. The dead man was washed white by the lamp. A small cloth was over his groin. The harsh light seemed to be making him less significant, nothing but a specimen.

Wenck continued, 'By economy I mean that the wound was inflicted by someone who knew how to do it. This injury displays no evidence that the knife's action had twisting or rocking components, which are common in knife wounds. And the blade penetrated the neck here.' The coroner pointed at one end of the wound. 'And it moved across the neck, only once, and not any further than was needed to accomplish the assailant's task.'

'Which was to kill him,' Müller said.

'Which was to cut both carotid arteries in the neck and the internal jugular vein.' Wenck moved his finger into the wound. 'This controlled cut resulted in almost instant death.'

'The same clean, quick knife work killed those three soldiers on the wall,' General Eberhardt said.

'Photographs, even good ones, are not a substitute for an examination,' Wenck said. 'But as far as I can tell, all the wounds – on the château soldiers and on the three agents – are virtually identical. So it is possible, perhaps probable, that the same person wielded the knife.'

General Eberhardt said darkly, 'The American is now in Berlin.'

Müller flipped a thumb toward Eberhardt. 'The general's so-called impenetrable wall around the city to keep this Jack Cray out was full of holes. The general has failed.'

Eberhardt straightened his backbone. 'While the Führer is alive, I have not failed.'

'And so far, Detective,' Müller glared, 'you have failed, too.'

'Jack Cray is in Berlin.' Otto Dietrich said the words slowly, tasting them. Then he asked, 'Is there anything more you can tell me, Doctor?'

'The assailant is right-handed,' Wenck answered.

'Why is that important to me?'

The coroner replied, 'Stay away from his right hand.'

Dietrich smiled. He nodded his thanks and turned to go.

'Dietrich,' Müller called after him. 'You have underestimated . . .'

Dietrich passed through the aisle of bodies, walked through an anteroom, then out onto Huzel Street. Peter Hilfinger and the car were waiting for him.

Dietrich opened the rear door and said, 'Peter, at the intersection, turn right, then go back to the station. I'll meet you there.'

The detective bent low, slammed the door shut, then in a crouch stepped back into the coroner's office. Hilfinger drove the car away. Decades of police work had taught Dietrich to trust his hunches. He stood inside the door, waiting.

Not long. A black Volkswagen sedan sped by his door, two men in the front seat, the passenger talking into a microphone, trailing Dietrich's car.

Dietrich walked onto the sidewalk, his gaze following the Volkswagen as it turned right and disappeared behind a rubble mound. The Gestapo was following Dietrich. Undoubtedly on Heinrich Müller's orders. Dietrich turned into the wind and began walking toward the station.

Katrin spun around, the rubble mounds a blur as she turned. She was lost, once again. She went up on her toes to try to look over a stack of concrete blocks, salvaged from a destroyed structure, but not yet carted away by salvagers. The pile was too high to peer over. She was less than three blocks from the Tiergarten's bird sanctuary, she was sure. Yet she did not know where the park was, did not know which direction was north.

Like most Berliners, she frequently became lost, sometimes only blocks from home, rubble piles obscuring the horizon, landmarks torn down, the location of the sun obscured by smoke and ash. She could not get her bearings. And because many buildings were crazily canted, the perpendicular was distorted, and Katrin found herself swaying in sympathy with the wounded structures. The war had taken away many things, none more surprising than the ability to tell which direction was straight up.

She tried to push her hands into her coat pockets, but they were stuffed with cheese and bread rolls. She had been without adequate food so long that she had been unable to leave her home without filling her pockets. The American had laughed at her, not in an unkindly way. But she needed to be near food, even if she had to wear it, and its weight in her coat was comforting. At the very least, she knew where her next meal was coming from. From her pockets.

She passed an elm tree lying on the street, its roots exposed, torn from the ground by a bomb blast. Two oxen pulling a Schutheiss Brewery dray crossed the intersection ahead of her. Perhaps she was near the brewery. Down the block a dozen French workers used block and tackle to pull reusable floor joists from a ruined building. Several loudly sang Maurice Chevalier's 'I'm a Lover of Paris,' probably to irk their two guards, who tried to ignore them by talking earnestly with each other. Painted on a nearby wall in a shaky scribble was, ENJOY THE WAR. THE PEACE WILL BE TERRIBLE.

From around a pile of fractured telephone poles came a stream of refugees, carrying knapsacks and cloth bags, silently tramping along, twenty or so of them, and every one looking beaten-down. Refugees always marched west – seemed to instinctively know the way – so Katrin took her bearings from them and started north toward the Tiergarten.

After another block she again felt her bearings slipping away, so she climbed onto a pile of fractured masonry, careful to keep her skirt tucked around her legs, and climbed unsteadily up the rubble mountain for a view from the top.

The war had turned Berlin inside out. Bits and pieces of lives that should have been concealed and comfortable behind walls and doors were rudely exposed to the gazes of passersby. Katrin stepped over a leather photograph album, open to the sky, its photos of marriages and christenings scattered about. Lodged between blue and black clinker bricks were a pair of men's long underwear, the legs missing from a blast. Also on the rubble pile were the upper half of a ceramic beer mug with a hinged pewter top, a pair of yellowed dentures, the head of a girl's china doll, a stack of letters held together by yarn, a brass weight and chain from a pendulum clock, a rouge brush, a shattered photograph frame, an empty bottle of India ink, a box of Christmas-tree ornaments, the blue glass balls fractured to the size of snowflakes and scattered across the debris, dully reflecting the day's gray light. Small tokens from broken lives. Berlin was awash in these mementos and trifles, abandoned and ignored in a city without roofs. She climbed over them without a glance.

At the top of the pile she could see over a neighboring row of rubble, just enough to find the flak tower near the bird sanctuary. She had her directions again. She carefully descended the wreckage, her shoes slipping on the damp bricks and concrete pieces. A swallow flitted by once, then again, perhaps looking for a recognizable place to land. A piece of torn camouflage netting caught her ankle, and she stumbled just as she reached the sidewalk. She caught herself on a telephone pole and started north.

She passed heap after heap of debris and one gutted building after another. She could ignore only so much. Her city – the destination of youthful dreams, the sacred place of her marriage to Adam – lay about her, trampled and burned, no more resembling a city than a rock quarry. The symphony of the city had been stilled. With a finger she dabbed at the corner of her eye, but there was no tear. She pressed the corner of her eye. Still no tear. She had shed the last of them, she supposed. And she was not alone. Berlin was beyond tears. Now only fear remained. Fear of Bolshevik soldiers, so close their campfires reddened the eastern clouds at night. Fear of the American and British bombers, which returned with numbing punctuality. Days and nights of fear.

Berliners wore their fear like a uniform. As she walked toward the park, passing many pedestrians doing their anxious errands in the predictable pause between bombing runs, Katrin realized that Berliners had grown to look alike. Drawn, bony, wan faces. Stricken expressions. Bent, furtive walk, like mice scurrying from one safe spot to the next. And as if by agreement, Berliners had surrendered their right to color. They wore gray or black, the clothes of mourning.

Ahead on the street were three wooden barricades. An errant bomb from the run on the Alkett tank plant in Ruhleben had blasted a hole in the street precisely the street's width. People waited in line to cross unsteady planks that had been rigged along the edge of the crater, which was filled with murky water from a burst main. Katrin stepped behind a Red Cross colonel in black boots, a slate-gray greatcoat, and a peaked hat. Even the Red Cross looked like the Wehrmacht. She waited her turn to use the planks. Buildings near the crater had been raked back by the blast. A dead horse was bobbing in the crater. A man in a chef's hat was in the water, pushing the horse carcass to the crater's edge, where a cart waited. A restaurant would be serving it by nightfall.

Katrin held her hands out like a wire walker as she negotiated the plank. The Red Cross colonel turned to offer his hand, and she used him for support the last few steps. She nodded her thanks, then waded through a knot of refugees waiting to use the plank, heading in the other direction. She glanced at her watch. She had twenty-five minutes.

A child's cry brought her up, a piercing wail. Huddled near an overturned Auto-Union truck was a boy, maybe four years old, wearing three gunnysacks for a shirt and a pair of rolled-up man's pants held around his waist by a rope. His face was screwed up with the realization that he was lost, that his parents had moved on without him. In his hand was a crudely carved toy truck. Porous shoes had allowed water to wick up his pants almost to his knees. Dirt or ashes smudged his face. The boy dragged an arm across his eyes, streaking the dirt.

What was one more lost child? One more orphan? Berlin was full of lost children. They go somewhere, eventually, she figured, though she didn't know where. Wars had their price, and children paid their full measure.

Katrin took three more steps before, with a huge sigh at her weakness, she turned back toward the boy. He stepped back at her approach, covering his eyes with his hands to make her disappear.

She towered over him. 'Where are your parents?' A little too gruff. Lord, she didn't want this little boy's problems.

He peeked up at her through his fingers, but said nothing.

'Are you German? Can you understand me?'

Tears had reached his chin. He nodded.

'Is your *Muti* alive? Your father?'

'*Muti*. But she's not here.' The boy's words ended in a thin wail.

A siren sounded from the next block, the mechanical wail weaving in and around the boy's cry. Kartrin no longer even turned her head toward sirens. She asked, 'How long have you been lost?'

His chin trembled. 'Ten hundred hours and minutes.' He tentatively moved toward her, two half-steps, and with that little movement, gave himself over to the kind lady who had asked after his mother. He was now hers.

Katrin understood this rule of engagement. She rubbed her hand alongside an eye, trying to think. Then it came to her. She looked at her watch. Twenty minutes. She had to hurry. 'What's your name?'

'Artur.'

She reached for his hand and gently patted it. 'Come with me, Artur.'

She led him through the street, past a restaurant where a sign in the window announced it was Eintopftag, One-dish Day, when it was required to serve only a tasteless stew. On the walk in front of the restaurant was a bundle of the *Völkischer Beobachter*, the Party's official newspaper, now down to one-page editions, and largely ignored except to kindle fires.

Another stray bomb had fallen that morning further down the block, felling two buildings, setting them on fire, and blowing much of their contents out onto the street. Katrin and the boy picked their way along, stepping around a blackened trumpet, half an accordion, dozens of loose ivory piano keys, and a French horn twisted even more than French horns are in their original state. The bomb had hit a musical instrument shop. The boy paused to put several piano keys in his pocket. The fire had been extinguished, and a crew was rolling up hoses. The street was slick with water.

A TeNo squad worked hurriedly in the rubble. TeNo was short for Technische Nothilfe, the Technical Emergency Corps, also called the Rescue Squad. Cable from an electric winch on a Phänomen truck's front bumper was pulling aside a beam. One rescuer moved his finger in a circle, and the winchman engaged the drum. The cable became taut, and the beam groaned as it was dragged from the ruin. A scream came from the rubble. The winchman threw the winch's clutch. With pry bars and axes, the Rescue Squad dug into the timbers. Artur tugged Katrin's hand to slow her so he could watch. The squad yelled encouragement to the trapped individual below. Two workers heaved on a wrecking bar, and two more reached deep into the wreckage. After a moment they gently pulled out the victim, who smiled weakly despite the blood on a leg. A gray-haired man in a tie. Perhaps from the music shop. A litter was passed into the rubble.

The boy said, 'That's blood.'

'Yes.'

'I seen it before.'

She pulled him along, around a piano leg, then over a saxophone that had been pressed as flat as a coin, the mother-of-pearl keys sprinkled about. Artur stopped for some of these, too.

Katrin again brought up her wristwatch. 'No wonder you lost your mother, Artur. You stop to pick up everything.'

A few moments later they were on the Kurfürstendamm near the blackened skeleton of the Kaiser Wilhelm Church. The zoo flak tower – the dark, indestructible obelisk that Allied fighters pock-marked daily – loomed just to the north. At this intersection were public notice boards, dozens of them, installed for government announcements – Jack Cray's face stared out from each panel – but lately plastered with private messages. A few boards displayed items for trade, but most were papered with layer upon layer of missing-person messages, hastily handwritten judging from the scrawls, often on crumpled scraps, most from refugees fleeing west, telling of a time and place to meet, hoping to hook up with the missing.

This was the place in Berlin where the lost might be found. A hundred or more people clutched their coats, went up onto their toes, and called out, hoping against hope that the war would for once relent and allow their loved ones to appear at this spot. Occasionally a crushing embrace was seen, but most often people drifted away, one after another, hoarse and heartbroken.

Even Berliners who had misplaced one another while shopping knew to meet at these notice boards. And Artur's mother had figured out that her son might end up here. She leaped from the crowd and grabbed her son, her face broadly creased by a smile. Artur whooped and clung to his mother's neck, the piano keys and saxophone buttons rattling in his pockets, his wood truck in one hand. She scolded him softy, but he laughed. Artur's two brothers – perhaps seven and nine years old – waited nearby. The woman was dressed in a filthy Wehrmacht coat that hung to her ankles. Her hair was matted, and a deep cut on her chin did not seem to be healing. But she hugged and hugged her boy. Katrin looked at her watch. She still had ten minutes.

Finally, Artur freed himself to point over his shoulder at Katrin. Artur's mother smiled tentatively. Artur wiggled out of her arms to join his brothers. His mother's mouth moved, trying to find the right words. Then she stepped to Katrin and gripped both of her hands in hers and whispered a thank you.

Katrin pulled two cheese rolls out of her pocket, and passed them to the woman, who may not have seen that much food in weeks. She grabbed them, then remembered to smile another thanks. Katrin dug further, and pulled out three Kaiser rolls. The woman also took these, and turned to join her sons. She herded them away. West, of course. An instant later they had disappeared in the crowd.

Katrin fairly ran past the ruined church toward Budapester Strasse. She reined herself in. To run in Berlin was to invite being stopped by the Gestapo. Wilhelm Becker had told her weeks ago that he was punctual. That in an emergency she could always find him walking along the park side of Tiergartenstrasse at four in the afternoon. He had given her precise instructions how to meet him, but only in a dire predicament. She hurried along the Landwehr Canal, then crossed a bridge to approach army headquarters.

And it was here she spotted Colonel Becker, emerging from the OKW building's double doors. But instead of turning north toward the park, for the stroll he promised he took every afternoon at four, he turned south, toward her. The distance between them closed rapidly. Other army officers moved in and out of the building.

She was startled by Becker's appearance. His shoulders were hunched protectively. His eyes were shadowed and remote, and, it seemed to Katrin, fearful, darting left and right. She had met him at several army social gatherings before Adam had been arrested, and the colonel had been animated, with an inexhaustible supply of expressions and gestures. But now his face was clouded, and his mouth was pulled back anxiously. Becker had the look of one expecting a blow.

Katrin stepped up to him. 'Colonel Becker?'

He started, his head snapping back. And he gasped, more a hiss, when he recognized her. 'What are you doing here?'

'I need to talk to you.'

He shook his head so violently he dislodged his peaked hat, and it rested on one ear. 'That's impossible. You've . . . you've put me in grave danger approaching me. I can't possibly – '

She fiercely gripped his elbow and turned him around. 'Walk with me to the park.'

When he balked, she pulled him along like she had done with Artur. The colonel ducked his head to hide his face under the cap's brim.

She said, 'You didn't respond to my message.'

His arm trembled under the pressure of her hand. He seemed so afraid he could not control his legs, and she guided him north, toward the Tiergarten. Fear was making him breathe like a runner.

'What has happened to you?' she demanded.

Becker coughed weakly, an excuse to hide his face behind his hand as a group of Wehrmacht officers passed. Two Mercedes limousines were at the curb in front of the headquarters buildings, and Becker tilted his cap to further hide himself. When he walked by the headquarters' doors, he quickened his pace, suddenly pulling Katrin along. Strung from telephone poles, overhead camouflage netting threw crosshatch patterns of shadows on the sidewalk.

He was silent, glancing over his shoulder every few steps. He licked his lips. Again he ducked his head as army officers passed. Katrin led him across Tiergartenstrasse and into the park. They walked toward the East-West Axis. The park resembled the dreadful, grainy newsreels she had seen of the Great War's trench lands; craters, uprooted trees, stones strewn about, lawns hidden under debris, nothing untouched by high explosives.

She conducted him toward a bench that had been blown backward. He stood mutely while she righted it, then swept dampness from the seat with her hand before sitting down. After a moment Becker joined her on the bench.

'You ignored the message I left in the milk box,' she said. 'You recruited me, and now you've cut me off?'

'You have no idea what has been happening.' Becker refused to look at her, staring at a bank of lilac bushes. Like a tortoise, he kept his head tucked back in his collar. He nervously dabbed at nothing at the corner of his mouth. 'My superior, General Etzdorf, has been arrested, and so have two others in my office. And many others in my branch. A purge. The general and I – '

'He is a member of your group?'

'There is no group,' he snapped. 'The general and I have . . . have worked together on certain matters. He was arrested, and he may soon implicate me. He is in a cell somewhere, and I know they'll come for me if he starts to talk, and . . .'

Fear had loosened Becker's tongue. His words gushed forth like water from a broken pipe. Katrin sympathized with him. She knew fear. All Berliners did. She patted his arm, just as she'd patted Artur's.

The gesture stopped Becker mid-sentence. He inhaled hugely. He turned on the bench and finally looked at her. 'Why have you come to me?'

'I need your help.'

He shook his head sorrowfully. 'That is impossible, Mrs von

Tornitz. I am no doubt under suspicion. Perhaps we are being watched right now, as we sit here.'

They were partly hidden by azaleas and lilacs, and could see only glimpses of trucks passing on Tiergartenstrasse.

He went on, 'I have ceased all activity in this regard. I no longer . . . no longer have the courage or strength to do . . . those things.'

Katrin removed a handkerchief from a pocket and passed it under her nose. She had had a cold for months. 'Colonel, I'm in over my head.'

'Aren't we all?'

'I need your help.'

'No longer,' he said quietly, averting his eyes. 'I can't. I simply can't.'

'You work in the office of army administration. You can easily get what I want.'

He shook his head.

'I need the roster for the soldiers and SS troopers assigned to the Chancellery.'

Judging from his reaction, she might as well have tried to set him on fire. Becker's eyes widened, his breath rattled in his throat, and he chopped the air with his hand, as if swatting away the absurd notion. Then he tried to rise, but she dug her fingernails into his arm and pulled him back down.

'You can get the Chancellery roster, can't you?'

'Impossible. I'm already a suspect.'

'You don't know that for sure.'

'They will break General Etzdorf and then they'll come for me, and then . . .' His tone carried an undignified pleading, and he clamped shut his jaw.

Her voice was a study in reason. 'Colonel Becker, you don't understand how important this is.'

He rapidly shook his head. 'It doesn't matter. I'm through with all that.'

With histrionic embellishment, Katrin reached to scratch the top of her head. So apparent was this a signal that Becker leaped from the bench and started toward the street.

He made only three steps. As if by sleight of hand, Jack Cray appeared in front of Becker, perhaps from the lilacs, and gently pushed him back to the bench.

The colonel's face blanched. Cray was wearing a Wehrmacht captain's uniform taken from Katrin's closet. A bandage hid one of his cheeks. The cap's bill was almost on his nose, hiding his eyes. Under the bill was a row of stitches covering the new gash on his forehead.

He sat on the other side of Becker. The colonel's gaze pivoted back and forth between Cray and Katrin.

She said, 'Colonel, I don't have time to fool with you. You are going to obtain the Chancellery roster and bring it to me.'

His breath was in his throat. He moved his head slightly, a negative.

'Take that bandage off,' she ordered Cray.

The American pulled off the wrap, wincing as the adhesive tugged at his skin.

'Colonel, look at this man,' she said.

Becker turned again to Cray.

She said, 'This is the man on the posters all over the city. This is the Vassy Château killer.'

Becker's face whitened even more. His mouth pulled back in a grimace of fear.

Katrin's voice was iron. 'He is going to slit your throat right now, right on this bench, if you don't agree to bring me that roster.'

Becker lost control of himself, leaning slightly toward Katrin.

Cray's face opened in astonishment. He blurted, 'No, I'm not.'

She persisted. 'Colonel, this American is a ruthless killer. His knife is in his sleeve, the same one he used at the château. And he is going to do what he does best, on you, right now, unless you agree.'

'No, I'm not.' Cray held up his palms toward her. 'I never said that.'

Katrin ignored him. 'Make your decision, Colonel.'

Becker stared at Jack Cray, weighing the American's face, with its stony angles and pugilist's nose and draftee's haircut.

Cray tried a smile. 'She's just teasing.'

'Colonel, are you going to do what I say,' she asked, 'or are you living your last seconds?'

Becker closed his eyes in surrender. His voice could just be heard above the rush of the wind. 'I might be able to get a copy of the roster.'

Katrin stood. 'Place it in the drop by tomorrow evening.' She stared at him levelly. 'If it is not there, I will anonymously telephone the Gestapo about your activities against the state. Then they will come for you, irrespective of what General Etzdorf tells them.' She started back toward the street, making her way around mud-filled craters.

Cray shook his head and said to Becker, 'She's been through a lot.'

'You are planning to suborn someone on the Chancellery roster, hoping to get into the Führer's headquarters?'

Cray said nothing.

'You are too late,' Becker said with some satisfaction. 'The Führer is leaving Berlin tonight.'

The American demanded, 'How do you know that?'

'When the leader leaves the city, hundreds of orders are issued to accommodate the move. One of them is that the Chancellery guard is drastically reduced. It happens every time, a pattern. I know it because orders regarding the Chancellery contingent are distributed through my office.'

'How will he leave Berlin?'

'Train or plane. Most rail bridges have been knocked out, so probably by plane.'

'Tempelhof isn't operating, is it? The runways have been dug up by bombers.'

'The Führer never leaves from Tempelhof. He uses an airstrip in the Tiergarten.'

'And you know this because you see the guard detachment rosters?'

Becker nodded. He glanced tensely at Cray's hands.

'Well, nuts.' The American pulled at his chin. 'Nothing's ever easy, is it?'

'Pardon?'

Cray smiled at Becker. 'Don't forget the roster. Put it in the drop.' He left the bench and ran after Katrin. At her elbow he asked, 'Will you kindly not do that again?'

'What?' she asked, all innocence.

'Use my face to frighten someone.'

As she neared the street, her shoes sinking in the mud, she turned to him. 'Don't you do whatever works? Isn't that what you commandos are trained to do?'

'Well . . .'

'That's just what I did.' She turned west, walking briskly along the sidewalk.

A convoy of Wehrmacht trucks passed, three of them still painted in the light swirling colors of desert camouflage, oddly cheery in drab Berlin.

He followed her. 'Well, you could hurt my feelings, doing that.'

She stopped cold. 'I cannot possibly have heard you correctly.'

Cray lifted his shoulders. 'I thought we were just going to talk to the colonel, not scare him to death. Just see what he could do for us. That's why we were meeting him in the Tiergarten.'

'Hurt your feelings?' She laughed brightly, so foreign and forgotten a sound that it startled her.

He smiled engagingly.

She walked on. 'It scares me, but with you here Germany may win this war yet.'

Cray kept pace with her. 'I didn't tell you all of it last night.'

'All of what?'

'About my wife, and what happened.'

'Maybe because I didn't want to hear it.' She picked up her pace. 'Maybe if I walk faster.'

'I've never told anybody else about it.'

His voice was suddenly devoid of his American boldness, and there was a touch of pleading to it. She slowed.

Cray said softly, 'I was the drunk.'

She stopped. 'What?'

'It was a one-car accident.' Cray forced his gaze up from the sidewalk. He looked into her eyes. 'I was driving.'

'You were the drunk?'

Only by force of will could Cray keep his eyes on Katrin. His voice was broken. 'We'd been at a restaurant, celebrating our second wedding anniversary. This was in the summer of 1941, almost four years ago. We held hands all night, even while we ate. I don't think my gaze left her once during the entire dinner. Our marriage was so . . .'

He stopped and turned away, toward a bank of ruined apartment buildings across the street. Her hand came up, hesitated, then touched his arm.

His voice was rough. 'I loved my wife.'

'I know.'

'That night, I never laughed so hard or talked so much. I'd never been funnier or more romantic. I had already swept Merri Ann off her feet, she liked to say, but I was trying to do it all over again. We were celebrating the good fortune of loving each other. And I never drank so much in my life. Christ, I drank too much.'

'What happened?'

'I drove us toward home, still laughing, her sitting so close to me in the car that I could hardly shift the gears. I was going too fast, not paying enough attention. I missed a turn on the country road above the Columbia River. Our car skidded off the road, then rolled down a ravine. It turned over and over.' Black grief was written on Cray's face. 'I was pinned behind the steering wheel, both my legs broken. Our car wasn't found for eighteen hours. I stared at my dead wife for those eighteen hours.'

'Were you prosecuted?'

Cray shook his head. 'The sheriff had been a friend of my father's. He didn't inquire into it.'

'So you ran away into the army?'

'After my legs healed.'

'And you've been angry at yourself ever since.'

'It has worked away at me ever since. Not an hour, not a goddamn minute of any day . . .' Cray's mournful voice trailed off.

'And so you've taken it out on my countrymen.'

'Something like that.'

'Your plan is to have a German soldier end it for you, rather than do it yourself.'

Cray said noncommitally, 'I don't know if I had thought it through that far.' He ran a hand along his temple. 'But I sure didn't expect to last this long in the war.' He tried a laugh, but it was feeble.

Katrin took him by the arm and continued walking. 'Well, why don't you wait until you get back to Wenatchee to kill yourself. So I won't have to think about it.'

He grinned crookedly. 'You can be quite a comfort, Katrin.'

She leaned into him as they walked. 'Don't make me think about you, alive or dead. All right? Is that too much to ask?'

'I don't know. You might end up thinking about me a lot. When I put my mind to it, I'm quite likeable.'

'No, you aren't.' But she squeezed his arm, and they made their way toward the Zoo Station. 'Not in the least.'

TWELVE

Heinz Burmaster tramped along, close on the heels of the Home Guardsman in front of him. Burmaster's antitank weapon, a Panzerfaust, bounced on his shoulder with each step. He had found a woman's scarf – hand-knitted blue wool with a cross-eyed gray cat in the center – and had placed it on his shoulder as a pad, and now at least the Panzerfaust's metal stock was not banging against his collarbone. Burmaster wore an old Italian army overcoat, stripped of insignia, and the white Volkssturm armband. His long face was covered with gray stubble. He still had that winter's cold, and with every few steps he wiped his nose with his sleeve.

Burmaster turned his head left. 'Getting older with each passing day is the natural order of the universe, wouldn't you say, Rolf?'

Rolf Quast walked beside Burmaster. He had become accustomed to Burmaster's jovial prattle, and only occasionally encouraged him with a grunt, which Quast did just then.

'Well, then, I have reversed the natural order, because I appear to be getting younger with each day.' Burmaster held up a hand to prevent Quast from interrupting, as if there were a chance of that. 'You ask, "How can that be, Heinz? Such cannot be the case, Heinz," you protest.'

Quast also wore a four days' growth of beard. His eyes were heavily bagged, and his earlobes had sunk with age and the wattles under his chin swung with each step. Quast and Burmaster were bringing up the rear of a double-file column of Home Guards, a hundred reserve soldiers walking at a desultory pace, their captain in front, bent over a city map, trying to study it while walking along, the map tilted toward the orange light from a burning building they were passing. Red Army shells fluttered overhead, sounding like tearing cloth. The moon appeared briefly, but then high clouds and low smoke obscured it once more.

The handle of Burmaster's entrenching tool was knocking his knee, so he yanked it along the belt where it hung next to his bread bag, which contained a fist-sized chunk of black bread. Before each time Burmaster bit into the bread, he tapped it against the side of his boot so the beetles would crawl out. Most of the bugs anyway, he hoped. Burmaster was usually too hungry to be particular about a few bread bugs. In the rucksack on his back was a blanket and a Bible and nothing more. The Panzerfaust was his only weapon.

He said, 'I was too old for the Great War, Rolf. I tried to enlist but the army wouldn't take me. Nor the navy. I lied about my age, but the recruiting sergeants saw the wrinkles around my eyes and laughed me away. And this was thirty years ago.'

Rolf Quast cleared his throat, which Burmaster took as an invitation to continue. 'But, as you can plainly see, I am not too old for this war. Hence, I must be getting younger.'

Quast harrumphed pleasantly.

Burmaster added, 'I don't doubt that Germany shall see yet another war in my lifetime, but by then I will be an infant, and too young to fight.'

Quast asked, 'How old are you, Heinz?'

'Sixty-six.'

'Two years older than me. We are both too old to be lugging antitank rockets around the city, I'd say. You ever fired one before?'

Burmaster followed the column to one side of the street to avoid a crater. 'We didn't have enough of them to waste them on training. So our instructor made us point them at a wood mock-up of a British Matilda, and pretend to pull the trigger, and yell out "Shoosh" to imitate the sound of the launch. Then the instructor would call out "Boom" to show I'd hit the tank. I'm a good shot, apparently.' He tapped the Panzerfaust affectionately.

The column of old men wound its way along Pleger Street, dodging some mounds of rubble, having to climb over others. British bombers had dropped fire canisters on the neighborhood, and they had landed haphazardly, igniting dozens of buildings along the street, sparing others. This was not the first time Pleger Street had been hit, and so some of the fires had to content themselves with devouring buildings that had already been tossed by high explosives while other fires worked away on apartments that had been inhabited until the air-raid sirens of two hours ago.

The fires marked the Home Guard column's way, each blaze casting brilliant, dancing light out over the rubble and ruin, which then threw black shadows further on. The guardsmen marched from light to dark to light again. They lingered when they passed through each pool of warmth, and the column stretched and compressed, stretched and compressed, like a worm. And it had been doing so for ten nights, a crisscrossing of Berlin that to Burmaster and Quast and the others seemed chaotic, but was in response to the Berlin commandant's best estimate as to where the city's defenses needed shoring up, an estimate that changed with each new bombing run and each new report of enemy troop movement. Burmaster had blisters on his feet, water on his knees, and so many aches that even his hair hurt.

He stepped over a bedspring and then pieces of a vase. The Panzerfaust was getting heavier with each step, as it did each night, and was biting into his shoulder, and when the sergeant blew the whistle to fall out for a break, Burmaster slid the damn thing off his shoulder and lay it against the trunk of a tree that had been blown out of the earth by a bomb, and whose roots now grasped at the air like gnarled hands. Quast placed his Panzerfaust next to Burmaster's, and then levered himself down to the cobblestones and leaned back against the tree, sighing heavily.

A few moments passed before Burmaster said, in a low voice, 'I'm never going to fire that thing. My Panzerfaust.'

'What do you mean?'

'I have lived too long to be blasted apart by a tank, which will surely happen should I engage in any impudent folly with the Panzerfaust. I'll miss my target, and the angry tank crew will turn its full attention on me.'

'So what are you going to do?' Quast rubbed his calves.

'I'm going to wait for the first chance I get, then throw up my arms in surrender, and pray our captain doesn't shoot me, and pray the Russians don't shoot me. And I may survive this war yet.'

'Maybe the Americans and Canadians and British will get to Berlin first,' Quast said. 'I've heard the Anglos are nice people, once they calm down some.'

'That's the first line of my evening prayer every night. Please, God, I pray, don't let that bastard George Patton's tanks run out of fuel.'

The whistle blew, and the guardsmen struggled to their feet, groans and curses rolling up and down the line. Heinz Burmaster grimaced as he placed his weight once again on his farm of blisters.

He turned for his Panzerfaust.

It was gone.

And so was Quast's. Nothing there, against the tree trunk.

'Rolf?' Burmaster asked. He didn't need to say anything more because both guardsmen saw the problem at once: no Panzerfausts where two Panzerfausts should have been, right up against the fallen tree where the guardsmen had left them.

Burmaster circled the tree. Nothing but shards of glass and fractured brick and bronze coffin handles. No Panzerfausts, and that was for sure. He looked over his shoulder at the dark ruins of a funeral home.

Quast drew air through his teeth. 'You don't have to worry about the Russians now, because the captain is going to shoot you and me, if he sees us without our weapons.'

Burmaster picked up a board from the curb. It might have once been part of a coffin. He placed it over his shoulder as if it were his Panzerfaust, then he stepped into line, Quast at his elbow. They began again their endless march, following the troops in front of them.

Burmaster said, 'The captain has other things to worry about, like figuring out where we all are. He's never even going to notice that our weapons are missing.'

Quast picked up a board, shouldered it, and walked beside him. He asked nervously, 'You think so, Heinz?'

Burmaster half-closed his eyes, then intoned in a low voice and in cadence with his steps: 'Please, God, don't let that bastard George Patton's tanks run out of fuel. Please, God, don't let that bastard George Patton's tanks run out of fuel. Please, God . . .'

Only for brief seconds when the moon shed itself of clouds could Cray see the entire length of the landing strip. At the west end, hidden under camouflage nets and tree branches, were a bulldozer and a grader, used to repair bomb damage. Cray could not locate a hangar, and he supposed that were such a structure to appear in the middle of the Tiergarten it would be bombed almost instantly. And he could not see a plane, not yet anyway. But there was no doubt this was the emergency landing strip Colonel Becker had spoken of. Fifteen hundred yards long, a hundred across. No trees, no debris. Cray shifted his weight against the crater bank. Mud at the bottom of the pit covered his boots. He lay on his belly on the sloping crater bank, the two Panzerfausts next to him. He had gathered broken branches to place over himself, and he would have been invisible to anyone standing twenty feet away, even had it not been a black night. His forehead felt like it had a row of upholsterer's tacks in it.

Cray studied one of the Panzerfausts. It was a simple weapon, with a steel launching tube containing a propellant charge. At the business end of the tube was a bulbous three-pound bomb that had spring-loaded folding stabilizer fins that would release as the grenade left the tube. On the tube was ACHTUNG FEUERSTRAHL (BEWARE FLAME JET) to remind the operator of the backblast. He had never before fired one, but it looked easy enough. Point and shoot, and stay away from the back end of it.

He was facing north, midway along the airstrip. An airplane taking off would have to pass within forty yards of Cray's position. The neighborhood to the north, across the Spree, had been hit by bombers that day and was still burning, a mile-long bank of fire that churned with liquid peaks and valleys. The inferno backlit the park, and black and broken trees stuck out from the ground at all angles. Refugee campfires dotted the Tiergarten, and low shapes huddled around meager flames. Other refugees moved between the blasted trees looking for shelter, blankets over their shoulders, a few pushing wheelbarrows, some leading children. Ash fell steadily, and Cray let it land on him, appreciating another layer of camouflage. Wind drew smoke from the fire and layered it over the park. Clouds of ash were kicked up by the wind, and drifts of it were growing against the bulldozer and grader and tree stumps.

A gray movement caught Cray's attention, something at the edge of the smoke, at the eastern end of the airstrip. A spark, then an orange flare, an intense point of light that instantly lit a soldier wearing a coal-scuttle helmet and a rifle over his shoulder who had a flare in his hand. The soldier walked several paces to the corner of the airstrip, placed the flare on the ground, then retreated out of the cone of orange light and was swiftly hidden by smoke and night.

A second flare came to life, carried by another soldier, again off to Cray's right. The flare was planted into the turned ground, and the soldier stepped away. Quickly two more flares were lit and set on the ground, these to Cray's left, at the west corners of the airstrip. The soldiers slipped out of Cray's sight. Flares now framed the landing field.

Cray looked at his wristwatch. Midnight. The low drone of an airplane could be heard above the fire's distant seething. The sound of an engine grew louder, and was soon a hollow pounding. Cray looked skyward, but saw only black haze and a weak moon. Then the plane slid out of the night at the west end of the airstrip and was almost on the ground before it formed out of the smoke. It passed Cray as it slowed.

It was a Fieseler Storch, a wing-over, single-engine plane with a fixed undercarriage. The model had proved itself scouting for Rommel in Africa. This plane had been reserved for the Führer. The engine gained power to turn the plane around, and then it taxied west along the airstrip, passing Cray again, its propeller blowing up dust and ash. A black national cross was on its fuselage and another under its wing. It bounced over stones as it made its way along. Cray could not make out the pilot.

The sound of other engines came from the southwest, from behind Cray and off to his left. The strident howling of motorcycles. Their headlights had been taped over to allow only slits of light to escape. Cray could see nothing but narrow beams that drifted across the park. Behind them was an automobile, it too sending forth only restricted shafts of light. This was a touring car, a Grosser Mercedes, with windows thirty millimeters thick and with seat backs and doors reinforced with eight millimeters of steel plate. The tires had extremely low air pressure so that vibration would not upset Hitler's sensitive stomach.

Earlier in his reign, the Führer had used an open car so that he could stand to appear before crowds lining the roadways, but Heydrich's assassination in Prague in May 1942 had convinced him that an armored roof might be useful, and this Grosser Mercedes was enclosed. Many of the automobile's parts – those not essential to the armor – were made of aluminum to reduce weight. Still, the heavy car seemed to plow like a ship across the soft ground, its tires sinking.

Two other automobiles followed the Mercedes, both black Horches. When the Führer's limousine stopped near the airplane, bodyguards emerged from both trailing cars to surround the Mercedes. They huddled around the car, forming a human shield. Cray could see only dimly. The guards were a smudge against the trees at the end of the airstrip. Some of them might have been wearing uniforms – straps across their chests and helmets – but Cray could not be sure.

The knot of bodyguards began moving at a slow pace toward the plane. They cleared the automobile. An interior roof light was now on in the Mercedes, and allowed Cray to see that the rear passenger door was open, and that the back seat was empty. When the guards reached the Fieseler Storch, one of them gripped the wing strut and stepped onto the landing gear. He opened the plane's passenger door. He, too, was forming a shield.

A man rose from the group of guards, many hands assisting him.

Cray could make out nothing but a suggestion of movement. Partly hidden by the guard on the strut, the man climbed into the plane.

Cray was acutely aware of the risks here in the Tiergarten. He was acting hastily on information from Colonel Becker that could not be confirmed. But if Becker's news was accurate, Cray's target was fleeing Berlin, and in a few minutes Cray would have failed entirely.

He had done what he could in the past two hours, walking around and through the Tiergarten, dressed like one of the thousands of refugees camped there, trying to spot something amiss, but had detected nothing. Still, coming to the Tiergarten on such sparse intelligence was a gamble. Cray had weighed the risk against the chance of success and had decided to act. The Panzerfaust's backblast would pinpoint Cray for the guards, but he also accepted that risk.

The Storch's engine began winding up as soon as the guard on the strut jumped down. Propeller wash whipped his coat. He and the others quickly retreated to their cars, holding onto their hats, their pants blown tightly against their legs. The small plane lurched forward, then gained speed, bouncing on the rough runway.

Jack Cray rose from his position, brought up a Panzerfaust, and placed it over his shoulder. The sight was a crude stick just behind the projectile. His hand found the trigger, and he centered the approaching plane above the aiming stick. The plane gained speed on the rutted runway. Cray's trigger finger came back.

Then the Storch's engine failed. At least, so it seemed to Cray, with the motor dying so suddenly. The plane slowed, tossing and swaying, and finally stopped, still a hundred yards short of Cray's position. For a brief moment Cray expected the doors to be thrown open, the pilot calling out his trouble to some mechanic, maybe back at the automobiles.

And then Cray knew his gamble was lost, that he had been set up. The Fieseler Storch – or, more accurately, the information that the German leader was leaving Berlin in a plane from this emergency landing strip – was the bait, and Cray had gone for it.

Cray slipped down into the crater, putting the Panzerfaust aside. He peered over the rim. The backlit refugees – black against the wall of fire to the north – had a new presence. New figures, also dark against the fire. The figures were forming up, solidifying out of the trees and refugees. A picket fence of men, surely soldiers, walked slowly in Cray's direction, still five hundred yards away, but closing.

He looked west toward the cars. The bodyguards had taken up positions at the end of the airstrip. He still could not see them clearly, but several appeared now to be carrying weapons, either rifles or submachine guns. Cray glanced over his shoulder. He couldn't make out anything of the night and smoke, but he had no doubt another phalanx of soldiers was closing in on him from the south. He was boxed in.

Next came the most fearful sound on a battlefield, the low rasp of armor, from Cray's left and right, and then from somewhere behind him. And across the airstrip several tanks and armored scout cars rumbled from down the street, the fires behind them, and the soldiers opened their ranks to allow the vehicles into their midst, into the box that held Jack Cray. Another tank crawled out of the darkness at the east end of the airfield.

Cray squeezed his eyes closed, and said under his breath, 'Nuts.'

Eugen Eberhardt's automobile arrived at the airstrip just as the Storch pivoted around to return to the west end of the airfield. The pilot killed the engine, and the Führer's stand-in, an RSD major in a brown raincoat, climbed down from the passenger's seat. Eberhardt's driver pulled up beside an armored car, and the RSD general emerged from his Horch. The false Führer's bodyguards, who were Waffen-SS, awaited orders.

Dietrich also climbed out of the Horch. Binoculars were in his hand. He stepped around the car's front bumper to Eberhardt.

'I think Jack Cray is in our square,' the general said. 'He fell for it. We've got him outgunned, with all the men and armor. I think we've got him.'

'He may be inside our square,' Dietrich replied gravely, 'but that doesn't mean we've got him yet.'

*

Cray pulled the pistol from his belt and scrambled up the crater's crumbling wall, leaving the Panzerfausts behind. He ran east in an infantryman's crouch. To his right came the sounds of soldiers closing in, heavy boots on loose soil and broken branches, a few sharp orders from officers, from back among the trees. Cray could see little, and ran with his left hand out to ward off tree limbs and brush. He knew what was coming. In a few seconds the airstrip and all that surrounded it would be lit as brightly as midday.

Cray dodged a fallen tree and sidestepped water-filled craters, sprinting east. A German voice called, 'Did you see someone?' Others barked replies, lost to Cray in the sound of his breath.

The most formidable weapon may also be the weakest. Cray was forty yards from the tank at the south end of the airstrip when the night was split by a dagger of harsh yellow light. Then another and another. Flares descending from the sky on parachutes threw flat shadows.

His legs churning, Cray glanced to the south, toward Tiergartenstrasse. Soldiers seeped out between the trees. They had been told this trap had been set for the Vassy Château killer, and they moved warily. They squinted against the sudden light. A few saw movement and brought up weapons. A smattering of shots.

Dirt and stones splashed up at the American's feet. The tank's commander was standing in the cupola, the upper half of his body protruding from the turret. This was a Panzerkampfwagen III, a medium tank, and fast, known for chasing Bernard Montgomery around northern Africa. The commander was wearing a black side cap and a radio headset. His sleeves were rolled up, and around his neck were binoculars. His eyes found Jack Cray just as Cray reached for a handhold on the spare track links on the tank's nose. The commander reached down into the cupola, shouting for his pistol.

The tank's loader also saw the American through a vision block, and he reached for the grip of his machine gun. Its barrel protruding from a hole below the turret, the coaxial MG-34 sprayed bullets that churned the ground, but behind Cray. The machine gun's traverse was limited, and as Cray crawled up the hull of the tank, his feet finding a platform on the tread fender and his hand using the barrel of the fifty-millimeter gun, he was inside the bullets' arc.

Clay launched himself at the tank commander, who was just bringing his pistol up through the hatch. Cray smashed the handle of his pistol into the German's temple. The black beret fell to the turret top, and the commander began to sag back down through the hatch. Cray straddled the cupola and dragged him out of the turret, his hands under the German's arms.

Running toward the tank, soldiers hesitated because Cray used the commander as a shield, but a few bullets clipped the air, and a few more clattered uselessly against the tank.

A second bank of flares lit the night. More shouts and curses and orders.

Cray threw the unconscious commander off the turret and jumped down through the hatch.

His feet landed on the commander's empty seat. Cray gripped the hatch rim, and let his knees buckle. He dropped fully inside the tank's fighting compartment.

The loader was bringing around a pistol. Cray lashed out at him with a boot, thrusting the loader's head back against the steel of the turret wall, and smashing it there. The loader slumped.

At the same instant Cray's pistol came around for the gunner, who was in his chair on the other side of the gun breech and recoil protector. One of the gunner's hands was still on the gun's elevating wheel. Two voice tubes were near his ear. He was unarmed. He spread his hands, his eyes locked on Cray's pistol. Behind the gunner was a gas-mask canister attached to the turret wall and in front of him was his traverse indicator. The turret was lit by dull yellow lights.

Cray barked, 'Tell the driver to back up the tank.'

The gunner had a burn scar along his cheek. Probably an Afrika Korps veteran. Tough, not someone who would bend easily. The gunner shook his head, just a fraction, and said, 'The driver – '

He didn't get another word out. Cray shot him through the arm, through the meat of his right biceps. The sound filled the turret and was gone just as quickly. Blood and bits of skin painted the turret wall.

'My next bullet goes through your head.' Cray brought the pistol to the gunner's nose. 'Do as I tell you.'

The gunner blanched and swayed but knew better than to hesitate. He pushed his mouth into the speaker tube and weakly called the order. Slumped on the fighting compartment floor, the loader groaned and grabbed for his head. Cray kicked him again, and the loader was still. Then Cray swung the hatch above his head closed and secured it with a lever. He was surrounded by steel thirty-four millimeters thick. He was sealed in. He felt better.

The hatch to the driving compartment began to open beneath Cray's feet.

'Walter?' the radio operator called.

When the metal door opened further, Cray yanked it out of the radioman's hands, aimed his pistol down into the compartment and sent a bullet into the radio operator's thigh. The man howled and slipped backward, clutching his legs, his headset slipping off him and dangling below the radio. He fell against a shell locker.

Cray moved the pistol several inches so that its snout was against the driver's beret. Staring down at the driver, Cray said, 'Get me out of the Tiergarten or none of you will ever leave this tank. Do you understand me? Back your tank up.'

'I can't see behind me.' The driver had a soft Bavarian accent. He looked up at the American.

'Do you think I give a good goddamn about what's behind you?' Cray prodded the man's forehead with the pistol barrel. 'The question is, have you just taken your last breath?'

The driver turned to face the vision block with the armored binocular hanging over it. With his right hand he pulled the gear lever back. In front of the driver, to the right of the vision block, was an electrically driven gyroscope direction indicator, and to his right was the instrument panel with a speedometer and an oil-pressure gauge and a water-temperature meter. Spilled sideways against the compartment, the radio operator gasped against the pain in his leg.

The driver wound up the Maybach engine, and the tank began to vibrate. Cray's compartment acted as a sounding board, amplifying and containing the engine's roar. The driver gripped the steering levers and released the clutch. The tanked lurched backward.

Blood rolled down the gunner's arm and through the hatch and onto the driver's beret. The gunner was breathing shallowly, his eyes fixed on Cray. Perhaps he had decided Cray had done to him all he was going to do. His breath whistling, he said, 'Goddamn Americans. You just had to come into the war, didn't you?'

Cray looked at him. 'Don't talk to me. Just sit there and bleed.'

Orders had apparently been given to sacrifice the PzKpfw III's crewmen, because a shell – perhaps from an armored car – banged against the turret, but it had hit it at an angle, and it bounced off. The sound was of being inside a bell when it is rung.

'You don't look as tough as in the posters,' the gunner sneered. 'Where's your knife, killer?'

Cray held up a finger like a schoolteacher. 'Let me explain a little of my philosophy: Shut the hell up.'

He shot the gunner again, this time his other arm, clean through it. The bullet smacked against the steel turret wall and slid to the deck. Cray picked up the flattened bullet and slipped it into the gunner's tunic pocket. 'Here's a little souvenir of the war. Now just sit there quietly and don't try my patience again.'

Gasping, the gunner slipped sideways.

The back of the tank rose as it climbed a tree, then leveled off as the tree toppled under the tank's weight. Then it did so again. Cray gripped the handle of the MG-34 and loosed a long string of bullets, the spent casings falling into a canvas bag below the breach, which prevented them from ricocheting around the compartment. The shots were warnings not to get close to the tank.

Cray's ears rang. He yelled down at the driver, 'Turn us around and head south across Tiergartenstrasse.'

The tank stopped, then wheeled about and took off again.

Cray shouted down into the driver's compartment. 'I've got a problem, driver.'

The driver braved a look up at the American.

'When I climb out of this tank, you are undoubtedly going to try to run me over or shoot me through. So I've got a problem letting you live.'

'Sounds more like my problem, frankly,' the driver replied.

Cray shoved aside the injured gunner to peer through his sighting telescope. He couldn't see anything but night. 'Where are we, driver?'

Crossing Tiergartenstrasse. Buildings straight ahead. Which way do I turn, east or west? Better tell me quickly or we'll ram the buildings.'

The tank tilted off the curb, and the fighting compartment filled with the sharper sounds of treads on concrete. The turret interior smelled of grease, exhaust, spent powder, and old sweat.

'Bombed-out buildings ahead.' The driver's voice rose. 'If you're the new goddamn commander, give me directions.'

Cray wet his lip. He knew soldiers would be following the runaway tank, but probably at a respectful distance. He also knew that in a battle the tank crew should avoid leaving their vehicle if at all possible because tanks draw fire, and that a crewman is never more vulnerable than when trying to climb out of the turret.

The American leaned back against a bag containing a 150-round belt of machine ammunition that hung from the turret. The loader stared at him with glassy eyes. Cray ordered, 'Straight ahead. Ram one of the buildings.'

'What, for Christ's sake?'

'Put your tank through one of those shattered buildings.'

Perhaps Cray's plan was immediately apparent to the driver, who saw a reprieve for himself and his crew, because he only nodded and said, 'Here we go.'

The tank ground forward, up the curb, then up two steps to the apartment building's door, knocking aside two cement planters. The building had been partly destroyed in a bombing run. The door was off its hinges and lying on the porch. The upper story had tumbled out over the street, leaving bricks and masonry about. The windows had been blown out and fire had charred the building's brick façade.

The tank charged through the wall, rising and plowing forward, bulldozing bricks and wood inward. Remnants of the second story collapsed onto the vehicle and out onto the sidewalk. The tank growled ahead, into the apartment's living room, crushing a sofa and table, then to the back of the room, where the treads gripped the wall and rose. Cray could hear wrenched timbers falling against the turret. The wall buckled, and the tank climbed higher, its blunt nose almost at the ceiling. Then the treads spun, without gaining more purchase.

'That's as far as we go.' The driver disengaged the gear. 'Now what?'

Cray unlatched the turret hatch, and rose to stand on the commander's chair to push open the hatch. Plaster and lath fell away from the cupola. He pushed away debris, then grabbed the rim to lift his legs out. Here, inside the fractured building, he was protected from gunfire as he exited the tank.

Cray quickly surveyed the ruined room. The tank filled it. A family portrait was still on one wall, but darkness hid the rest of the room. Shots came from outside, from across the street in the park. More orders were called. Armored vehicles rushed along the street.

He bent back through the hatch. 'Don't try to follow me, driver.'

The driver shook his head. 'The notion hadn't occurred to me.'

Cray slipped off the turret to the fender, then down to the room's floor. The tank's weight had bent the room's back wall, revealing beams and sky above. The treads and wheels had sunk into the floor as if it were water. Exhaust from the tank's engine filled the room. Carrying his pistol, Cray stepped over a lampshade and through a door to a kitchen where utensils were scattered over the floor, then out a back door. He sprinted along the alley, then onto a side street where the night took him in.

PART THREE

The Range

THIRTEEN

Otto Dietrich's desk was cluttered with tokens of appreciation. He would diminish them with a shrug when asked about them. But he was too proud of them to consign them to a box on a closet shelf. The largest was a glittering brass fire nozzle. Etched into the brass was TO DETECTIVE INSPECTOR OTTO DIETRICH WITH ETERNAL GRATITUDE FROM THE FIREMEN OF CHARLOTTENBURG STATION NO. 2, OCTOBER 12, 1938. Dietrich had caught the gem-setter who, in a fit of pique resulting from a denial of a raise, had burned down his employer's jewelry store. Three fireman had died when a floor collapsed.

A bronzed glove was on a polished walnut stand. The glove – before being bronzed – had been floating on the Wannsee, the first trace of evidence that Baroness Maria von Hinton had done anything but journey to Baden-Baden, as was her routine at that time of year. When the lake was dragged, her body was found wrapped in enough chain to anchor the *Bismarck*. The coroner, Dr Wenck, had determined that the baroness was alive when dropped into the water. Her family had presented the glove to Dietrich upon conviction of the notorious playboy Count Erich von Stöln, who had wrapped the baroness in iron and thrown her in the lake, two bottles of brandy having altered his perception of an acceptable frolic. Also on Dietrich's desk were an inscribed pair of brass knuckles inlaid with diamonds, a silver-plated hatchet head, a crystal decanter containing a human ear (a row of teeth marks clearly visible), and other mementos.

Dietrich seldom sat at his desk, but he did now, still weak from his time in the prison. He asked mildly, 'How many Jack Crays are out there now?'

Detective Peter Hilfinger stepped to the window overlooking Alexanderplatz. The day was fading, with red in the sky, some from the sunset, some from that day's bombing-raid fires. 'Nine, looks like. With some of the Jack Crays in uniform, it's hard to tell them from their guards.'

Hilfinger's back was to the desk but Dietrich knew he was working to suppress a laugh. Dietrich picked up a gold-plated letter opener that at one time had also opened a kidney. 'I hadn't anticipated this, Peter.'

'Perhaps both of us should have,' Hilfinger said charitably. 'But with the American's face covering almost every vertical surface in Berlin, we are getting an average of fifteen sightings and three arrests an hour.'

'I have supervised city-wide manhunts before.' Dietrich leaned back in his chair. 'And you have assisted me. We know how to do it.'

'Of course.'

'Berliners will not tolerate a knife-wielding killer walking their streets.'

'No.' Hilfinger turned from the window. His face was inappropriate for a policeman, all in the department agreed. His eyes were set merrily, and the corners of his mouth permanently turned up. Hilfinger was eager and enthusiastic and helpful. He used his happy countenance to his advantage, Dietrich knew, particularly during interrogations. Just like everyone else, criminals wanted to befriend him.

'And that's why we've had this flood of reports.' Dietrich thought his own words lame. The truth was that his manhunt had failed.

'Inspector?' The voice came from the doorway. 'Will you check this man out?'

Dietrich's chair squeaked as it turned toward the door. The detective rubbed his eyes before looking at the door, hoping whoever stood there would disappear.

Detective Egon Haushofer shared the door frame with a blond refugee wearing a miner's cap. The refugee kept his head bowed and repeatedly ran his lips over his tongue. He had a thick chest and rugged hands cuffed together. He had a passing resemblance to Jack Cray.

Detective Haushofer explained, 'He was turned over to me by three SHD men, who spotted him on Keller Street near the armory.'

The Security and Help Service were part of the air defense system, conscripted reservists who were required to sleep every other night in their barracks, which they most gladly tolerated because they were exempt from the armed services.

'Are you German?' Dietrich asked.

'From Stettin,' the prisoner replied.

Dietrich went through the motions. 'What is the name of the six-hundred-year-old church in Stettin?'

'St James.' The refugee almost smiled. Perhaps he could feel the handcuffs loosening.

'What is the longest ship moored on the Oder?'

'The aircraft carrier *Graf Zeppelin*. It's been there for years, but it isn't finished.'

'What's the name of the building across the roadway from the *Graf Zeppelin*'s moorage?' Peter Hilfinger asked.

'The Western Pomeranian Museum.'

'Release him,' Dietrich ordered.

Detective Haushofer pushed his key into the handcuffs to snap them open. The refugee rubbed his wrists. He nervously looked right and left.

'What's your name?' Dietrich asked.

The refugee again lowered his eyes. 'Ewald Schack.'

'Where were you going when you were arrested?' Dietrich knew the answer, of course.

'West. With my wife and daughter. We lost our home in Stettin and . . .' His voice trailed away.

Dietrich asked, 'I don't suppose you have any identity papers on you?'

Schack hesitated. 'My Wehrmacht ID.'

'Anything to show why you aren't with your unit? Any travel passes?' With that Dietrich conveyed to the refugee that he knew he was a deserter, had left the army to return to Stettin to try to take his family to safety.

For an instant the man looked like he might try dashing down the stairs. Haushofer moved his hand to the small of the refugee's back.

Dietrich reached for a piece of stationery and a pen. He wrote several lines, then passed the paper to Schack. 'This will help. Good luck to you.'

The refugee stared at the stationery, which below the Berlin Police Department's impressive logo and Dietrich's imprinted name and rank, read, 'Ewald Schack is working for the Berlin police. I have Reichsführer Himmler's authority to order that Schack and his family are not to be disturbed or delayed in their travels,' followed by Dietrich's signature.

The refugee gripped the letter as if it were a life ring. He mumbled his thanks and backed away from Hilfinger, then disappeared down the hallway.

Detective Haushofer asked, 'Want me to bring up another Jack Cray?'

Dietrich rubbed a human skull on his desk that had a hole in the temple precisely the diameter of an alpine climbing pick. 'Maybe later.' Dietrich gripped the fire nozzle and slammed the desk with it, so uncharacteristic a gesture that Hilfinger and Haushofer glanced at each other.

Dietrich exclaimed, 'I thought we had that bastard last night at the Tiergarten airstrip. Thought General Eberhardt and I had him trapped, goddamn the American anyway.'

After a moment he was able to release his fingers from the nozzle. He looked sheepishly at his subordinates, clucking his tongue by way of apology, then to the document on his desk, marked boldly in red across the first page 'State Secret' and 'Top Secret,' below which was the title, 'Führerbunker Firefighting and Rescue Plan.' General Eberhardt had provided him with the copy. It set out which organization had which responsibility, and who would make the determination to initiate firefighting or a rescue or an evacuation. General Eberhardt had the ultimate responsibility for the decisions, and was to consult with the guard captain at the bunker. The document was signed by the Führer, so presumably Hitler would comply with whatever emergency decisions Eberhardt might some day have to make. Any rescue would be attempted by the Technical Emergency Corps from their station closest to the bunker, on Kaiser-hofstrasse near the Hotel Kaiserhof. Firefighting teams would come from Berlin No. 1 Station on Mauerstrasse. If either the Rescue Squad or the firefighters were ever called to the bunker because of Jack Cray, it would of course mean that Dietrich had failed.

'There's something about the American I can't figure out,' Hilfinger said after a moment, pushing aside a telephone so he could sit on the front of his desk facing Dietrich.

'Only one thing?'

'Why didn't he hide his progress toward Berlin?' Hilfinger asked. 'I mean, he had that conversation with that old lady, and he let those two Wehrmacht soldiers live, Sergeant Keppler and Private Enge. The American must have known they'd report to the authorities.'

'I think it's Jack Cray's way of boasting. He is telling us we can't catch him, even if he gives us glimpses of himself.' Dietrich scratched his chin. 'Or maybe he doesn't care if we catch him.'

'What sense does that make? Why would he go to all the trouble of traveling to Berlin if he doesn't care if we find him? He could have saved himself and us a lot of trouble by getting caught nearer Colditz.'

Dietrich shook his head by way of an answer.

'Do you think Jack Cray is a feint? That the enemy has another plan underway, and Cray's purpose is only to distract us? Maybe that's why he let those folks live, when he knew they'd report him.'

Dietrich replied, 'Maybe he let those people live because he doesn't like to shoot down someone in cold blood.'

'You're suggesting Jack Cray is a nice guy?' Hilfinger laughed.

'I don't know if he is or not, and I hope never to have to put that suggestion to the test. But, feint or not, I'm only in charge of finding Cray.'

Hilfinger said, 'We'll have our hands full with just him, it looks like.'

'General Eberhardt can worry about the others, if Cray is a feint.' Dietrich toyed with the fire nozzle. 'One of the few things I'm certain of is that Jack Cray is almost certainly still disguising himself in a German uniform. Not in a refugee's clothes, or some other civilian's clothes.'

'What makes you think so?' Hilfinger asked.

'Jack Cray is most comfortable in a uniform. Soldiers the world around think and act alike. Cray knows the soldier's walk and mannerisms. Because he doesn't have to be an actor when he's in a uniform, his job is easier.'

'What else do you know, Inspector?' The new voice at the doorway was dreadfully recognizable.

Dietrich spun in his chair to see Rudolf Koder, who had pushed aside Haushofer. Dietrich tightened, as if expecting a blow.

The Gestapo agent smiled, perhaps in recognition of his effect.

'This is my office,' Dietrich managed, trying to make himself sound angry rather than afraid. 'Get out.'

'I'm your case officer,' Koder said in a tone of finality, as if that explained everything.

'I'm done with you.' It was more a prayer.

Koder lifted half-frame reading glasses from his coat pocket and inspected them a moment before replying. 'You are unfamiliar with our procedures, Detective Dietrich, and for that I apologize. We close a file only upon the death of the subject. As long as you live, I am your case officer.'

Peter Hilfinger demanded, 'What are you doing here?' Berlin police detectives could spot a Gestapo agent as readily as blood on snow.

Koder grinned, a malevolent crease that split in half his narrow head. 'Detective Dietrich, you were a little too clever, shaking our car outside the medical examiner's office. So General Müller has ordered me to assist you.'

'To watch me,' Dietrich corrected.

Koder pursed his lips. 'Your organization and mine have different methods, to be sure. We in the Staatspolizei are a bit more' – he hesitated, apparently searching for the precise word – 'direct. But I can be of help in your search.' He added pleasantly, 'While I watch you.'

Dietrich stared at his tormentor. Then he reached into his coat pocket, pulled out Himmler's letter, and held it up so Koder could read it. 'Now go away.'

'That's truly impressive. I wish I had a letter like that.' The Gestapo agent shook his head with transparent sadness. 'But I report to General Müller, and can't take orders from anyone but him.'

Koder lowered himself to a captain's chair below a bulletin board. To his right was a floor-to-ceiling map of Berlin, with colored pins stuck here and there. A row of lockers lined the north wall. Three other detectives were at their desks in the room. Somewhere nearby the telephone poles were down, so lines had been jury-rigged through a window near Dietrich's desk. A wadded coat had been plugged into the gap around the phone lines. Because the office had no heat, the detectives were wearing overcoats. Around Hilfinger's neck was a blue scarf his mother had knitted.

'I'll ask again, Inspector,' Koder said. 'What else do you know?'

Peter Hilfinger's face had gained the pink hue of anger. He had learned his craft from Dietrich and revered the man. Like all detectives in the room, Hilfinger knew the circumstances of Dietrich's disappearance into the Gestapo dungeon. And here was one of the devils, in their own midst, bullying the great man. Hilfinger's hand slid toward the lead-filled sap in his coat pocket as he sidled toward the agent. A look from Dietrich froze him.

'I've learned nothing else,' Dietrich answered.

'And is that why, even though a barbarous killer is roaming the city, you and your boys are sitting here, rather than out on the streets looking for him?'

Reassured that Koder had not arrived to escort him back to Lehrterstrasse Prison, a modicum of courage returned to Dietrich. 'Koder, how many reliable people do you have reporting to you on, say, the Schiffbauerdamm?'

This street, near the Spree, was where Berlin shipwrights had lived and worked during the reigns of the Great Elector and Frederick the Great.

Koder studied Dietrich, perhaps wondering how he was being asked to incriminate himself. 'Three or four.'

'Three or four in the entire neighborhood.' Dietrich glanced at Hilfinger. This lesson was for him and Haushofer and the others. Rudolf Koder was beyond lessons. 'In the summer of 1941, I arrested Gotthard Henneberg, a house painter who had murdered three young women on the street over the prior twelve months. Henneberg was convicted of the murders and executed.'

'Is there a point to this nice little story?'

'The neighborhood was relieved and grateful, and now I have two hundred people on the Schiffbauerdamm who report to this office the slightest of peculiar circumstances. You rely on fear. I rely on respect.'

'Jack Cray is still out there,' Koder said flatly.

'But he can't evade me long. Not in Berlin. I have thousands and thousands of pairs of eyes looking for him.'

When the telephone sounded, Dietrich lifted the handset to his ear. 'This is Dietrich . . . Yes, I remember you, Captain.'

The detective grabbed for a pencil and rose from his chair as he dashed off notes on the back of an envelope. 'Von Tornitz? I don't know that name . . . His widow? Are you sure?'

Dietrich dipped his chin at Peter Hilfinger, who picked up an extension to listen in.

'And the American?' Dietrich asked. 'A bandage over his face?'

Dietrich cupped his hand over the phone. He ordered Hilfinger, 'Adam von Tornitz. A Wehrmacht captain, dead now. Lived in Berlin. Get his address.'

He turned his attention again to the telephone. 'That's all? . . . Thank you, Captain. You'll hear from me again.' Dietrich lowered the telephone. He grinned meanly at the Gestapo agent. 'One of my pairs of eyes saw the widow of Adam von Tornitz walking with the American near the Tiergarten.'

Hilfinger ran his finger down a page of the city directory.

'Von Tornitz?' Koder asked. 'I know that name. He was involved in a plot against the Führer. He was hanged, as I recall. I might have witnessed his execution on Lehrterstrasse.' He waived his hand airily. 'But perhaps not. They are hard to remember, one from another, after a while.'

Hilfinger wrote down an address. 'It's in the Nikolassee.' He handed the address to Dietrich.

Dietrich dialed, then barked orders into the telephone. Still grinning, waving the address like a prize, he sped past Koder on his way out of the office, a line of detectives following him.

'Have you seen him?' Dietrich whispered, even though the house was sixty meters away. He had just gotten out of his car. Night was almost complete, with only faint purple left of the day in the western sky.

The plainclothes policeman shook his head. 'I've been here ten minutes. There's someone in the house. At least I think so. A shadow crossing a window is all I saw. My men have had the house surrounded for those ten minutes, so if he's in there, he can't get out.'

'You look silly, carrying that machine pistol,' Dietrich chided easily. 'Detectives and machine pistols don't mix well.'

'Then you dash into that house with just your puny handgun, sir.' The policeman's name was Erwin Nolte. He quickly added, 'With all due respect.' He wiggled the weapon. 'I'm going to keep this damned thing right in front of me, with the trigger half pulled back. That American scares the crap out of me.'

'Me too.' Dietrich carried binoculars in one hand and a pack radio in the other. He sucked wind through his teeth as he watched three cars pull up along Kenner Street, a block west of the von Tornitz house. Peter Hilfinger and Egon Haushofer climbed out of the first car. Hilfinger gave directions to policemen who began to array themselves around the house, but at a distance, joining the police already there. More cars were arriving to the north, policemen spilling out.

'Sir,' Nolte blurted, 'he's coming out. On the front porch.'

Dietrich lifted the binoculars to his eyes, saw nothing but black, hastily removed the lens covers, and tried again. Jack Cray was abruptly centered in Dietrich's field of vision, stepping between two potted plants down the steps to the front walkway.

Dietrich breathed. 'It's him, all right.'

Jack Cray must have had superb hearing, because just then his head jerked up. He cocked an ear. Dietrich heard nothing. For a moment. Then from the south came the low growl of an engine. Dietrich turned to see an armored scout car roaring down the street.

'Goddamn that idiot.' Dietrich spun toward the house, in time to see Jack Cray rush back inside and close the door.

'Where'd the armor come from?' the policeman asked.

'On the orders of a Gestapo agent whom I'd murder if I hadn't spent a career chasing murderers.'

A black Horch rolled up next to Dietrich. Rudolf Koder and two other agents emerged from the car. At this stage in the struggle, Gestapo agents seldom traveled alone.

'That the von Tornitz house?' Koder demanded.

The armored car – a three-axle Mercedes-Benz with two-centimeter gun on a rear turret – came along the street, followed by two identical armored cars and three troop trucks. In the lead armored car a spotter wearing a tanker's black beret threw open the hatch and rose just enough to glance at Koder.

'You seen the American?' Koder yelled at Dietrich over the grind of the armored cars' engines.

Dietrich was silent, furious that the Gestapo agent had muscled into his police work.

Erwin Nolte replied, 'He's in that house. Just went back through the front door.'

Koder signaled to the spotter, who slipped back down into the Mercedes-Benz. The car lurched forward down the block, then rolled up the curb, plowed through three azalea bushes and knocked over a lamppost to park in front of the von Tornitz house, thirty feet from the massive oak front door.

Blackout curtains were drawn over all the windows, but power was on, and slits of light escaped from the bottoms of the curtains. The porch light was dark. The house was accented with heavy timbers on the first floor, and expanses of whitewash on the second, crisscrossed by more timbers. It was old and rambling, with dormers and gables, four chimneys, ornate cornices, and small oculus windows. The house was large and confused and comfortable.

SS storm troopers emerged from the trucks. When platoon leaders signaled, the troopers spread out around the house, joining the policemen. They carried Schmeissers and rifles, and moved with a confidence that indicated they were veterans of a front. A machine-gun team set up an MG-42 on a tripod on the west side of the house. The Berlin detectives watched gravely.

Anger clipped Otto Dietrich's words. 'Who gave you authority to use the SS on this operation, Koder?'

'General Müller, of course.'

'This is my goddamn job.'

'The American is in the house, and the house is surrounded. He cannot get out. Your job looks at an end, doesn't it?' Koder smiled at him. 'So who knows what you might be doing tomorrow, or where you'll be.'

When this mission was over, Dietrich would be once again of no worth to the Reich. He had not been promised a pardon were he to capture the American. Still, perhaps if he brought Jack Cray in, rather than allow the Blackshirts and the Gestapo to do his job, some fate other than a return to the cell might await him.

'I'm going in after the American,' Dietrich said.

'You are a policeman, not a soldier,' Koder said with some satisfaction. 'You don't have any idea what's waiting for you in that house.'

Dietrich walked toward the front porch. Pilasters were on both sides of the arched door. 'Better Jack Cray than you and your guillotine.'

'At least let me help you with the door.' Koder gave an order to the armored car's spotter.

The spotter yelled down into his hatch. The two-centimeter gun roared, yellow flashes dancing at the tip of the barrel. The sound was similar to a lightning storm: a sharp crack followed by a deep bellow. The door of the von Tornitz house and the pilasters and the frame blew inward, leaving a ragged, smoking hole at the top of the steps.

More armored equipment came noisily down the street. The gauleiter in a neighboring house pushed aside his blackout curtain to observe the scene.

Dietrich motioned for Hilfinger to join him. They slowly circled the house, beginning along a walkway between a laurel hedge and the house. Troopers held their weapons on the windows and a side door that exited to a garbage bin. A trooper was repeatedly plunging a bayonet into the garbage. He shook his head.

'The American's not under there,' Dietrich told him. 'He didn't have time to get outside. He's in the house.'

The trooper stabbed the bayonet several more times, all the way up to the rifle barrel. 'I was told to stab, so I stab.'

The house had been built on a slope, and the detectives stepped downhill along the walkway, passing basement windows and more of the SS troopers who had surrounded the house. The troopers kept their distance from the house, posting themselves behind trees and bushes. Along the back of the house was a rose garden. A dog run was also in back, where a Gestapo agent was poking his pistol into a clapboard doghouse. Several more troopers stood under a trellis that was ensnared by rose vines. The troopers wore gray fatigues and coal-scuttle helmets. They were almost invisible in the darkness. Two Gestapo agents were standing near a greenhouse, which was made to look Gothic with wrought-iron curls along the corners and ridgeline. Dietrich stared at the greenhouse a moment, thinking it odd for a reason he could not immediately determine. Then he realized that in Berlin he seldom saw so many undamaged panes of glass in one place. The detectives passed the coal and ash gates – both too narrow for a man to squeeze through, but nevertheless guarded by a trooper pointing a Schmeisser at the gate. More troopers watched the back door. Their lieutenant was standing behind them, the red point of his cigarette rising and falling in the night. Other troopers surrounded the garage. Dietrich's detectives stood apart from the troopers and Gestapo agents.

Dietrich and Hilfinger completed their circuit and paused at the front door. The armored car spotter asked from up on his machine, 'Are you two waiting for me to make the hole bigger?'

A second armored car drove onto the lawn. Instead of a two-centimeter cannon, this car had a blunt nozzle that Dietrich had not seen before. Rudolf Koder was giving directions to the second car's driver, who peered out from a rectangular slot. The car pulled up closer to the house.

'Damn, I don't want to go into this house,' Hilfinger said. 'I thought being a cop meant I was exempt from this kind of Skorzeny stuff.'

Pistols in hand, Dietrich and Hilfinger slowly stepped through the door, ducking under shattered boards that hung down. The bitter smell was of spent explosives. The armored car's shell had done its work on the hallway, also, which was tossed and shattered and filled with rubble like a Berlin street. They stepped around an overturned Chinese chest and a gilt-framed mirror that had been blown off the wall. Shards of mirror lay all along the hall. The chest was too small for a man, but Dietrich looked into it anyway, pushing aside a door that was off-kilter. The chest was filled with china dishes, now mostly fragments. Rudolf Koder and six storm troopers followed them, Koder in the rear, a pistol in his hand.

Dietrich led them into the good room, then into the kitchen. They pulled open cabinets. On the counter near the sink was a bottle of wine that was half full, ten sausages on a string, and hard rolls.

When a trooper came to the closed pantry door, rather than open it blindly he pulled back the bolt on the Schmeisser and loosed half a clip through the door, the weapon roaring and bucking, stitching the wood up one side and down the other.

Then he kicked in the door and bulled his way inside to find nothing but a few empty jars and bins.

'Learn that technique in Warsaw, did you?' Dietrich asked mildly.

He led Hilfinger and the troopers up the stairs. The detectives peered into the bathroom. A trooper with a bayonet on a Mauser stepped by Dietrich, opened a towel cabinet, and jabbed the bayonet into the piles of neatly stacked towels. In the hallway, the

Schmeisser-carrying trooper covered an armoire while Dietrich opened its door to reveal folded linen sheets and pillowcases. The bayonet was plunged into the linen. Rudolf Koder watched from the top of the stairs.

Troopers and several detectives now crowded the hallway. Dietrich entered the front bedroom, checking the two armoires, looking under the bed, turning back the mattress. The trooper followed him, sticking his bayonet into the armoire and through the mattresses. Hilfinger and other troopers searched the three back bedrooms while Dietrich climbed to the servants' quarters in the garret. They opened closets and dressers. Armoires were opened and pierced through with bayonets.

The basement was next. Lightbulbs had been unavailable in Berlin for months, and they had apparently been purloined from this little-used basement for the sockets upstairs. Dietrich was passed a flashlight. He held it to one side, presenting a target away from his body as he descended the stairs, the pistol in his other hand. Koder followed. In the darkness only vague outlines were visible. Dietrich's eyes adjusted slowly. The basement was filled with boxes and bins, two bicycles, a pedal sewing machine, a ringer washer, and a laundry hopper. Hilfinger and Koder had also obtained flashlights, and the thin, moving beams threw exaggerated shadows against the boxes and the walls.

Dietrich moved toward the furnace room. He stuck his flashlight and gun into the room at the same time, sweeping the light left into the coal bin.

'Nothing, not even coal,' he whispered to himself.

He brought the beam of light down to the ash bin below the furnace's iron lip. The ash was gray and fine and a film of it lay on the furnace-room floor. A trooper squeezed by Dietrich and thrust his bayonet twice down into the ash box, the weapon sinking each time until the front sight was below the ash.

Dietrich lowered himself to his knees to peer into the furnace's combustion chamber. He couldn't see up into the furnace, but nothing was on its floor. And he couldn't think of a way a man could get into it, anyway.

The bass cracking of a Schmeisser filled the basement. Dietrich turned to see the water heater leaking from eight holes. When he stepped away from the furnace, the same trooper used his weapon to perforate the furnace, up and down, then back and forth.

'Don't fire that again unless I order you to,' Dietrich said wearily. 'I want to talk to this American first.'

'I take my orders from Kriminalrat Koder, sir,' the trooper replied.

'This is my goddamn investigation. I run it my way. I search a house my way.'

Koder stared at him.

Dietrich detested the weakness in him that compelled him to explain further, 'There might be evidence here we can collect. There's no sense destroying the house during this search.'

'Evidence?' Koder appeared genuinely at a loss.

'And we don't know how involved this woman is.'

'We have learned her name is Katrin von Tornitz,' Koder said. 'She is the wife of an executed traitor.'

'But that doesn't mean she herself is a traitor. And so we shouldn't be in such a hurry to destroy her home. There's a less destructive way to search a house than to shoot up everything.'

Koder smiled. Then he snapped a finger at the troopers.

Three of them turned their submachine guns on the cartons and bins. The roar pushed Dietrich back against a wall. Wood splinters leaped into the air. Masonry chips shot out from the walls. The boxes shattered inward, revealing old clothes and bric-a-brac from prior household moves. Bullets spun the bicycles and then threw them on the floor. The water heater and furnace were further perforated. A collection of bottles from the last century and three old vases blew apart. A glass-front bookcase ruptured. A duffel bag containing rags was shot through. The ringer washer was almost cut in half. A storage closet danced under the onslaught, and its door sagged open, revealing old clothes that were further punctured. Spent shells skittered across the floor. Gray gunsmoke gathered along the ceiling.

Then the troopers picked through the debris and pulled aside the bullet-riddled clothes and kicked in the boxes.

One of them said unnecessarily, 'The American isn't here.'

Dietrich's ears were ringing. He crossed the basement and climbed the stairs. Three Gestapo agents were in the kitchen, and four more in the good room, all of them rooting around, pulling items off shelves, flipping through a stack of letters and examining a pen-and-ink set.

Peter Hilfinger had been searching through back rooms, and he joined Dietrich at the door. He returned his pistol to his belt. 'I feel like I've been run over by Blackshirts.'

'It's clear to me now,' Dietrich said in a low voice, 'that although I was given control of the search for Jack Cray, and even though I've got Himmler's letter in my pocket, the Gestapo have also been given their orders, and when they and I conflict, I'm expected to give way.'

Hilfinger followed Dietrich from the house and down the front steps. They walked between the two armored cars. The crews had climbed out of their vehicles and were sitting on the hoods and turrets. More equipment had arrived, filling the street, including a light tank, a bulldozer, and more troop trucks. More than three hundred soldiers and policemen now surrounded the house.

'So where is Jack Cray?' Hilfinger asked.

Dietrich turned abruptly so that he could again look at the von Tornitz house. 'Peter, I saw him come out, and go back into that house.'

'So did I.'

'He is still inside, goddamn it. But I don't know where.'

Rudolf Koder emerged from the house, leading a line of agents and troopers. His black coat was shiny in the night, looking wet. His mouth was a grim line. He marched to the second armored car and yelled an order Dietrich couldn't hear over the sound of its engine.

The troopers and agents backed away from the house, giving the armored car a clear field of fire.

Dietrich rushed up to Koder. 'What in hell are you doing?'

'The American is in that house.' Koder did not bother looking at Dietrich. He walked away, hands casually in his coat pockets. 'He won't let me find him, so he leaves me no alternative.'

The sudden blare was of a bellows, a loud windy howl. The night lit up, painting Dietrich and Hilfinger and all the others in orange light. A stream of fire gushed from the second armored car's nozzle. The flood of liquid flame surged across the lawn and coursed up the steps and into the house. The fire stream roared and popped, and it splashed against the house as the gunner swung the nozzle left and right. The force of the flood blew in the front-room windows, which instantly filled with flame. The blazing spray climbed to the second story and poured into the windows. Fuel dropped in puddles onto the lawn under the fiery stream, and ignited, leaving a trail of fire to the house. The flame thrower was then directed at the base of the house, covering the porch and even the azaleas with flame. Dietrich shielded his eyes from the furious light. The armored car filled the hole where the door had been with fire.

Within seconds, nothing of the front façade could be seen. Fire rose three stories and beyond, swirling in the air above the house, and sending sparks even higher. Black smoke churned up from the fire, but was quickly lost in the night. Everything – the dormers and parapets, the flues and chimneys, the cornices and shutters, the roof cresting and door casings – was lost behind the boiling curtain.

Fire enveloped the house, which became a torch, nothing visible but flames. Golden washes of flames peaked fifty meters above the roof. In his robe the gauleiter had joined the Gestapo agents, giving a series of orders they ignored. The von Tornitz house was still surrounded by Blackshirts and Gestapo agents and policemen, but they had to withdraw, away from the heat, into the street and adjoining yards. They watched the conflagration. Where was the American?

Dietrich and Hilfinger retreated to the far curb. Even here the heat was on their faces. Behind them was an elm grove that partly hid a vast and dark house that had once belonged to a Berlin banking family.

Staring at the backlit figure of Rudolf Koder, Dietrich muttered, 'If I had anything left of myself, any courage at all . . .'

Hilfinger leaned toward him to hear, but Dietrich let his words trail off, even left the thought uncompleted.

For half an hour they watched. The blazing house fell in on itself, and continued to angrily burn, the red core getting smaller and smaller. Clouds of smoke lifted skyward. The fire sighed and hissed.

The troopers returned to their trucks. The armored cars and the tanks and fire trucks and motorcycles receded, all loudly, all with the neighbors watching from dark windows. Even the gauleiter went home.

Koder crossed the street. 'Where's the American?'

'Dead in the ashes.'

'No person – not even this crazed American commando – can sit calmly in a fire and burn to death. He should have cried out. He should have made a run for safety.'

In the tone of one addressing a child, Dietrich said, 'He was in the house, and the house burned down.'

Koder's eyes dug into Dietrich, who would not look down, not like all the times in the prison. Finally the Gestapo agent turned toward his car and walked away.

'Are we done for the night?' Peter Hilfinger asked.

'Maybe more than just for the night.' Dietrich stared at the remains of the house, much of it still glowing and steaming. He chewed on nothing for a moment. 'Goddamn it, Peter. If I know anything, it's that I trust my eyes.'

Hilfinger nodded. 'I trust your eyes, too.'

'Jack Cray is in that house.'

'There is no house anymore. Only fire.'

'Then Jack Cray is in that fire.'

'Bright and early tomorrow, then.' Hilfinger turned toward a car where other plainclothes policeman waited for a ride back to the station. 'They'll find his body in the ashes after they cool.'

Dietrich nodded. He walked toward his car, along the wooded lane, the fire still spitting and crackling behind him. With the fire dying down and Dietrich walking away from it, the night had become bitterly cold and fully dark.

Otto Dietrich would go to his grave wondering how he heard utterly nothing and saw utterly nothing. He was alone on the sidewalk, surely. But he wasn't.

An arm came out of the night and wrapped itself around Dietrich's neck, pulling him back against a man's chest, a big and solid man.

The detective gasped and might have cried out, but he felt cold metal press into his neck, right into the soft spot next to his Adam's apple.

The accent was strong. 'What did you want to talk about?'

Dietrich blinked. He was about to die – bubbling blood rushing from a slash in his neck, and he'd resemble the appalling body at Dr Wenck's morgue – and all he could think of was that Jack Cray's German was fairly good. And that Cray was as quiet as snow. And that Cray simply must have been incinerated in the von Tornitz home.

'What did you want to say to me?' The voice of his killer again.

Dietrich's mind was blank with fear. He finally managed to gasp, 'Nothing.'

'Better think of something.'

Was the American making fun of him? Dietrich stammered, 'I . . . I wanted to ask if you were a show-off.'

'I've been called that before.' The flat voice was right at Dietrich's ear.

The detective could see a portion of Cray's shoulder, covered in dirt and ash.

Dietrich was still alive. He willed his mouth – dry as a kiln – to work. 'How did you escape the fire?'

'In the furnace ash pit.'

'The ash pit was stabbed with a bayonet, a couple of times.'

'I was stabbed with a bayonet, a couple of times.' Cray held his left arm over Dietrich's shoulder so the detective could see it. The uniform sleeve was matted with ash. Blood leaked from the arm onto the ground. 'Clean through my arm. It hurts, I don't mind saying. I've got another long cut, a graze, right along my backbone.'

'How did you survive the heat?' Dietrich could feel his own

pistol on his belt, pressing into his side. It seemed a long way away. The American was talkative, for Christ's sake.

'I opened the coal gate. Cool air came in, sucked in by the flames. All the fire was above me. I dug down into the pit, and it was fairly comfortable. Except for being stabbed, of course.'

Was the commando mocking him? It didn't seem professional. On the verge of death, Dietrich was indignant.

'I could hear you in the basement,' Jack Cray said. 'You sounded like a policeman. Not a soldier.'

'I'm a detective. A homicide detective.'

'Would killing you be legal, then? Would it be a lawful wartime action?'

'No, surely not.' The American was having a fine old time at Dietrich's expense. The detective asked, 'Are all Americans as cocky as you?'

'You should meet our pilots.'

'We Berliners meet them every day,' Dietrich said.

'How'd you set me up last night in the Tiergarten?'

Dietrich hesitated, but when the knife scraped his neck as if it were shaving him, the German said, 'We had the Chancellery issue orders as if the Führer were leaving Berlin. It is always a complicated process, with hundreds of people involved in preparation for Hitler's departure. We figured somewhere there'd be a leak and you'd find it. We were right.'

'That was good,' Cray said. 'I like that.'

'Thank you.'

'Now what do I do with you?'

'You're going to let me live because you want someone to be able to tell how clever you were escaping the fire.'

'I'm going to let you live because you argued against destroying her house.' The pressure at Dietrich's neck lessened slightly. 'Stay away from me. You'll get hurt if you get close again.'

The knife was removed. Dietrich could sense the American receding into the night. He waited a few heartbeats to be sure. Then he pulled his Walther from his belt and turned around, the pistol leading the way.

He saw nothing, as he had known he would. Nothing but night and the dark shadows of a few trees and down the street a few licks of flame and purple sparkling embers, all that remained of the house.

Dietrich pushed the pistol back into his pants. His hands were shaking and he had trouble drawing a breath. He could still feel an echo of the appalling knife at his throat.

Finally, 'Bastard American show-off.'

FOURTEEN

'Can we trust the names from the milk box?' Katrin tapped on the door.

Cray replied, 'I hurt too much to think about that.'

'I thought you commandos don't feel pain.'

'I'm about to weep from it.' Cray held his left arm in his right hand. Blood had dried along the length of the coat sleeve, stiffening the fabric and turning it dark.

She gently touched the sleeve.

'Ouch.' He jerked his arm away from her.

'Commandos say "Ouch"?'

The brass sign to the right of the door read FREDERICK HOLENBEIN, MEDICAL CLINIC. Katrin knocked on the door again, then she saw the bell cord and pulled it. The sound of chimes came from deep within the office.

A bulb flicked on above them, from the second floor, spots of light visible through holes in the blackout curtain. After a moment the door opened, just a crack, an eye visible above the taut safety chain.

'Dr Holenbein?' Katrin asked. 'We were told you would help us.'

The doctor hesitated, vast indecision apparent in one visible eye. Then the safety chain's catch scraped against its anchor. The door swung open. A flannel robe flapping behind him, the doctor led them through the reception area into his surgery, glancing nervously over his shoulder several times.

She had been out making a radio broadcast. When she returned, her home was surrounded by policemen and troopers and ablaze from front to rear. She had watched and watched from down the block, seeing her home turned to ash and smoke. Over the winter she had burned her furniture for heat, and now this fire was taking away all the rest, everything she owned, every memento of Adam. Her sorrow had rooted her to the sidewalk.

And only after a moment had she remembered that the American was in her house. She had stared at the twisting fire. There could be nothing left of him. Perhaps Jack Cray's death should have seemed inconsequential to her – a foreigner thrown at her as her life was collapsing – but she had been surprised by her sadness that the American was surely dead, under the ashes of her home. She had never met anyone who had been on first sight more suggestive of wild trouble. His crazed grin, his animation, his unwavering focus. His stupid cheerfulness. Jack Cray would have led her to ruin, perhaps would have cost her her life. Yet for a while, watching the embers die, she had been sorrowful that he was gone.

Watching the fire, she had surprised herself with that emotion, the flutter of grief. She had thought herself no longer susceptible to such sentiment. Another soldier's life tossed into the war's grinder. What possible difference could it make to her?

But after a few more moments gazing at her burning home, her sensibilities had callused over again. Jack Cray had come and gone. Even though her home was gone, she was still alive. In Berlin, another day of life was a victory.

Then when everyone else had retreated from the destroyed house, and when she had turned to wondering where she would spend the rest of the cold night, she saw Jack Cray rise from the ashes – a ghoul emerging from the center of the earth – and make his way toward the last remaining policeman, who was standing by his car.

She had been transfixed by the American's movement, utterly silent, yet almost as fast as a sprinter, and somehow eerily hard to follow with her gaze, merging with the shadows, darkness on darkness, and she then understood why the Hand had called on him. This was the skill, probably one of many skills, that his American fatuousness concealed. His exuberance and affability were doubtless feigned, a professional fakery designed to lull whomever he dealt with.

Watching Jack Cray move toward the policeman, she had been reminded once again that the American was nothing more than a proficient killer, a weapon of war loosed on Berlin, just like a B-17. But less philosophical and repentant. He was going to kill again, this time the policeman by the car.

But then the crazy American said a few words into the policeman's ear and then let the man go. Just turned him loose. Jack Cray was continually complicating her assessment of him.

The doctor walked to the far side of his examining table before he turned to look more closely at them. When his eyes settled on Jack Cray, his face turned pale in blotches and his shoulder hunched protectively. His face slackened and his lips parted, and a small sound escaped him, perhaps the beginnings of a plea for mercy. Then the doctor saw the blood, and realized that the American whose face littered Berlin had come to him for the same reason everyone else came to him. Slowly the doctor's face came together again, wrinkling around hostile eyes.

'He's been stabbed in the arm,' Katrin said. 'And along his back, though it's a slight wound there.'

'Easy for you to say how slight it is.' Cray's jaws were clamped with pain. 'It's not your back that's hurting.'

Katrin had seen firsthand the resources the Hand was committing to its mission, and knew that the American had been entrusted to her care, and so sensed that she had been invested with substantial authority, however undefined it was for her.

So she said bluntly, 'We are in a hurry. Clean his wounds and do whatever else you need to do, and do it quickly.'

The doctor scowled blackly at her, but he must have thought better of protesting or making an inquiry, for he reached for Cray's arm, but tentatively, across the wide distance between him and the American, afraid to get closer to the killer.

'Is this your knife hand?' Dr Holenbein asked pointedly.

'Nah, fortunately,' Cray replied.

Katrin stared at Cray.

'Can you take the coat off?' the doctor asked.

During the day, the doctor hid his baldness with several carefully placed strands. In his irritation and haste, he had forgotten to arrange his hair, and the long strands hung down one side of his head almost to his shoulder. His eyebrows were vast and black, covering a good portion of his forehead. His eyes were shallow and close together. His salt-and-pepper goatee looked carefully tended.

In a glass case against a wall was an otoscope, a blood-pressure gauge, and holders for thermometers and syringes and medicine droppers. The door to the stairs to his private quarters was in one wall. An eye chart was on another wall.

When Cray struggled with the coat, the doctor assisted, still maintaining a distance. Cray grimaced as the sleeve was slipped along his arm and the coat lifted off his shoulders. Next came the uniform blouse, stained dark brown on one sleeve and along the hollow of his back. The wound lay open to the light, the entrance hole on top of his upper arm, the exit hole below. Clotted bits of blood hung from the lower wound. A pistol was in Cray's belt. Katrin wondered where the knife was. Cray had prisoner's ribs, clearly defined, the skin sunk deeply between them. Blond hair on his chest was in tight curls.

'Sit on the end of the surgical table.' Holenbein glanced around at the blackout curtains, all in place, then flicked on an examining light. He placed a mirror on his head and leaned over the wound. After a moment he said, 'I must open the wound to abrade it properly. Do you know if you have reactions to anesthesia?'

'No anesthesia,' Cray said.

'I'm already impressed,' Katrin said. 'You needn't do anything more.'

Cray smiled at her.

Dr Holenbein said, 'I cannot clean and mend this wound while you are conscious. It needs to be properly opened – the wound enlarged – to satisfactorily rid it of dirt. Otherwise it will pus out, and quickly.'

'I can't afford to lose the remaining motion in my arm. Clean the hole as best you can without opening it any further, without tearing the muscle any more.'

'Mr Cray, I am better with a knife than even you, believe it or not,' Holenbein said magisterially. Like all Berliners, he knew Cray's name. 'So kindly do not tell me how to practice medicine. You need a general anesthesia, and a full probing and abrading of your wound.'

Cray said, 'Doctor, I'm leaving your office in three minutes. Do you have a bottle-washer?'

'Pardon?'

'Do I have the wrong phrase in German?' Cray asked Katrin. 'A long wire with bristles all around at the end, used to clean the inside of a bottle.'

'A bottle-washer?' Then the doctor's eyes grew small with understanding and amusement. 'You cannot be as badly wounded as I had supposed, making such a jest.'

'Get a bottle-washer,' Cray ordered.

'I have them here.' Holenbein lifted a wire bristle brush from a drawer under an autoclave. 'For test tubes and beakers.'

'What do you have to kill germs on a wound?' Cray asked.

'Alcohol is all I have due to the shortages.'

'Dip the brush into the alcohol.'

Dr Holenbein opened a jar of rubbing alcohol. 'I'm going to enjoy this little spectacle. I only hope your friend here,' he nodded toward Katrin, 'will help me lift you from the floor, where you will fall senseless from the pain.' He dipped the brush into the fluid, and brought it up again, the bristles dripping. He held it out.

'Americans don't use anesthesia.' Cray glanced at Katrin, his eyes alight. 'We view it as a European indulgence.'

Cray took the brush by the handle, and held up his wounded arm. He stared at the raw wound a moment, his jaw tight, the humor gone from him. Then he rammed the brush into the wound, through the wound, so that bloody bristles popped out under his arm.

Katrin thought she could see his fist shake, could see his jaw tremble. Cray plumbed the wound, just as if he were cleaning a rifle barrel. In and out went the brush, carrying clotted and fresh blood and bits of tissue and damp ash. Katrin studied him, looking for signs of pain or distress. His mouth pulled back, but only a little. Nothing more.

The American passed back the bottle brush. His words were serrated by pain. 'Sew it up.'

Katrin said flatly, 'You are an exhibitionist.'

Cray suddenly sagged to one side but caught himself on the operating table. He pushed himself back to his feet. He blinked rapidly, his teeth sunk into his lower lip. He held out his arm again. 'Sew it up.'

Dr Holenbein clucked his tongue. He lifted a needle and a vein of silk thread. 'I'm impressed, even if she's not.' He pulled the silk through the needle's eye. 'You won't need anesthesia for the stitching either, I would imagine.'

The room suddenly filled with glass and bits of plaster and splinters of wood, thrown about as if in a high wind. Jack Cray tackled Katrin and drove her to the floor before the sounds of the shots registered on her. A machine gun, two machine guns, outside the surgery's window. Cray was on top of her, then he was crawling toward the surgery's back door, dragging her across the floor like a flour sack. Beakers shattered. A wheelchair against a wall skipped about. Pockmarks raced across the wall opposite the window, then back again. Fractured cabinet doors flew open. Dr Holenbein fell to the floor, his trunk almost severed by bullets, blood spilling from him.

Cray grabbed a fistful of Katrin's dress and yanked her upright, still tugging her toward the rear of the room, between the medicine sideboard and the X-ray machine and into the back hall.

He released her. 'Through the door.'

In one hand was his pistol, and the knife had appeared in the other. The top half of the office's rear door was a frosted panel of glass. Cray shot twice through it, the sound sharp in the small hall. Then he shot two more times through the wood panel below. He threw the latch. He rushed out and she followed.

Slumping to one side was a Gestapo agent, two of Cray's bullets in him. Cray leaped down the steps and fired twice into a dark Mercedes sedan parked in the alley. The agent in the car had been trying to climb out, but now, new holes in him, he sank back, sightless eyes on the American. Cray used his knife as a grapnel to hook the agent under a rib and pull him aside.

He turned for Katrin, who was stepping to the car door, too slowly. He almost lifted her off the ground as he threw her into the cab. He ran around the front of the car toward the driver's side. The engine was still running. He slid into the seat behind the wheel, then stepped on the clutch and pulled the gearshift back, the pistol resting on the knob.

The sedan rolled away from the back door. Shots came from behind, one punching out the rear window and exiting through the roof. Cray yanked on the steering wheel, taking the car around a corner onto Hemplemann Street. More shots sounded behind them, but distant.

Katrin tried to breathe, but could not work her chest. Ninety seconds had passed since the doctor had held up the needle, prepared to stitch closed Cray's wound. She had not had time to be afraid. The car passed a shuttered bakery and a bank that had sandbags up to its second story.

Finally she said, 'You left your coat and shirt behind.'

He looked down at his chest. 'Well, that's one more damned thing I have to think about.'

She stared at him. That dumb American grin returned to his face.

He said, 'You do this enough, you begin to like it.'

Cray swerved around potholes.

'You won't be satisfied getting just yourself killed, will you?' she asked dully.

Cray glanced at his arm. 'Know where I can get a needle and some thread?'

'You'll get me killed, too.'

'I can sew this up myself. I've done it before.'

She persisted, 'I can't get away from you, can I?'

'And it's cheaper than having a doctor do it.'

A wall of rubble blocked an intersection, so Cray turned north.

He slowed the car. The sedan's headlights were taped. Little could be seen out the front window, shadows and smudges, mostly darkness.

'You are insane,' she said. 'I only suspected it before, but now I know.'

He finally looked at her, his smile fading. 'I'm good at what I do. That's not being insane.'

'You are good at what you do. But you are also insane.'

The smile again. 'I find it helps.'

'You are on the list, Inspector,' the SS guard said, pointing at a line on a clipboard. 'This man is not.'

'Wait here, Peter.' Dietrich handed his Walther to Hilfinger, then spread his hands and feet for a search. The moon was hidden by high clouds. British bombers had not made their appearance that night yet. Any moment now.

Hilfinger stepped back to look again at the mammoth concrete block in the garden. 'I think I'd rather stay out here, anyway.'

One of the guards checked his watch, then nodded at Hilfinger. 'You can step inside the blockhouse with us when the British bombers appear.'

Dietrich followed an SS guard past a telephone box and through the doors into the block. As he descended into the bunker, Dietrich felt his faith in his ability as a detective being shaken. He prided himself on his knowledge of Berlin. More than anything else, knowing the city's streets and alleys gave the detective an advantage over lawbreakers. And an advantage over fellow detectives, an edge Dietrich savored, truth be told. Other detectives knew Dietrich had better eyes and ears than they did. Friends and informants on those streets made sure that little in the city escaped Dietrich.

Yet here was an enormous structure – apparently the seat of the German government – that Dietrich had only heard rumors about but had never been able to confirm. Right in the center of Berlin, a short walk from his own precinct station. It made Dietrich wonder what else he had missed.

The guard led him to the bottom of the stairs, where two more guards started to search Dietrich, but gently, showing more deference than they did to Wehrmacht generals. At this point in the war, men possessing all their limbs and wearing civilian suits were doubtless powerful.

The escorting trooper turned back, climbing the stairs. One of the guards at the metal door must have seen the wonder in Dietrich's eyes because as he patted down the small of the detective's back, the guard said, 'It's called the Golden Cage. Or the Catacombs. Take your pick.'

'How long has this bunker been here?' Dietrich asked, spreading his arms.

'State secret.' The guard grinned as he searched Dietrich's coat. 'That and everything else about the place. You may go in.'

Dietrich stepped through a door that must have weighed more than a Panzer, must have been ten centimeters thick, solid steel. An SS orderly was on the other side of the door, checking his wristwatch as the detective entered.

The orderly said, 'One moment, if you will, Inspector.'

Dietrich stared down the hallway, recognizing people he had seen only in newsreels and on posters and in newspapers. Dr Goebbels was speaking with General Keitel. When Goebbels turned toward the hallway's rear door, Dietrich noticed that the man walked with a limp. One of his feet was turned in. The detective wondered if Goebbels had been to the front, and been wounded in the leg. He looked at the little man, with the slicked-back hair and choppy chin and terrier's eyes. No, never to the front. The minister of propaganda – the most visible man in the Reich now that the Führer had largely disappeared from public view – had a club foot, was born with it, and Dietrich had never heard of it. Again Dietrich was disturbed.

Also in the hallway were Minister Ribbentrop and a tall, hatchet-faced man Dietrich knew to be Ernst Kaltenbrunner, head of the Reich Main Security Office, who had replaced the assassinated Heydrich. And he recognized Friedrich Hatzfeldt, who had replaced Alfried Krupp von Bohlen und Halbach as head of Krupp industries when Krupp had been arrested by an American patrol a year ago.

Hatzfeldt was bent in conversation with Theodor Steinort, director of the Mariupol electro-steel works in Breslau. All appeared to be waiting. The hallway also contained a dozen senior SS officers and Wehrmacht generals Dietrich did not recognize, and a number of lower-ranking personnel Dietrich took for valets and orderlies. A high-pitched whine seemed to come from all directions. The air was dank.

After two primly dressed women carrying secretarial pads emerged from a door on Dietrich's right, the orderly at Dietrich's elbow pointed at the same door and said, 'Go in, please.'

Kaltenbrunner's eyebrow rose, and others in the hall turned to examine Dietrich, a man in plainclothes who apparently had precedence over all the rank in the hall. Dietrich walked into a small study, filled by a table covered with maps. Dietrich was alone with Adolf Hitler.

The Führer was wearing reading glasses, which Dietrich had never seen in posters or photographs. The detective knew Hitler was fifty-five, but he looked two decades older, shrunken, the skin on his face mottled. Hair hung down across his forehead, and it appeared greasy, needing to be washed. The mustache was uneven, bitten and dull, with speckles of gray. Hitler's left hand rested on a map, and it trembled with enough force to make the map rattle.

The Führer looked up. 'Detective Inspector Dietrich.' Not a question.

'Yes, sir.'

'Would you like some refreshment?' Hitler removed the spectacles and put them into his uniform pocket.

'Yes, sir.'

'Come with me.'

Hitler led the detective into a back chamber, a sitting room. The Führer motioned to a blue-and-white horsehair sofa set against a wall under a portrait of Frederick the Great that was framed by two ventilation grates. Below a grate was an oxygen bottle on wheels, its mask resting on the controls at the top of the bottle. Dietrich lowered himself onto the sofa while Hitler reached for a silver teapot. He poured tea into a tiny engraved silver cup, then passed it to Dietrich.

Dietrich sipped it. 'What is this?'

Hitler smiled. Never had Dietrich seen a photograph of Hitler smiling. The man had bad teeth, yellow with some green, and small.

'It is just as well you did not join the Party, Inspector. Asking what refreshment is being served is not the proper protocol, and indicates a dangerous independence.'

Was Hitler making a joke? Humor was a characteristic Dietrich had never before associated with the Reich's leader. And it was ghastly.

Hitler returned the teapot to the stand, grabbed his left hand in his right to hold it close to his body, then with a slight groan sat in a leather chair behind a cluttered desk. Near a lamp with a green glass shade was Schopenhauer's *The World as Will and Representation*. Hitler's eyes found Dietrich.

Found him with the force of a blow. Despite Hitler's appearance of age and infirmity, the eyes were blue, a milky blue, penetrating, yet at the same time warm and guileless. So powerful was the gaze that it was a presence entirely apart from the decrepit, ailing man sitting across from Dietrich. The detective felt pushed back into the chair by the eyes, and laid bare.

'You never joined the Party, Inspector.' Hitler's right leg trembled so violently that his boot danced on the rug. 'You would have done better at the Berlin police had you been one of us, had been one of the Old Fighters.'

'Yes, sir.' Was that all Dietrich could say? Didn't Hitler's comment deserve some caustic retort, an observation that the Old Fighters had caused Berlin to be plowed up and turned over? The words would not come. Something to do with Hitler's eyes.

'You noticed my leg.' Hitler patted it with his good hand. 'It shakes a little.'

'Yes, sir.'

'It's not from the bomb at my field headquarters, like everybody thinks. My doctor says I have a touch of the grippe.'

Dietrich had never heard of a bomb at a headquarters.

'But I don't suppose I need to apologize for my health to a Berlin policeman.'

'No, sir.' Dietrich's face warmed with anger. At himself. Hitler was deliberately charming the detective, and it was working. Two decades resisting the National Socialists, and now to be enchanted in sixty seconds by their leader. Dietrich fought it, and stared at the Iron Cross on Hitler's coat rather than into the eyes.

'You have been assigned to search for the American killer.' Hitler spoke with his lower-Bavarian accent.

'Yes, sir.'

'You missed him earlier this evening.'

'I didn't miss him. That was the Gestapo. Apparently they are running an operation entirely apart from my own. And, if I may say, they are interfering with mine.'

'It's apple-peel tea, by the way,' Hitler said. 'You should never drink real tea or coffee. They'll kill you.'

'I'll keep that in mind.' Dietrich cleared his throat. 'I wasn't informed that the American had been spotted again walking with the woman, and had been seen entering that physician's office. The information went to the Gestapo, instead of to me.'

'Well, they can be a bit aggressive.'

Dietrich again brought his gaze up to Hitler's face. Was this more humor? Dietrich quickly surveyed the small room. It was spartan. Little more than the desk and sofa and dresser and bed. A photograph of Hitler's mother was on the desk, and two telephones.

'You expected something more grand,' Hitler said, lifting a hand to indicate the room.

'I heard a rumor you believed in the occult, sir.' Had Dietrich ever said anything more foolish? 'I expected tarot cards and an astrology chart.' He smiled weakly.

'I allow rumors to spread if they are useful. If my enemies think the phases of the moon affect my decisions, all the better.'

'May I ask why I was summoned here, sir?'

'Goering sees things as an officer. But I see them as an enlisted man.' Hitler brought up a finger, indicating the silver service. 'I forgot my tea. Would you mind?'

Dietrich rose quickly, poured tea into a cup, and handed it to the leader.

'It's a little difficult for me to move about, with the grippe and all.' Hitler sipped the drink, holding the silver cup under his nose for a long moment. 'As I say, I see things as an enlisted man.'

'Sir?'

'Goering and many of the others want me to flee Berlin. I could never do that.'

'Because enlisted men expect their leader to remain in the center of things?' Dietrich was determined to add more to the conversation than a series of 'Yes, sirs.'

'And there's another reason.' Hitler again sipped the tea. 'I have nowhere to go.'

Dietrich said nothing.

'Our enemies believe we have a fortress in the Bavarian Alps, an enormous fortified redoubt where we will defend ourselves once Berlin falls. Where crack Waffen-SS troops are waiting. Where I will flee once the enemy appears at the city's gates.' Hitler paused. 'There is no such place.'

An orderly appeared at the door with a fistful of messages on paper of three different colors. 'My Führer. Dispatches.'

Hitler waved him away.

Dietrich was immensely flattered. And angry once again.

'Do you believe in fate, Inspector?'

'I've not given it much thought, sir.'

'One day during the Great War when I was eating dinner with other soldiers in a trench, I heard a voice in my ear. It said, "Go over there, quickly." It was so insistent – much like an officer barking an order – that I obeyed automatically, moving twenty yards down the trench. And just then a deafening report came from behind me. A shell had burst over my comrades, sitting there eating from their tins. All of them were killed. Fate spoke to me that day. Fate spared me.'

'Yes, sir.'

'I believe in fate, and my fate is tied with my city, Inspector.' Hitler lightly rubbed the side of his chin. 'I will never leave Berlin.'

Another small smile. 'And there's that other factor: I have nowhere to go.'

'Yes, sir.'

'Do you know the story of Leonidas at Thermopylae?'

'Of course, sir.'

'And Horatius at the bridge?'

'Yes.'

'The lesson of these great men is of the power of the will. The will conquers all.'

'Leonidas died at Thermopylae, sir.'

'Don't ruin my story, Inspector.' Another quick smile. 'The Reich's resources are diminishing by the hour. Yet my will must prevail.'

'Yes, sir.'

'And for that to happen, I cannot meet my end at the hands of an assassin.'

'Yes, sir.'

'As I said, Inspector, I think like an enlisted man. And here is another example of it. It would never occur to an officer to personally thank his men. But an enlisted man knows the power of gratitude. I asked you here to thank you.'

Dietrich stared at the leader.

One more smile. 'And to encourage you to work a little harder.'

'I will, sir. Work harder.'

Hitler struggled to rise from the chair. Dietrich resisted the urge to rush to him to help, to put a hand under his arm to help him up. What happened to those who dared to touch the Führer?

Using the seat back for support, Hitler moved to the desk. He opened a side drawer to pull out a gilt picture frame. He held it out to Dietrich.

In the frame was a photograph of Hitler. Dietrich gingerly accepted it.

Hitler said, 'My health is poor, Inspector.'

'Yes, sir.'

'It will be much poorer if that American gets near me.'

'Yes, sir.'

Hitler escorted Dietrich back into the conference room.

'Goodbye, then. And send Keitel in. My meeting with him won't be as pleasant as this one, I assure you.'

Minister Goebbels blocked the door into the hallway. He gripped a piece of paper in both hands. His smile was wrapped around his bony face, so wide it seemed to hang from his ears. He fairly danced on his one good leg. 'My Führer, Roosevelt is dead.'

Hitler's eyes widened. He inhaled quickly, his breath hissing. 'Roosevelt? Dead?'

'Dead.' Goebbels was trembling with the news, the dispatch shaking in his hand.

'By God, we are saved, Goebbels.' Hitler's voice rose like a storm. 'The Reich is saved.' He breathed heavily. The news straightened his backbone and put color into his face. He slapped a fist into a hand, then again and again.

Dietrich moved to step around Goebbels, but Hitler arrested him with a gaze. 'Detective, do you know of Empress Elizabeth? What her death meant to the Fatherland?'

'Yes, of course.' Once again Dietrich tried to step around Minister Goebbels. Christ, he wanted out of here.

But Hitler grabbed his sleeve. 'In 1761, Frederick and fifty thousand soldiers were surrounded by Russian armies.'

Goebbels added exuberantly, 'Frederick was suicidal, his armies were about to be annihilated.'

'And then Frederick's archenemy Empress Elizabeth died on the Russian Christmas Day,' Hitler said. 'Her nephew and successor, Czar Peter III, was an admirer of Frederick, and the first thing he did as the new czar was to order the Russian armies home. Frederick was saved.'

'The death of just one person can rescue a civilization,' Goebbels concluded. 'That's Frederick's lesson to us.'

Hitler rasped fervently, 'It was foretold to me, Goebbels. I have long known I would be taken up from these ashes. And now it has happened.'

'We go forward from here, my Führer.'

Hitler turned away, back to his study. Goebbels followed him like a lapdog.

Dietrich had been instantly forgotten. He stepped into the long corridor. Keitel's face darkened when Dietrich indicated he should enter Hitler's rooms. Dietrich was oddly satisfied by the general's reaction. The orderly escorted Dietrich back up the stairs, and out the blockhouse door. Dietrich stepped between the SS guards into the garden.

Peter Hilfinger was waiting for him. 'You returned. I had my doubts.'

'So did I.' Dietrich filled his lungs with the outdoor air. 'President Roosevelt is dead.'

Hilfinger chewed on the news a moment. 'It won't make any difference.'

Dietrich nodded. 'Not to you. Not to me. Not to anybody belowground in that bunker. Not to Germany.'

They walked away from the concrete structure, toward the empty fountain. The British had come and gone, hitting a neighborhood somewhere upwind. Soot and smoke carried in the breeze.

Hilfinger asked eagerly 'What's he like? The Führer.'

Dietrich stared at the framed photograph. 'He almost convinced me, almost had me.'

'What?'

Dietrich pulled at an earlobe. 'I don't really know what happens in his presence, but . . .' His voice trailed off.

Hilfinger stepped around a puddle on the walkway. 'What do you mean?'

'I almost fell for him, like some schoolgirl.' Dietrich glowered, then tossed the framed photograph onto a pile of gravel near the concrete mixer. The glass shattered, a tiny sound by Berlin standards. 'Like some goddamn swooning schoolgirl.'

Dietrich slid hangers along the pole in the closet. 'Cray would take a military uniform, if there was one. Anything on that? A husband or son in the military?'

Hilfinger looked at his notes. 'She was a widow. Husband dead fifteen years. So even if she didn't throw his clothes away, there probably wasn't a modern uniform here, something that wouldn't stand out.'

'There's some man's trousers in here. Civilian. So maybe he's dressed again as a civilian.'

Dietrich and Hilfinger and Egon Haushofer occupied most of the small bedroom, and they picked through the old lady's belongings, looking for evidence of Jack Cray's destination. During the night Dietrich's detectives had searched city records for Katrin von Tornitz's relations, and had found that she had two sets of uncles and aunts and two adult cousins living in the city, at least at the start of the war. The detectives had driven to the addresses, and all of them had been destroyed, reduced to piles of debris. Then the policemen had dug further into the records, this time at the Berlin Graves Registration Office, and had found more evidence of Katrin von Tornitz's relations, including a great-aunt who lived in the city, information that was waiting for Dietrich and Hilfinger when they returned to the station at three in the morning.

They had rushed to Dahlem, Dietrich wondering again whether the American was part of a feint, an intricate ruse designed to tie up the Reich's scarce resources. Sometimes Cray left an obvious trail. Other times he moved invisibly. Thousands of men and women were looking for him. Perhaps this was the American's only purpose.

The great-aunt's home was a brick structure from the last century, covered with vines, and still standing. It was dark – all Berlin houses were dark – but not shuttered. Dietrich had sensed they were too late and, after spending almost an hour approaching and entering the house, the detectives covering each other, Dietrich's suspicion had been confirmed. Dietrich had found a pair of Wehrmacht uniform trousers with ash and a few spots of blood on them. Cray had been in the house, and had already gone. Blood meant Cray was injured.

The Gestapo had told Dietrich nothing about their raid on the physician's office. He had learned of it from the precinct watch officer, who had investigated the clinic after the Gestapo had left, and had then telephoned Dietrich. Dr Holenbein had been a casual acquaintance of Dietrich. Early in the war their wives had volunteered for bandage-packing gatherings, and had dragged their husbands to the coffee klatches afterward. The doctor had once spoken of his brother, a professor of architecture at the University of Berlin. After the watch officer had hung up, Dietrich had telephoned the doctor's brother and had told him what had happened, and that the Gestapo would undoubtedly be rushing through the professor's door at any moment, casting their net wide and gathering in many innocents, and that if the professor and his family had anywhere they could repair to for hiding, they had better do so immediately. The professor had thanked Dietrich profusely, but quickly, and was frantically calling his wife to wake her before his telephone receiver was back on its cradle.

Dietrich stuck his finger into a blue ceramic washbasin. The water was cool and stained red. Cray had tended his wounds here. Small clips of sewing thread were on the washstand, and a needle. So the American hadn't been treated successfully at Dr Holenbein's office before the Gestapo arrived.

Hilfinger rifled through a sewing basket, then the drawers of a desk. 'Here's an address book.' He dropped it into a canvas satchel he had brought with him. 'And Christmas cards. A lot of return addresses on them. Maybe Katrin von Tornitz and her great-aunt have mutual friends, another place Cray might hide.' The cards also went into the satchel.

Haushofer fingered a miniature doll collection. 'You know why I became a detective?'

Dietrich answered, 'So you can lawfully snoop around other people's bedrooms?'

'Precisely.'

'You don't follow orders, do you, Inspector?' A new voice, abrupt and coarse.

Dietrich turned to find Heinrich Müller at the bedroom door, with Agent Rudolf Koder at his elbow.

The Gestapo chief stepped into the room. 'How long have you known about this address?'

Dietrich feared this man, but he would not let Hilfinger and Haushofer see it. In a level voice, he replied evenly, 'About an hour.

Rather than spend time contacting whomever at your office, I thought it best to rush over here. We were still too late, as it turns out. The American has been here, and gone.'

Koder entered the room.

Müller rose on his toes, a bucking motion, his hands behind his back. 'I specifically ordered you to report all your leads to me.'

Dietrich sucked on a tooth before answering. 'With Himmler's letter, I unordered myself.'

Hilfinger smiled at his boss's dangerous impudence.

So did Heinrich Müller, but narrowly, meanly. 'It is a lack of respect, isn't it, Inspector? You simply do not respect my organization, and this leads to a lack of cooperation.'

Dietrich idly rubbed his jaw.

Müller bit down with such pressure that his lips paled. A signal must have passed, but Dietrich did not see it. Nor did he see the pistol in Koder's hand.

Koder took one step toward Peter Hilfinger, placed the muzzle of the pistol against Hilfinger's temple, and pulled the trigger.

Hilfinger collapsed to the floor. Blood and bits of his brain dribbled down the wall above the desk. Koder swung the pistol toward Haushofer, freezing the detective's hand as it reached under his coat for his weapon. Hilfinger's perpetually bemused grin was still on his dead face. Blood snaked across the floor toward the window curtain.

'Perhaps you won't forget to report next time, Inspector,' Müller said pleasantly. He walked out of the old woman's bedroom.

Koder shrugged and put his palms up, perhaps a gesture seeking understanding, the pistol still in one hand, then backed out of the room, following Müller.

FIFTEEN

'Skin is just like cloth, isn't it?' the old lady asked. 'Just poke and pull.'

'Take it easy, will you?' Cray spoke through clenched teeth. 'This isn't as much fun as it looks.'

'Do you want me to sew you up?' The lady was cheery. 'Or are you going to walk around with holes in your arm?' She pricked his skin again, then pulled the needle through, the thread trailing behind.

Cray grimaced. He was sitting at the woman's feet, leaning back against her overstuffed chair. She was bent over him, legs to one side, the needle gleaming in her hand. The bulb of a gooseneck lamp was bent almost to Cray's shoulder. She worked quickly, professionally.

'Are you going to tell me how you got these holes in your arm?' She tugged at the thread, closing the wound.

'A bayonet.'

'Didn't your mother ever tell you not to play with bayonets?'

Cray glanced over his shoulder at her. She smiled with strong yellow teeth. The skin of her face was sallow, and was wrinkled like an elephant's leg. Her hair was too black – badly dyed – and pulled into a bun at the nape of her neck and secured by a red ribbon. She wore a shawl over a red print dress with ruffles at the neck. Her eyes were daylight blue and bright with humor. She was enjoying her work. On a lamp table next to the woman was a black Bakelite radio from which came a Deutschlandsender broadcast of Wagner.

The American said, 'You're pretty good with a needle, ma'am.'

'I don't want you to think I was always a seamstress, young man.' She again slid the needle into his skin. 'I didn't always make my living sewing the *Klamotten*.'

'I don't know that word, ma'am.'

'It's Berlin slang for clothes.' She narrowed her eyes at her needle, wiping off a drop of blood between her fingers. 'I once had a home on the Graf Spee Strasse, and I was a friend of the Casardis and Fürstenbergs, the della Portas and Meinsdorps.'

'Never heard of them.' Cray winced. 'Take it easy, will you? You're killing me here.'

'But when the bombs came, my friends all boarded up their windows and left the city. Some to Rome, some to country villas. Our family has been a bit embarrassed for a generation, if I may say, and I don't own a country retreat.' Her words were becoming clipped as anger rose at the unfairness of it all. 'When my house was destroyed – it was sucked off its foundation by a bomb blast – I found this apartment in Bleibtreustrasse. And now I take in alterations and repairs.' She yanked the thread through Cray's skin.

Cray yelped, 'Kindly don't take it out on me.'

'Before my society disintegrated, I was known for my table and my wit. Now I'm known for my sewing.' She stabbed him again.

Cray sucked wind through his teeth.

'What are all these purple punctures? Must be a hundred of them. And these stitch scars?'

'A dog.'

'Just one dog made all these teeth marks? Did you just stand there and let the dog eat you?'

'It was three dogs. The stitches are where they tore away the skin. I've got more on my buttocks, not that I'm likely to show you.'

'Not that I'm likely to ask.'

'You probably were going to ask,' Cray said. 'I've heard things about you countesses.'

She giggled. 'And I've heard things about you young Americans.'

'They are all true.'

After a moment she said, 'You must despise dogs now.'

'Not at all,' he replied. 'Those long little dogs you have around here, the ones that look like sausages.'

'They are called *Tekels*. The British call them dachshunds.'

'Little salt and pepper. They wouldn't be too bad. Served with some rice or potatoes.'

'Oh, you.' She slapped his shoulder.

The small room was cluttered with mementos from her prior station and evidence of her new one. In one corner was a Louis-Quinze armchair. On a fern stand near the chair was a bronze bust of the Roi Soleil. Four Dresden china parrots lined the top of a bookshelf, and on a pedestal table were two Augsburg silver candleholders and a candle snuffer. These suggestions of the Grande Époque were surrounded by the more common paraphernalia of the seamstress. A treadle sewing machine was under a framed portrait of Martin Luther hammering his ninety-five theses on the door of the Wittenberg church. Cloth scraps were scattered about the floor near the sewing machine. Colorful snips of fabric filled three woven baskets. A pincushion was on the armchair and another on the woman's lap and another on the table with the candlesticks. Bolts of cloth leaned here and there, some brightly dyed, but many were of the somber colors of the uniformed services. A sewing basket rested on the lady's lap, scissor handles showing above the rim. When she jerked the thread, thimbles in the basket clinked together, and Cray bared his teeth.

An ironing board was in front of the windows, which were hidden by blackout curtains. Under the board was an open box of spools of thread, arranged by color, light to dark. A pile of patterns lay on a chair. Beads of different sizes and shapes were displayed in two dozen small bottles. A headless wood mannequin stood at the end of the ironing board, a tape measure draped over a shoulder. KARSTADT'S DEPT STORE was stenciled on the mannequin's belly.

Cray looked at a pole suspended horizontally from two wires. Perhaps twenty outfits including Wehrmacht and SS uniforms hung from the bar on hangers.

She followed his gaze. 'Senior officers come to me to tailor their uniforms. Sometimes they never come back to collect them. Killed in action, I suppose. I've got a nice collection. You are welcome to them.'

'I might take you up on that. Nothing less than a captain, though. I have certain standards.'

She laughed, pushing her needle through his skin again. 'But most of my work is taking in women's dresses and men's pants. There's no food in Berlin, and so my customers are losing weight. Pleats in the skirts, darts in the pants. That's most of my business now.' She guided the needle into his skin again. 'Just a couple more stitches. This is going to leave a scar. You won't mind, judging from the looks of you.'

'Ma'am – '

'I'm properly called "Countess." Countess Gabriella Hohenberg.'

'Countess, how is it you know Katrin?'

'Her mother and I were friends since childhood. We used to ride together.'

Cray said, 'Katrin calls you "Auntie." '

'Just a nickname.'

'You aren't related?'

'No, but Katrin has known me all her life.' She reached for a pair of scissors. 'It's unlikely anyone would make the connection between her and me, if that's what you are wondering.'

'Are you still in touch with Katrin's mother?'

'She died several years ago. Didn't Katrin tell you?'

'She doesn't tell me much.' Cray looked again at his shoulder. 'I'm surprised you didn't use some fancy double stitch, make me suffer a little more.'

She cackled, and clipped the thread. 'You're a nice young man. I'm glad to see Katrin has found someone.'

'She didn't find me. I found her. And I'm none to her liking.' After a moment Cray added, 'I don't know why.'

'It's probably your looks.'

He smiled. 'That's it.'

'Would you like some coffee?'

'What's it made of?' he asked.

'Acorns.'

'I'll pass.' He picked up his uniform tunic. 'Can you repair this sleeve as well as you did my arm?'

She held the tunic to the light. 'Blood is hard to get out. And it's filthy. With what?'

'Soot, mostly.'

'I've got the cloth to make you a new shirt. Or, better yet, I'll alter one of the uniforms belonging to a dead customer. Won't take me any longer than it would to wash and dry and mend this one. You can borrow another shirt from that pile.'

Cray found a blue flannel shirt that had long sleeves. While he was buttoning it, the sound of footfalls came from the outside hallway. His hand touched the pistol in his belt.

A key sounded in the lock, then Katrin entered the apartment. Her coat was cinched tightly around her waist, and the shoulders were damp from rain. She was using both hands to carry a burlap bag, and was breathing quickly from hauling it up the stairs. She lowered the bag in front of Cray, brushed drops of rain from her shoulders, then pulled an envelope from under her coat. Katrin had received a coded message on her pack radio, an address on Kordt Street, where she was to find an envelope in a milk box, and a burlap sack near the box.

From the bag Cray pulled out three Tellermines, German antitank mines each containing twelve pounds of the explosive amatol. They were olive green, about a foot in diameter, with carrying handles. On the underside of the mines were antilifting switches so they would explode when disturbed. Also in the burlap bag was a canvas pouch, which Cray opened to reveal three blasting caps, a roll of electrical wire, and a battery.

'Just what I ordered,' he said.

Cray then used the countess's pinking shears to slit open the envelope. He pulled out the envelope's contents: three typed pages and several photographs. 'It's coded. More work for you.' He passed the typed pages back to her, retaining the photographs.

He sat back down on the floor to share the lamplight. He studied the photographs. One was an aerial shot of Berlin, taken from perhaps three thousand feet, showing the center of the city from the

River Spree on the north to Tempelhof Airport on the south. The runway was cratered. The second photo, taken at a much lower altitude, was of the Reich Chancellery – some of it open to the sky – and the garden behind it. A square blockhouse with two guards standing at each side of its entryway was clearly visible. The remaining photographs were of POWs, three of them. Each of these photographs showed a prisoner standing next to a camp guard. The prisoners wore Wehrmacht uniforms stripped of insignia. Judging from the guards' uniforms, two of the photos were taken in an American POW camp while the third one was from a Soviet camp. All three POWs looked confused and vulnerable.

Katrin pulled off her coat. 'Auntie, may I heat some water? I found a little tea at the market. I think it's real.'

'I've got the water, but not the heat.'

Katrin stepped around a basket of yarn and entered the small kitchen.

The countess didn't look up from the buttons. 'You look like her husband. Did she tell you that?'

Cray lowered the photos to look fully at the old woman. 'No. She didn't.'

'He was more handsome than you, of course.'

'Of course.'

'But he had the same size, same hair color. Same wicked smile.' She glanced hopefully at the American. 'I'll bet you had a way with the ladies, over there in America.'

'Not really.' Cray ran his finger along his chin.

'I'd guess you've some stories to tell about the American ladies,' she tried again. 'A fairly handsome young man like you.'

'I'll never tell. And don't try to break me. I'm too tough for that.' Cray returned to the photographs. The one taken from the greatest height had numbers printed along the top and letters along one side.

Katrin came in from the kitchen with three glasses of cold water, each with a sprinkling of loose tea leaves floating in it. The pages were under her arm. She handed a glass to the countess and one to Cray, then pushed a hassock into the circle of light near the old lady. She dug into the scraps in a basket near the countess's feet and retrieved the onetime pad. She sipped the cold tea, then began the transcription.

'I visited Philadelphia once, over in America,' the countess said. 'Did Katrin tell you?'

He glanced at Katrin. 'As I said, she doesn't tell me much.'

'This was in 1912. I was younger back then. Had fewer wrinkles.'

'I haven't seen a single wrinkle.'

She playfully tapped his arm. 'You do have a way with the ladies, just as I suspected.' She reached for her scissors. 'Your country does not have nobility, and so I was entirely uncomfortable there. No one with titles and, worse, no one who understood titles. I don't think I was called "Countess" once in all the time I was there.'

'How dreary.' Cray smiled again.

'That's why I loathe that little man with his tidy little mustache who has taken over the Reich Chancellery. He is not sensible to Germany's thousand-year heritage. He doesn't understand the courtesy due to his betters.'

'Some people think he's done worse things.'

'I met him once. Did Katrin tell you that?'

'She didn't mention it.'

Katrin was bent over the pad. She might not have been listening. Her pencil scratched at a piece of paper.

'This was back in thirty-four, when Hitler was still trying to present himself as respectable. It was at a garden reception for Princess Maria Metternich-Wittenberg on her return from a year in Cairo. I'm one of the few people ever to see Hitler in a suit and a Homburg. He arrived in a Mercedes cabriolet. The Brownshirts who had followed him in a second car weren't allowed into the garden, but Hitler strolled right in, hat in hand. He was introduced to me.'

Cray's eyes were now on the countess. 'What's he like?'

She returned the scissors into the basket. 'Nice voice. He could have been a singer, if he hadn't become a dictator.'

'Anything else about him you remember?'

'He looks directly at you when you speak. He doesn't look over your shoulder or look away. And he seems to be listening to your every word. Weighing it. His eyes are peculiar. They are compelling, curiously so, unlike any other eyes I've ever looked into. In fact, as he looked at me, I stammered out my "How do you do?" and could hardly get out my question about how he kept his hat on in the open car.'

'What else did he say?'

'Nothing to me. He moved along, the princess introducing him to other notables. I watched him for a while, though, standing near him. When a butler arrived and asked Hitler if he could take his hat, Hitler replied, "Take it where?" I laughed, but hid it behind my hand. I think he noticed, though. He glared at me, but only for an instant. He was looking for Prince Metternich-Wittenberg, the hostess's husband. I think Hitler wanted something from him.'

'What else do you recall about him?' Cray asked.

'Nothing, really.'

Katrin passed Cray her completed transcription. 'The Hand works fast.'

Cray read to himself a moment.

Then she asked, 'How do you think it came up with this information?'

'It took Colonel Becker's list of Chancellery workers we sent it, and compared those names with records it procured from the American and English and Soviet POW administrations. It must have taken a roomful of intelligence agents, sitting at desks, churning through documents.'

She leaned close to follow his finger on the page. 'And the Russians helped?'

'The Hand somehow managed to get Soviet cooperation.'

'What's your sleeve length?' the countess asked.

'Long.'

'That doesn't help. Hold your arm up.'

When Cray complied, she lay a tape measure along it. She nodded to herself.

Katrin's handwriting was large and looping, requiring a second page, which Cray turned to.

Cray summarized the message aloud, slowly, as if tasting the news. 'The Hand has found a second bunker in Berlin, under the barracks of the SS honor guard, on Hermann Goering Street, at right angles to the Reich Chancellery.' He looked at the photograph of the Chancellery. 'It's here, several hundred yards across the garden from the main bunker. The Hand thinks this second bunker is a backup, and says Hitler would probably retreat to this SS bunker were the main one knocked out.'

'How did it discover the second bunker?'

'POW interrogation, I suppose. Probably a German officer who has been inside the bunker earlier in the war. Or maybe somebody who helped construct it. It says here that the source does not think there is an underground tunnel connecting the two bunkers.'

'What's your neck size?' the old woman asked.

'Thick.'

'That doesn't help, either.' She looped the tape measure around Cray's neck. He was still sitting on the floor, so she had to bend low to read the measurement. 'You're right. It is thick.'

The countess lifted herself from her chair with a dignified grunt, then crossed the room to the hangers. She searched for a uniform tunic of a certain size. She pulled one out. 'Here's a colonel's. Why don't you just be a colonel?'

'I don't want a lot of people saluting me, noticing me.'

'I'll put your old patches on it, then.' The countess returned to her chair and began plucking at the stitching on a collar patch. 'You are going after Hitler, aren't you?'

Cray stared at her. 'I never said anything like that.'

'A man whose photograph is plastered all over Berlin – the Vassy Château killer – appears at my apartment with a pistol in his belt, and he receives photos taken from an airplane of the Reich Chancellery. You didn't need to say anything, but I know.'

'Well . . .'

'And I wish you luck. I don't like people glaring at me at garden parties. It's rude.'

'Well, I'm not really – '

'And I remember one more thing about Hitler from that day, from when he was standing there in the garden, surrounded by admirers. He is shorter than photos of him lead you to believe.'

'Yes?'

She added, 'So be careful not to aim too high.'

Cray lay on the dirt, the scent of German loess rich and close. He was at the edge of a woods, and was concealed by juniper bushes. Ahead was a clearing, then a chain-link fence. A pathway of beaten-down grass, made by patrols, paralleled the fence. The night was still dense, but the first grainy light of dawn was coloring the eastern sky. Cray could hear Red Army guns in the east. To the south the clouds were a soft orange, reflecting the fires from that night's bombing raid on Berlin. Clouds also hid the moon, and Cray could see no further than the fence. He had left the countess's apartment at midnight and had pedaled a bicycle four hours north.

He cupped an ear and closed his eyes to concentrate on the sounds of the night. Cray knew that sentries patrolling a secured area are usually noisy. He heard nothing. He opened his eyes. Gossamer strands of concertina wire topped the fence, glittering in the starlight.

With another look to the left and right, Cray rose from the brush and sprinted across the clearing. The links were too small for footholds, so he gripped the fence and pulled himself up, hand over hand. Cray had experience with razor wire, and knew if there was no time to cut it, it could only be ignored. But he had expected the wire and had not come unprepared. Using pliers to draw the needle, the countess had sewn heavy oilcloth onto the palms of a pair of black gloves. Cray was also wearing a black pea coat and black dungarees.

He reached the top of the fence and gripped the razor wire, his feet scrambling against the chain link. The wire was in loose coils, offering no support, so Cray spilled onto it, toppling forward, cart-wheeling over and down, the wires' sharp edges slicing into his arms and legs. He plummeted down, the wire slashing at him. His right arm caught in the snare of two crossed wires. He was jerked back toward the top of the fence. He braced himself with his legs jack-knifed horizontally against the fence. With his free hand he pried apart the wires, then fell to the ground, the wire raking him.

Cray sat there a moment, taking inventory. His dungarees were wicking blood from slashes on his thighs. The back of his right wrist was gashed, and both ankles were bleeding. He'd been hurt worse, he decided.

Cray rose and hurried on, bent low like an infantryman. When he crossed thirty yards of soft earth he encountered a second fence, this one with no razor wire atop it.

He had bantered with the countess about dogs. But since his attempted escape from Colditz, where the guards' dogs had set upon him, Rottweilers and Dobermann pinschers had become his nightly companions, and in those dreams Cray never got the best of them. He would awake, shaking and damp. Jack Cray feared dogs, as much when awake as in his dreams.

And parallel fences at a military base often meant a dog run.

The sound came at him from the north, a huffing and hissing, and a low rasp, louder in an instant. A churning, rushing rumble, closer and yet closer.

Cray leaped wildly, his fingers snaring the links. He yanked himself higher, swinging his legs to the side to get them away from the ground. He was too late.

A dog sank its fangs into his ankle and held on. Another dog leaped, its teeth slashing at Cray's calves, snagging the pant leg and his muscle, but then twisting and pulling away, falling back to the ground. Cray climbed hand over hand, the first dog attached to his foot like a bear trap. The dog bucked and arched, trying to bring down its prey.

Cray's hand found the fence's top bar. He braved a look down. Dobermann pinschers, two of them, one stuck to him like some ghastly new appendage. His foot was a flare of pain. The dog's eyes were eerily red, as if lit from within. Foam flew from its mouth as it jerked and scrambled with its legs, trying to topple Cray. The other Dobermann leaped and leaped again, attempting to find purchase somewhere on the trespasser's body, maniacally barking and howling and growling.

Cray kicked at the attached dog with his free foot, first in the head, to no visible effect, then to its lungs. The Dobermann grunted, but held on. Cray kicked again, viciously, using the heel of his boot, and it sank into the animal. Again and again he kicked. The dog loosened its grip, and Cray lashed into it again. The animal slipped off, crashing to the ground near its partner. The Dobermann instantly leaped again. Both dogs lunged upward, snapping their jaws, Cray's blood dripping down on them.

Pulling himself up, Cray lifted a leg over the bar, then slid down the inside of the fence. The dogs – inches from him but separated by steel strands – pressed against the links on their back legs, their fangs working furiously. One of the dogs had blood on its dewlaps, Cray's blood.

Cray drew his pistol and put it at that dog's head, aiming through the fence. Then he thought better of it and glanced up and down the dog run. Still no sentries.

Shuddering, he glared at the dogs. He whispered, 'You two need a little work on your manners.'

When he limped away from the fence, his ankle felt as if it were a bag of broken bones, pumping pain up his leg with each step.

He lowered himself to the ground fifty yards from the fence, in tall damp grass behind a tree. The wind was blowing idly from the direction of the dogs, so his scent would not continue to rile them. The Dobermanns barked and paced, staring in Cray's direction with their villainous eyes. Cray suspected the dogs had not been on guards' leads, and that no sentries were approaching. But he waited, his pistol in front of him. The dogs simmered and barked.

The night began to lift, pale blue light seeping across the land from the east. Cray gingerly touched his ankle. The sock was wet and warm. Puncture wounds. Cray didn't know how many. He rotated his foot. The pain was sharp, as if the dog was still latched onto him, but the ankle worked well enough. The Dobermanns glared one last time, then drifted away, back the way they had come. Still no sentries.

Cray rose from the ground and started north again, traveling between fir and oak trees, and over damp ground made soft by moss and decomposing leaves. He pushed through banks of holly and juniper that dampened his pants. He was moving well, and the pain in his chewed foot settled to a low throb, hardly causing him to limp. His boots had absorbed most of the dog's fury, he decided.

The woods ended abruptly. Cray stepped onto a field that had a double horizon. The lower one was grass, acres of it, surrounded on all sides by forest. A second horizon drifted above the first, this one white and geometric, forming perfect grids. They were crosses, ranging off in all directions, marking dead soldiers in the ground below. Cray walked between rows of grave markers, his damaged foot squishing in his boot. Flagpoles at the center of the military cemetery were bare.

As he crossed the graveyard, the carefully arranged wooden crosses and stone markers gave way to rows of unpainted crosses, many leaning in the soft ground, and many with crude lettering. These were the more recently dead. Then Cray passed several long berms, where dead soldiers had been buried together in shallow rows, without coffins or ceremony. Sacks of quicklime were piled nearby, several broken open, coloring the morbid ground with patches of shocking white. A horse cart contained a load of picks and shovels. The rot of corroded flesh percolated up from the ground.

Cray left the cemetery to enter the woods again, paralleling a service road. He came to the base's motor pool, four buildings that had been blown apart. Nothing remained but concrete foundations covered with blistered truck parts. Poles were at each corner of the foundations, and fragments of failed camouflage netting hung from them, idly swaying in the soft wind. The strike had been precise – perhaps dive-bombers – because the nearby ground was craterless and neighboring trees were standing and green.

For a hundred yards he followed the gravel road away from the motor pool, passing what had once been a gasoline and diesel dump, but which was now a hole in the earth. Here the blasts of exploding fuel had pushed trees back as with a giant hand. The concussions had stripped the trees of limbs and leaves and left them resembling a flight of arrows. Dawn filled the woods with fragile blue light.

Through the trees came a sharp yell, then another, followed by a volley of curses and then a shouted order. Cray recognized the voice. They were the same the world around. A drill instructor. Cray pushed aside laurel branches.

The parade ground was a flat expanse of gravel. On the western edge of the grounds had been rows of barracks, perhaps forty clapboard buildings, every one of them flattened by bombs. The recruits lived in tents concealed in nearby trees. Reveille had been sounded. Hundreds of recruits were forming up in lines and were being harangued by four instructors who ranged back and forth in front of them. The recruits were boys, maybe fourteen and fifteen years old. Their uniforms were odd-lot castoffs. Some pants trailed on the ground. The hands of many of the boys were hidden by overlong sleeves. Only a few wore caps. Some of the boys had red stripes down their seams, dress trousers reclaimed from some prior war. This was a new class, and the morning light was reflected by tears on some of the boys' cheeks.

Cray skirted the parade ground, staying in the forested area, stopping to study the map Colonel Becker had drawn for him. The base, near Schellenberg just north of Berlin, was the home of the Wehrmacht's Third Army. Through the bush Cray could see the camp hospital, its white wall painted with an enormous red cross. Ambulance trucks were parked to one side, each with a red cross on its roof. Beyond it were the ruins of an administration building. Planes had caught automobiles in front of the building, and their blackened hulks had been pushed onto a nearby field. A soldier was raising the national flag on a pole in front of the building.

Cray moved north through the brush and trees. Early in his commando training he learned that he was safer when traveling. At first he thought it was only because a moving target is harder to hit, but then he determined his reactions were better and his decisions more sound when he was moving. Cray was more comfortable and capable passing through the world than when anchored to one spot. Traveling seemed to give him an advantage, and he had never figured out precisely why. Maybe it was just momentum.

He jumped a creek, then the rotted remnants of a pole fence, indicating the land had been a farm before being appropriated by the army. Birch trees grew where wheat and oats once did. Though it looked deserted, Cray gave a wide birth to a tumbledown farmhouse. He passed a one-blade plow, rusting away and sinking into the ground. High in the trees a flock of starlings clicked and trilled.

The forest opened to a long rectangle of pasture. Cray stayed inside the cover of the brush, but edged close to the field. The area was about a mile long and four hundred yards wide. Bombers had mistaken it for an airfield, and it was cratered from one end to the other. So many explosives had fallen on the field that the remaining grass was in narrow strips resembling walkways between the craters. The bomb pits had gathered the rain and were filled with mud. Trees edging the ruined field swayed slowly in a light wind. A footpath of beaten grass lined the field on Cray's side.

The sound might have been a hummingbird. Sailing overhead, a soft buzz, east to west, and gone quickly. Then, chasing the sound from the east, came a flat and muted clap, the echo rattling in the trees before fading away.

Cray settled to his haunches behind an oak tree, a few feet from the edge of the cratered field. And then he began to disappear. Jack Cray did not believe in the mystical. His universe was well contained within the horizon of his senses. He was impatient with the inexplicable and only amused by the occult. So he could not explain how he could almost vanish. He was so silent and still that the trees and brush and damp ground seemed to soak him up, and he became part of his surroundings, more foliage than flesh. As he waited, he was invisible to anyone more than five feet away.

The low drone soared overhead again, a murmur so swift that it was gone almost before it registered on Cray. Then another dull report that filtered down the field.

The flyaway sounds told him he had found the right place on the army base. Cray waited, invisible in the bush.

*

Corporal Ewald Hegel lay on his belly on the straw mat, his chin against the rifle's checkered stock, his eye at the telescope's ocular lens.

'Don't let your face drift close to the scope, Corporal.' The instructor stood above the shooter, his hands around a pair of binoculars. 'The scope will kick back and cut your cheek and forehead to the bone.'

'Yes, Sergeant.'

'And can you feel the pulse in your finger? Look for the pulse.'

'I think so.'

'Wait until you do. Pull the trigger between pulses. Otherwise the pumping of your heart will draw you off the target.'

The corporal squinted into the scope. 'Yes, Sergeant.'

The instructor moved to a second shooter, who was also prone on a mat, a rifle in front of him. The sergeant bent low to correct the position of the second shooter's finger on the trigger. 'The side of your finger shouldn't touch the trigger at all. It'll nudge the rifle sideways as you pull it back.'

The second shooter replied tonelessly, 'Yes, Sergeant.'

Behind the prone riflemen and the instructor were eight other Wehrmacht soldiers, each with a rifle on a sling over his back. They waited their turns at the firing line. A second sergeant stood on an overturned crate, binoculars in one hand and a megaphone in the other. He was the rangemaster. He once had a proper tower for his work, but dive-bombers had destroyed it, and destroyed it again after it had been rebuilt, and all that remained of the tower was a pile of fractured wood fragments along the firing line. Near the rangemaster was a wooden box containing flags of several colors.

The targets were above the butt six hundred meters downrange. A cratered wasteland separated the shooters from the bull's-eyes. Corporal Hegel's weapon was a Mauser, but resembled the standard-issue Wehrmacht rifle in name only. The barrel was made of Norwegian steel – the entire steel plant had been barged across the North Sea to Germany – and was fully a centimeter wider than a regulation barrel. The wooden stock and grip – which snipers call the furniture – were also heavier than those on the standard Mauser. The weight added stability.

'Hegel, you've got a crosswind.'

'The rifle is clicked left two points, Sergeant.' Hegel waited, trying to sense the pulse in his arms. He thought he had it. He counted along with his heart, then brought back his finger.

The Mauser barked and kicked up. Snipers know that even smokeless powder smokes. A translucent globe of smoke trailed away from the barrel.

'I could see your finger fidget from here,' the instructor said as he brought up the field glasses.

Downrange, a black circle on a pole rose from the butt and covered the new hole in the target.

The sergeant peered through the binoculars. 'A wart. Second ring, six o'clock.' A wart was a shot that was on the white but touching the black ring. 'You've got a way to go, Hegel.'

'Yes, sir.'

'Let's rotate the pit, Sergeant.' The rangemaster brought up the megaphone and called out, 'Cease fire on the line.'

He brought out a red flag and waved it above his head. When, six hundred yards away, a red flag answered by crossing back and forth in front of the target, the rangemaster announced, 'The range is closed.'

'Hegel, you and Pohl are due in the target butt.'

As the instructor turned to his other sniper students, Corporals Hegel and Pohl rose from their firing positions, slung their Mausers over their shoulders, and started for the target butt, a journey they had made once a day since their sniper training had begun two weeks ago.

Hegel was eighteen, and graveyard thin. His camouflage smock – brown and green and worn over his field uniform – hung on him as from a hanger. His face was long and his mouth was turned down at the corners, and so his friends in his unit thought Hegel carried the world's problems with him, but in truth Hegel was just built with a mournful face. He trotted along, the stock of the Mauser bouncing against his hip. At this stage in the struggle, when Russian guns were in earshot, full kits were worn even during training. Under Hegel's smock were three stick grenades, an entrenching tool, bullet dumps, and a canteen.

Hegel asked, 'You think they'll finish with us in time?'

'In time for what?' Corporal Pohl followed in Hegel's footsteps toward the target butts. The path was at the edge of the range, wedged between the trees and the bomb craters.

'In time for the war.'

Pohl laughed. 'We'll probably finish our sniper training just as the Red Army gets to the camp. That way our unit won't have to be shipped anywhere. We can put our education to use right here.'

Roland Pohl wore his field cap back on his head, showing tufts of blond hair. He had tried to join the Wehrmacht two years ago, but was rejected because he was too short. He had showed up at the recruiting office again six months ago, and discovered that, as the Red horde got closer to the Fatherland, he was still growing or the Wehrmacht was lowering its standards, probably the latter. He was little taller than his rifle. His good cheer at being accepted into the army had not quite worn off. He also wore camouflage.

Walking along, the mud sucking at his boots, Pohl said, 'We're going to be ordered to do the impossible, you know that, don't you, Ewald?'

'What do you mean?'

'You and me and these rifles are going to be told to stop the entire Russian army. We'll be put out on the line to cover a Wehrmacht retreat, sure as anything.'

'Well, if that's our duty, then we'll do it.' Hegel held his arm out for balance as the path narrowed and he had to negotiate around the crumbling side of a bomb crater.

'We'll be put out there, given a pocketful of cartridges, told to do as much damage as we can and slow the crazed Bolsheviks for as long as we can, and then we'll be forgotten while our army retreats.'

The clouds above were broken, revealing patches of white spring sun. A crow wheeled overhead, its shadow climbing Pohl's back then speeding on.

Pohl went on, 'We might as well be submariners, for all the chance we have of surviving the war.'

'Didn't our Wehrmacht oath contain something about not complaining?' Hegel laughed. 'We are going to do what we are told and if that's – '

Ewald Hegel would never be able to recall what happened to him at that instant, would have no memory of it whatever. One moment he was chatting with his friend Roland, walking along the path toward the target butts, and the next he was kneeling at the bottom of a bomb crater, gasping for breath, his head feeling as if a grenade had gone off in it, mud dripping off him and splashing into the brown pool of water at the base of the pit. The corporal coughed raggedly, then wiped mud out of his eyes.

Roland Pohl was next to him, on his back, the stock of his Mauser protruding above the surface of the water. Pohl groaned and rolled to his stomach, then brought his legs up to try to stand. He wobbled, then collapsed to the mud, sitting there a moment as if taking in the sun at a beach.

Finally Hegel asked, 'What . . . happened?'

Pohl looked as if he had been rolled in mud. His cap floated nearby. After a moment he could offer an answer. 'The edge of the crater must have collapsed.'

'Then why does my head hurt so much?' Hegel pressed his temple. 'My goddamn head was hit by something.'

Corporal Pohl pulled his weapon out of the mud. 'The sergeant isn't going to like this, Ewald. Look at my Mauser. He's going to see the water and mud, and court-martial us. I'll bet the scope is ruined.'

Hegel pushed his hands through the mud, first in front of him, then to both sides. 'Where's my rifle?'

'Under the water, probably.'

'And my grenades? Where are they?'

They searched for several minutes, feeling their way through the mud. Then they climbed out of the crater, shivering, their uniforms dripping steadily, to search the edge of the range.

After a moment of looking through the brush and around the trees, Hegel said darkly, 'My rifle is gone. And my sticks.'

'It can't be.' Pohl brushed mud from his sleeves.

'Someone stole my rifle. Knocked me in the head and took my rifle and grenades.'

'We'd better go tell the sergeant.' Pohl carried his muddy Mauser by the stock.

'The sergeant is going to kill me,' Hegel said in a rough voice.

They walked back the way they had come.

'He's going to kill me,' Hegel repeated.

'Well,' Pohl replied, 'it'll save the Russians the chore.'

SIXTEEN

'Every time you show up here, you've got more holes in you.' The countess chuckled, staring down at her knitting. The needles clicked together rhythmically. 'You're like a big pincushion.'

Cray was sitting on a hooked rug, leaning back on his elbows. Katrin was bent over his punctured foot. A bowl of reddened water and a bottle of iodine were at her right hand. She held the foot up for better light, and probed a wound with a cotton swab dipped in the antiseptic. Cray's pant leg was rolled up. His right foot had six other wounds. He looked at Katrin, not his foot. Her ebony hair framed her face. Her features were delicate without being weak. Her mouth was pursed as she concentrated. In the dim light her eyes were wine dark. Her brows approached each other a trifle.

She said, 'I'm surprised you can even walk.'

He bit his lip as she dug the cotton into another perforation in his foot.

She looked up. 'Where did you learn to walk like you do?'

'One day when I was a baby I got tired of crawling.'

She slapped the bottom of his foot. 'That's not what I mean, and you know it. I saw you sneak up on that man, the one who told you he was a detective. You didn't seem connected with the ground. You were as quiet as growing grass. And moving fast.'

'I learned it in Wenatchee.' Cray's mouth pulled back with pain. 'You're killing me with that swab. It feels like you've got barbed wire wrapped around it.'

'I'll be gentle,' she said. 'They walk differently in Wenatchee?'

'My mother and father and I lived in the Columbia River valley, north of town. For those years between planting our first apple trees and harvesting our first apples, we were poor.' He hesitated, his eyes distant, settled now on a scarf hanging on the back of the door. 'I don't know how my parents made it through those years. No money, little food, never anything store-bought.' He looked back at her. 'Have you ever been poor, Katrin?'

'One winter we didn't go to the south of France because our villa near Cannes had been damaged in a storm. Is that poor?'

'How you must have suffered.' Cray stared at her. 'One Christmas I received an orange and a pair of work gloves, my mother weeping that it couldn't be more. That's poor.' He bunched an edge of the rug in his hand, fighting down a bolt of pain. After a moment he added, 'Because we didn't have any other food, I learned to hunt. We ate venison, pheasant, even bobcats, anything I could shoot. But I was still a kid. Eleven, twelve years old. So I'd also play games.'

The countess looked up from her knitting. 'I remember that winter. You all went to Danzig instead, isn't that right? Visited Baron Esten at his estate?'

'Games out in the wilderness?' Katrin asked.

'I taught myself to sneak up on animals. I'd move through the brush, testing the ground with each step, rolling my feet, crouched, utterly silent. I'd often get close enough to a deer to tap it on its flank.' Cray laughed lightly. 'You've never seen anything as startled as a deer that's been snuck up on. They don't like it. It offends their sense of how things should work in the woods. They'd bolt away, and I swear I could see them blushing.' He laughed again, then his mouth pulled down when she punched the cotton into another hole in his foot.

'The baron, he was a dandy.' The countess leaned forward to unroll more yarn in the basket at her feet. 'I had a fancy for him, I don't mind telling you.'

'Once I snuck up on a badger.' Cray held out his right arm to roll back a sleeve. 'It didn't take to the surprise too kindly. This nice little scar on my forearm was the result. I'm lucky I got away with my fingers.'

She worked on his foot, apparently lost in the procedure.

The countess said, 'And one day I counted the candles in the chandelier in their dining room. Over four hundred.'

'Now you tell me something in return,' Cray said.

Katrin looked up. 'Pardon?'

'I told you my family was poor.' He smiled gently, but his eyes were straight and untamed. 'I don't talk about things like that easily. Now it's your turn.'

Her eyes flitted around the apartment, searching for a thought. 'I broke a boy's leg once.'

The countess lowered her needles. 'You did what?' Her eyes glowed with the prospect of a bit of history of her best friend's daughter.

'Do you remember Freddie von Vietinghoff, Auntie?'

'The count's boy. A rascal, as I recall.'

'One day – I must have been fourteen – he put a ladder to my dressing-room window to try to watch me change clothes. I spotted him, and shoved the ladder away. He broke his leg when he landed below my window.'

Her hand at her mouth, the countess exclaimed, 'My Lord, is that how Freddie broke his leg? We all thought he fell from a horse.'

'I was mortified,' Katrin added. 'I thought I'd go to jail. Freddie might have been a sneak but he was also a gallant. I made him swear he'd never tell anyone, and he never did.' She looked swiftly at the countess, then back at Cray. 'And I've never told anybody about that little episode.'

'Not even Adam?' Cray prompted.

Her smile faded. 'Except Adam. Now you. I don't know if you deserve to know it.' She wrapped his foot in a band of cotton then tapped his toes. 'That's as good as I can do mending you.'

Cray stood to try his foot. 'Feels like new.'

The countess looked over her needles at him. 'Your foot must hurt terribly.'

The American lifted his shoulders. 'I'll be able to move about as well as in the old days in the brush in the Columbia valley.'

Katrin's eyebrow lifted. 'You'll just sneak up on him like a deer?'

Cray smiled that mad smile. 'And slap him on the flank.'

Sergeant Ulrich Kahr dropped a handful of potato peelings into the meat grinder bolted to the workbench, then turned the grinder's long handle. He grunted as he worked, cranking the handle around and around. Pulpy, mashed potato skins oozed out the spout and dropped into a wooden bucket. The bag of peelings was on the bench. He wound the handle and added more peelings to the feeder cup.

Kahr was searched each time he entered the garden and the Chancellery and the bunker, but only given a glance when he left them, just to make sure he wasn't walking out with the candelabras.

The staff took slops from the Chancellery kitchen. They dug through the wastebins and retrieved whatever was edible, took it home, if they still had a home, and fed their children with cast-off scraps. Same with the wastebins in the bunker. Halves of pears and apples, steak bones with meat left on them, coffee grounds that had only been used once, jars with fruit preserves still stuck to the sides that could still be scraped out with a spoon. Took them home in cloth bags. The guards would glance in the bags, see rubbish, maybe stick their hand in to make sure one of Adolf's paperweights wasn't hidden below, and wave them on. One time a guard said Kahr must be hungry as a goat, him taking home potato peels.

It wasn't hunger that prompted Kahr to bring home the potato skins and orange rinds and bread crusts. It was thirst. The sergeant could make alcohol out of almost anything. His still was in the goat shed behind his farmhouse, just east of the Havel, near the Hamburg road. The duty roster allowed him three days at home after seven days living in the Chancellery barracks and serving the bunker's generators and ventilating systems. Getting to his farm was harder with each passing week, with most bridges underwater and buildings lying across the streets, but Kahr always found a way, twice rowing across the Havel.

Kahr scooped the potato-peel pulp into a wooden bowl, where

he ground away at it with a stone shaped like a pestle, crushing out the liquid. Then he poured pulp and fluid into a bucket along the shed's back wall. He had nine buckets of various sizes, most used at one time for chicken feed or to carry scraps to the pigs. He had spotted two of the buckets among ruined houses on his walks from the city. Now they all contained fermenting mash. Three with potato peels, three with apple parts, and two with citrus rinds. Kahr had no idea how the Chancellery found oranges and lemons with the Allies now occupying the citrus orchards in Italy. The last bucket held assorted berries and jams he had scavenged, and whatever else he could find to throw in, including half a pomegranate. He called this the surprise bucket, because he never knew quite what the result would taste like.

He sat on an upturned nail barrel near his boiler, then brought kindling from the wood rack and carefully placed it on the fire. It wasn't a boiler, really, just a ten-gallon hot-water heater, but it worked well enough. The heater was held over the fire by an angle-iron contraption Kahr had fashioned using the vice on his bench. A pipe ran from the top of the heater to an automobile radiator, which sat in a barrel of cold water. Vapor from the boiling mash traveled through the pipe to condense in the radiator. Kahr had learned how to make a still when he worked at the mustard-gas plant near Cologne during the Great War. He and the crew maintained a still at one end of the plant, and were careful not to confuse the two products.

With the tip of his boot, Kahr pushed a few embers back into the fire. On the workbench were bottles and a bag of corks. Kahr drank much of his output, but he also traded it for food, something other than army food. Half a kilometer down the road, Widow Wenner would swap a bottle of apple spirits for a platter of doughnuts, which were at least edible, unlike the Wehrmacht variety, called 'sinkers.'

Kahr didn't know which gave him more comfort, the whiskey or tending the fire. It was a small fire, just enough to warm his corner of the shed and bring the mash to a boil. The fire demanded just enough attention to dull his misery. With his family gone – all his sons – he spent more time in the shed than in the house a hundred meters away. Every piece of furniture and every corner of the house brought back memories, so he preferred the goat shed. The place was lit by five oil lamps. It smelled of sour mash, old leather harnesses, and a hundred years of goats. The boiler gurgled in a satisfying way. Though he could not see the steam, Kahr could picture it drifting along the pipe toward the radiator. Slits of night could be seen through the walls, and Kahr sat there with his coat on.

The farm had been his father's, and his father's father's before that. The tools along the wall – the pitchfork and shovels and harnesses and scythes – were older than Kahr. The farm no longer had any animals. They'd all been sold off or eaten, even the goats who once lived in this shed. Nothing to tend anymore on his farm, except the still. He lifted a handful of straw to toss onto the blaze. Kahr liked the spurt of fire that resulted.

His head came up. He knew the sounds of this place, and he'd just heard a noise that wasn't of the shed. He pivoted on the barrel to face the door. Its hinges were as old as the farm, and couldn't even be looked at without squeaking. Had it been the hinges? No, something else, a wood sound. Someone stepping on wood, or tripping on it. Maybe out at the stack of firewood. Kahr listened, wishing for once the fire and boiler didn't make so much noise. He looked at the bottle near the barrel he was sitting on, wondering if he'd drunk too much. Then the noise came again. Closer. Someone outside the goat shed who couldn't see in the dark, and was tripping over wood or stepping on shavings, something.

Kahr rose from the barrel and lifted the pitchfork from its wooden pegs. The fork had three prongs, each half a man long. The wooden handle was shiny from use, years of lifting hay from the rick and tossing it to ungrateful cows. He edged toward the door, bringing up the pitchfork and cocking his arms. Anybody coming through the door was going to wear a pitchfork.

'Sergeant Kahr?' A woman's voice. Somewhere out in the night. 'Sergeant Kahr, may I speak with you?'

Kahr was silent. He didn't know any women except Widow

Wenner, and the widow wouldn't be out walking around his farm in the mud at night. And the widow had a frog's voice, a bass crackle. The voice outside the goat shed was young. And cultured. Kahr could tell in just those few words.

'Come near the shed,' he called in a gruff voice, trying to sound armed. 'Where I can see you.'

Katrin von Tornitz stepped into the circle of frail light coming from the shed. Her blue coat was tight around her waist, and her arms were out for balance on the slippery field. Her shoes were slight and cut low, and muddied, and her coat had shiny buttons and large lapels. Her dark hair was cut to her shoulders. This was a city girl, no question.

'Sergeant?' She smiled at him. 'May I have a word with you?'

'Are you alone?' Kahr stepped through the door to look left and right. 'What are you doing out here?'

'I've come from Berlin, and I rode a bicycle all the way. Can I come in out of the cold?'

'Into the goat shed?' Kahr lowered the pitchfork.

'Maybe it's warmer in there.'

Kahr glanced over her shoulder. 'You alone?'

'It's important, Sergeant Kahr. You'll profit by it.'

He hesitated, then said, 'Sure, come in.'

The sergeant led Katrin into the shed. 'It's not much, but it's better than where I serve my army time.' He turned over another barrel, then dragged it toward the fire. He brushed clinging straw and dirt from the barrel. 'Have a seat. Do you want something to drink?' He waved toward the bottles. 'A lady like you might not appreciate what I stir up here, but they'll do the job for you.' He sat across from her, lifted his bottle, and swallowed gratefully.

She shook her head at the offer, then said, 'Sergeant, I don't want you to be frightened.'

His chin came up. 'I'm not frightened.'

'Well, you are going to be in a minute, as I was the first time I saw him. As everyone is, when they see him.'

'Who? Who are you talking about?'

'And it isn't as if I had a choice to be with him.'

'Who?' Kahr glanced at the door. Nothing outside but darkness.

'The war has forced him on me. I wouldn't tolerate him otherwise.'

'Who?'

'If it weren't for this terrible struggle, I'd find his presence intolerable. My association with this man should not be held against me.'

'Who?'

From the shed door came a new voice. 'Will you just make the introductions, for God's sake?'

Katrin added, 'I just don't want you to be afraid, Sergeant.'

Sergeant Kahr had seen the posters in Berlin, and now he saw the man standing at the door. Terror lifted him from the barrel as if by the nape of his neck, and his face bunched with fear. He backpedaled, bumping into the boiler. At first he could do nothing but stare at Jack Cray, but then he scooped up the pitchfork and held it up, the points at the level of Cray's neck.

The sergeant glanced reprovingly at Katrin. 'You said you were alone.'

'No, I didn't,' she replied. 'But when I'm with this American, I wish I were.'

Cray said to the sergeant, 'This lady is nicer than she acts.'

'What are you going to do?' Kahr's voice was windy with fright.

'What do you have in those bottles?' Cray nodded toward the workbench where the glass dully reflected the lamplight.

'Some of it is schnapps. Some of it is vodka. And some of it, I don't know what to call.'

'May I have a drink?'

The pitchfork was lowered slightly. 'That all you want?'

'I want to talk.'

Kahr peered at the American. 'What kind of talk? The kind you did at the château?'

'About family.' Cray pushed the tines aside and stepped to the workbench. 'And what it's like to lose a son.'

Katrin said, 'We know your son is gone.'

The sergeant snorted. 'Not just one. All three of them. All dead within a year.'

'What's this?' Cray held up a jar of clear fluid.

'Made of apples. Apple peels and cores, actually.'

Cray sipped from the bottle, then sharply drew in air through his teeth. 'Could use another ten or fifteen minutes of aging.'

Kahr glanced at the pitchfork in his hands. He had heard tales of German commandos, how they trained and how rugged they were. And the legendary Otto Skorzeny had visited the Führer in the bunker, and everyone down there had talked about Skorzeny and his men, how they had rescued Mussolini. This American was much like Skorzeny, must be, with his operation against the Vassy Château. And he looked as tough as Skorzeny. Kahr decided a pitchfork was useless against the American, would have all the effect of spitting from a flatcar. He hung the fork back on its pegs.

Cray wiped his mouth with the back of his hand. 'Where I'm from, we call this applejack.'

'I tried to make it taste like schnapps.' Kahr returned to his upturned barrel. 'Sometimes I add spices to the mix, when I can find them.'

The woman was staring with disapproval at the American. Finally she said, 'We didn't come all the way out here for you to drink liquor.'

Cray took another swallow. 'There's a taste of lead in it.'

'From the automobile radiator. I flushed it out as well as I could, but the lead flavor is still there.'

With the bottle still in one hand, Cray dragged a sawhorse to the circle of warmth around the boiler. 'Drink enough of this, the lead will make you blind.' He passed the bottle to Kahr.

'I'm not going to live long enough to worry about it.' The sergeant took the bottle and brought it to his mouth. 'No survivors where I'm posted. We're all going to fall, right to the last man. That's what my Schutzstaffel friends tell me, not that they're really my friends.' He added happily, 'The Russians are going to kill every one of them when the Red Army gets to Berlin. I only hope they run out of bullets before they get to us regular army folks.'

'I ever tell you my father once made a barrel of this stuff?' Cray leaned back, bringing his feet to the fire to warm them. 'Tasted about like yours.'

'Yeah?' Kahr sipped from the bottle again, then passed it back to the American. 'I'll bet he didn't have the problems that I do finding yeast for the mash.'

Katrin cut in, 'What is this talk?'

Cray took another pull from the bottle. 'He'd use red delicious apples from our farm, in the state of Washington. Place called Wenatchee, right on the Columbia River. The best apples in the world, some of them almost the size of my head, their color as glorious as a sunset.'

'I used to grow those big red ones myself, between the wars. Right out there.' Kahr waved at a wall. 'Sixty-four trees in perfect rows. A lovely sight. But when I was called up into the army in 1943 – an old gent like me, so I knew the Wehrmacht was getting desperate – I didn't have the time to work the orchards. Prop up the apples. Do the culling.'

'My dad even had an apple press.' Cray smiled at the recollection. 'And I'd help him by turning the crank . . .'

She interrupted again. 'Two men, sitting around a fire, drinking, having a fine time, like in some beer hall. That's not why we came out here.'

Sergeant Kahr stared morosely at her.

So did Cray. He said to the sergeant, 'She's been a lot of fun, you can tell.' He passed the spirits back to Kahr.

'To business,' Katrin insisted. Her hair reflected the fire like obsidian.

Cray rubbed the side of his nose with a finger. 'You've lost three sons, Sergeant.' Colonel Becker had reported Kahr's missing sons to Cray.

Kahr nodded. 'No one to leave the farm to now. I can't think about it much. I . . . I don't have . . .' His voice was just audible above the crackling of the fire. 'So I sit out here in the goat shed.'

Cray smiled broadly. 'I'll give you one of them back.'

The sergeant's brow furled.

'One of your sons,' Cray said.

'That's a poor joke, friend.'

The American pulled an envelope from his jacket pocket. From it he withdrew a photograph. He held it up to the sergeant and said grandly, 'Wehrmacht Corporal Max Kahr sits in a Russian POW camp six hundred kilometers from here.'

Ulrich Kahr stared at the photo, his knuckles white on the bottle. 'That can't be him.'

'Look closely.' Cray smiled again. 'This photograph was taken within the past week.'

For a long moment the sergeant looked blankly at the photograph, unable to take in all that it conveyed. Then his voice was the ghost of a whisper. 'I was told my boy was dead.' Kahr blinked repeatedly, but he could not stop the tears. Finally he had to dab at his eyes.

Katrin said, 'We can get him released from the POW camp, Sergeant Kahr.'

'And returned to you,' Cray added. 'In a matter of days.'

Kahr was breathing quickly, the joy flooding him. Forgetful of himself, he swayed, first right, then left. Cray put a hand on the sergeant's knee, lest he might topple.

The sergeant intoned, 'You have no idea . . . no idea what my boys mean to me. . . . My last boy . . .'

'Well, there *is* one small catch,' Cray said, almost apologetically.

And it brought Sergeant Kahr up as if he had been snagged by one of Otto Skorzeny's grappling hooks. 'A catch? What? What is it you want?'

Cray held out his hands, palms up, a gesture of complete equanimity. 'It's nothing.'

'Nothing?' Kahr repeated.

Cray smiled again, reaching for the bottle. 'A small thing, really.'

Half an hour later they left Sergeant Kahr to his distilling and walked around his farmhouse, then out the driveway with pasture on both sides. The moon's shadow was dappled by the boughs of elms that lined the driveway. The boundary of Kahr's small property was marked by a stone wall. Cray and Katrin approached their bicycles, which were leaning against the wall near Kahr's mailbox at the main road.

Cray pointed. 'What direction is that?'

'West.'

'How can you tell?'

'See the orange clouds that way?' She pointed, too, but at a ninety-degree angle off Cray's direction. 'Berlin burning, a reflection of the fires. Orange clouds are our unfailing compass.'

Cray glanced east. 'Do you hear something?'

She followed his gaze. 'The wind.'

'Are there train tracks near here?'

'I don't know.'

He looked at her, an impish cast to his eyes. 'Thanks for the date tonight. I had a good time.'

'Date? What date?'

'You and me, sitting in front of the fire, having a couple drinks.'

She was brought up. 'That wasn't a date. And you weren't really drinking. You tasted his liquor, and after that were pretending to drink. I noticed that after a while.'

He kept on walking, nearing the bicycles. 'Then why did I have the most fun in two years, if that wasn't a date?'

'That was a . . . a business meeting.'

'You had a couple of drinks, you can't argue that.'

'Only after the sergeant forced them on me. He seemed so happy, I couldn't refuse his alcohol. I didn't want to spoil it for him.'

'And we were sitting in front of a cozy fire.'

She glanced at him. 'The fire was heating a still.'

'And the scent of spring was in the air.'

'It was the smell of old goats.'

'So it sounds like a date to me,' he said. 'You and me. A romantic evening in the Prussian countryside.'

'And we weren't even alone,' she protested. 'The sergeant was there, and once we made our deal, he did most of the talking. About old times. No, it wasn't a date. Nothing of the sort.'

'Sure it was.'

'Not at all.' She laughed.

'There. You laughed.'

'I did not laugh. I'm a war widow. We never laugh.' She laughed again.

'Sergeant Kahr's fire and liquor and hospitality. And my company.' He righted her bicycle and gave it to her. 'You had a good time for a few minutes. You're laughing, and that proves it.'

'I'm laughing because I'm stuck out of doors on a cold night in the middle of a war with a crazy foreigner. I never thought my life would turn out like this, that's for sure.'

Cray was suddenly sober. 'That sound. It's trucks, quite a few of them. Coming this way.'

Katrin turned to the sound. 'What do we – '

He grabbed his bicycle. 'Get behind the wall.'

The sound was louder. A low growl and a deep grinding.

Cray led her off the mud driveway and into the high grass. The stone wall separated Ulrich Kahr's pasture from the road. Cray lay his bicycle on the grass and lowered himself to his haunches. She put her bicycle down and knelt beside him.

Rocks on the top of the wall had spaces between them, leaving gaps like archers' slits. Cray peered through. 'I still can't see them. They've got their headlights covered. They're traveling at night so they won't be found by dive-bombers.'

The noise was now a rush of engines and treads, closer every instant, a mechanical yowling. Katrin gripped her coat to herself and leaned against the wall. A frightening sound, and she closed her eyes.

'They aren't after us.' Cray blew on his hands. 'An armored column on the move, is all. Moving west to east, so the High Command must think the eastern lines need shoring up.'

Two motorcycles sped by, then two more, and then several Horch scout cars, and then a dozen Opel Blitz half-track conversions the Wehrmacht had nicknamed Mules.

Cray rose to look through a gap in the stones. Then he leaned close to Katrin so she could hear him. 'This unit has been hit hard. Their equipment is a mess. Burn marks and bullet holes. Lots of welded patches. I don't see any spare treads riding on the tank fenders. I'll bet they left most of their equipment behind as junk. A couple of the trucks are towing scout cars.' He paused. 'And there's a Panzerjäger also being towed.' A tank hunter.

Next, several trucks with mounted antiaircraft guns rolled by, and then a dozen troop trucks, the canvas sidings down. Next came Henschel 6×4 trucks pulling tanks on trailers. The ground shivered under Cray. Diesel fumes rolled over the stone wall.

Cray said, 'Five tiger tanks. One of them has a turret that's skewed to the side, and showing marks of a rocket attack.'

The Henschels rolled east and were followed by two more motorcycle escorts. After a moment Cray gripped several rocks on the wall and pulled himself upright. The rumble of engines and treads faded in the east.

When Katrin offered her hand, Cray helped her to her feet. She brushed the back of her coat.

Cray shook his head. 'That armored column was probably once an entire brigade, and that's all that's left.'

'I feel sorry for Sergeant Kahr.' She tucked in her chin against the wind.

'He's lost a lot.' Again he reached for her bicycle and rolled it to her. 'Like you.'

'Do you think the sergeant will go along with what we want?' Katrin asked. 'He said he will, but do you think he really will, when the time comes? He's a German, and he no doubt loves the Fatherland. And he's taken an oath.'

'He wants his son back. Wants him back more than he wants life itself.'

Katrin pushed the bike toward the end of the wall. She stepped out from behind the wall and onto the road.

She said, 'And will he have the courage?'

The sound of the receding armored column had masked the approaching Kübelwagen. It had almost come to a stop in front of the driveway before Cray saw it. The squat vehicle was the Wehrmacht's equivalent of the American Jeep, and was manufactured by Volkswagen. The passenger – an SS officer in field gray – stood at his seat, gripping the vehicle's window frame with one hand and holding a Luger in the other. Once the vehicle was stopped, the driver pulled a Schmeisser from under his seat. The passenger covered Cray as the driver climbed out of the wagon.

Cray's cap was low over his eyes. He let his bicycle fall to the road.

The officer called, 'Get your hands away from your sides. Get your hands up.'

Cray lifted his hands.

The officer swung the pistol to Katrin. 'You, too.'

The officer and driver approached them. The Schmeisser's muzzle was aimed at Cray's sternum.

Katrin stared balefully at them. 'I'd heard this, but I didn't believe it until now. The SS follows army columns, looking for deserters. Shooting them.'

'Your papers,' demanded the officer. His collar tabs identified him as a Hauptsturmführer, the equivalent of a captain. 'Quickly.'

Katrin's voice was oddly calm, 'We were just out on our bicycles.'

'I will not ask again,' the captain said. 'Give me your papers.'

Cray still carried the documents manufactured by the Colditz escape committee. He moved his hand toward his jacket pocket.

Then the captain recognized him. He barked, 'Don't move, you.' He stepped forward, and pushed back Cray's cap with his pistol barrel. The captain smiled meanly. 'I'll be damned, Jürgen. It's the château killer. I'll be goddamned.'

The driver – a corporal – stepped back to better cover Cray with the submachine gun. 'Let's kill him now, Captain. It'll be easier to take his body back than him back.'

'Maybe the general will want to talk to him.'

'This American is too dangerous, Captain. You heard the same briefing I did. Stand back and let me do it. The lady, too, for all that matters.'

The captain appeared to think about the suggestion. He had a smooth face, with a nose as straight as a blade and thin, bloodless lips. He asked Cray, 'Do you have weapons on you?'

'A few.'

The captain laughed. 'I would imagine so. Get up against that wall and spread your legs. You too, lady.'

Cray stepped to the wall, spread out his hands, and leaned against the stones. Sergeant Kahr's farmhouse was down the lane, and was dark. Cray could see some of the goat shed behind the house, leaking strings of light through the siding. Katrin stood beside Cray, her arms out. She glanced fearfully at him. The corporal moved closer, his weapon roaming between Cray and Katrin.

The captain pressed his pistol into the small of Cray's back, then Cray could feel the man's hand begin with his boots.

The SS officer said grimly, 'Here's a knife.' He held it up to show the corporal. 'I wonder if it's the famous one, the one you used at the château.'

He continued his search, yanking Cray's pistol from his belt. He tossed it away, and it skittered on the mud road. After he had patted Cray's back, he moved to one side to rudely explore the crotch of Cray's pants.

'Nothing here you don't know about, that right, lady?' The captain laughed again. 'All right, get over to the wagon.' He stepped against the wall to roughly shove Cray toward the Kübelwagen. 'Get going.'

And those were the last words he ever said. The tines of a pitchfork emerged from the captain's coat, three of them in an even row, sliding out of him. He looked down at his coat, his jaw drooping, his eyes wide with the puzzle.

From the corner of his eye, Cray saw Ulrich Kahr at the handle of the pitchfork. Run through thrice, the SS captain lifted his gaze to Cray.

'Sir?' the corporal asked. Katrin blocked his view of Kahr.

The captain sagged. His hand tried for Cray's shoulder for support, but Cray was no longer there. He had lunged for the corporal. The Schmeisser was coming around, but not fast enough. Cray's fist hit the corporal squarely on the nose, the sound as loud as a shot. The corporal collapsed instantly.

Kahr had pulled the pitchfork out as his victim had fallen. Carrying the pitchfork, he walked along the wall to his driveway, then onto the road. He stood over the corporal. 'He's still alive.'

Gripping his fist in his other hand, Cray grinned at Kahr. 'The corporal's face is going to hurt when he comes around. As much as my hand hurts, if there's any justice.'

Kahr stared down at the SS corporal. The Schmeisser lay in a puddle. 'When he wakes up, he talks his head off about this farm, and me and you.'

'Yeah, well . . .'

Ulrich Kahr jabbed the pitchfork into the corporal, lifted it out and did it again, then again, moving the tines around, stirring the corporal's bowels like soup. He lifted the pitchfork, and blood dribbled down the tines. 'No sense risking that.'

Cray stared at him. 'Christ, he was just a boy. There wasn't any need to do that.'

'What were you going to do with him?'

'Well . . .'

'I just solved a big problem for you.' Kahr pointed the bloodied tool at Cray. 'I want my son back. We've made our deal. You go and do your goddamn arranging or whatever you have to do. I'll take care of these two bastards and their wagon. I might chop them up and turn them into liquor.' He laughed brightly.

Katrin and Cray walked their bicycles away from Sergeant Kahr. When Cray glanced back, Kahr was lifting the SS captain into the back of the Kübelwagen.

'You know your question?' Cray asked. 'Whether Sergeant Kahr will have the courage.'

She replied. 'Forget I asked.'

SEVENTEEN

'They match?' Eugen Eberhardt bent over the table. 'I don't see it.'

With a pencil Dietrich pointed at a portion of the photograph. The pencil trembled. 'Half a centimeter in from the edge of the heel imprint, right at the back of the heel. It's the trace of a nailhead. A piece of the nailhead is missing, so the imprint looks like a half-moon. The cobbler probably used the damaged nail because he was short of them.'

'And you see it on this photo, too?' Eberhardt adjusted the gooseneck lamp, centering it over the second photograph. He didn't wait for the detective's answer. 'Now I see it. Looks like the same imprint, same nail print. Just like you say.'

'The first photograph was taken near Katrin von Tornitz's destroyed home, near the spot Jack Cray had his little chat with me. The second photograph was taken at the rifle range, where those two snipers were attacked.'

'And you're sure that the rifle is missing?' Eberhardt lowered himself to a folding chair. The truck was cramped, and his knees were pressed against a metal cabinet.

'On my instructions, Third Army military police turned the camp upside down. That boy's rifle is gone. And so are his three grenades. Two of them were TNT, and one was a smoke grenade.' Next to Dietrich was a leather rifle case.

'We almost missed this, Inspector.' Eberhardt pinched the bridge of his nose.

Dietrich nodded. He grabbed the table edge with both hands. Since witnessing Peter Hilfinger's murder, he had been unable to keep his hands from shaking. His old fear – his constant companion in his prison cell – had returned with such force that it was overwhelming the grief he should have felt for Peter's loss. Sorrow could not surface through Dietrich's fear, and he was again ashamed of his weakness. Eberhardt had expressed his sympathy, and was now doing Dietrich the service of being briskly professional to keep Dietrich's mind on the job at hand.

'You know, there was a time when hardly a bullet could disappear in Germany without my learning of it', Eberhardt said. 'It was my job to make sure that the tools of assassination were accounted for. My office knew where everything was, and when weapons or ammunition or explosives disappeared under mysterious circumstances, I learned of it immediately.'

'The war has changed that, I suppose.' Dietrich leaned against a bank of radio equipment.

Eberhardt and Dietrich were inside a Funkwagen, a mobile command post built for the military services by Volkswagen. The vehicle was twelve feet long, and squat, with two rod antennas and a bedstead aerial attached to its roof. An RSD radio operator was also in the cargo bay, hovering over an array of dials and switches, his face reflecting the green light from the instruments. A faint cackle came from a radio speaker. Behind him a fire extinguisher was hung above a gas-mask case. Eberhardt sat at the metal table, where a rim prevented documents or other items from sliding off when the vehicle turned tight corners. On one wall was a converted wrought-iron wine rack filled with rolled maps. Near Eberhardt's elbow was a microphone on a hook, connected to loudspeakers on the roof. A sawed-off shotgun was mounted on the back door near the handle. On another wall was a clipboard containing a cordoning-off order. Like an armored car, the Funkwagen had rifle slits cut into its sides and rear door. Behind the radio operator was a bulletproof window through which the driver's head could be seen. Eberhardt's office on Potsdamer Platz had been destroyed the night before, and he had been promised a new one – somewhere – by noon. Until then the RSD director would conduct his business in the Funkwagen.

'With the war going the way it is, rifles disappear all the time,' he said. 'So do machine guns. Even explosives, trucks of them. There's no way to track it all down anymore. And so I'm not protecting the Führer as well as I once did. So the Third Army's General Epp telephoning me was just luck. And I contacted you immediately.'

'There's something else we found out from Jack Cray's prints at the firing range,' Dietrich said. 'He was limping as he crossed the base, from the fence to the firing range. He had been hurt.'

'How do you know?'

'We found some blood – quite a lot of blood – where Cray climbed the base's second fence. Paw prints showed that the patrol dogs were in a frenzy there. From Cray's boot prints, my tracker determined that after Cray was inside the second fence he was favoring his right foot. So one of the dogs must have gotten hold of the American's foot or leg as he was going over the fence. But that's not the point I find interesting.'

'No?'

'My tracker found Cray's prints again as Cray was leaving the base, by then carrying the sniper rifle, we believe.'

'Who is your tracker?'

'Senior Hunting Master Werner Eismann, who is in charge of the Schleswig-Holstein forest preserve north of Hamburg, near the village of Volsemenhusen. He is employed by the Office of the Forest Master.'

'One of Goering's subordinates?' Eberhardt asked skeptically.

'But competent. I've worked with Eismann for years. He could track a man across a pavement three days later. Eismann thinks Cray was injured by one of the Dobermanns. He was limping badly. Then, a while later, when he's leaving the base, he's not limping at all.'

'You sure those were Cray's prints leaving the base?'

'Same boots with the odd nail. And everybody walks a little differently, Eismann tells me. These tracks had the same distance between steps. Same gait, rolling a certain way. Eismann swears it's the same man. But Cray's limp goes away as he walks.'

'So what do you make of it?'

Dietrich chewed on his lower lip a moment. 'I saw the wound on Cray's arm.'

'When he was giving you that affectionate bear hug?' Eberhardt laughed.

'You laugh because it wasn't you,' Dietrich said bitterly. 'The château killer's knife under your chin, him casually deciding whether you are going to meet God today.'

Eberhardt flicked his fingers by way of apology. 'So what about the wound in his arm?'

'It was a bad one, a gaping hole put there by a bayonet. It would've meant time in a hospital for any soldier. And I'd bet his foot was hurt just as badly by those Dobermanns.' Dietrich leaned against a panel that contained dials and switches for the generator. 'And we know from interviewing the Colditz commandant that Cray was severely injured trying to escape. Dogs got him there, too. And Cray refused a stay in the castle's hospital. After he was cleaned out and sewn up, he went straight to the isolation cell.'

'So you have concluded that Cray is tough. I already knew that.'

'It is more than being tough. I believe the American is indifferent to pain.'

'How is that possible?'

'I don't know,' Dietrich replied. 'But I've met one or two people like that. Criminals. They don't allow pain to affect them. Nor bad weather, nor being tired, nor being under the pressure of being hunted. All they care about is reaching their goal.'

General Eberhardt ran his hand along the metal table, flicking away unseen dust, his expression hard with thought. 'That's bad news for us, Otto.'

'And here's more bad news.' Dietrich unbuttoned the rifle case to bring out a rifle with a scope mounted on it. 'The base commander loaned me this Mauser. It's identical to the one Jack Cray took off the young sniper.' He passed the rifle to General Eberhardt, then said, 'I don't know whether Jack Cray is a trained marksman. But even an average shooter has a range of five hundred meters with this weapon, and with any training at all, his range would be seven or eight hundred meters.'

Eberhardt's expression suggested that perhaps his boots were too tight. 'Do you realize how vastly more complicated my job has become, with Cray having a sniper's rifle . . .'

The general was interrupted by the sudden blare of an air-raid siren on a pole just outside the Funkwagen. Even though the vehicle was armored with steel plate, the noise filled the cabin.

Eberhardt muttered, 'Goddamn, I get sick of this, every day and every night, never failing, as regular as the postman. Let's go.' He reached over to the bulletproof window to signal to the driver to follow them, then opened the Funkwagen's door.

The vehicle was parked near the Stadtmitte U-Bahn station. Dietrich and Eberhardt and the RSD driver and radio operator joined the flow of people heading for the subway entrance. Berliners poured out of office buildings and shops. The office workers and military personnel walked without panic, but steadily, converging on the subway station. The station was near the government quarter, and many who converged on the subway station carried briefcases and notebooks with them, intending to work during the air raid. Turnstiles had been removed at the entrance so as not to impede the foot traffic. In a stream of people Dietrich and Eberhardt descended the stairs and entered the long concrete cavern.

Four yellow subway cars were already parked next to the platform, the drivers having been alerted of the impending raid by signal lights in the tunnel. Earlier in the struggle dozens of benches had been brought belowground, and many iron double cots, manufactured especially for air-raid shelters, were against the gray wall, hiding the advertising billboards. People checked their wristwatches. British raids lasted forty-five minutes. The Americans took much longer, the raids often two or three hours, which many Berliners viewed as a glimpse of the American character, spending all the time necessary to make sure they killed you properly. No sense hurrying such a task.

Dietrich found a place on a bench, then ceded it to an elderly woman wearing a scarf around her head. She smiled at him with gray teeth. He leaned against a wall next to Eberhardt. No deference was paid to Eberhardt's uniform. No salutes, no one offering space on a bench, not when there were probably twenty generals in the station, and not with the war going so poorly.

Lights on the ceiling cast the station in an amber glow. Many of Berlin's children had been taken to the country, but a few were underground, running around, treating the raid as a recess from school. A lady near Dietrich breastfed her infant, the baby's head hidden by a scarf. Office workers sat in circles, speaking in low tones, anxiously glancing at the ceiling, as if they could detect the approach of the bombers through the concrete and earth. A Kriegsmarine captain in a blue reefer jacket with four gold stripes on each sleeve walked along the platform.

'There aren't any boats left in the navy,' Eberhardt said under his breath. 'I wonder what that captain does to earn his pay.'

Dietrich chuckled, liking the RSD general.

Both men stared for a while at a striking brunette in a Luftwaffe Signals Auxiliary uniform. The navy captain had also let his eyes settle on her.

Eberhardt said, 'You know, in a way, I owe you for my son's life.'

Dietrich's back was pressed against the station's chilled wall. He stood upright to get away from the cold. 'I'd be interested in learning how you figure that.'

'My boy – his name is Ritter – used to follow your exploits in the Berlin newspapers. He'd read about some ghastly crime, and your capture of the perpetrator. He followed your career with some relish. And he became a policeman, maybe due to your unwitting influence. He is now a police officer at the Prenzlauer precinct. So he has been spared the front lines.'

Dietrich shook his head. 'Don't know him. But I'll accept your thanks, however faulty your logic.' He hesitated, then added, 'And in return I'll ask a favor.'

'Sure.'

'Can you get Müller off my back? Him and one of his agents, an idiot named Koder?'

Eberhardt took a long breath. 'Otto, I've got my own problems with Müller. Severe problems. I'll try, but I don't think there's much I can do.'

Dietrich rubbed his hands together. The station was colder than the Berlin streets. He said softly, 'I'm afraid of Müller.'

'So am I,' Eberhardt admitted after a moment. 'You met with the Führer. Talked with him personally. You've got Hitler's ear, sort of. Doesn't that make Müller hesitate?'

'Not that I've seen.' Dietrich searched for a handkerchief in a pocket, but found none. He sniffed loudly. 'Hitler thanked me, sure. But maybe he also wants me to still be terrified of the Gestapo.'

The walls abruptly shifted, then shivered. Bombs were falling. The station fell silent, except for a distant rumble that was fed into the station from the subway tubes. Berlin was built on alluvial sand, and so bombs had a rippling side effect through the earth. These explosives might be falling a kilometer away. The platform bucked, and people grabbed bunks and signposts and walls for support. Mortar dust fell from ceiling cracks, and in a few places water began seeping down the walls. Women hugged their children. Some Berliners stared at the ceiling, holding their hands up against the dust. Others closed their eyes, grimacing. The sounds coming from the subway tunnels eerily changed pitch and timbre. The smell of cordite drifted from the tunnels into the station, mixing with the scents of concrete dust and oiled railroad ties.

Eberhardt asked, 'Did you know that in America underarm deodorant is advertised on the radio?'

The detective looked at him. 'Really?' He pondered that a moment, then said, 'Well, they sure make good bombs.'

The long moments passed, Dietrich with his hands jammed into his pants pockets, staring at the back of a bench, watching it tremble. Finally the quivering stopped, and a few minutes later the all-clear sounded from speakers on the wall. Berliners rose from the floor and the benches and cots and surged toward the exits. Dietrich again followed General Eberhardt, swept along by people desperate to leave the tomb of the subway and return to whatever was left aboveground.

Dietrich and Eberhardt stepped through the doors into a cloud of smoke and ash that hid buildings fifty meters away. The government quarter had not been hit – no new debris or fires – but it was downwind of today's target. The smoke was harsh in the detective's throat. He walked toward the Funkwagen, squinting to keep the drifting ash out of his eyes, almost running into a fire hydrant that emerged from the smoke. The sky was so low he could not see the tops of lampposts. Ash the size of envelopes curled out of the sky. The sharp scents of high explosives and ruptured sewage lines carried in the breeze.

From the haze came the sound of an automobile's worn brakes, metal on metal, or so it sounded to Dietrich. Then it came again, an agonized wail, more a bleating, and so out of place among the ruins that the detective could not identify it. A vast patch of the haze shifted, and then was pushed aside by a mammoth presence. A trunk and tusks formed out of the smoke, then the rest of the elephant, moving fast, throwing one enormous foot out in front of the other.

Even though the animal was more than fifty meters from them, Dietrich and Eberhardt jumped back. Wisps of smoke trailed behind the animal like the wake from a boat. The elephant bleated again, at once fierce and pitiful.

'It's Fritzi, from the Tiergarten Zoo,' Dietrich said. 'He's gotten out of his pen.'

'Goddamn it, he's been hurt.' Eberhardt stepped toward the elephant, as if he could help it, but the creature continued to run, first one way, then the next, perhaps looking for its tormentor, or looking for help.

A gash the size of a door was open on the elephant's side, running diagonally from the shoulder behind his ear down to his hind leg. White ribs were visible, and torn muscles, and blood was gushing from the elephant, leaving a wide trail. Fritzi bleated again and again.

'My boy and I used to feed Fritzi peanuts,' Dietrich said emptily. 'Damn it to hell.'

'My children and I did the same thing,' Eberhardt said. 'Everyone in the city did.'

The same bomb that had ripped open Fritzi's pen had ripped open Fritzi. The elephant had been running in fright and pain for blocks, but was now at its end. It lurched against an automobile, righted itself, and raised its trunk to cry out. It sank slowly and ponderously on its front legs, shuddered, and then toppled onto its side. Its huge chest rose and fell once, and then the animal was still.

Emerging from the veil of smoke and ash, Berliners gathered around the animal. Fritzi had been the star attraction of the Berlin zoo for twenty years, a favorite of Berliners. Now the terror flyers had killed it. Men and women began to weep openly, and gently touched the giant animal, trying to comfort it in death.

Dietrich touched the dampness at the corner of his eye. He said quietly, 'It's not like losing your wife, is it? A dumb zoo elephant.'

Eberhardt stared sadly at the elephant. 'This'll all be over soon. All of this destruction.'

The detective glanced at Eberhardt. 'Are you and I lengthening the war or shortening it, General? By trying to catch Jack Cray.'

'That's not for us to worry about, Otto.' Eberhardt turned toward the Funkwagen. 'We've been told to catch Cray, and that's what we'll do.'

'You don't look any better as a brunet,' Katrin said, her arm in his, leaning into him as if guiding him along the sidewalk. A scarf hid her hair and much of her face.

'I used up all the countess's dye on my hair and eyebrows.' Cray adjusted the bandage that hid the right side of his face.

He was wearing a Wehrmacht officer's uniform borrowed from the countess. A corner of the bandage was fitted under his peaked hat. Smoke rose from the block ahead of them, and in the east was a wide smoke column.

She said, 'You've had practice with a cane, looks like.'

Cray limped along, using a black walking stick and favoring his right leg. 'I broke my foot once.'

'How?'

'Trying to kick down a door. My foot broke instead of the door. I learned my lesson.'

'You learned a lesson?' A trace of amusement was in her voice.

'I'm encouraged. I don't suppose the lesson was to renounce all violence and to live in peace.'

He looked at her. 'The lesson was to use explosives on a door, not my foot.'

She pursed her lips. 'I keep forgetting who I'm talking with.'

They walked by an automobile turned over on its back like a turtle and stepped around a fresh bomb crater, then avoided a newly killed dog – the carcass had not been taken away for someone's dinner – and rounded a corner to come upon an apartment house that had collapsed in on itself. Across the street from it was a burning row house. Two pumper trucks were in the street, and firemen were rigging nozzles to a hydrant. They wore Prussian-blue greatcoats, and their helmets had polished metal combs centered on top and leather flaps that hung to their shoulders.

The east end of the row house had been hit by a bomb, and was fractured and exposed to the street. Fire was bubbling up through the windows, and quickly eating its way toward the neighboring house. A wall collapsed inside the house, sending a cloud of black dust and sparks out shattered bay windows onto the street. Flames crawled beneath the overhang. Smoke curled skyward. At the coner was a telephone pole with a poster showing Jack Cray's face.

'The rest of the homes and stores along the street weren't hit,' Katrin said. 'Just those two.'

'Maybe these stray bombs were jammed in the plane's bomb bay, and were kicked loose by one of the crewmen.'

Her voice was dark with resentment. 'I'd hate to have one of your planes return to England with unused bombs.'

A Borgward 4×4 rolled down the street to stop near a pumper. Painted on the olive door was TECHNISCHE NOTHILFE. The canvas flap was pushed aside and six men in off-white herringbone uniforms spilled out of the truck's cargo bay. Several carried axes and mauls. Another opened a tool chest mounted behind the driver's door and brought out bolt cutters with handles the length of his legs. One of these men conferred with a fireman, who pointed at the house, then moved his hands in measured gestures, perhaps indicating the movement of the fire.

'Who are those men in the white uniforms?' Cray asked as he led Katrin across shattered glass.

'They call themselves the TeNo. Everybody else calls them the Rescue Squad.'

The TeNo workers wore black berets and black belts that cinched in the white tunic. The white pants were loose and made of rough drill material, and stained from earlier rescues. Black cuff titles identifying the unit were on the left sleeves.

The TeNo men entered the home next to the burning unit. The fireman at the hydrant cursed, then spun the nozzle off the spigot. Bombs had disrupted the mains, so there was no water to be had. He dragged the hose back to the pumper to attach it to the outlet. The truck's tank carried four thousand liters of water. It would not last long. The fireman checked the pressure gauges, then pushed back the hose bed tarp to reach for more hose.

When Cray stopped to watch, and resisted Katrin's trying to pull him along by the arm, she said, 'Honest to God, you are a child. Stopping to gaze at a fire.'

He replied, 'I rarely see one I didn't start.'

The muffled roar of a collapsing ceiling came from the burning building, then the squeal of timbers wrenched down by the weight of debris. Two TeNo men ran out of the neighboring building, chased by a swirling smoke cloud. They yelled at their supervisor – the only TeNo worker wearing a black greatcoat – and one of them pointed with agitation back toward the building. Fire in the neighboring building was drawing near. When a fireman turned the handle on the nozzle, a stream of water from the pumper arced into the building, to little effect.

Katrin flinched when the cry of a man came from the neighboring building, a ragged wail, choked off by pain. She breathed, 'My God, someone's still in there.'

A TeNo worker climbed into the truck, then emerged a few seconds later carrying a three-meter pry bar, so heavy that he could not jump to the ground with it, but had to lay it on the bed, climb down, then retrieve it. Other TeNo men pulled gas masks from a wooden compartment under the toolbox. They removed their berets to secure the masks to their faces. Glancing anxiously at the next building, where fire was gaining despite the stream of water, the Rescue Squad reentered the building.

Another cry came from within, a strangled shriek. Jack Cray edged closer to the building, as far as the first pumper truck.

'What are you doing?' Katrin asked, still at his elbow.

'Someone's in that building, and the fire is moving into it.'

'That's why the Rescue Squad is here.' She gripped his arm more tightly.

'Someone's going to be parboiled.' Cray moved nearer to the buildings, stepping over a fire hose.

'This is none of our business, Jack.' She was startled she had used his first name.

But he drew closer to the fire, to stand next to the TeNo leader. A double row of silver buttons was on the leader's greatcoat. He wore a black beret. He glanced at Cray, then stepped toward the door of the house where the man was trapped inside. He was met by a Rescue Squad member holding the pry bar as he emerged from the house. The man pulled off his gas mask.

Katrin hung back when Cray walked toward them, as if he were suddenly part of the Rescue Squad.

The TeNo man was saying, 'When I jam the pry bar into the fallen wall and jack it up, it just sags around it. The stuff is too soft. Every time I pry, more weight goes onto the man's arm.'

The troop leader asked, 'Would a pulley and chain work?'

'Nothing solid overhead to hang it on, and you've still got the problem of the crumbling plaster around his arm.' The TeNo man looked over his shoulder into the building. Timbers creaked and groaned. 'He doesn't have long, Lieutenant. I can already feel the fire when I'm in there, right through the wall.'

The lieutenant ordered, 'Get the saw.'

'Will you do the sawing this time, sir?' the pry-bar man asked. 'I've had it with the saw.'

Another TeNo worker passed the saw to the lieutenant. It was a carpenter's tool, with crosscut teeth.

The lieutenant slipped a gas mask over his face. His words were muffled. 'Get the litter ready. Hans, you come in with me, and you yell if the ceiling is about to give way, and don't be shy about it.'

The lieutenant may have been surprised when the Wehrmacht officer followed him toward the building, but he said nothing. Cray left Katrin on the street and climbed four stairs to the door, and then stepped from the cool day into a hot house. The east wall – papered with maroon flowers – was bubbling and peeling from the fire in the adjacent home. This was a living room, but the furniture had been tossed when the room buckled from the bomb that hit next door. And the back wall had collapsed, as had some of the ceiling. Timbers and plumbing hung down, and electric wires. Plaster was everywhere.

A man was on his back next to the collapsed wall. A timber lay across his arm, pinning him. On the floor below the arm and beam was crumpled plaster. His eyes were wide and glassy. His mouth opened and closed. His other hand was gripping the corner of a throw rug. He was wearing a blue knit sweater, and it rose and fell quickly as he breathed.

'See what I mean?' The TeNo man jabbed the big pry bar under the beam, then heaved on it. The bar's blade only dented the weakened floorboards under the man's arm, and didn't raise the offending beam.

'You can't just push the beam back?' Cray asked. He held his gloved hand to his face, trying to keep the heated vapors out. He breathed quickly, as if that might make the air cooler. He had not bothered with a gas mask.

'Too much weight behind it,' the Rescue Squad man replied.

The lieutenant stared at Cray's bandaged face. 'Who are you?'

Cray lifted his collar to look at the tabs. 'I'm a major. Go turn off one of the fire hoses and bring it in here. Turn it off at the pump, not the nozzle.'

The lieutenant knelt next to the man on the floor. He brought up the saw. 'I've got to take the arm off. He's not going to last. None of us is going to last if we don't get out of here.'

The man groaned. The sound of falling timber came from the

floor above. The room shivered. Glass shattered somewhere in the next room.

Cray reached for the lieutenant's hand, halting the saw just as it was about to bite into the trapped man's arm.

'Go turn off the fire hose and bring it in here.'

The lieutenant hesitated.

'I'm an engineer.' Cray had to raise his voice over the sounds of the burning and collapsing structure. 'Berlin Polytechnic. Now go get the fire hose.'

The TeNo lieutenant released the saw to Cray, then sprinted from the room to the street. Cray tossed the saw aside. He knelt next to the man. 'We'll have you out of here in a minute.'

The wounded man breathed raggedly. He nodded.

Yells came from outside, the lieutenant cursing the firemen who were reluctant to follow his orders and relinquish the hose. Cray looked toward the door but smoke hid it, and obscured even the nearby walls.

Cray coughed against the smoke and said to the wounded man, 'Is it hot in here or what?'

The man managed, 'Yeah, it's hot. And my arm hurts.' After a moment he added, 'I'd ask you to get out of here and save yourself, but I'm not that brave.'

Licks of fire came through the wall near the ceiling behind them, then gushed into the room, spreading along the fractured ceiling. Flames churned above them like an angry sky.

The lieutenant rushed back into the room, dragging the hose behind him. Water dripped from the brass nozzle.

'Drop the hose to the floor,' Cray ordered.

The lieutenant did as he was told, and Cray stepped on the hose, pressing the water out of it and flattening it. The lieutenant copied him, stomping on the hose. Water dribbled from the nozzle. Then Cray knelt to close the nozzle.

'Help me press the hose into the crack,' Cray said. 'Hurry now. You' – he pointed at the TeNo man in the gas mask near the door – 'when I give the signal, tell the firemen to turn the water back on, full pressure.'

Cray jammed the hose into the narrow space under the beam. He wedged it in, much like filling a gap with a bead of caulk, kicking the hose into place.

Then the lieutenant understood. He carried a portion of the hose over the trapped man, to his other side, and began inserting it into the crack that held the man's arm.

'Get it good and tight,' Cray said unnecessarily. 'Ready?'

The lieutenant nodded.

Cray called over his shoulder, 'Open the pumper nozzle.'

Using his hands as a megaphone, the Rescue Squad man relayed the order. A side wall in the neighboring room fell, sending a blast of hot air through a door. Burning debris from the ceiling began falling on them.

'Have I said it's hot in here?' Cray asked.

'You did, yes.' The wounded man almost smiled.

Then the hose filled with water, expanding and rising, and lifting the beam all along its length. With a grinding groan the weight of the fallen wall shifted, and the cavity opened, freeing the arm.

Cray grabbed the wounded man's legs and the lieutenant brought up the man's shoulders. They carried him out of the room, his maimed arm trailing across the floor. Clumps of burning ceiling fell behind them.

They put him on a litter, a Rescue Squad man at each end. He was carried toward an ambulance that had arrived while Cray was in the room. Katrin was still standing near a pumper.

Cray breathed the cool air, wiping his forehead with a hand.

The lieutenant removed his gas mask. He fixed his eyes on Cray, then said, 'Sir, the makeup on your eyebrows is coming off, dripping down your face, from the heat in the building.'

Cray dabbed at a brow and looked at his hand. A black smudge.

The lieutenant's words were barely audible above the fire's sibilance. 'That was nice work with the hose in there, Captain Cray.'

He stared at the lieutenant.

'I'd never have thought of it.'

'Like I said, I'm an engineer.' Cray's pistol was in a belt holster under the greatcoat.

'The radio in my truck is broken,' the lieutenant said, 'and it's going to take me at least ten minutes, maybe fifteen, to find a telephone to report your location.'

The American nodded, then turned for Katrin and quickly led her away from the burning buildings. The sounds of buckling wood and falling lathes and plaster followed them along the street.

EIGHTEEN

The bombers had returned half an hour after their first run, an unusual double punch for one morning. Katrin and Cray had not been near a shelter, so they had climbed into the basement of a ruined building and huddled in a corner under a table, mouths open and fingers in their ears. When the all-clear sounded, they emerged to find that smoke and drifting ash had swallowed Berlin. Their ad hoc shelter had been at the edge of the target area, and the new fires and craters and shattered buildings were to the south, the direction they needed to travel.

They picked their way along, no one else on the street yet. For a few minutes after each terror raid, Berlin stood in mute shock, like a man just slapped, incapable of comprehension, yet full of helpless outrage. Then Berliners slowly emerged from their hiding to begin again their inventory. The Allies destroyed, Berliners made an accounting, an endless cycle.

Smoke was as thick as cotton, and Cray could make out nothing beyond the reach of his arm. Katrin coughed into her hand. He led her around a cluster of tortoiseshell spectacle frames, blown from an eye doctor's office by a bomb blast, then past a dozen white linen napkins tied together with a red ribbon. They passed shattered seltzer bottles, a pencil sharpener ripped from a desk, a silver teapot and a brass coronet, scattered across the street. They carefully stepped through new fields of brick and plaster, and around timbers, some still on fire. Above them the sky was a sulfurous yellow, the sun hidden in the haze.

'Do you smell perfume?' Katrin asked.

'Lilac, smells like.'

'Some woman's perfume bottle was vaporized by a blast, probably, and now the smell wafts down the street.' She sniffed. 'I can also smell fresh bread and mothballs, and there's a whiff of ammonia, maybe someone's kitchen floor cleaner. It's always like this after a bombing. The air smells of better days.'

'I don't smell any of that.'

'Take a big breath, and tell me the scents you detect.'

Cray breathed deeply, pondered for a moment, then announced, 'Cordite and gelignite and HE residue.'

She looked at him. 'Have you ever had a romantic thought in your life?'

Katrin had been contacting the Hand twice a day since Cray had appeared. The Hand had given her no information during her last three broadcasts. The American had speculated that either the Hand was learning nothing to pass on, perhaps because of the purge Colonel Becker had referred to, or perhaps the Hand was saying nothing because Cray's mission was only a cover for some other operation, and so the Hand had other, more pressing concerns. Still, she would continue to make her broadcasts, hoping for something useful.

They passed a row of three cars, all on fire, beacons in the gray smoke. The buildings near the cars had just been destroyed and were now nothing but tumbles of wood and wire. Cray could see their remains only when the wind pushed a hole in the smoke.

'I'm hungry,' he announced. Much of his face was hidden behind a bandage, and he was walking with an exaggerated limp. 'You'd think if the Hand is putting us to all this trouble, it'd send us something to eat.'

Katrin's hands were on his arm. Her face was well hidden by a scarf. She asked abruptly, 'Have you ever read Kant?'

He shook his head. 'Did you say you smelled bread?'

'Or Leibniz or Hegel?'

'Not enough pictures in those books.'

She slowed their pace. 'What do you read?'

Cray shrugged.

'Do you read?' she demanded. 'Anything at all?'

'*Popular Mechanics*.'

She hesitated. 'What's that?'

'A magazine about how to make crystal radios using junk found in the kitchen drawer,' he said. 'I must have made a dozen of them when I was a kid.'

'I'll try again.' Her tone was of vast patience. 'Clearly you don't know our literature or philosophy. But do you know anything about us Germans?'

'I aim and fire at them. What's to know?'

After a moment she said, 'Is it just that your German is rough, or is it possible I'm speaking with a moron?'

'Now I'm smelling the bread, too. It's making me salivate like a dog.'

A few Berliners crept out of cellars onto the sidewalks to squint against the gauze of smoke, craning their necks, trying to determine what was left of their neighborhood. Then more and more people emerged, some brushing off their coat sleeves, others pulling wadded paper plugs from their ears, others coughing at the dust in their throats. Some swatted at the smoke, to no effect. No one paid attention to the wounded Wehrmacht major, even when they could glimpse him through the smoke. Berlin was brimming with injured servicemen. Wooden stumps, eyepatches, empty sleeves, halting limps, purple burn scars, crutches – the city was choking with them.

Katrin and Cray waded through someone's library, the books tossed along the sidewalk, some shedding pages in the wind. Then they stepped around a row of shattered pigeon cages, the birds inside and dead. Then around a tangle of brassieres and two headless mannequins.

'Adam and I had wonderful conversations,' she said finally.

He looked at her. 'Is that what this is about? Trying to have a conversation with me to replace the ones you once had with your husband?'

'It was a laughable idea, come to think of it.' She dabbed a glistening eye. 'An absurd notion on my part, trying to get some conversation from you.'

They passed an elderly man pushing a perambulator filled with bread loaves.

'What's so absurd about it?' Cray's gaze followed the bread, then turned back to Katrin. 'I can have a meaningful discussion, probably just as well as Adam could.'

'Try it.'

They stepped over a wad of singed blankets, then from the sidewalk out into the street to avoid the heat of a burning building, which creaked and groaned from the fire's assault.

Cray pulled at the earlobe that wasn't covered with the bandage. He had repaired the damage to his eyebrows. He was again a brunet.

'Go ahead,' she prodded. 'Make some intelligent conversation.'

'Well, I can't talk about Hegel or Kant, if that's what you're waiting for.'

'Something easier, then. How about your childhood?'

Cray thought for a moment. 'I knew I was going to be an engineer when I was very young. Maybe ten or eleven years old.'

They passed a rolling pin, then stepped over wooden coat hangers.

She nodded, encouraging him. 'What made you think so?'

'Future engineers do one of two things. They play with radios or they play with chemistry sets. And they become either mechanical or chemical engineers.'

'So what did you do?' Her voice was warming, and she walked a bit closer to him.

'Radios. I built them and I took them apart and I put them together again, when I was a kid. Endlessly.'

'You had a childhood. Somehow I didn't think so.'

'There wasn't a wire or a tube in a radio I didn't know. I rigged an antenna on our house, but it wasn't high enough, so I put one up on the barn. I could hear stations as far away as San Francisco.'

'I thought you maybe sprang from the ground, fully formed, carrying a knife and a grenade and a pistol.'

His look was of crushed dignity.

'I'm teasing.' Her voice was light and warm. 'Go on. I like this.'

'For years our house near Wenatchee had radio parts scattered throughout it. I made a transmitter, and bought a microphone at an auction of used police equipment. There was a while when San Francisco might've been able to hear me.'

She laughed.

'It amused my mom and dad, having all those tubes and condensers and dials and switches all around.' He paused. 'Until one bad day. A very bad day.'

'Yes?'

'I made a radio detonator.'

She stiffened. 'Aw, damn it, don't go ruining this little talk.'

'And discovered – purely by accident, I told my dad – that match heads inside a length of pipe could be detonated at a distance, and would indeed destroy a tool shed.'

'Weapons. Is that all you ever think about?'

'Shovels, hoes, planting pots, rakes, shingles, bits of window-panes, the works, all blown into the air. Some landed on our lawn, some I don't think ever came down.'

Katrin sighed heavily.

'Well.' He brushed his hands together. 'I do enjoy a nice chat, after all.'

'Now you are just teasing me.'

They worked their way around a tangle of roof rafters and collar beams that had fallen from a building.

She asked abruptly, 'Have you ever examined your life?'

'Why would I do that?'

She waited, silently coaxing more from him.

Finally he said, 'A person shouldn't look too closely at himself.'

'Why not?'

He said nothing.

'You are a better person than you think, Jack,' she said with emphasis.

That stopped him. He looked perplexed, but only for a moment. He smiled at her, an American grin, full of teeth. 'I've always said so.'

She added, 'But that doesn't mean you aren't a moron.'

Her hand was on his arm as they walked, and now Cray put a

hand over hers. He said in a diminished tone. 'I can get you out of here when this is over, Katrin. Out of Germany.'

Her eyes shone with emotions he could not read.

He said gravely, 'Even if the Gestapo doesn't find you, the Red Army will be here soon. The horrors have just begun for Berlin.'

Her mouth moved, trying to find the right words.

'I can get you out,' he repeated.

'You won't be able to get yourself out, much less me.' She smiled to take the edge off her words.

'I guess I've been too subtle around you.'

'Subtle?' She laughed, a bright chirrup. 'You? You're as subtle as a belch in church.'

'You try to get me to talk, so you can examine me, figure me out.' His mouth was still turned up. 'But you still don't know me.'

His face was abruptly as cold as a carving. His urbanity seemed suddenly stripped away.

Alarmed, she dropped her hand from his arm. 'Why do you say that?'

'If you knew me,' he said, 'you'd know that once my mission is accomplished, I'm going to be like a horse turned back to the stable. I'll be coming hard, and those who try to stop me will fare poorly.'

'I don't . . . I don't think I know what you mean.'

His gloss of civilization abruptly returned. His eyes became gentle again, and an arm – as thick as a hawser – went across her back as they walked around a scattering of bricks. 'I can get us out, both of us.'

She shook her head. 'I'm not leaving Germany. I know a few places I can hide.'

'We can talk about it later.'

'There's no need to. I'm not leaving.'

'Later.'

Lifted by a breath of air, a curtain of smoke rose in front of them, revealing yet another building with a collapsed façade. Cinder blocks and glass and shingles had fallen into the street, and a commercial baking oven was halfway out a shattered window, balanced on the window apron, the baking racks having spilled onto the street. The bomb had yanked off the building's fixtures, and deposited them here and there: doorknob, a mail drop, two brass light fixtures, strips of wood siding, lengths of vent pipe, and pieces of window casing. A cash register lay near the oven, on its side with its drawer sprung open and a few Reichsmarks fluttering about, but they were ignored by the knots of people hurrying toward the bakery. There was nothing to buy in Berlin.

Cray pointed. 'That's where the smell is coming from. Looks like lunch.'

Cray led her toward the fractured bakery. Berliners were following their noses toward the wrecked building, pushing their way through the smoke. The scent of freshly baked bread drew them as if hands were tugging their lapels. More and more Berliners crawled out of cellars, turned their noses into the wind, then began brushing their way through the smoke and slapping aside leafy ash, desperately searching for the source of the intoxicating scent. Cray glimpsed them through twisting ropes of smoke, an eerie, gathering assemblage, pushing through drifting ash and trailing swirling wisps of smoke.

'It'll be first come, first served in that bakery,' Cray said.

He rushed ahead of Katrin, through the opacity, careful to preserve some of his limp. He pushed by an elderly woman walking with a cane, and joined four others who climbed into the bakery through the shattered window, squeezing by the oven, scrambling over fallen timbers, crushing glass shards under their feet, and then ducking under sagging beams. Cray scaled a loose pile consisting of baking trays, an overturned mixer, and flat wood spatulas. Against the back wall were the cooling trays, rapidly being emptied by frenzied Berliners, twenty people and more every moment, some in uniform – two Red Cross nurses and auxiliary postal drivers and a bus conductor – and others in rumpled civilian clothes. They yanked loaves from the trays, jamming them into their coats and under their arms, balancing them in their hands, piling themselves high with bread. Light fixtures dangled from the ceiling, and water poured from the wall where the sink had been ripped away.

Cray muscled his way through the throng, almost too late. He was able to find one loaf, which he pulled from the rack amid a cluster of grasping hands. He tucked the bread into his belly like a fullback, and shoved his way back through the crowd.

Despairing shouts and groans came from Berliners who had arrived in the bakery too late. A few scuffles at the edge of the crowd, and more yells. The scavengers quickly fled the smashed bakery to disappear into the smoke, lest they be forced to account for their good fortune.

Cray slipped by the oven again on his way out. Katrin was waiting near a fire hydrant, her hands in her pocket, looking at once embarrassed at the looting and grateful that Cray had found the bread.

The old woman with the cane stepped around an empty flour barrel into Cray's path. 'You should share that loaf of bread, young man.' Her hair was gray and tightly curled like a schnauzer's. She wore a gabardine coat and a wool shawl. She held out her hand, the cane in the other. 'Give me some of that bread, in the name of the Fatherland.'

'No, thanks.' He could say the short phrase entirely without an accent. He sidestepped her toward Katrin.

The old woman might have had bound-up hips, requiring the use of a cane, but there was nothing wrong with her shoulders and arms. She brought her cane around in a tight arc and cracked it against Jack Cray's temple just below his Wehrmacht cap.

Cray yelped and brought up his hands to his head, dropping the bread. The old lady swung again, and this time her cane found Cray's cheekbone. Cray blindly spun to the source of his torment, but the woman shoved the cane between his legs, and he toppled to the cobblestones.

The old woman used her cane like a broom to scoot the bread away from Cray. Then she braced herself on the cane to reach for the bread. She grunted politely, her hips creaking.

As she hobbled away, the loaf under her arm, she said over her shoulder, 'You should be ashamed, trying to take bread from an old woman, and my husband a veteran of the Great War.'

Several bystanders laughed, but they moved on, and the smoke hid them quickly.

Cray sat on the sidewalk, amid the rubble, his legs inelegantly out in front of him and his hands to his throbbing cheek. His teeth showed with his grimace of pain.

When Katrin knelt to him, Cray said in a hiss of suffering, 'Don't say anything, please.'

Her smile was puckish. 'I wasn't going to say anything.'

Cray rose to his knees, a hand still at his cheek.

'Just a question.' She helped him to his feet.

'Don't ask.'

'Do you suppose Hitler's guards are as tough as that old woman?'

He adjusted his bandage, that small motion seeming to chase away his pain. A red welt on his cheek resembled a smear of lipstick. The half of his smile not hidden by the dressing was sheepish. 'No. Surely not.'

Dietrich and Eberhardt stood in front of the barber's chair, which was brought into the room once a day for these few minutes. The barber was an SS noncom who handled the straight-edge with infinite care, starting below the left ear. White foam covered the Führer's face, except for the narrow mustache. The barber expertly drew the blade down Hitler's cheek.

Dietrich had never made a mental connection between the Führer and anything tonsorial. He had sort of assumed the Führer was born with a mustache. But here Hitler was, getting a shave, under the smiling and careful attention of an SS barber. Hitler's teeth were an appalling green, in contrast with the white shaving foam, and his eyes the yellow of old snow. A bib was across his chest, and Dietrich thought it peculiar that the bib was camouflage brown and green. Under the bib, Hitler was wearing a black satin morning robe over white pajamas with blue piping. On his feet were black patent-leather slippers. Hitler's left arm trembled under the bib.

'You again, Inspector,' Hitler said, the foam parting at his mouth.

'Yes, sir. And General Eberhardt.'

'General Eberhardt has been working for me for thirteen years, Inspector, and not once has he brought me welcome news,' the Führer said. 'What is it this time, General?'

The barber lightly gripped Hitler's head as the blade slid along the cheekbone. The razor was wiped on a towel hanging at the barber's belt, then brought up again. The barber had a high, blank forehead and pinprick eyes, and his face was squeezed in concentration. A fern stand next to the barber had also been brought in for the occasion, and on it were a bowl of steaming water, white towels in a rumpled pile, a lather cup, and a horsehair brush with a silver handle. A strop hung by a metal clip from an edge of the table. The marble bust of Frederick watched the operation dispassionately.

'I must be blunt, my leader,' Eberhardt said.

The foam below the mustache moved again. 'You always are. I've yet to determine if I appreciate it.'

'We believe the American – Jack Cray – has obtained a sniper rifle.'

While General Eberhardt informed the Führer how such an event came to pass and how it had been discovered, Dietrich sensed movement to his right, and so risked a glance around the room. This was Hitler's bedroom, one room further into the catacombs than the map room. A Dresden vase and Carlyle's biography of Frederick the Great were on a nightstand near a low bed. Across from the bed was the blue horsehair sofa.

Another person was in the room, standing at a dresser. A woman with hair the color of straw and a flippant nose. She was rearranging tubes of lipstick and vials of perfume on the dresser, taking too long, perhaps with nothing else to do. She had a shade too much rouge on her cheeks, and her eyebrows were penciled darker than her hair. She wore a bright blue dress with white ruffles at the neckline. The dress fit her snugly, showing her figure.

And when Dietrich – feeling like a thief for having glimpsed this woman – quickly turned back to the barber's chair, Hitler startled the detective by raising an eyebrow, just fractionally, but plainly and purposefully nonetheless. It was the silent and common question one single man asks of another: She's something, isn't she? Eberhardt continued with his briefing, and might not have seen it.

The familiarity and bawdiness of Hitler's little motion pushed everything useful from Dietrich's head. He stood there at attention, as straight as a shinbone, while Eberhardt talked about the rifle and all that the weapon connoted. The detective wondered if he would be able to escape Hitler's sway this time. Last time – down here in the bunker – it was very close.

'So he will try to flush me out of the bunker?' Hitler was again all business.

Dietrich's attention returned to the conversation.

'There is no other reason to obtain a sniper's rifle.' The RSD general spoke succinctly, a professional briefer.

'How will he do it, Inspector? How will the American try to make me flee to the open air?'

The barber waited until Hitler had finished the question before scraping the blade across his chin. Strip by strip, the Führer's face was emerging from the foam.

'Perhaps a massive bombing raid on the garden above us, and on this structure.'

Hitler raised a hand from under the bib to point at the nearest wall. 'This place is impregnable.'

'The Allies have a new weapon,' Eberhardt countered. 'A bomb that penetrates several feet of concrete before exploding. It has been used with success on airplane runways. Perhaps it works on bunkers.'

'This roof is considerably thicker than a runway, and on top of all the concrete is another ten meters of earth,' Hitler said as the barber drew a damp towel across his face, wiping away the last specks of lather.

Eberhardt said, 'Perhaps the bombers' goal will not be to destroy this facility entirely, but to chase you from it, to make it uninhabitable and dangerous, so you will be forced to emerge.'

'Where Jack Cray will be waiting,' Dietrich concluded. 'With the sniper's rifle.'

The barber used an index finger to tilt Hitler's head, searching for missed spots. Then he snapped the towel to one side, his signal that his mission was accomplished.

Hitler rose unsteadily from the barber's chair. His face was pink and shiny. He pushed aside his forelock using his entire hand, the outsized gesture of a boy. 'My engineers tell me this bunker cannot be pierced by a bomb, any bomb. I trust them to be correct. So I will stay in this place. Forever.'

'You are never leaving?' Dietrich asked.

'Last time you were here, Inspector Dietrich, I told you I would never leave Berlin. Now I am telling you I am never leaving this bunker. Even if the terror flyers have a bomb big enough to make the bunker come down around my ears.'

Dietrich moved his jaw, his face impassive.

Hitler read it anyway. 'I've just made your task easier. Yes?'

The inspector nodded.

'This American . . . what is his name again?' Hitler asked.

'Jack Cray,' the detective replied.

The blond woman crossed the room to sit in the blue davenport. She picked up a magazine. She was either entirely bored with this business or superb at hiding her interest.

'Jack Cray won't have a target.' The Führer's blue eyes were as flat as paint. 'He'll be out there, with his new rifle, waiting and waiting, and he'll never have anything to shoot at. And so all you need do, Inspector, is catch him. You don't need to concern yourself about me.'

The barber lifted the chair with one hand and the table in the other. He crisply bowed to the Führer and left the room.

Thinking himself dismissed, Dietrich moved to follow the barber.

Hitler's hand on his arm brought him up. 'Tell me, Inspector. Are the Bolsheviks in mortar distance of Berlin?'

Dietrich again was startled. How could the Führer not know this? 'Soviet shells are landing on the city, all day and night.'

Hitler nodded.

Again, Dietrich found reserves of courage he did not know he possessed. 'Don't your generals tell you?'

'Some do and some don't,' the Führer replied tonelessly. 'It's a matter of who to believe. That's how I've come this far, Inspector. Knowing who to believe.'

Dietrich sensed he was witnessing the tide turn, the waning of reason and the waxing of something more dangerous. He had heard rumors of these sea changes. He hastily turned to go, Eberhardt at his heels.

'And amid all the traitors, I can trust you, Inspector.' Hitler's voice gained half an octave, and inklings of hysteria were at the edges of his words. A flood was coming. 'They have never told me the truth. They lie to me. And worse, they conspire with each other to lie to me.' Hitler's face was turning red in splotches. Spittle formed at the corner of his mouth. His voice rose like a stormy wind. 'That's all I hear down here. Lies and more lies.'

The Führer caught himself. He shuddered with the effort to control his passion. He breathed quickly, air rattling in his throat. He turned to the blue sofa like a jerking marionette, his ruined body not cooperating in even this small motion.

He said over his shoulder, 'Send another one of them in as you leave, Inspector Dietrich. Any one of them, outside the door there, waiting for an audience, sniveling in fear, hoping I haven't discovered their treachery, but of course I have.'

Otto Dietrich held two corners of the map laid over the car's hood, and Eugen Eberhardt pinned down the other two corners. They were near the Food and Agriculture Ministry's building on Wilhelmstrasse. A company of Eberhardt's RSD troops were cordoning off the intersection and two hundred meters of Behrenstrasse, setting up wooden traffic barricades and giving gruff responses to the few passersby who asked anything. Most pedestrians on the sidewalks hurried along without even a glance at the operation. Camouflage nets hung from lamp poles made Wilhelmstrasse seem like a tunnel.

'It's all a matter of angles, really.' General Eberhardt raised a hand to ward off the sunlight, made white and blinding by the high smoke. He stared down Behrenstrasse toward the church. 'We'll give Jack Cray a few, and we'll take away a few.'

'And you're sure the Führer would exit the bunker only by these three routes?' Dietrich was bent over the hood, studying the map.

Also on the car hood, pressed under his left palm, was an aerial photo of the middle of Berlin, from Gestapo headquarters on Prinz Albrecht Strasse north ten blocks to the Brandenburg Gate, showing the neighborhood that was the Reich's administrative heart.

'He has told us he is not leaving the bunker. I take him at his word. I have overseen his departure from the Chancellery hundreds of times, and these would be his routes were he to leave. He usually gets into the limousine in the Honor Courtyard, and the limousine then exits the complex east through the automobile gate onto Wilhelmstrasse. But occasionally the limousine pulls up in front of the building, where he leaves from the Great Marble Gallery, nearer his office.'

'And that exit is on Voss strasse, to the south of the Chancellery?'

'You aren't familiar with the New Chancellery? Have you ever been inside it?'

'Never been invited.' Dietrich smiled ruefully. 'And I avoid the government quarter when I can.'

'The Marble Gallery is a hundred and fifty meters long, twice as long as the Hall of Mirrors at Versailles, the Führer told me. Boasting a bit, you see.'

'General, are you certain you know of all the secondary bunkers, those places the Führer would go if the Chancellery bunker were rendered uninhabitable? Himmler or Goering wouldn't have a bunker you don't know about, would they? A bunker Hitler could flee to in an emergency?'

Eberhardt stiffened, lifting his hands from the map so that it flapped in the breeze. 'It's my duty to know these things. The SS bunker across the Chancellery garden would be the first refuge. And the Wehrmacht command bunker in Zossen would be the second.'

'How would the Führer travel to them? Could he walk to the SS bunker?'

'Of course. It's just across the garden.'

'Would he drive there?'

'It would take longer to drive, especially if it were an emergency and the driver and bodyguards hadn't been given advance notice, hadn't brought the cars up from the garage.'

'Can the Führer get from the bunker where he is now – the garden bunker – to the SS bunker through an underground corridor?' Dietrich asked.

'At one time the SS was planning on connecting the two with a fortified tunnel, but it was never completed.' Eberhardt repinned the map with his hands.

Dietrich continued, 'And to get to the Zossen bunker, he would have to drive, of course. It's quite a distance.'

'My men have practiced such an evacuation many times. But the roadways are always a surprise these days. Each day I send a driver to survey the escape route to Zossen. And he never fails to report that he had to take a new route because of new rubble or a new crater.'

Cray traced a route with his finger. 'So if Jack Cray can force the Führer out of the garden bunker, the only place Cray can count on the Führer being in the open will be as the Führer walks across the garden toward the SS bunker, or when he is at the motor gate or the Marble Gallery entrance. Is that right?'

'Yes, but you are supposing Jack Cray knows these things, that Cray has learned of the bunkers and the Chancellery entrances the Führer uses, knows the Führer's escape routes.'

Dietrich said, 'We speak of Cray as if he were one person, as if just one commando were closing in on the Führer. But we must presume that the Americans and English have put a vast intelligence machine at Cray's disposal. And so we must assume Cray knows the Führer's escape routes.' Dietrich's face creased into a grin. 'And you have told me you always anticipate the worst.'

The RSD general nodded. Every part of this conversation had been spoken before by these two men over the last two days, and more than once. They acted as each other's cross-examiner, searching for Cray through the power of their intellects, sifting through the meager clues Cray had left behind. And Dietrich and Eberhardt talked to buck each other up. They were working on little sleep and no encouragement and the prospects of a bleak future should they fail.

'And another thing, Otto.' Eberhardt had begun using the inspector's first name and the familiar *du*. 'These three places where Hitler might emerge – should Cray somehow force him up from underground – are several hundred meters apart. The garden, the Wilhelmstrasse gate, and the Marble Gallery exit. Cray can't know where Hitler will come out, and Cray can't cover them all, not even with the long-range rifle, because it can't shoot around corners.'

Dietrich began folding the map. 'There's a chance the sniper rifle is a ruse, Eugen.' The detective began folding the map.

Eberhardt drew in a quick breath.

'Maybe Jack Cray stole that rifle as a smokescreen. And his plan is something else entirely.'

'We can only work with what we've got.' The general pursed his lips. 'If we assume it's a ruse, what do we do then, Otto? Go home and make a fire in the grate? We simply don't have anything else to work on. And Cray went to a lot of trouble to get that rifle, and was injured in the process. I don't think it's a ruse.'

An RSD man blew his whistle twice, then yelled a final warning through a bullhorn. Down Behrenstrasse other whistles sounded, indicating nearby buildings and roads were clear of people. Another RSD man pulled a last sandbag from the back of a truck, and added it to a low wall of them.

The man with the bullhorn called, 'Ready when you are, General Eberhardt.'

Dietrich pulled at his chin, letting the map flutter. 'I'm stumped by that, too, Eugen. Even if Cray knows of the three exits, he can only cover one of them with his rifle.'

'So is Cray accepting a thirty-three percent chance of getting the Führer in his crosshairs? Is the American just hoping to get lucky? Or maybe he has accomplices. We know he's working with the woman, Katrin von Tornitz. I've got a lot of my men looking for her.'

'Nothing in her background indicates she can use a rifle.'

'Other people, then. Maybe the Allies sent three Jack Crays, and each will cover a bunker exit.'

Dietrich shook his head. 'We'd have crossed their trails by now. There's just one commando, I'm convinced.'

'And, Otto, how – just how – is Cray going to make the Führer flee the bunker? A massive bombing? That doesn't seem likely. It's not sure enough.'

'I don't know how Cray will do it. I just trust that he will.'

The detective followed General Eberhardt toward the sandbags. An RSD man waited there, one hand on the plunger of a detonator and the other around a pair of binoculars.

As he walked, Dietrich said in a low voice, 'You saw him down there, the Führer.'

'I see the Führer rather frequently,' Eberhardt replied, a touch of the bureaucrat in his voice. 'It's my duty.'

'It's insane up here, on the streets of Berlin, Eugen. Look at these streets, look at every street in this city. Fires and craters and smoke. Satan's hell will be just like this.'

'What's your point, Inspector?' At the whiff of defeatism, Eberhardt reverted to using Dietrich's title.

'It's also insane down in that bunker.'

'You shouldn't speculate—'

'For God's sake, you heard him down there, Eugen. Talking of traitors and cowards, talking of his loyal soldiers like that, soldiers who've given their lives and families and homes to Germany. And their leader is raving and rolling his eyes, spit flying from his mouth.'

'Otto, these are dangerous things you are saying. Said to the wrong people . . .'

'I always wondered about the Führer's war aims, Eugen. Wondered about almost everything he did. It all seemed insane. Now I know why.'

'Otto . . .'

'It's because he's crazy, down in that bunker.' Dietrich found his voice rising, just as Hitler's had. 'He's a certifiable lunatic. You saw it yourself. You must see it every time you meet with him. I never knew it until now, and – '

The RSD general gripped Dietrich's arm with more force than required. With an effort that strained his every muscle from toe to temple, Dietrich shut off the flow of words.

'Otto, listen to yourself. If the wrong ears hear you, you'll be back in that dungeon before the hour is out. Get hold of yourself.'

Prickly sweat had formed on Dietrich's back. His view of General Eberhardt and the street was through the fine red mist of suffused anger.

Eberhardt counseled, 'Let's do our jobs, Otto. The rest of it is beyond us. Let it be.'

Dietrich was having trouble breathing.

'Are you going to help me now?' Eberhardt asked quietly, the priest inquiring of the penitent.

'Yes.' Dietrich wiped his mouth with the back of a hand. 'Yes, of course.'

They stepped behind the sandbag wall. Eberhardt held his hand out for the field glasses, then peered through them down Behrenstrasse, to the century-old church with its high steeple, high enough so that a man could stand on the bell platform and see over the Old Chancellery into the garden, to the walkway in front of the blockhouse entrance to the bunker. Many other buildings along the street were in ruin, but the church had so far escaped the explosives. Not this day.

Eberhardt nodded at the RSD man, who pushed the plunger handle. The grind of the small generator inside the box was immediately followed by the roar of dynamite from the church's roof. Smoke and splinters erupted from the base of the bell tower, and the tower sank, then toppled forward. The church's roofline snagged the spire, flipping it so it fell top first. The tower landed on the cobblestones, crashing and falling in on itself, trailing smoke and bits of debris and raising dust, quickly obscuring itself, its bell tolling a last mournful note. The bell tower had become a trifling scrap of rubble in a city that was little else.

Dietrich and Eberhardt rose from behind the sandbags, splinters of the tower still landing all around. Eberhardt said, 'I wish we could have just posted a squadron of my men at that church, and so spared the bell tower.'

The detective replied, 'Cray might have gotten by them, killing some, maybe.'

Eberhardt sighed wearily.

'We can't cover every single firing site Cray might use.'

'Of course.'

A gleam entered Dietrich's faded blue eyes. 'But we can cover two or three.'

The RSD general nodded.

And Dietrich added with relish, 'And then maybe once – just once – Jack Cray will appear where we want him and when we want him.'

NINETEEN

'You ever heard of her, Egon?' Dietrich asked, his hand on the dashboard, bracing himself. 'A Countess Hohenberg?'

'Not that I recall,' Detective Haushofer replied. 'She's not related to Katrin von Tornitz, then?'

'Not that we can find. I suspect the countess was a friend of Katrin von Tornitz's mother, but that's a guess.'

The Mercedes lurched and sank, then bounced up and dipped again as it rolled over rubble on Heuwingstrasse. Dietrich's hat flattened against the car's roof and slid off his head to the seat.

Dietrich's men had started watching the homes of all Katrin von Tornitz's relatives days ago, figuring she and the American might be staying with one of them. They found she had several cousins in Berlin, and some north of the city in Mecklenburg, where the family once owned an estate. The decades had dispersed the family, so Berlin detectives had been watching sixteen homes. With no luck at any of them.

Heuwingstrasse was a narrow ravine between inclines of rubble, all that remained of the three- and four-story apartment buildings and shops that had once lined the street. It had also been a neighborhood of breweries, and the scent of malt still lingered. This street had been newly ruined, and the scree was still precarious, falling into the street when prompted by gusts of wind. A bulldozer had pushed aside the debris like snow, so smaller hillocks of bricks and boards lined the sidewalk.

Dietrich commented, 'We got a break on this.'

Haushofer nodded. 'We needed a break.'

A woman who lived on the floor below the countess happened to be peeking out her door when Katrin von Tornitz was walking up the stairs. She had recognized Katrin from the posters along the street.

'One of those old ladies who monitors the morals of her fellow tenants, I suppose,' Haushofer added. He pulled on the steering wheel, and the Mercedes wound around a file cabinet and sofa in the road. A drumroll of rain sounded on the Mercedes's roof. Haushofer leaned forward to wipe his hand against the window. Haushofer's skin had a cloistered pallor. His eyes were red-lined from lack of sleep. His chin was large and uncompromising. The wiper blades beat back and forth.

'Are Cray and Katrin von Tornitz still there, you think?' Haushofer asked.

'The snoop said she hadn't seen them today, so probably not. But I want to talk with the countess.' Dietrich stopped himself from rocking back and forth to encourage the car to go faster. 'Hurry up, will you?'

Haushofer grinned and pressed the accelerator. The car bounced over a clot of rubble, sending Dietrich against the roof. He held up his hand like a traffic cop, and Haushofer eased the pressure from the gas pedal. The canyon ended at an intersection, and the car drove between low apartment buildings. This portion of Heuwingstrasse had been spared.

Dietrich squinted through the rain. 'There's her building. Pull over.'

The clouds suddenly parted, revealing the sun. The road began to steam. Dietrich left the car and ran to the door to check for her name on the mailbox. HOHENBERG. He pushed open the door, ran past an empty glass vase on a lampstand, and began ascending the stairs. He drew his pistol. On the third floor a narrow crack between the door and the frame revealed the snoop's wide eyes. Breathing in gulps, Dietrich climbed to the fourth floor.

The countess's door was open. Dietrich could see into her apartment. Saw a hatstand and an umbrella holder. He stepped nearer, his Walther up and ready. The old woman was in a chair against the window. Knitting needles were on her lap, and a ball of twine and a sewing basket at her feet. Scraps of cloth were all around. She was staring through the door at Dietrich, and her mouth was pulled back in a curl of fear.

Dietrich thought she must be afraid of his pistol, so he moved it behind his leg. He stepped to the door's threshold and leaned forward to peer inside. Nothing but old furniture and pieces of fabric, and uniforms and coats and dresses hanging across a bar. The old woman was a seamstress.

'Countess Hohenberg?'

She croaked piteously, 'Please don't hit me.'

Dietrich allowed himself a smile, a friendly one, he hoped. 'I wouldn't think of it. I'm Detective Inspector Dietrich. I just want a few words with you. May I come in?'

Her face was white. Her eyes were old and leaking, and mirrored a wild fear.

Dietrich stepped inside the apartment. The place smelled of perfume and ironing. 'Countess, I'm just a police officer here to have a few words with you. There's no reason to be afraid of me.'

Rudolf Koder stepped in from the kitchen. 'But she has good reason to be afraid of me.'

Dietrich's pistol involuntarily swept to Koder.

The Gestapo agent grinned at the weapon. 'We are on the same side, remember?'

Dietrich shoved the Walther into his pants, and only then did he notice Koder was carrying a meat cleaver, a heavy blade on a bone handle.

'Don't hit me again,' the countess intoned. 'Please.'

Koder smiled at her and lifted a palm in a gesture of understanding and sympathy. He said to Dietrich, 'She won't answer my questions about the American.'

Color rose in Dietrich's face. 'How did you find out about this lady?'

A vulpine smile. 'We listen to your telephone. I thought you knew that.'

Dietrich could see Koder's knuckle imprints on the countess's cheek.

The Gestapo agent said, 'I know full well Jack Cray slept here last night. He left a pair of socks in a corner of the kitchen, in a bag. One of the socks had blood on it. But the so-called countess here won't tell me where he and Katrin von Tornitz are.'

'Maybe I can talk with her.' Dietrich sensed movement behind him. He turned to see another Gestapo agent, who had been standing on the stairs up to the next floor. This one's pistol was out, its snout pointed at Dietrich. The Gestapo agents had been expecting Dietrich, had probably been watching him from the countess's window as he arrived.

'She won't say anything. I've already tried to persuade her, but it wasn't enough.' Koder brought up the cleaver. 'Never let it be said that distaste for a task dissuaded me from my duty.'

With speed that belied his banker's manner, he snatched the countess's hand, slapped it against her sewing table, and held it there as he viciously brought down the cleaver. The blade clapped loudly against the tabletop, and two of the countess's fingers fell to the floor where they curled like grubs.

'I must apologize,' Koder said to her, still holding her hand. 'No doubt that smarts. But maybe it will freshen your memory.'

The countess's eyes were wild and white. She moved her jaw but no sound came. Blood dripped from her hand across the table, then fell into her sewing basket.

Dietrich rushed forward. 'There's no damned reason to do that . . .' He brought up his pistol, unsure what he would do with it.

Koder swung the cleaver in a tight arc, catching Dietrich's jaw with the flat of the blade. The detective staggered, then collapsed to his knees, dropping the Walther. A fog of pain blurred Dietrich's view of Koder and the countess. The Gestapo agent again planted her hand on the table. A trill of pain and fear escaped her.

Koder raised the cleaver. It hung in the air, shimmering with reflected light. His voice was as passionless as a cashier's. 'The American was here last night, and you know where he and the woman are. Tell me.'

Dietrich held up a hand. The pain in his head was echoing back and forth, and his mouth was woolly. His words were chopped with suffering. 'Don't . . . don't.' He tried to rise from his knees.

Koder glanced over his shoulder. His brows approached each other a trifle, a man irritated at a minor interruption. He dipped his chin at the agent in the doorway, who slammed the butt of his pistol into the detective's head. Dietrich pitched into a black void.

An age passed, or perhaps only a minute. The veil of darkness lifted in fits and starts, allowing Dietrich vague and puzzling glimpses of the countess's apartment as seen from the rug. Dietrich blinked, and that tiny motion sent a bolt of pain from his eyes back across his head and down his neck. He groaned, a sound that barely escaped his lips. He tried to push himself up from the carpet, but nausea surged from his belly into his throat, and he sank back to the floor.

He coughed raggedly, and again tried to rise, but his legs would not hold him, so he rolled to his seat. His head pumped agony down his neck and into his shoulders. The countess – several countesses – drifted in front of him. Her sewing basket and table shifted before him, and all of it was red. He dragged a hand over his eyes. The red haze contracted and swelled with each of his heartbeats, then began to fade. He blinked several times, and the room came together.

The countess's fingers lay across the floor like spilled cartridges. Dietrich's vision still was not good enough to count them, but he trusted the Gestapo to finish a job, and there would be ten of them lying there. The countess was still sitting in her sewing chair. Her hands hung down on each side of the armrests, the frayed stumps of her fingers dripping blood like rows of little spigots.

A hand found Dietrich's shoulder. Egon Haushofer asked fearfully, 'Inspector, can you stand?'

Dietrich grunted a reply.

Haushofer pulled on Dietrich's arm, wrestling him to his feet. 'Take it easy, Inspector. I'll get you to a hospital. Are you all right?'

'No, hell no, I'm not all right.' Dietrich tried to stay above his feet, but he swayed into Haushofer, who pushed him back to standing. The floor seemed to be rolling like the deck of a ship.

Dietrich palpated his head, and brought away blood. His eyes found the countess's seamed face. Her old and leaky eyes were open, and stared at Dietrich in the sightless reproach of death. A clean, perfectly symmetrical bullet hole was centered in her forehead. Her brains were gray and scrambled and seeping down the back of her chair.

Haushofer's words tumbled out. 'I wasn't away long, just while I parked the car, and I was still down the street when I saw those two Gestapo bastards leave the apartment, and . . .'

His head a furnace of pain, Dietrich waved away the explanation, a flick of his fingers that said it didn't matter. He stared bleaky at the countess's body.

'Egon,' he said softly, his head in so much pain his tongue hurt as he worked it, 'what am I doing?'

Haushofer hesitated, searching Dietrich's expression. 'You all right, Inspector? I'd better get you to a doctor.'

Another toss of Dietrich's hand. 'Look what they did to this poor woman.'

'Do you know where you are, Inspector Dietrich?'

'Yes, I know.'

'Your pupils are dilated. I think you've got a concussion.' He gently took Dietrich's arm to turn him to the door. 'Come on, Inspector. We'll get you patched up, then back we'll go after Jack Cray.'

Dietrich touched away dampness at his eyes. 'Yes, Jack Cray. The American.'

Haushofer tried to lead Dietrich from the apartment, but Dietrich said, 'Let's look around here. If he's been here, he's surely left things, left part of himself, though he probably doesn't know it, things the Gestapo would miss.'

Not once in his subterranean service had Sergeant Kahr attempted to smuggle contraband into the bunker. The list of forbidden items was long, and included weapons, writing materials, cameras, food and drink, and cigarettes and matches. He was sneaking such a common item, and tiny. Kahr thought he'd be able to calmly walk up to the SS guards at the blockhouse entrance, receive the usual insults as they patted him down, and enter the blockhouse.

He had rehearsed this entry into the bunker a hundred times in his mind. But as he stepped to the SS guard, Kahr's bit of contraband – a box of matches no larger than his thumb, taped high on his right thigh – seemed to expand in size and weight, slowing him down, forcing him to walk peculiarly, and making him glow like a machine-gun barrel. He felt as if all the Nuremberg spotlights had picked him up as he raised his arms for the pat-down. Five other SS troops milled about. A Red Army shell fluttered overhead, but they were so common, no one looked up. Ash spiraled down as thick as alpine snow, and the SS guard at the door wore it on his shoulders and cap.

'I forget,' the guard said. 'Do you have to go through the toilet room to get to your generators, Sergeant?'

That passed as high humor for the other guard, who laughed mightily, but sobered quickly when a Wehrmacht general with a steel hook for a hand stepped into line behind Kahr. The sergeant held his breath while he was patted down. The guard's hand came close – maybe touched – the matches, but the guard was searching for pistols or grenades, and he searched five hundred people a day, so he missed the matches, just as Kahr had prayed he would.

'Go ahead, Sergeant.'

Kahr moved toward the door into the concrete blockhouse. He heard the Wehrmacht general growl at the guard, 'SS prick. One of these days I'm going to take that probing hand of yours and stick it up your ass.'

'Yes, sir' – words dripping with contempt – 'I'll be here.'

Kahr entered the blockhouse and started down the dimly lit stairs. Berlin had fallen into such dark chaos that the bunker no longer seemed so gloomy by comparison. At least he could escape the ash and the hollow rattle of Bolshevik shells and the scent of sewage from the ruptured lines, though the bunker's toilets often backed up, fouling the air. He turned on the landing and continued down, his stomach still tied up.

The SS guard at the antechamber door frisked him. Coat pockets, inside his coat, up and down his sides, small of his back, his armpits. Then up and down his pants, all of it rough, the guard not giving a damn about offending. This guard didn't find the matches either. Kahr could hear the Wehrmacht general coming down the steps behind him. To hide his nervousness while the guard studied his identification card, Kahr swatted ash from his shoulders.

'Enter,' the guard ordered, passing back the card.

Kahr stepped through the door, breathing for the first time in an hour. The bunker was so crowded he could not see the door at the far end of the hallway. And he gasped at the disarray. Three SS officers in green-and-gray camouflage were in a corner, sharing a bottle of schnapps. Four untouched dinners on a tray sat on the floor near them. General Gotthard Heinrici was raging at Foreign Minister Ribbentrop, his hand pumping like a locomotive's main rod. The minister's face was professionally blank, but his back was against the concrete wall and he could retreat no further. A card table had been set up outside the Führer's door, and two generals were hunched over it. An eastern territorial official – who were all called Golden Pheasants because of their golden-brown uniforms – was slumped forward on a folding chair, elbows on his knees, an empty bottle at his feet. On another table was a gramophone, playing Brahms. A cake with green frosting was next to the record player. An SS adjutant was wiping away frosting and letting the Führer's dog Blondi lick it off his finger. The ecstatic dog banged his tail against a leg of the table, and when the gramophone's needle jumped, Brahms began the bar over again, then again and again as the needle bounced in time to Blondi's tail. His eyes glassy, a Wehrmacht major general in a soiled field uniform sat on another folding chair, blood seeping down his trousers into his boot, a report on his lap. Sipping tea and chatting, three of the Führer's secretaries stood near the door to his conference room, waiting for their shift to begin. Another general – the rose-pink of his greatcoat lapel facings identifying him as being from the Luftwaffe's Corps of Engineers – leaned against a wall, cleaning his fingernails with a pocketknife.

Kahr pushed his way into the hallway, stepping around a tank-crew lieutenant in his black uniform, looking overwhelmed, who probably had been brought underground to receive a medal. Dr Goebbels was looking up at his wife, his lips pulled back in a rictus showing his yellow horse teeth. Mrs Goebbels was lecturing him on something, but Sergeant Kahr was afraid of him – and her – so he steered himself along the other side of the hallway.

He squeezed by General Steiner, who was speaking with another general whom Kahr did not recognize, and was lamenting, 'My total forces consist of six battalions, including some from an SS police division and the 5th Panzer, and the 3rd Navy Division, but we can forget the sailors, who are great on ships but useless for this kind of fighting, so . . .' Kahr moved along, out of earshot.

He walked by the Führer's open door, and the nasal, rasping screech coming from the room could scarcely be identified as Hitler's voice, but of course it was. Only one person belowground was permitted to carry on like that. Kahr flicked his eyes right to glimpse the man. The sight startled him. Hitler was bent over the map table, spavined and frothing, his neck and face as red as paint. His head bobbed violently, and his forelock slapped his eyebrows. Hitler's ordeals had shrunken him. His uniform seemed like a tent over him. At his side were Keitel and Bormann. The sergeant could not see who the Führer was denouncing.

Kahr glanced around. Nobody else in the hallway seemed perturbed by the Führer's ranting. Kahr almost bumped into Armaments Minister Speer's back. Speer was bent low in conversation with Berlin's commandant, General Raymann, who apparently had been summoned from his headquarters on the Hohenzollerndamm and, like all the rest, was waiting his turn for an audience. His chief of staff, Colonel Refior, stood at his elbow. Raymann's burden was such that he always looked as if he had just been beaten up. Holding a clipboard, Gestapo Müller was speaking softly with an SS general, the two leaning toward each other, their faces only inches apart.

The sergeant passed the door to his generator-ventilator room, then exited the main hallway, where an SS guard Kahr recognized was idly flicking his holster's flap. Three pump fire extinguishers were behind the guard on the floor. Kahr climbed the circular stairs and entered the servants' quarters and kitchen wing of the bunker. The central hallway here was used as a dining room, and benches and chairs – including six gilt Louis Seize chairs – and two long rows of tables filled the area. A dozen men and women were eating. Kahr recognized Erich Kempka, Hitler's chauffeur, and Hans Baur, Hitler's pilot, dining on soup and speaking with each other in soft tones. Kahr walked to the end of the dining hall, then turned into the kitchen.

'So you are back again, Ulrich?' A cook smiled over her rolling pin. 'Couldn't stay away, could you?'

'I'm on business today, Helena.'

'You are never on business when you come into my kitchen.' She smiled, put the rolling pin to one side, and wiped her hands on her apron. A circle of dough lay on the table in front of her. Baking trays were stacked on a shelf under the table. Six other cooks were working in the room, one holding a wooden spatula the size of a snow shovel, about to remove bread from an oven built along the back wall. Helena Stalla pulled out a tray of chocolate éclairs from a rack next to the pastry oven, then plucked one from the tray and put it into Sergeant Kahr's hand.

'This is why you visit me,' she said with mock petulance. 'My food. Just my food.' Her smile was both flirtatious and long-suffering. She was wearing a white apron, a short-sleeved white shirt, and a white skirt. Her arms were agreeably flabby. Her hair was hidden under a white bandanna. Dainty streams of sweat flowed from her temples down to her cheeks. 'I always know when you'll show up in my kitchen, Ulrich.'

'You do?'

'Sure. You control the ventilation for every room in the bunker. So you turn off the air in the kitchen. It's hotter than a brick kiln in here now. And then you wander in here, knowing I'll give you food just so you'll turn the fans back on. It's blackmail, is what it is.' She smiled, encouraging him.

Kahr normally appreciated Helena's modest attempts at being a coquette, and would linger awhile, but today he had work to do.

He ate the éclair in two bites, and mumbled around the pastry in his mouth, 'You are stockpiling flour, sounds like.'

'All the time. And sausages and cabbage and venison, everything.'

Kahr licked chocolate from his thumb and index finger, hoping this little concern with cleanliness would disguise his agitation. 'Well, I've been told I've got to share my office with some bags of flour.'

She cackled. 'You call your roomful of pipe an office?'

'I've been ordered to take as much flour off your hands as I can cram into my room. You'll get another load tomorrow.'

She clapped her hands together, raising a cloud of flour. Her teeth showed sourly. 'So now we are hoarding? Is it because access to the warehouse on Kremnitz will soon be impossible? Are the Russians that close?'

Kahr swallowed. His fear had given the éclair – the Führer's favorite dessert – a rancid aftertaste. He tried to be chatty. 'The end has been near since 1942, but don't tell anybody I told you so, lest I'm dragged before a court martial. Let me into the pantry, Helena.'

She untied her apron and hung it on a towel bar. Her keys were on a cord around her ample midriff. Silk stockings were still available to those who had the keys to the Führerbunker pantry and didn't mind passing out butter tins and jars of preserves and a few links. Helena's thighs swished together loudly as she led the sergeant from the kitchen back into the dining hall. The cut-faced Austrian, Kaltenbrunner, had just arrived, and was placing his coffee cup next to Gestapo Müller. At another table Generals Krebs and Burgdorf were huddled over plates of noodles. Krebs eyed Kaltenbrunner uneasily. A few servants were now also eating in the room. Making motor noises, one of the Goebbels children ran along the wall, a toy airplane held over his head.

When Helena came to the supply-room door, she inserted her key, pushed open the door, then reached inside for the light switch. He followed her through the door. Barrels and crates and bags and bottles filled the room. Rounds of cheese, racks of wine, casks of olive oil, kegs of beer, shelves of spices, baskets of oranges, and combs of honey. Eggs, potatoes, raisins, tea, condensed milk, and peppermints. At the back of the pantry was a door to the refrigerator room.

'The flour sacks are there.' Helena pointed.

The sergeant stepped around stacked boxes of carrots. He grunted as he lifted a bag. He guessed it weighed thirty kilograms.

'I'll be back for more.' He brought the sack up to his left shoulder.

The crowd in the dining hall was rapidly growing. Kahr stepped along behind a row of chairs. He did not draw a glance.

At the stairs the SS guard demanded, 'What's in the sack?'

'Flour. I was told to store some bags in my generator room. As many as I could get in.'

The guard drew his knife, and pricked the side of the cloth sack. He pinched a bit of exposed flour between his thumb and forefinger and put it to his mouth. 'It's usually a plate of wurst or pigs' knuckles that the cook gives you.'

With that the guard turned his attention back to the stairs. Kahr carried the sack into the main hall, as crowded as ever. General Busse emerged from the Führer's conference room, his face a mash of chagrined rage. He bolted for the stairway to the garden, a Wehrmacht aide rushing after him. The pretty blond woman – whom Kahr had heard called *die Blöde Kuh*, the stupid cow, and whom the sergeant had once seen absently reach for the Führer's hand, which he jerked away as if her hand had been a sizzling brand – was sitting in a chair, teaching the eldest Goebbels daughter how to apply mascara. Kahr pressed the generator room's buzzer with that day's code, three rings then two.

After a moment – always just long enough to irritate him – Sergeant Fischer threw the bolts and opened the door.

Kahr shouted above the whirr of the fans, 'We've got to keep company with the dry goods. Orders.'

Fischer did not understand much, but he understood orders. He said sullenly, 'First it's canaries, and now it's the stores.'

Kahr lowered the sack to the floor, then pushed it against the base of a generator. When he left the room to return to the pantry, Fischer locked the door behind him.

The sergeant made five more trips to the pantry. Helena flirted with him a little each time, and the SS guard at the circular stairs tasted a sample from each bag. At the end of his labors, Kahr had moved 180 kilograms – about 400 pounds – of flour into the generator room, Sergeant Fischer's scowl deepening with the start of each of Kahr's journeys back to the pantry because he was anxious to escape the bunker.

When Kahr finally relieved Fischer and locked himself into the generator room, he noticed that his exertions with the bags – throwing them off his shoulder onto the concrete floor – had resulted in a fine veil of flour on the generators. The sergeant pulled out a rag and began wiping down his machinery, those big Benz generators and the fan boxes and the air purifiers, and all the red and green pipes. He knew it was to be – one way or the other – the last time he would ever do so.

RSD General Eugen Eberhardt stepped down from the Funkwagen, the cordoning-off order in his hand. He had overseen security for all of the Führer's public appearances and at his residences and headquarters for thirteen years, and the guiding principle had always been the same: erect a wall of guards between the Führer and potential trouble. In years past, tens of thousands of Germans would flock to any wreath-laying or Knight's Cross ceremony, and SS troopers would be stationed at such small intervals that each could grip the belt locks of the men to his left and right. Three other cordons would also be established, using the SS and RSD, the BDM, and Hitler Youth, even the Female Police Auxiliary Helpers. Eberhardt understood and was comfortable with these massive shows of force. But today's cordoning off order was new entirely. It was less an impenetrable wall than it was a knotty scheme. Eberhardt didn't like it.

Otto Dietrich was waiting for him on the street. The detective's driver, Egon Haushofer, was leaning against his car's fenders, a dandelion cigarette in his hand, burned down almost to his knuckles.

Eberhardt waved the four-page cordoning-off order as if he were about to throw it away. 'Otto, I never thought you'd side with the

Gestapo, goddamn them, anyway. Not after the knock they gave your head.'

The back of Dietrich's head hurt so much he could not wear a hat. 'This plan is better, General.'

Eberhardt stared at the order another moment. Smoke drifted by in long and winding loops. A tire plant upwind was burning, and the scent was foul and inescapable.

His voice as mournful as an undertaker's, the general said, 'You know, Otto, there was a time early in my career when I thought protecting the Führer was simply an all-out, full-blown effort, and that all I had to do was to stop a bullet or defuse a bomb. But I learned quickly – and I'm reminded again today – that it involves endless negotiations, and that politics and appearances and territories must be accounted for. And now . . .' He held up the cordoning-off order. 'And now this goddamn mess of an order.'

Dietrich exhaled quickly against the new and caustic scent of ammonia. So the terror bombers had found – somehow and against all odds – a working factory, this one a chemical plant – to destroy. Berliners found no irony in the bombers' Germanic thoroughness.

Dietrich said, 'Preventing Jack Cray from a attempting to assassinate the Führer won't be enough, because Cray will try and try again. He must be caught.'

'He must be killed.' The new voice belonged to Gestapo Müller, who moved into their circle as if he'd been invited. 'I agree with the inspector. If we cordon off the entire government quarter with fifty thousand men, so that the Chancellery is entirely out of sniper-rifle's range, the American will simply come back another day. We must let him think today is like every other day regarding the Führer's security. Let the American have his chance with his rifle. Or, at least, let him think he is getting his chance.'

Dietrich added, 'And we'll be there when he tries. We've left him five firing sites, three that look into the garden, and two that look onto the Vosstrasse Chancellery entrance. There is no site remaining that looks onto the Wilhelmstrasse motor gate.'

Eberhardt knew all this, of course. He and Dietrich had overseen the destruction of fifteen structures that looked upon the Chancellery. Most of the buildings had already been damaged, and Eberhardt's crews had pulled down the buildings' husks.

Dietrich said, 'Jack Cray will appear at one of those firing sites today. I am sure of it.'

'So am I,' Müller said. 'Those sites will be like hornet traps. Cray will find them easy to enter, but impossible to escape. We have ten troops at each one of them. Well armed, well trained, and hidden.'

'And you are sure he is going to try for the Führer today?' Eberhardt knew Dietrich's theory, but he wanted to be convinced.

'The old lady told us so,' Müller said.

Another Gestapo vehicle appeared out of the smoke – unmarked black vehicles with sufficient gasoline to move about were invariably the Gestapo these days – stopping across from the Funkwagen, near a burned-out delivery truck, the name of the vendor – BREMEN PRODUCE – just distinguishable under black soot covering the side panels. Rudolf Koder emerged from the car. He put his hands in his coat pockets and leaned against the front fender, eyeing Dietrich with disdain, and apparently waiting for Gestapo Müller.

General Eberhardt said, 'Your man had no call to murder that woman, that countess, Müller.'

'Would you rather have sacrificed the Führer's life? That was our choice, wasn't it? Either she talked, or the American would have been successful. Do you deny the logic of the choice?'

'Well, that doesn't mean you should – '

Müller cut him off. 'Once again the Gestapo had to do your job for you, Eberhardt. You needed to know when Jack Cray was going to make his move, and you didn't have a clue. Now you do, thanks to Agent Koder over there.'

'We still don't know.' Dietrich felt the need to defend the RSD general. 'Not really.' The detective made a swift noise in his throat, angry at himself, and embarrassed. He did not have the courage to argue with Gestapo Müller, to argue that the murder of the countess was an outrage, or that the ends did not justify the means.

'Jack Cray said goodbye to the countess this morning, meaning he would not be sleeping at her apartment another night.' Müller rocked on his heels. 'Cray believed the countess's place to be secure.

He wouldn't tell her he would not be returning if he were staying in the city any longer. Cray is going into action today.'

Dietrich wished he could fault Müller's reasoning.

'And we think Cray's plan will begin with a bombing raid.' Müller nodded along with his own words. 'And the American planes always come between nine and noon. Any other time, we'd be suspicious.'

Dietrich glanced again at Rudolf Koder. Blood rose in the detective's face.

Müller had a pavement voice. 'General Eberhardt and Inspector Dietrich, your conclusion is a house of cards: Cray using a bombing run to try to chase the Führer from the bunker. But this speculation on your part is the best we have, as you say yourself.'

Somewhere in the distance the wail of an air-raid siren began, a wavering tinny trill. Then another, and another, until the sound had rushed to every corner of the ruined city.

'Here come the Americans, then,' Heinrich Müller announced needlessly. He started toward Koder's car without saying anything more.

'We'd better get belowground, Otto.' Eberhardt walked toward the underground station. 'If our theory is correct, these bombs are going to fall on the government quarter, all around us.'

Dietrich followed at Eberhardt's elbow. His anger bubbled up. 'I'm going to kill that son of a bitch Rudolf Koder when I get the chance.' He was instantly abashed.

Eberhardt turned to grip the detective's arm and gave him a corrosive look. 'The Russians will be here any day, and they'll surely do that work for you.' After a few more steps he added, 'Koder and his boss Müller are too dangerous for us to fool with. So don't do anything to get yourself hung, Otto.'

TWENTY

'Will I be seeing you again?' Cray looked up from the blanket he was about to roll. In the center of the blanket were the clothes the countess had made for him. Near the blanket was the burlap bag containing the antitank mines and the stick grenades. 'After I leave here in a few minutes . . .' His voice trailed away.

'I can't go with you.' She wrapped her arms around herself. 'I've already told you so.'

Cray threw onto the blanket a roll of cheese, a loaf of bread, a canteen, and a gas-mask container. The masks were issued to Berliners early in the war. This one had belonged to the countess, and she had never taken it out of the box. Cray gathered up the blanket's corners to form a bundle. He was wearing refugee clothing, two pistols in his belt under his coat, and the knife tucked into a sleeve. Once again the left side of his face was covered with a smudged bandage, and his hair and eyebrows were dark. On his head was a filthy workman's cap that covered the bandaged gash on his forehead. He would be indistinguishable from thousands upon thousands of other refugees fleeing west through Berlin's tortured streets, everything they owned on their backs.

'Where's the rifle you went to so much trouble to get?' she asked.

'It's already where it should be.' He was always vague.

An air-raid siren down the street began a shrill piping, joined after a few seconds by another.

Cray brought up his wristwatch. 'Right on time.'

She shivered. 'Do you know the one thing I'm going to miss about you?'

'My looks?'

She didn't even smile. In the smoke-filtered morning light, her face was as pale as candle wax. 'The sense of invulnerability you give me. When you first showed up, I was frightened beyond my wits. I knew I was in immense danger every second I was with you. But your brainless bravura is infectious. You've convinced me you will live forever, and are no more vulnerable to the German war machine than those American bombers on their way here now. I've come to feel safe around you. As safe as I've felt since my husband died and I started working for the Hand. I'm going to miss that.'

'Not my looks? You sure?'

'Can you be serious one second?'

He looked away a moment, out the window. They were in the second floor of a burned-out clothing store. Most of the roof had been ripped off by an HE blast, and the fire that followed had charred everything else. Rolled in blankets, they had slept that night in the one corner of the room that still had a roof. Puddles of rainwater filled sagging points in the floor. Scavengers had stripped the store of everything but coat hangers, and they lay about the floor and stairs where Cray had placed them to prevent anyone stealing up on them as they slept. They were on Kellner Street, nine blocks from the Reich Chancellery.

He said quietly, 'I tried to be serious with you. It didn't work.'

'You were serious? About what?'

'About what is going to happen to Berlin in a few days, a week. What might happen to you if you stay here. You didn't give me any reason to hope I could change your mind. So now I'm back to my good-natured self.'

She stared at him, her expression softening. Suddenly she laughed. 'Can I predict your future?'

'Sure.'

She looked through a gap in the ceiling. The sun was pale, silver instead of gold. Her eyes found him again. 'Someday back in the United States you'll trick some woman into marrying you, Jack. Some young lady who'll have no more idea who you really are than you do.'

He smiled, then rose to his feet, lifting the blanket pack and the burlap bag to his back.

'What a terrible trick you'll be pulling on her,' Katrin said, trying to smile. 'I don't know whether I should be sorry for her or envious.'

'Do one more thing for me?' Cray asked. 'Meet me at the Tiergarten airstrip, near the East-West Axis.'

'I can say goodbye here as well as there.'

'It'll give me one more chance to convince you. Maybe you'll change your mind between now and then, and leave Berlin with me.'

'I won't. I belong here.'

'Seeing me board that plane might change your mind.' He grinned. 'Might break your heart and change your mind.'

She could not help but smile with him. 'I'll be at the park, if you'd like. But I won't go with you, Jack.'

The bundle and bag over his shoulder, stepping across coat hangers and around an overturned desk, Cray said, maybe to her, maybe to himself, 'I can be pretty convincing.'

He descended the stairs, made his way around debris on the first floor, walked outside into the watery sunlight, and started in the direction of the Reich Chancellery.

Ulrich Kahr knew the air raid had begun when his desk started to shiver. Only a little at first, then the old Wehrmacht-surplus oak desk began to dance toward the generators, and the sergeant had to grab it and drag it back. His chair shifted under him, wanting to scoot toward the door, sliding as if it were on ice. His pencil box vibrated and moved to the edge of the desk, then fell to the floor. The control panel, with its luminous dials and toggle switches shifted in front of Kahr's eyes like a kaleidoscope. When he rose from his chair, the floor shifted under his feet like beach sand pulled by waves.

The room went black, a disorienting, impenetrable black. Kahr moved unsteadily toward the door, to the flashlight that hung on the wall near the door frame. The room quieted as the fans wound down. He moved the beam of light to the fan box. He tripped the fan switches so that when the bunker again had electric power the fans would remain still.

Then the light beam found the starter engine. He knew the routine well enough, but never had the room trembled so violently, and when he reached for the starter engine's cord, it shimmied in front of his hand and he had to stab at it several times before he could close his hand around it. He planted his feet squarely – the floor vibrating under him – and yanked the cord. The little engine popped several times, then blared like a trumpet.

The sergeant let it warm up for the prescribed sixty seconds before pulling the clutch lever that engaged the belt to the first diesel engine, which began a low grinding. In a moment the diesel would be warm enough to run without the aid of the starter engine.

Kahr withdrew a service knife from the desk drawer, then pulled the mattress from its cot onto the floor. He stabbed into the mattress and raked the ticking with the blade, then again and again, shredding it, his arms throwing outsized shadows on the pool of light from the flashlight. He lay the knife aside to tug out the stuffing, all of it, until the mattress cover was limp.

He interrupted himself to disengage the starter motor. The diesel hummed satisfactorily. He pressed the kill button on the starter engine and threw the main switch. The overhead bulbs flickered on in the room, and throughout the bunker, not as brightly as with outside power, but adequately.

The sergeant carried the mattress wadding the few steps to the second generator, this one not running. He put most of the wadding to one side, but retained a handful. He lifted his helmet from the desk. The fuel line was interrupted by a drain valve near the filter. He held the upside-down helmet under the valve, then opened the line. A thin stream of diesel oil fell into the helmet. Kahr dropped the wadding into the helmet, and let the fuel soak the fabric. When it was saturated, he put it aside on the floor and dipped another tuft of wadding into the diesel. After a few moments he had soaked all of the wadding, and it lay on the floor, oozing fuel.

The lightbulbs abruptly regained their full brightness, and then a buzzer at the control panel indicated power had been restored to the bunker. Normally, Sergeant Kahr would now shut down the diesel generator. This time he left the big machine – all green and brass and glorious – droning along.

He looked at his watch. The room continued to twitch and ripple as the earth carried bomb shock waves to the bunker. He was to wait five minutes from the first blasts. A few more seconds. The entry buzzer sounded with the correct sequence. Kahr ignored it. The canaries sang unknowingly.

Another glance at his watch. At the control panel he threw five switches, each engaging an electric motor that closed a gate in the ventilation system. After a few seconds signal lights on the panel indicated all five gates had worked. Instead of bringing in fresh air, his system was now recycling old air, taking it out of the bunker, circulating it through his pipes, and returning it again to the bunker. If Kahr were to do no more, and if the air purification system remained off, it would be several moments before occupants of the bunker noticed that their air was becoming warm and foul.

But he had more to do. He opened a service gate on one of the green pipes, then pushed wads of the damp and reeking mattress stuffing into the pipe. He compressed them a bit, making sure the wet wads were not entirely blocking the pipe. Then he opened another green gate, and stuffed another wad of diesel-impregnated fabric into it. He repeated the procedure nine more times, until each green pipe contained his preparations.

He unbuttoned his pants and yanked on the matchbox. He grimaced as hairs came away with the tape. He opened the box to fish out a match. Again he checked his wristwatch. The time had come. He struck the match against the box, and it flared to life. He pushed the small flame into the opening of a green pipe until it was against the fuel-soaked wad. The material caught fire. He quickly closed the gate, trapping the fire inside the pipe. It would burn slowly until it had new air.

He set another clump of fabric on fire in a second pipe, then flicked his hand to extinguish the match when it began to cook his fingers. He tossed it aside and lit another, and in the next few minutes set all the wadding on fire.

Next, Sergeant Kahr engaged the fans, but at a low speed, not so fast as to extinguish the pipe fires, but enough to move the black diesel smoke from his fabric fires through the system and into the bunker. He pulled his gas mask from its box and put it over his head.

And now he waited. The entrance buzzer sounded again, and he heard a muffled, 'Sergeant Kahr. Open the door.'

But still he waited, listening to the fans as they filled the bunker with smoke. Black haze began pouring into his room through the grates. Once again up came his wristwatch. Five minutes more, and he would turn his attention to the red pipes. He sank into his chair and glanced at the bags of flour. Pounding at the door became louder. 'Sergeant Kahr.' One voice, then three voices, all yelling his name. Fists beat on the metal door and the buzzer sounded again and again. He waited.

The bombers had come from the northwest, then wheeled over the Havel River, and had followed its tributary, the Spree, into the center of Berlin. The city offered a bomber pilot's dream: unmistakable landmarks close to the target. Dead center in the vast expanse of the Tiergarten was the Victory Monument, and at the northwest corner of the Tiergarten was the burned-out Reichstag and, just south, the Brandenburg Gate. These structures stood out like beacons. The target – the government quarter – lay at the east end of the Tiergarten, and the route to the quarter was as clear as the creases on a B-24 navigator's palm.

The bombing run was unusual for the Americans in the spring of 1945. They came in low – at two thousand feet, unheard of for B-24s – and they came with only twenty planes. And these twenty planes aligned themselves like ships of the line, rather than in their box formation. They roared over the Reichstag and over Joseph Goebbels's home and across Unter den Linden, right into the Mitte between Wilhelmstrasse and Mauerstrasse, precisely on target, bomb bays open and sticks falling.

A swath of chaos and destruction on the ground chased the

planes' shadows. Upper Wilhelmstrasse buckled and then turned over as if by a giant plow. The Science and Education Ministry disappeared in a cloud of dust and fragments. The Justice Ministry received two bombs through its roof, and every window and door blew out in bursts of fragments, followed by its front wall, the stones crashing down onto Wilhelmstrasse.

On Mauerstrasse the Paris Restaurant ceased to exist in a white flash, nothing remaining larger than twisted forks. The House of Furniture also vanished, leaving only a crater filled with furniture splinters and shiny brass drawer handles. On Wilhemplatz a water main was exposed, and torrents of water swept across the plaza toward the Chancellery. The walls of the Chamber of Culture cascaded to the street, and the floors sank one on another like spoons placed in a drawer. The Finance Ministry was hit for the second time in the war. Half of the building was blown out onto Kaiserhofstrasse, and fire swept through the remaining half, fueled by rows of document-filled filing cabinets. The enormous Postal Ministry building was instantly transformed into a knot of wreckage. Hotels and shops and apartments were shaken or blown or vacuumed apart, and then fire swept into the remains.

The earth lurched and reeled. Shock waves sped through the ground like a shaken blanket. Superheated air swept along the street, yanking off awnings and signs, sucking out windows, and carrying deadly debris. Power lines collapsed and lay across the street, sparking and hissing. Automobiles were tossed about like windblown leaves. Cobblestones and bricks rained down. Some light poles were bent double, others were ripped from the ground. The iron picket fence with its gilded spikes that had protected the Propaganda Ministry flew through the air like spears. Timbers and pipes and masonry shrieked and groaned. Ribbentrop's Foreign Office – just next to the Reich Chancellery – was torn in two. And just south of the Chancellery, the Transportation Ministry suffered three direct hits, gutting the building. The trees on Kaiserhofplatz – opposite the Vosstrasse motor entrance to the Chancellery – were stripped of their new spring leaves.

Then the planes were gone and the bombs had spent their fury.

An eerie quiet settled over the area, broken only by the crackle of fire and the occasional beam or post giving way. Scents of cordite and sewage and plaster dust and newly turned dirt were carried away from the target area by the wind.

Berliners hiding belowground could not have known then of the careful placing of the bombs. Ruin had been vast in the Mitte, but not one bomb had sailed into the Reich Chancellery or its garden.

They were left alone. They were left for Jack Cray.

General Eberhardt ran up the steps from the bomb cellar below the Air Ministry, four RSD men behind him. They emerged at a service entrance on Leipzigerstrasse. They sprinted east along the street toward the intersection, dodging the new debris and craters. Eberhardt carried a radio in one hand and a pistol in the other. His troops were armed with Schmeissers and rifles. The air contained the sharp odor of high-explosive residue. The all-clear had not yet sounded, and no one else was on the street. Eberhardt knew another team would be closing in on the Teller Building from the other direction, further east on Leipzigerstrasse.

He personally could cover only one of the five potential firing sites, as Eberhardt well knew. But he prayed Jack Cray would choose this one, the six-story office building with a view of the Chancellery's motor-court entrance. This building was Eberhardt's best guess, the most likely of the five sites, the one Eberhardt would choose were he up to such business. He wanted to be the one to waylay the American commando.

With a combat team, Otto Dietrich was covering another site, and was hoping with a fervor equal to Eberhardt's that his – Dietrich's – spot would be chosen by Cray. Because of the knife at his throat near Katrin von Tornitz's home, Dietrich had gained an animosity toward the American unusual in someone as professional as he was. Eberhardt had humorously chided Dietrich about it, but the detective would not be amused.

At first Eberhardt's plan was to hide in the Teller Building's cellar during the bombing run. Then he determined that was probably where Cray would keep himself safe – presuming this building was his firing site – and so the general had chosen the nearby Air Ministry. And now he had to hurry. He stung his ankle on a brick, but kept running, turning left and right through a maze of overturned automobiles and skirting a new crater at the intersection of Wilhelmstrasse and Kaiserhofstrasse. He passed a human torso – no head, no legs – belonging to someone who had risked that the bombers would not hit the government quarter today. Glass shards lay over the street like dew on grass.

An RSD sergeant from the other team was already at the Teller Building's front door. He held his submachine gun like he knew how to use it. It was not for a general to be the first through the door, and Eberhardt knew it and so did his men. He did not have their proficiency, which he had made sure was unequaled in the German services. When Eberhardt nodded, the RSD troops rushed into the building and began up the stairs, their weapons in front of them. The rear of the building – which was a wall shared with the neighboring restaurant – had been exposed by the bomb that ruined the restaurant, explaining the scent of horse stew in the Teller Building's lobby.

Eberhardt was breathing through his open mouth when he reached the sixth floor. His men – younger and more fit – were already inside the room that overlooked the Chancellery's motor entrance. The general swore to himself when he saw they were milling about, their weapons at ease. Desks and filing cabinets filled the room. He had been wrong. Cray had chosen another site. Other RSD men were searching the rest of the floor. Through the window Eberhardt could see the Chancellery's motor entrance three blocks away.

He put the handset to his mouth and dispensed with radio protocol. 'This is Eberhardt. Anything at number two?'

A crackling voice. 'No, sir. Nobody.'

Eberhardt demanded, 'Number three?'

A different voice, made weak by the reception. 'Nothing, sir.'

He called out the other numbers, each a potential firing site, his scowl deepening as each team reported seeing nothing.

Then one of his soldiers entered the room, holding a scoped sniper's rifle, a Mauser with a thick barrel. Eberhardt groaned, but only to himself.

'I found the rifle two rooms down, sir. This was with it.' The soldier handed Eberhardt a piece of paper.

The general read aloud, ' "You can have this rifle back. I won't be needing it." '

And then – his face crimsoning – General Eberhardt understood why Dietrich had taken a personal dislike to Jack Cray. And Eberhardt knew he and Dietrich had been wrong – perfectly and wildly wrong – about Cray's plan.

TWENTY-ONE

The intercom on Sergeant's Kahr's desk was buzzing and the telephone there was ringing and it sounded as if SS guards were working on the steel door with a pry. Kahr had helped design the door, and he knew it would hold for the few more minutes he needed. Black smoke was coming through the ventilator grates, the same smoke that was pouring into all the rooms of the bunker, and it was getting thicker.

Kahr coughed into his mask. The two filter canisters hung almost to his belly. With levers he engaged the fan box that pushed air through the red system. He played with a dial until the fan was moving air at half capacity. Then he twisted the valves on the water pipes, closing down the bunker's sprinkler system.

He opened a grate over the uppermost red pipe on the wall. Air flowed through the pipe in a steady stream, but it too was smoky because the red backup system was drawing air from the bunker and returning it to the same place. Kahr ripped open a flour sack, glanced for the last time at his wristwatch, and then started pouring flour into the pipe. It fell in a steady stream, and was just as quickly sucked away along the pipe. After only a few seconds his first bag was empty. He lifted the second bag, balanced it on his knee to yank out the thread, and spilled its contents into the pipe. And then the third bag, then the fourth, pouring steadily, the white powder disappearing down the pipe. He emptied the last two bags. And now the flour began to drift back into his generator-ventilator room through the air ducts.

Kahr brought out his box of matches and scratched a match against the score.

Foreign Minister Ribbentrop struggled with his gas mask. A strap was caught on his ear. He wrestled with it, swearing and coughing. Finally the goggles were squarely over his eyes. He lit a cigarette, perhaps figuring no one would notice, and he lifted his mask momentarily to draw on it.

Keitel had found the captain of the guard, an SS-Hauptsturmführer who was overseeing three men working a pry bar at the ventilator-generator room door. Keitel yelled at them to hurry, then tugged at his high collar and gulped the blackened air. He jammed his thumb against the door buzzer again and again.

The bombing raid had just ended, and the bunker had stopped its trembling. But it was filling with acrid black smoke that obscured the walls and ceiling. Fumes gushed from the grates along the hallway.

'Keep at that door.' The guard captain began walking the hallway, demanding at each door, his voice muffled by a gas mask, 'Report any fire.'

Martin Bormann emerged from the conference room and held a handkerchief to his mouth. Bormann was called the Brown Eminence because of his cunning and his brown uniform, one of the last of the Old Fighters to wear brown. An SS orderly rushed up to Bormann to give him a mask. Bormann pulled it over his face.

On the guard captain's orders, guards had assumed their emergency stations. At each end of the center hallway an SS guard wearing a gas mask stood near the door, a submachine gun in his hands. Another guard stood precisely in the middle of the hallway, holding a pistol, and yet another posted himself outside the door that entered Hitler's conference room and bedroom, the guard's Walther ready and his head – hidden under a gas mask – moving left and right like a metronome.

Smoke was thickest near the ceiling, and the throng appeared headless to Minister Goebbels, who was shorter than everyone else in the hallway. General Speidel helped one of the Führer's secretaries into a mask, then gestured that she should kneel to get below the densest smoke. Gasping, another secretary stumbled into a folding table, spilling three bottles and a deck of cards onto the floor. One bottle shattered, and wine sped along the floor. The pilot, Baur, lifted his mask to wipe his eyes with his fingers.

Noise in the bunker was ear-rending. The ventilators had again started their dentist-drill whine, pushing smoke into the area. The Führer's dog, Blondi, howled and barked at the smoke as he paced in front of the conference room door. The SS crew frantically worked on the ventilator-room door – metal on metal – and the door squealed in protest. Goebbels had found someone to yell at – a hapless Propaganda Ministry aide – whom Goebbels, it was suspected, employed for that very purpose because he had no luck shouting at his wife. The gramophone played a piano solo, one of the Führer's favorites, Schumann's *Kinderszenen*, too loudly. And all the coughing and swearing and arguing, all of it echoing in the long concrete tunnel.

Alfried Jodl stepped into the hallway, breathing stertorously, tears running down his rounded cheeks. He called, 'We must evacuate. Give the order.'

'No, sir,' replied the guard captain. 'Our orders are to remain belowground if at all possible, and it is still possible.'

Jodl was six ranks above the captain, but the captain was in charge of bunker security. Jodl abruptly turned away, bumping into Minister Speer, who was standing in the middle of the hallway staring through his mask goggles at a ventilator grate with evident detachment, his hands clenched behind his back, the smoke still flowing from the grate. He knew of the backup system because he had helped design it. Black smoke was rushing from half the grates. The other half was not in operation, not moving smoke or fresh air.

The crew at the ventilator-room door jammed the pry bar's blade into the space between the steel door and the steel frame, but it was a question as to whether the door or the pry bar would give first. Two guards yanked on the bar, but it lost its purchase, and the guards had to catch themselves to prevent spilling backward. The captain plunged the bar again into the crack.

Smoke flowed from half the grates, now darker and more dense. It hid the ceiling, and more of the acrid haze was sinking toward the floor.

Keitel could not restrain himself. He marched over to the guard captain. 'I order you to evacuate the Führerbunker, Captain.'

He let up on the pry bar. 'Sir, there is no fire belowground.'

Keitel's chin went up. The dueling scar on his cheek was magnificent, even in the smoke. 'I will not stand for impudence from a – '

'If there's no fire, we stay here.' A new voice.

The captain was relieved to see RSD General Eberhardt, who had just entered the bunker. Eberhardt's countenance was grim. He slipped the straps of a gas mask over his head.

'Eberhardt, we cannot breathe this air,' Keitel said. 'It is time to leave the bunker.'

Not wanting a trace of self-pity to color his words, Eberhardt spoke carefully and firmly. 'I have failed to stop the American commando. He is still out there, and I have no doubt he is nearby.'

Keitel's black scowl dissolved as he coughed, a rattling hack that bent him over so that his medals hung away from his coat, and that ended in a whistling wheeze. He managed, 'Look around, for God's sake, Eberhardt. We can't stay down here. We'll suffocate.'

General Eberhardt's voice was weary. 'Your mask is secure against the smoke, sir.'

Still staring at the ventilation grates, Albert Speer said, rather idly, his words lost in the tumult, 'What's that new material? Chalk dust? Coming from the second set of vents.'

Speer did not have long to wonder, and perhaps no one else belowground noticed the white powder.

At that instant, in the locked ventilator room, Sergeant Kahr dropped the match into the red pipe and slammed shut the cover.

The flour-air mixture in the pipes ignited. Fire roared through the system.

The guard captain heard the muffled explosion, and turned from the ventilator-room door to see fire pour out of grates that lined both long walls of the bunker hallway, flame rushing into the hallway from six grates and spilling to the floor.

He opened the sprinkler valves at his station in the corridor, twisted both valves to their fully open position. A few drops of water came from overhead sprinklers, but nothing more.

'Extinguishers,' yelled the guard captain. He pushed the nearest SS guard's shoulders and pointed at the door to the kitchen wing. The guard hurried through the door for them.

Fire pooled in the hallway beneath the grates, then spread across the floor like rushing water. A secretary screamed. Speer removed his jacket to try to douse one of the lakes of flame. A patch of rug caught fire. An orderly turned to run but knocked the gramophone off the table, and it shattered on the floor. The dog fled. Smoke was thick and choking. Fire crawled up the cement walls, blackening them. Flame leaped about, as if searching for combustibles. A gilded chair that had been under a grate was a ball of flame. The air temperature in the bunker rose quickly. There were more screams and confused shouts.

The guard captain punched the TeNo button on a wall box, then, not satisfied, lifted a telephone handset from the wall. He yelled into it, 'We need fire and TeNo crews in the Führerbunker immediately.' He listened a moment, then added, 'I don't give a goddamn if your entire building just blew apart. I mean right now. This is no drill.'

Eberhardt caught the guard captain's eye. Patches of fire were along the hallway and in many of the rooms. More fire came from the grates. But perhaps this was the worst of it. The smoke was dense, but everyone had gas masks. With Jack Cray outside, Eberhardt was still reluctant to order the bunker evacuated, despite the heat and smoke and turmoil. The guard captain understood, and nodded his agreement.

General Eberhardt brought up his wristwatch, close to his mask's eyepieces. The fires were spreading. Two sofas were burning, and more of the rug. Eberhardt had no idea whether the bombing run had caused the smoke and fires, or whether someone in the generator-ventilator room had done some mischief. He and the guard captain could wait another two or three minutes before deciding whether to evacuate the bunker.

And hope soared within the general. Perhaps the American had failed. Perhaps this was Jack Cray's attempt to flush the Führer from the bunker, and this fire and smoke were the worst Jack Cray could do. Fire was spreading, but it might be contained. The American hadn't chased the Führer to the surface yet. Not yet.

Blood came away with the receiver when TeNo Captain Klaus Dreesen lowered the telephone. A gash along his temple was spilling blood. A splinter from the wall, he guessed hazily. Dreesen heard shouts from his squad members, then a muffled scream from one of them trapped in back of the building. He pressed his temple below the wound, trying to bring his thoughts together. Blood dribbled onto his fingers.

The captain's Mauerstrasse building was the headquarters of the Technical Emergency Corps unit that was to respond to an emergency in the Führerbunker. His unit was held in reserve for just such a summons.

Twelve months of training for this moment, for a real emergency in the bunker, and all Dreesen could think of was how much his goddamn head hurt. And then, after the alarm had sounded, the Führerbunker guard captain had telephoned to yell at him, as if Dreesen needed to be told his job. Dizzy and staggering, he turned toward the ruin.

He and his men were already in uniform, as they were during each air raid. The bombs had sounded like they were landing blocks away, but one must have dropped late from a bomb bay, and hit the building next door to the north with a force that blew in the squadron's headquarters' wall and dropped much of the second floor onto the ground floor. Half the building was in ruin, with dust and smoke still billowing and timbers still swinging. A pipe had broken, and water rushed across the concrete floor. Fire was working on a pile of wood fragments that had a moment before been lockers, and two of Dreesen's men were putting it out with pump extinguishers. A wall clock was in pieces on the floor, the face lying on its scrambled springs. The bomb had shredded several TeNo uniforms that had been hanging near the lockers, and mangled strips of white herringbone fabric were sprinkled across the room.

One of Dreesen's men sat on the hoses, his mouth open, blood flowing from an ear. Another TeNo member searched for his spectacles in a pile of boots, groaning softly, one arm hanging limp and useless. Beams hung through the ceiling, and several were hanging down almost as far as the trucks. A stack of portable street barricades had been tossed together with half a dozen stretchers. Chunks of the ceiling were still falling.

Even so, even in the ruin, the months of drill began to pay off. His crew was responding to the bells, was emerging from the smoke and rubble, some donning their masks, others putting on tool belts, some carrying pry bars and axes, some limping, others grimacing against injuries. A squad member pulled on the chain to raise the door. Because of the bombing run, it was as smoky outside as in. Another crewman pushed rubble from the top of the pumper, then climbed in and started the engine. A second vehicle – the generator truck – cranked into life. Two TeNo men were already in the cab. Captain Dreesen climbed onto the running-board.

The trucks pulled onto Mauerstrasse. Curtains of smoke rose and fell. Debris was scattered across Kaiserhofplatz, the plaza that separated TeNo headquarters from the Reich Chancellery. Buildings in various states of ruin – the Propaganda Ministry, the Chamber of Culture, the Hotel Kaiserhof, the Transportation Ministry – drifted in and out of Dreesen's view. Two blocks east, fires consumed a row of buildings, but Dreesen could see only an orange haze through the smoke, seemingly suspended in the air at the rooflines. Sirens wailed from every direction.

A dozen more of Dreesen's men hurried out of the building, some in masks, others holding cloth to their faces against the smoke, forming out of the haze from a neighboring flat that was used as a barracks.

Dreesen barked an order, unnecessarily. His men knew the

procedure. Debris was scattered across the plaza. A few TeNo men hopped aboard the trucks, but most began running toward the Reich Chancellery, knowing they would make better time than the vehicles.

Captain Dreesen glanced at his watch. He smiled with cold pleasure. Three minutes since the alarm, and they were underway. Despite the bomb blast that had gutted his headquarters and had injured some of his men, his TeNo squad was rolling in three minutes.

The ceaseless drills had just paid off. The trucks lurched around a fallen masonry arch. The smoke shifted, and the Chancellery was suddenly visible. Dreesen grinned again.

Otto Dietrich picked up the telephone, rubbed the handset nervously a moment, then without using it returned it to the cradle behind the SS guard's booth. The detective had heard a muffled explosion, the sound made hollow and metallic by its route up the stairwell, followed by thicker smoke pouring from the door. General Eberhardt – sixty feet under Dietrich's feet in the bunker – would call if there was anything Dietrich needed to know.

The massive blockhouse was in front of Dietrich, with its steel door open. Smoke continued to drift up the stairs and out through the door, joining the haze that filled the garden from the bombing run, obscuring the walls of the Chancellery. Six SS guards stood near the door, and two more by the booth. The guards knew of Dietrich's authority, knew of Himmler's letter in his pocket, and knew he had the Führer's ear. Still, they looked at the plainclothesman with suspicion. Dietrich paced, ignoring the guards. A young guard watched from a tower, appearing and disappearing in the dense smoke. Rudolf Koder no longer bothered to hide that he was trailing Dietrich. He waited near the blockhouse, watching the detective.

The telephone sounded. An SS lieutenant lifted the handset, said, 'Yes, sir,' and replaced it on the cradle. He told Dietrich, 'The Rescue Squad has been summoned.'

'Has an evacuation been ordered?'

'Not yet. They can hold out a while longer, General Eberhardt thinks.'

Dietrich nodded. He suspected Eberhardt would rather allow everyone to be parboiled than expose the Führer to Jack Cray out in the open.

And Jack Cray was out in the open. Cray was within one hundred meters of him, Dietrich was certain. Somewhere in the Reich Chancellery, in the ruined wing, maybe even in the garden, hidden somewhere, waiting for Hitler to emerge. Cray's sniper rifle had been found, along with the note, and so Dietrich's deductions regarding Cray's plans had been entirely wrong. Now Dietrich simply had no notion how and where Cray would strike. Dietrich had failed.

Guards at the motor entrance pulled open the iron gates. The guards were made spectral by layers of smoke that dipped from the sky, hiding their heads and shoulders, then lifting to reveal them again. TeNo men ran through the gate, followed by a TeNo pumper truck with yellow flashing lights on top of the cab. A generator truck followed. The TeNo uniforms were the precise color of the smoke. Some of the Rescue Squad carried axes and pry bars. Many wore gas masks, and others were just now putting them on.

When the first truck arrived at the blockhouse, a TeNo officer jumped from the running-board and held his identification card up to the guard at the door and said, 'Captain Dreesen.'

The TeNo captain's gas mask was hanging around his neck. The SS guard had worked with Dreesen before during rescue drills, but he still studied Dreesen's face, comparing it with the photo on the ID.

Finally Dreesen barked, 'Get out of my way, asshole.'

The SS guard waved Dreesen and his men through. A line from the generator truck was clamped to an electrical box. If needed, the truck would provide electricity for emergency lights. Another TeNo man placed a pack radio on the walkway near the bunker. Two TeNo radiomen entered the bunker, one carrying a second radio, and another unwinding wire from a reel. Should the bunker's telephones fail, the TeNo crews above- and belowground would still be able to communicate.

More Rescue Squad members trailed in from the haze. Several wore fire-resistant canvas vests with 'TeNo' stamped on them in white. Some carried coiled ropes, others hauled oxygen bottles, pry bars, and sledgehammers. The SS guards stood aside as they passed through the door into the blockhouse.

And then it came to Otto Dietrich, came with a force like a blow to his chest, crushing the wind out of him.

The SS guards had checked the TeNo captain's identification, but were allowing his men into the bunker without being screened.

TeNo men had come into the ruined garden as a group, and were entering the bunker as a group, all in their white herringbone uniforms, some wearing gas masks, all hauling equipment, rushing underground as they had rehearsed time and again. And as the SS guards had witnessed time and again.

No one was examining each TeNo face.

'Arrest them,' Dietrich yelled, waving his hand wildly. 'All of them. All the TeNo men.' He dug into his coat for his pistol.

The SS guards glanced at Dietrich with indecision, but only for an instant. They brought their weapons up, and stepped across to bar the blockhouse door.

Outraged, the TeNo radioman began to loudly protest but was choked off when the bore of a Schmeisser found his nose. The guards quickly surrounded the Rescue Squad members still aboveground.

His pistol in front of him, Dietrich tore off the nearest TeNo man's gas mask. A dark-haired man with black stubble across his cheeks and chin. Looked nothing like Jack Cray.

Guards shouted orders. The TeNo crew dropped their axes and bars and ropes, and lifted their hands above their heads.

Dietrich ran to the telephone at the blockhouse door. He lifted the handset and pressed the button. He yelled into the phone at the guard captain, 'The American is in the bunker. Jack Cray is in a TeNo uniform.'

Then the detective grabbed a gas mask from a guard and ran into the blockhouse and down the stairs, into the smoke and gloom.

Dietrich descended blindly, unable to see through the rising smoke, roughly pushing aside TeNo men slowed by their equipment, awkwardly trying to put on the mask. The detective knew any one of them might be Jack Cray working his way into the bunker, but Dietrich suspected the American would have been one of the first TeNo men down the stairs. Cray was already in the bunker, Dietrich was certain. Koder followed Dietrich down.

From below came cries of alarm, shouted orders, a dog's barking, and the crackling of fire. Heat rose in the stairwell. Dietrich held his pistol in front of him. His mask leaked and smoke stung his eyes. He reached the antechamber where two SS guards held their weapons on TeNo men, keeping them from entering the bunker. Smoke drifted among them, collecting in the antechamber before being pulled up the stairs. When the detective held up his ID, the SS guard glanced at his face, then nodded that he could enter.

'Arrest the TeNo men,' came the harsh voice of a guard captain who had been yelling the order again and again since Dietrich's call sixty seconds before. The captain was hidden in the gray clouds somewhere down the corridor. 'Block them from entering the Führer's quarters.' His voice rose even more. 'Block them.'

'What the hell?' the TeNo captain yelled. 'Who gave that order?'

'Arrest all TeNo men,' the guard captain yelled again. 'The American commando is one of them.'

A shot came from somewhere in the bunker corridor, a sharp slap that echoed back and forth in the underground compound. Screams, then a curse, and orders for calm.

Dietrich stepped from the antechamber into the central corridor, Koder behind him. Fire worked along the floor in many places. The carpet burned, sending runners of smoke into the already thick air. Dietrich could see little beyond his hand. He heard the pumping of a fire extinguisher. He bumped into Gestapo Müller, who was coughing into his hand. Kaltenbrunner was doubled over, breathing in deep rasps and struggling with a mask.

The detective waded through the smoke. His foot caught on a leg. The body of a TeNo man. An SS guard with a pistol blocked the door to the Führer's map room and bedroom. He had just shot the Rescue Squad member.

The TeNo leader, Captain Dreesen, emerged from the smoke to kneel over the wounded man.

'What are you doing, goddamn it?' he yelled up at the SS guard.

And now the SS guard swiveled the pistol and fired at Captain Dreesen, whose face registered rage and shock as blood gushed from his chest. He slid sideways into a card table. Smoke closed over him.

Chaos. The commando's tool. General Keitel screamed order after order, slapping his field marshal's baton against his thigh. He was ignored. Sounds of metal prying metal came from deep in the smoke, where men were frantically working to open the ventilation-room door. A TeNo man dropped to the floor, felled from behind by an SS guard, who roughly kicked the TeNo man onto his back to rip off the gas mask. It wasn't the American.

'Don't shoot the TeNo, for Christ's sake,' the guard captain called. 'Arrest them. Round them up . . .'

His orders were drowned out by the scream of a woman, a secretary who swatted at the flame that had caught the fringe of her dress. A Luftwaffe general wrapped his uniform jacket around her legs, smothering the fire.

General Jodl stepped toward the SS guard blocking the door to Hitler's rooms, but the guard raised the pistol. No one was to enter. The German shepherd howled and tried to enter the Führer's room, but was kicked back by the SS guard. Not even the dog was going to get in.

A TeNo man carrying a pressure extinguisher emerged from the smoke directly in front of Dietrich, who held up his pistol and ripped off the man's mask. Not the American. Dietrich pushed him aside and stepped toward the pistol-wielding guard at the door, his shoes stepping in the TeNo man's blood. He yelled over the turmoil, 'Where's General Eberhardt?'

Something clinked near Dietrich's feet. A skittering sound. Metal tumbling across the floor.

Dietrich glanced down. A stick grenade flashed by, visible one instant, then swallowed by the smoke. Then a second grenade slid along the floor and disappeared into the haze. It oddly registered on Dietrich that the head of the second grenade was a different color than that of the first.

Dietrich had long known he did not possess the instincts of the soldier. He should have shouted 'Grenade.' Given the warning. Told everyone to get down. But fear slowed him, and the warning caught in his throat. Others beat him to it, maybe the generals who were up from the trenches, shouting a warning.

'Grenade,' came from Dietrich's right.

'Down, down,' from somewhere near the door to the antechamber. A rush of movement. More yells.

The detective lunged away from the SS guard toward the opposite doorway, which was to a dressing room. Just before he entered the room, the smoke opened for an instant and he glimpsed a TeNo man in a gas mask with his back against the corridor wall, holding an SS guard in front of him, the TeNo man's thick arm around the guard's neck. The TeNo man was using the SS guard as a shield. Jack Cray must be in that TeNo uniform.

Dietrich tripped on an overturned chair and fell into the dressing room. A rug burned at the back of the room, and fire was spreading to a rack of uniforms.

The first explosion was muffled, nothing like Dietrich had feared. Maybe a dud, he thought, lying there at the feet of General Jodl, who had also dashed into the dressing room and dived to the floor. But the corridor instantly filled with spewing, acrid green-gray smoke, and clouds of it poured from the corridor into the rooms off the hall, pushing aside the gray smoke. Dietrich stared into the new smoke toward the corridor, seeing nothing.

General Jodl's face was the color of the new smoke. His cigarettes had fallen from his pocket and were scattered across the room. Dietrich pushed himself up to sitting.

The second grenade detonated.

The first had been a smoke grenade. The second contained TNT and shrapnel. The corridor filled with a brilliant white flash. The sound was of a sledgehammer hitting an anvil, a metallic peal so loud it seemed to stab Dietrich's head. Air in the bunker pulsed.

Dietrich's ears rang. His pistol was still in his hand. He rose unsteadily and returned to the hall, walking into a wall of smoke.

Two seconds of silence. Then moans and screams. Shrapnel had swept the room like a scythe. The SS guard used as a shield was sprawled face up on the floor, blood oozing from a dozen lacerations on his chest and belly and legs. Near him on the floor, blood pumped from punctures in the SS guard who had stood at Hitler's study door and shot the TeNo men. His mouth silently opened and closed. Smoke rolled over them. Dietrich looked up, across the narrow corridor to the entrance to Hitler's study and bedroom.

The smoke thinned for an instant. The TeNo man stood there. Jack Cray. Face hidden by a gas mask, but surely it was him. Pistol in one hand, knife in another. Just standing there, next to the door into Hitler's quarters.

But just for that second. Then the smoke throbbed and the air clapped and Dietrich felt metal cut into his thigh and leg. The detective spilled forward, onto the body of an SS guard. He tried to catch himself but slipped on the gore. Lacerations in his leg shot pain up into his body. He clamped his jaw and rose, grunting with pain. Cray had thrown another grenade into the study, maybe inside as far as the bedroom. And now the American spun from his place against the wall and charged into Hitler's study.

Dietrich staggered after the commando, across the hall and into the study, slipping on someone's entrails. The grenade had reduced the study's table and chairs to splinters. Another SS guard had been in the study. His legs were against one wall and the rest of him was against the opposite wall fifteen feet away. The barrel of his Schmeisser was bent in two like a jackknife. Bits of maps floated in the smoke.

The detective high-stepped over the fragmented furniture, his leg in agony. The American commando's back was dead ahead, framed in the doorway to Hitler's bedroom. Cray was raising his pistol.

Cray twisted violently, ducking, just as a shot sounded from the bedroom. Then the American's knife arm slashed forward, out of

Dietrich's sight. Cray stepped ahead again into the bedroom, the weapon at the end of his arm coming up.

The sound was of a melon dropped onto the floor. Then another. The commando pitched forward into the bedroom, his gun and knife hitting the rug just as he did. Dietrich moved through the smoke toward the bedroom.

The commando was sprawled face down on the rug.

General Eberhardt stood near the pedestal, the bust of Frederick the Great in his hand. The general's handgun was on the floor, and his right hand was bleeding from a slash of his forearm.

Eberhardt smiled grimly. 'I hit him with Frederick.'

The detective grimaced with pain as he bent to the downed man. He rolled the commando over and pulled off the gas mask. 'It's him,' Dietrich breathed. 'Jack Cray. I'll be goddamned. You got him.'

'We got him,' Eberhardt corrected kindly.

Hitler appeared in the smoke. He was holding a small oxygen mask close to his mouth and nose. The tube was connected to a bottle on a roller. He asked drily, 'That was a little close, don't you think, General Eberhardt?'

Gestapo Müller rushed into the room, his face a mask of pain and rage. His uniform was dappled with blood. Shrapnel had creased his neck, and blood oozed over his shirt. He demanded, 'Is he alive?'

As if in answer, Cray moaned. His arm moved a fraction.

Müller said, 'I'm going to take care of this son of a bitch right now.'

'I want to talk to him,' General Eberhardt said, his voice muffled by the mask. 'See how he got this far, and – '

'Your job is over, Eberhardt,' Müller cut in. He yelled over his shoulder, 'Koder, get in here.'

The RSD general returned the bust of Frederick to the pedestal. 'My Führer, an interrogation – '

'I'm not interested in what the American has to say, General. The commando is now Müller's.' Carrying the oxygen mask, Hitler turned back to the blue sofa. He said over his shoulder, 'And now that you've got the American, tell the TeNo to stop dawdling and put out the fires. It's a little warm in here.'

Rudolf Koder rushed into the room and bent to grab Jack Cray's legs to pull him away. Dietrich put his pistol into his belt. When Cray's eyes fluttered open, Müller viciously kicked him in the head. An SS guard stepped into the study to take Cray's other leg. He and Koder dragged the American through the study's wreckage and into the smoky corridor, pulled him over the bodies of two guards and an SS colonel, sliding him across the blood-soaked rug. Smoke hid even the near walls. A team of guards was using a sledgehammer on the door to the vent room, the sound a rhythmic ring of metal on metal. Speer was sitting on the sofa, wearing a detached expression. The shrapnel had missed him entirely.

General Eberhardt stepped into the hallway. He called to the guards, 'The assassin has been taken. Let the TeNo crews in to work on the fire and smoke.'

Gestapo Müller followed Koder and the SS guard as far as the antechamber. Carrying firefighting equipment, TeNo men again flowed into the bunker.

Müller ordered Koder, 'Do it near the south end, near the wrecked offices. A bullet in his head. Take the body to a pit in the Tiergarten.' He turned back into the bunker's central corridor and was quickly lost in the smoke.

Agent Koder paused in the antechamber, pulled his Walther to check the load. He loudly snapped the clip back into the handle.

He and the guard pulled Cray feet first up the stairs, the American's head bouncing on each step, the gas mask around his neck. Limping from the shrapnel wound, Otto Dietrich followed them up, leaving behind the bunker's turmoil.

General Eberhardt returned to the corridor from Hitler's rooms. He gulped air through his gas mask. He had done his job, by God. Had caught the American commando. It had been close, sure. The American had made it close. But the Führer was as alive today as he was yesterday. Eberhardt's only role in the war had been to keep Germany's leader alive, and he had just succeeded in his mission. Eberhardt was giddy with relief.

Cray had turned into the Führer's room, was bringing his pistol around, and hadn't seen Eberhardt standing near the pedestal bust hard to Cray's right. Eberhardt had fired his pistol, but the general had never been much of a shot, and Cray was moving fast and had spun out of the way, and in the smoke the general had entirely missed. Cray's knife hand swept out, catching Eberhardt's arm and sending the general's pistol across the floor. And then – enraged that he had failed and that there stood the cocky American, in the safest, most secure spot in the Reich – damned if Eberhardt hadn't simply snatched the bust and lashed out at the commando. Smashed it twice into Cray's head. And down went the American. Eberhardt would have laughed aloud had the wound on his arm not hurt so much.

A sofa had caught fire, and was pumping black smoke into the green-gray haze generated by the grenade. Eberhardt stepped over the body of a TeNo man toward the ventilation-room door. The guard captain was overseeing the crew trying to pry open the steel door. Gestapo Müller was now there, an SS guard at his elbow, pointing a Schmeisser at the door.

Müller said to the RSD general, 'The ventilation technician is going to meet the American's fate up in the garden. Just as soon as we open this goddamn door.'

A heavier pry bar had been found, and the corner of the steel door had been bent several centimeters, enough for the bar to gain purchase higher on the frame. A TeNo man heaved on the bar. The door groaned but didn't give.

That was their problem. Eberhardt turned away from the door. The ventilation equipment had apparently been sabotaged, and the smoke was still so thick that he could not see as far as his hands. The bunker was still in loud confusion, with shouted orders and calls for medics and ragged gasps and shrill screams, the fire still working on the rugs and pictures and some furniture. TeNo men and SS guards rushed about, appearing and disappearing in the haze.

But it was over. The American was upstairs, dead or dying. The Führer was safe. General Eberhardt had never been to the front in this struggle. But the front had come to him. And he had prevailed. Right before the Führer's eyes. To the RSD chief, even the acrid, blinding, swirling smoke in the bunker corridor was sweet.

*

The last Rescue Squad member to enter the bunker could see no better than any of the others, with the smoke acting as a film across his eyes, so he turned right and took six steps to the wall, then followed the wall past the cloakroom door and the conference-room door to the third door. Bodies lay in front of the door. Like other TeNo troops, this Rescue Squad member wore a herringbone white uniform. The gas mask hid his face.

The American commando had been captured. The Rescue Squad's job was now to secure the bunker against fire and offer aid to the injured. This TeNo man walked into the room, brushing by another Rescue Squad member who had checked the room and was now leaving it. No one else was in the study. He stepped over the ruined furniture and blackened pieces of maps and reports, and walked into Hitler's bedroom.

The Führer was sitting on the blue sofa, a small mask covering his face, with a tube to an oxygen bottle on a stand near his feet. He was wearing the field-gray jacket that symbolized his role as supreme commander of the German armed forces. Hitler flicked his hand to dismiss the Rescue Squad member, silently indicating he did not need help. He turned back to the document in his hand.

Then Jack Cray removed his gas mask. He brought out a pistol from the folds of the Rescue Squad uniform.

Hitler again looked up. He pulled off the mask and put it aside. His face was blank. With difficulty, he stood.

'You are back. The Vassy Château killer,' the Führer said, his voice echoing in the concrete room. The Iron Cross on his chest, won in the trenches during the Great War, testified to his bravery. He showed it now. 'I thought I was rid of you. But I underestimated you. You got past them all, again. Got into the bunker, again. How did you do it?'

Cray smiled. 'I'm not much at chatting.'

He fired the pistol. The sound was a flat clap. A hole opened between Hitler's eyes and his brains dappled the portrait of Frederick the Great. Hitler collapsed to the blue sofa, his arm hanging to the floor, blood streaking the fabric.

Cray spun to a movement at the corner of his eye, bringing the pistol around. A soft cry came from a woman in a blue print dress who had appeared from the adjacent dressing room. She was wearing a gas mask, and her hand came up to the mask, and then she flew across the room to the body, ignoring the killer.

Cray returned the gas mask to his head, then backed out of the room and sidestepped the table in the study. The pistol was back inside his uniform when an SS guard rushed into the room.

'What's happened,' the guard demanded.

'The Führer,' Cray yelled.

As the guard hurried into Hitler's room, Cray reentered the central corridor. He could see little through the smoke, and instantly was lost among the milling Rescue Squad troops and others. The corridor was still in a noisy uproar. No one was yet tending to the wounded or taking away the dead. Blood was everywhere. Fires still burned. Some had heard a shot, others had not. In the echoing hallway few could determine the shot's direction.

Lost in the smoke, someone cried out, 'Who fired?'

The guard captain called, 'What has happened? Report.'

A scream came from down the hallway, then an answering scream, and a shout for order. Panic was again stirring.

Cray pushed through the green-gray blur, straight across the hall – he had been told the route with precision – to the opposite wall, where he turned right. The SS crew had failed to pry open the steel door and were looking about for further instructions, one holding the bar. A guard held a submachine gun in front of him, pointed at the door.

'New code,' Cray said. He pressed the buzzer. Five short, two long.

Instantly bolts scraped and the door opened. Wearing a mask, Ulrich Kahr stepped into the hallway. He cried, 'The ventilators have failed. Where's the mechanic?'

Cray said, 'Come on.' Short clipped words, hiding his accent. The Schmeisser-wielding guard hesitated.

Blood from his neck wound soaking the front of his tunic, Gestapo Müller rushed by the SS guard. He stabbed a pistol at Kahr. 'You. I'm taking you upstairs.'

Cray shot the Gestapo chief in the stomach. Müller folded and sank to the floor. The Schmeisser guard saw Cray's gun hand come around, and the guard ducked back into the smoke. Cray fired again at other SS guards. One sank to the floor and the other leaped back and was quickly swallowed by the haze. Cray yanked Sergeant Kahr toward the exit, cutting through the smoke. From somewhere in the smoke, the submachine gun fired. Bullets pocked the wall where Cray had been an instant before.

Shrieks and shouts came from all directions. Sounds of running footsteps and scuffling. Gray haze hid everything but suggestions of movement. Wild faces appeared and disappeared in the smoke. Glimpses of armbands and peaked caps.

Cray was four steps to the stairwell door, Kahr on his heels, when a general's hand found Cray's shoulder.

'You,' Eberhardt demanded. 'Where did you come from? From the Führer's rooms just now?'

Cray stepped up to the general so their noses almost touched, and stabbed the pistol barrel at Eberhardt's solar plexus.

'Say another word and I'll kill you,' Cray spat. 'Go out the door and up the stairs.'

When Eberhardt hesitated, Cray said, 'Don't you read your own posters? I'm a bastard. Get up those stairs.'

Eberhardt turned for the door, Cray and Kahr right behind. Cray's pistol once again disappeared. They walked through the haze into the stairwell, past the SS guards, who did not give them a look because they were peering through the smoke into the corridor trying to discover the source of the resurgent furor. A second TeNo crew was noisily descending the stairs, and they brushed by Eberhardt and Cray and Kahr. The RSD general's back was rigid as he climbed the stairs.

At ground level in the blockhouse, the pistol was in Cray's hand again. 'Go back down the stairs, General.'

Eberhardt did not look relieved at the dismissal. 'I have failed to protect the Fürher, haven't I? I have failed in my duty.'

Cray grinned. 'And will you count to a hundred before you alert anybody?'

The general's voice was full and bitter. 'You are a cocky son of a bitch, just like Dietrich said.' He started down the stairs, but turned back to Cray. 'What did you do to Inspector Dietrich?'

Another smile from the American. 'Go back down the stairs, General.'

Cray and Kahr waited thirty seconds before stepping through the blockhouse door into the smoke-blanketed garden, the guards nervously pacing at their posts, speculating about the green-gray smoke rising from the bunker, indifferent to the Rescue Squad man and the Wehrmacht sergeant who walked by them and then across the garden toward the motor-court entrance.

TWENTY-TWO

Cray stepped into a foyer in the ruined west end of the Chancellery. The all-clear sirens were still quiet and no Chancellery workers were aboveground. He held up a hand, indicating Sergeant Kahr should wait for him there. Then Cray opened a door that had a shattered glass panel and walked into an office, pushing aside rubble hanging from the splintered second floor. Cray ducked under a broken beam and dangling floorboards, stepped his way around a masonry wall that had collapsed into the room, and trod carefully over a shattered umbrella stand and a flattened desk and a cluster of overturned chairs, making his way toward an interior door.

He entered a second office and said, 'Let's go, Inspector.'

Otto Dietrich was holding his pistol on Rudolf Koder and the SS guard who had helped Koder drag Cray up to the garden. Koder and the guard were sitting on the edges of chairs, bent slightly forward because Koder was wearing his own handcuffs behind his back, and the guard was wearing Dietrich's. The room was filled with file cabinets spilled onto their sides. Smoke from the garden seeped in through the shattered wall. Rudolf Koder glared malignantly at Dietrich.

'So you got back into the bunker?' Dietrich asked.

'In and out like grain through a goose.'

Dietrich shifted his glance to the American. 'And?'

Cray looked at him with mock incredulity. 'Slick as a whistle.'

'What does that mean?'

'The trouble with you Germans,' Cray said, 'other than that you are a warrior race, is that you don't have enough slang.'

Rudolf Koder's voice was tight with hatred and fury. 'You are a traitor, Dietrich. A traitor to the Fatherland.'

Russian shells landed on the plaza outside, and cobblestones rained against the Foreign Ministry's wall.

Cray lifted a finger toward Koder. 'This fellow know you, Inspector?'

Dietrich nodded. 'His name is Rudolf Koder, a Gestapo agent. He is my case officer. He had my wife arrested and sent to a camp, where she came down with typhoid fever and died.'

Koder bellowed, 'A traitor to the Führer and to your homeland.' He jerked against the handcuffs, his face the color of blood.

'And he tortured me in a prison cell, day after day, until I was released to chase after you.' Dietrich breathed heavily, and then ran a hand down his face, fighting the memory. 'He almost killed me, reduced me to nothing, nothing human. I'd like to shoot the bastard.' The detective spoke slowly, convincing himself of the correct and lawful course. 'But I've spent too much of my life hunting down murderers to kill somebody in cold blood. It would haunt me the rest of my life.'

'It's not going to bother me at all.' Out came Jack Cray's pistol. He pulled the trigger, and Rudolf Koder bucked back in the chair, then spilled sideways. Blood pumped from the hole in his chest and leaked from the exit hole in his back. Twisted sideways, his hands still behind him, Koder stared in surprise, stared without seeing.

'What about the other one?' Cray asked. 'The SS trooper?'

'I don't know him,' Dietrich said. 'Never seen him before.'

Cray wagged his pistol at the trooper. 'Lucky for you, eh?'

The American used a key to unlock the trooper's handcuffs from one hand. The trooper's eyes darted between Cray's hands, searching for thc fabled knife. Cray attached one cuff to an exposed pipe, the trooper still sitting in the chair.

The American picked up his pack, then led Otto Dietrich through the wing's maze of ruin.

As they reached Sergeant Kahr in the lobby, the all-clear sounded, and Cray looked at his wristwatch. 'There'll be another air raid in thirty minutes. We'd better be there.'

He didn't say where, and Dietrich and Kahr had to satisfy themselves by following him. They turned south to Leipzigerstrasse, then onto the plaza, then past the Hotel Esplanade, heading for the Tiergarten.

Detective Dietrich could not help himself. 'Look around. Your bombers did this.'

They were walking through a sea of rubble, along a narrow path cleared to allow pedestrians to pass. On both sides of them fire-blackened building façades stood like tombstones. Wreckage filled the eye to the horizon without the relief of a single undamaged structure or bit of color or a standing tree. Gray and brown debris and nothing more.

Cray said, 'Well, you did your part to stop it, back there, letting me go.'

Dietrich stepped around a pile of books that had been tossed onto the street by a bomb's concussion. 'Agent Koder was right. I'm a traitor to the Fatherland.'

'Yeah, maybe so.' He led them around a delivery truck lying on its side.

Dietrich raised his voice in exasperation. 'Isn't it incumbent on you to argue that I'm a patriot and not a traitor?'

'It's incumbent on me to see that we don't die in the next few minutes. I'll worry about your feelings later.' Cray narrowed his eyes, searching out the next intersection. He had heard something.

Looking for deserters, an SS patrol rounded a mound of rubble, three storm troopers, two of them carrying submachine guns. One trooper signaled for Cray and Dietrich and Kahr to stop.

Cray shifted his pack to his other shoulder, then said under his breath, 'Unless you have a better idea, Inspector, I'm going to kill all three of these fellows five seconds from right now.'

'Wait.'

The troopers surrounded the trio. The leader, an SS sergeant, ordered gruffly, 'Show me your papers.'

Moving his hand slowly, Dietrich pulled out Himmler's letter and showed it to the Scharführer, who rasped, 'Sorry, sir. Thank you.' He saluted either Dietrich or the letter and led his men away.

Cray and the others crossed Tiergartenstrasse and entered the park. Bombs had turned the Tiergarten over as thoroughly as if it had been done with a giant plow. Little remained of the level – only holes and mounds of dirt. Acres and acres of craters and hillocks of blasted earth had replaced the lovely grass fields.

'Slow down,' Dietrich said, panting. 'My leg is killing me.' His pants were bloodstained from the knee to his shoe.

Cray glanced at Dietrich's wound. 'Hell, I've been hurt worse playing poker with my Ranger buddies.'

As they passed the remnants of a pergola, Dietrich grabbed Cray's arm to stop him, perhaps too roughly. The knife was instantly in the American's hand, held politely, almost out of sight. The detective said, 'You are the only person who will ever know my reason for turning my pistol on Koder and the SS guard and freeing you to go back into the bunker after trying desperately to stop you. I want you to listen to me a minute, without any of your ghastly American optimism or dumb wisecracks.'

'I'll try.'

The air-raid sirens began again, drifting over the Tiergarten, their tones shifting with the breeze.

'The Reich killed my wife. She died in front of my eyes. It didn't break my loyalty to the Fatherland. Not then. It took some time, working on me every day and night. And I could push it aside, chasing you, doing my job. That's all I had after she died, my job. And so I did my job, pushing away the senselessness of Maria's death.'

Cray was looking around, moving his head right and left, searching for the SS or the Gestapo.

The detective grabbed his arm to get his attention. 'Listen to me, goddamn it.' He wet his lips. 'But my rage worked like a worm inside me. And when I saw you dragged into the garden, I broke. Müller was going to toss me back into prison anyway, and I owed the Fatherland nothing, not anymore, not after they took my wife from me. I just broke, right then, just as Koder was about to shoot you. And I knew how to strike back. Through you. So I drew my pistol on Koder and the guard, and let you go back down into the bunker with Koder's pistol.'

Cray reached for Dietrich's arm. 'I'm touched, really. Now let's get to the airstrip.'

Dietrich asked harshly, 'Are all Americans as tough as you?'

'The tough ones are over fighting the Japs.'

Dietrich hurried after Cray, Ulrich Kahr in the rear.

Cray pursed his lips, his eyes at an amused angle. 'It had become personal between you and me, hadn't it? You weren't going to allow yourself to break until you had bested me.'

Dietrich admitted solemnly. 'Yes. It had become personal.' After a few more steps he asked, 'How'd you infiltrate the TeNo squad?'

'I knew exactly when Sergeant Kahr was going to fill the bunker with smoke and fire. And I knew the Mauerstrasse TeNo station responded to Chancellery and bunker emergencies. So I put detonators into several mines, and half blew up the TeNo squad headquarters just as the emergency call was coming in. In the resulting smoke and confusion at the TeNo station, I joined up.'

'You joined up?'

'Some TeNo men were injured, most confused. I walked out of the smoke into their midst, wearing a gas mask like many of them. I crossed the plaza with them, covered by smoke from the bombing run. I wasn't given a second glance.'

'Where's the plane?' Ulrich Kahr asked urgently. They were walking across sawdust, where Tiergarten trees had been sawed into fireplace-sized pieces. 'I can't see anything. Too much smoke.'

Cray led them to an area in the park west of Bellevue Allee, a road that cut diagonally across the Tiergarten. A short landing strip was wedged between craters. The strip had been cut into the park at the beginning of the war, and bulldozers immediately repaired the runway each time it was bombed. The Allies had guessed that this tiny field would be used by Hitler to flee Berlin. Cray and Dietrich and Kahr approached a copse of shattered trees, their trunks broken and split like trodden straw.

Katrin stepped from the trees. Her arms were across her chest.

She was not carrying anything, didn't bring anything to take with her. Cray knew then he had failed to convince her to leave Berlin.

Cray said, 'I'm glad you've come.'

'To say goodbye. And to see what other strange things you'll say, to prolong my amusement a little more. Sort of an antidote to the war.' She paused, then added, 'And I have nothing else to do.'

Cray slipped the pack off his shoulders and unbuttoned it. 'Put on these shirts.' He handed the Germans large white dress shirts, and began putting on the fourth shirt.

Kahr nervously looked over his shoulder, across the park to the row of ruined buildings on Tiergartenstrasse. 'These white shirts will make us conspicuous.'

'Anyone not wearing a bright white shirt or any vehicle which approaches our plane is going to have a world of trouble.' Cray's shirt – from the countess's closet of unclaimed tailoring – was much brighter than his Rescue Squad uniform. The tails hung out. Katrin put on a white shirt over her coat.

'Why do you have three shirts?' Dietrich asked. 'You weren't expecting me to come along. This woman – Katrin von Tornitz – won't join your escape?'

'No.'

Dietrich looked at her. 'I heard reports from Danzig and Stettin. Terrible things have happened to German women. Russian soldiers won't treat you kindly. You'd better go with the American.'

She shook her head.

Dietrich shrugged, then held out the white shirt. 'I'm not going, either.'

'The Gestapo is going to hunt you down if you remain here.' Cray buttoned his shirt. 'And then there'll be the Russians after the Gestapo is gone.'

'I'm not going to England or the United States. I'm a German.'

'You'll be a dead German in short order, you don't come along.'

'I have a few places I can hide.'

Cray argued, 'You can't hide from the Gestapo. You told me so yourself. There's no point martyring yourself when the end of the war is so near.'

Dietrich shook his head. 'I'm not going.'

Cray said only, 'Suit yourself.'

'There they are.' Ulrich Kahr pointed north.

The wind had torn great windows in the smoke. A bomber wing was approaching the Spree from the north. The B-17s were escorted by a dozen or more fighters, looking like gnats hovering around the bombers. At the Spree the bombers veered west to do their business elsewhere, maybe Spandau. But most of the fighters maintained their southerly course, flying right at Cray and the others in the Tiergarten. The fighters – P-51 Mustangs – grew quickly, the roar of their Rolls-Royce Merlin engines racing out ahead of them.

Otto Dietrich looked back at Tiergartenstrasse. 'Cray, they've found us.'

Two black automobiles were making their way along the street, winding around clusters of rubble.

An armored car emerged through a gap in the rubble and fell in line behind the cars.

'A bulletin must have gone out from the bunker.' Dietrich pulled out his pistol, but it looked tiny and useless in his hand, so he returned it to his waistband. 'Maybe a call from the bunker. That SS unit we came across probably reported our direction. Or maybe someone recognized you. Or maybe the Gestapo just figured we would head here, to this airstrip. But here they come.'

'The Russians are within a couple of kilometers of here,' Cray said. 'You'd think the SS and Gestapo would clear out while they had the chance.'

Dietrich looked at him. 'You don't understand them. You're from America. You don't know anything.'

'Where's our plane?' Kahr demanded.

He stared at the convoy, which had jumped a curb and was crossing the park. A side window came down in the lead car, a Horch, and out came a hand holding a pistol. The armored car took a new bearing, heading more westerly, to block an escape attempt. Their engines could not be heard over the rising and falling wails of the air-raid sirens and the increasingly louder bellowing of the Mustangs.

'Where's our plane, goddamn it?' Ulrich Kahr yelled. 'Where's the plane you said would be here?'

It dropped out of the sky from a parting bank of smoke, smaller and more nimble than the usual hardware over Berlin. It fluttered down, resembling a leaf in autumn. A twin-engine transport made by Douglas and called the Skytrain, often used to ferry generals and their staffs around.

'That's a fine pilot,' Cray said.

'Christ on his cross, Yank, the Gestapo is coming for us.' Kahr's head jerked left and right, searching for an avenue of escape. 'They're a hundred meters away. Eighty meters. We're going to end up on a meat hook.'

'Don't worry about them.'

'What?' Kahr exclaimed furiously. 'Do something.'

Cray smiled. 'Those Gestapo agents aren't wearing white shirts.'

The lead Horch was fifty meters from Cray when the ground near it began to bubble. Clots of dirt burst into the air. Then the projectiles found the car, and cut it in half, side to side, ripping through metal and glass and upholstery and flesh. The Mustang pilot lingered with the auto in his sights, letting .50-caliber bullets reduce the vehicle to scraps. Then the fighter soared overhead, the pilot wiggling his wings in glee.

Gestapo agents bailed out of the second car, fleeing the next plane's target. But they were too late. The second Mustang in the strafing formation loosed long bursts at the car and all around it. Limbs and heads and trunks were pierced through and flicked into the air and dashed to the ground, and then the car was shredded. The gasoline tank burst and doused the car's remains in fire.

The armored car turned sharply, its driver trying to find cover behind a mound of dirt. Bullets ruptured the vehicle, turning it inside out, then dismantling it. The car sank on its axles. Not one of the SS troopers inside made it as far as the door latches.

The Skytrain miraculously pulled out of its dive and plopped down on the runway. A crewman opened the fuselage hatch as the plane was still rolling.

Katrin turned away from the smoking wreckage of the armored

car. She stood there, her eyes glistening, until Cray held out his arms and she stepped into them. She tucked her chin into his neck and held him around his shoulders, and he held her tightly, but they were out of practice, and it was all a bit awkward.

She whispered into his ear, 'Goodbye, Jack.' Her tears were on his neck.

Cray's arm jerked. Katrin's head bounced forward, and she slumped into Cray's arms. In his hand was his pistol. He had just sent the butt into her temple.

'Help me,' he ordered.

When Cray started dragging her, Ulrich Kahr lifted her legs. They carried her to the Skytrain, then handed her up to two crewmen.

Cray hollered over the roar of the plane's engines, 'Buckle her into a seat.'

Prop-wash flattening his clothes against him, Cray returned to Dietrich.

The detective said, 'You're doing her a favor, taking her out of here.'

Cray said quietly, so that Dietrich had to lean forward to hear, 'I'm not doing it for her. I'm doing it for me.' Then he scratched his chin. 'You know, I don't have a lot of friends.'

'That's entirely understandable,' Dietrich replied, a bit stiffly. Katyusha rockets rose into the eastern sky, as close together as piano strings.

'I'd hate to lose one.' The pistol appeared again in Cray's hand, and he lashed out with it, slamming the butt against Dietrich's temple.

Cray caught the detective as he fell. He laughed and said to Kahr, 'You Germans sure are slow learners.'

Kahr lifted Dietrich's legs, and Cray had him under his arms, and they retraced their route across the ruined ground toward the Skytrain. Mustangs covered them, soaring low over the transport, then rising and banking north to come around in tight circles. The Skytrain's propellers were still turning.

The pilot pushed back the side window. 'Who is that? I wasn't told about a third man.'

'A friend of mine,' Cray announced.

Ulrich Kahr climbed through the Skytrain's hatch, then turned to pull up Dietrich. Cray shoved and prodded, and between the two of them and the crewmen Dietrich was put quickly into a flight seat.

The pilot turned to look at them as they strapped themselves in. 'I just saw you coldcock that fellow there. You sure he's a friend?'

'He's a pal of mine, all right,' Cray said over the engine nose.

The pilot wound up the engine, and the crewmen strapped themselves in, ogling Katrin. The Skytrain began down the runway. It bounced once, then again, and lifted into the air. Within seconds it was over the Brandenburg Gate, where it turned north. Mustangs hovered around it.

Cray looked at Dietrich. The side of the detective's head around his ear was purpling. 'Though he might not know it yet.'

As the Skytrain approached the airstrip near Wittenberg – field headquarters of the US Ninth Army – Sergeant Kahr began rocking back and forth in his seat, as if that might hurry the plane. The Skytrain sank toward a field of tanks and self-propelled guns and armored cars and a checkerboard of tents, a staging area for the next push west. At the north end of all the equipment was a landing field with mobile AA batteries along its perimeter.

Ulrich Kahr's forehead was pressed against the side window. 'I don't see him. Where is he?'

Cray opened and closed his jaw against the increasing air pressure. Otto Dietrich was slumped in his seat, rubbing his temple, looking only at his knees. Katrin was pressing a towel to her head and glaring at Cray. When she had come around, he had told her – with a grin that gave the lie to his words as he spoke them – that a Russian mortar round had blacked her out, and he couldn't just leave her lying there on the runway.

Dozens of pilots and mechanics were at work below. Rows of Mustangs and Thunderbolts lined the field, and trucks and tool carts were between the planes. The Skytrain touched down, then taxied toward the north end of the field, where three soldiers stood, two with M-1s and the third in a tattered Wehrmacht uniform, cramming food from a bowl into his mouth as quickly as he could swallow.

'That's him,' Kahr shouted. 'That's Max. My God, look how thin he is.' Kahr turned in his seat to look at Cray. 'You did it, by God. That's my boy there. You sprang him from the Bolshevik camp.' Kahr might have been about to add his thanks, but his eyes were abruptly damp, and he could say no more, so he roughly patted Cray's knee. Then he shouldered open the door and leaned out of the plane, gripping a hatch frame until the Skytrain had stopped. He leaped to the ground and sprinted toward his son.

Perhaps Max Kahr had not been told why he had been plucked from a POW camp in Russia and brought to this airfield. Or maybe his hunger was such that he could not force his gaze up from his bowl until his father's arms were around him. But then he held his father tightly, still holding the bowl. The American guards smiled.

The air was calm, so the pilot could take off from either direction. He braked the plane into a half-circle, then shoved the accelerator knob forward. The Skytrain bumped down the runway until its wheels lost contact with the ground.

Cray looked down as the plane banked north. Sergeant Kahr and his son were still standing next to the field, and still in each other's arms.

The Skytrain was pointed toward the airfield near Eastwell Manor in Kent. Cray could see the rose garden with its trellises to one side of the building, and the topiary bushes and fountains on the long grassy slope behind the manor. The pilot said something into his radio.

'They'll never let it out,' Dietrich said abruptly, more to himself. The blood on his pants was dry and caked.

'What?' Cray asked.

'That the Führer was assassinated. It doesn't fit into the legend that he carefully crafted for himself. He told me so himself. He said he couldn't meet his end at the hands of an assassin. So they'll say he committed suicide.' Dietrich thought again about the pretty blond woman who shared the Führer's bunker suite. She knew Hitler had died at the hands of an assassin, rather than by noble suicide. Dietrich suspected she would not be allowed to tell the tale, and would never leave the bunker alive.

Cray shrugged. 'What're your plans, Inspector? Where you going to go?'

'You mean I'm not a prisoner of war? I'm not going to a POW camp somewhere in England?'

'Why would you become a POW? You're a policeman, not a soldier.'

Dietrich said just above the sound of the Skytrain's engines, 'Then I'll be a policeman. That's all I know how to do. I'll go back when things have settled down. Maybe work for the occupation forces. They'll need homicide detectives in Berlin after the war.'

Cray said, 'The war won't have made much difference to murderers, I suppose.'

'And you won't be in Berlin, so it'll be safer.'

'I'm going back to Wenatchee, Washington. Ever heard of the place?'

'Only in my file on you.'

'I own an apple orchard there,' Cray said. 'Inherited it from my parents. I've leased it to a neighbor, but I might take it over again. Might try apple-growing.'

'You? Growing apples?' Katrin laughed from the seat behind Cray, then winced and gently touched her head. 'That's not an image that comes easily to mind.'

He turned to her. 'Well, I'm sick of all this engineering I've had to do in the army, I'll guarantee you that.'

The Skytrain's engine dropped to a purr, and the plane began its gliding approach, flying toward Eastwell Manor's twelve chimneys, descending quickly.

Cray announced to Dietrich, 'Katrin is coming with me. To help me out in the orchard. Eat some of my cooking. See what happens.'

'What?' From the back seat.

'Come with me to Wenatchee.'

'To Wenatchee, Washington. I can't even pronounce the name.'

'It's a good idea, it seems to me.'

'A stupid idea,' she said, but without heat. 'I'm a German.'

'Germany doesn't exist anymore. It's been destroyed. Everything you ever loved about your country is gone.' Cray looked out the window at the reception awaiting them. Three people in suits. No uniforms. He had no idea who they were. An ambulance was also there. He twisted in his seat back to her. 'And what else are you going to do, Katrin? When this plane lands in a few seconds, where do you go?'

'Me, helping you raise apples in rural America?' Katrin laughed again. 'That's a crazy notion. Besides, I can just barely tolerate you.'

'I grow on people.' Cray grinned again. Goddamn that grin. 'I can be a pretty good convincer. All we need is a little time together.'

'I've already spent a little time with you. It seemed like half a century.' But her eyes were pensive. He looked back at her. That optimistic and brash and compelling American face. That beat-up face. Someone who cared for her, even if he was crazy. And an American.

She exhaled suddenly, loudly, her mind running away from her, running into absurd territory. Those wild thoughts, and what they abruptly revealed to her about her heart, had a force that pushed her back into her chair, as if the plane were taking off rather than landing.

The plane touched down on the plowed field, and the ruts grabbed the wheels and guided the Skytrain along. The plane pulled up to the three men waiting for them, and the pilot shut down the engines.

The pilot was first out of the plane, and was immediately surrounded by the men, who were all grinning and who one after another shook his hand. Dietrich followed the pilot out of the hatch.

Cray had a foot on the ladder, about to climb down, but Katrin touched his shoulder. 'What kind of apples, did you say?'